THE STANDING STONE

Erected by a forgotten people, it catches the light of summer sun, its shadows briefly spelling words that none among the living remembers how to read:

> *The truth of this dreaming world is the turning of the stars, and as the seasons return after long rest, this marks the land where dream returns to its native ground, truth. Here reigns the true ruler of these islands in memory and in promise. Great is the burden of this care.*

The planet turns, the shadows lengthen, and the words are gone again. . . .

"By far the most lyrically written of the recent Arthur books. . . . Achieves moments of aching emotion. . . . Fresh and engaging."

—*Magazine of Fantasy & Science Fiction*

BY A. A. ATTANASIO

The Dragon and the Unicorn
The Eagle and the Sword
The Wolf and the Crown

Published by HarperPrism

The EAGLE *and the* SWORD

— ❦ —

A. A. ATTANASIO

HarperPrism
A Division of HarperCollinsPublishers

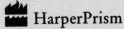 HarperPrism
A Division of HarperCollins*Publishers*
10 East 53rd Street, New York, N.Y. 10022-5299

This is a work of fiction. The characters, incidents, and
dialogues are products of the author's imagination and are not to
be construed as real. Any resemblance to actual events or
persons, living or dead, is entirely coincidental.

ISBN 0-06-105839-4

HarperCollins®, ®, and HarperPrism®
are trademarks of HarperCollins*Publishers*, Inc.

Cover illustration © 1998 by Danilo Ducak

A trade paperback edition of this book was published
in 1997 by HarperPrism.

First mass market paperback printing: May 1998

Printed in the United States of America

Visit HarperPrism on the World Wide Web at
http://www.harperprism.com

❖ 10 9 8 7 6 5 4 3 2

For my sister—
Elise
—a true Christian

Arthur was cruel from boyhood, a horrible son,
a horrible bear, an iron hammer.
—Nennius

The
EAGLE
and the
SWORD

Preface

Born of Uther Pendragon, king of the Britons, and Ygrane of Tintagel, queen of the Celts, Aquila Regalis Thor—Arthor—has grown to young adulthood unaware of his royal destiny. This is the first book in his story, in which the orphaned youth discovers himself, physically and emotionally, on his journey to Camelot.

The Dragon and the Unicorn, the volume that preceded this, recounts the magical events that culminated in Arthor's birth, and the following Prologue touches on the consequences of that story and the coming of Merlin.

Arthor, of course, is the eagle of this book's title: an apt symbol, this solitary lord of raptors, for the most solitary king of legend. And the sword is the most famous sword of all—the blade that held darkness at bay for a generation of magic, chivalry, and peerless love.

Prologue

An angel stands atop a rocky summit in western Britain at noon on a summer day in this year of the Lord 490. To mortal eyes, he is invisible, his face a shaft of sunlight, his robes bundles of wind stirring the gorse on the higher slopes of the mountain. Yet in his eyes, nothing is hidden. He sees the stuttering flames of all living things. The dead and the unborn draw near his fire in a frail mist. The hosts of the forests flicker like stars before him, and under his gaze every sparrow strung on its thread of song is stitched brightly against the blue curve of heaven.

Patiently, the angel stares south over the verdant, rumpled land and watches the sea turning its pages on the Saxon Coast. He reads there the coming Dark Ages. Flat-bottomed boats slide off the sea and hiss onto the sand, disembarking furious warriors in wolf pelts and cloaks woven from human scalps. The drums they beat have been stretched from the flesh of those they conquered, and their music is low and weighted as fog.

Directly in front of him, Roman ruins dot the landscape like the crazed pieces of a shattered puzzle.

Huddled within the slanting and skewed stone walls of these decrepit villas, thatch-roofed hamlets await unawares the torch of the coming invaders. Oblivious clerics cower in their mud huts, miscopying Plotinus and Lucretius again and again. Only the blind eyes of broken statuary watch as grunting farmers drag their crude plows across gravelly fields.

Sitting among bluebells on a slope of the angel's mountain is an ancient notch-stone erected by the nameless Neolithic people who lived here before the Celts. It catches the light of summer noon and casts along its length crooked shadows that suddenly and briefly spell words none among the living knows how to read.

The angel remembers what it says.

The truth of this dreaming world is the turning of the stars, and as the seasons return after long rest, this marks the land where dream returns to its native ground, truth. Here reigns the true ruler of these islands in memory and in promise. Great is the burden of this care.

The planet turns, the shadows lengthen, and the ephemeral words smear away and are gone, not to return for another year. The significance of what they say remains, and the angel directs his attention toward where the notch-stone points. Below, on a broad table of land backed by forested mountains and facing a deep river gorge that opens into a vista of southern lowlands, a fortress is under construction. This will be the citadel belonging to "the true ruler of these islands"—if the promise of the angels is ever to be fulfilled.

Much has yet to be accomplished for this dream

to return to its native ground, and the angel stands atop this peak as mute witness to all that remains undone. The river below and the sea beyond lift under the hooks of the moon and carry the long, low-draft ships of Saxon raiders forward. These are the warriors of the north tribes, who worship spirit powers other than the faith of angels. The Furor, their ardent war god, so passionately covets these islands that he has inspired his followers with a murderous frenzy that the angels alone are powerless to counter.

For the angels there is no choice: To help stave the tide of the Dark Ages, they must fight. They fight to preserve their dream of truths yet to come, for their lofty cathedrals and city-states and glass towers of the future, for their nations of prosperity destined someday to defeat poverty and sickness and eventually even death. This desire to exalt humanity to the stars drives them to keep on fighting. And to aid them in their struggle, they have found one ally alone, in the last place any would think to look: among the demons.

The demons call him Lailoken. Once an incubus fierce with hatred for all life, he now lives in human guise as the wizard Merlin. Empowered still with a demon's strength and cunning, he has learned love from the woman he once tried to rape; Optima was her name, a saint whose womb received his demon energy and who, with the help of the angels, wove him his mortal body of uncertain age. At this moment, as the angel gazes down from his peak, Merlin labors below with caliper and rod, serving as chief architect and builder in the construction of this modern stronghold.

The angel watching over him was the very one who worked closest with Optima, transforming Lailoken into the wizard Merlin. It was one of his prouder achievements. But now the angel is afraid. Fifteen years have passed since the destined king was born and the construction of his castle begun, and the demon-wizard has reached that dangerous time when, according to prophecy, he must deliver to the throne "the true ruler of these islands." In the meantime, the Furor and all who defy the angels have hardly been idle. They know as well as the angels do that nothing is definite, no prophecy certain. Will Merlin remember this? Already, the angel sees approaching Merlin's enemy, Morgeu the Fey, the sorceress who has sworn to spend her life destroying whatever the wizard builds.

To the angel, she appears as a smear of moonlight in the forest darkness. Her physical body lies entranced far to the north in a cirque of magical stones veined with the roots of tropical trees, dwarf shrubs of lime and orange that unfold their blossoms in the sun for the plunder of the bees. Glistening among the sweet flowers, the bees fill the air with their mumbled joy, lulling the sorceress into a trance deep enough to unstring her wraith from her flesh. Distance is nothing to her now, and she drifts free as a thread of mist, needling through the pine beds and the mighty coves of oak that remain dark even at noon, dark as the hidden places of thunder.

The angel sees that Merlin is absorbed in building the castle of his king and seems unaware of the approaching wraith. To all the world, and even to the angel himself, the wizard appears no more than a lanky old man with a long white beard, his haggard face imprinted with a hawk's scowl, his shoulders heavy with weariness. Only his bent conical hat with its floppy brim and his midnight blue cowl embroidered in fine crimson filaments stitched with planetary sigils and alchemic signatures indicate his magician status.

How constraining and frail are mortal limits, the angel thinks, observing Merlin leaning heavily upon his gnarled wooden staff as he moves among the colossal stone walls. The angel knows well the dangers of these physical restrictions, for he, too, remains bound by the limits of his energy. The angels have given everything they have to build the worlds as they are now, and they must yet work unrelentingly to maintain their fragile creations against the destructive efforts of the demons. There is precious little power to spare. Having given everything to install Lailoken in a human body and transform him into Merlin, the angel does not have enough energy left to aid him further. He is too weak even to hinder the sorceress Morgeu, let alone thwart the malignant strategies of the Furor. Merlin must rely on his own resources now to establish his young king and hold back the minions of chaos.

Rising, the angel disappears in the wind. His shadow trawling after him through the hot day becomes rain in the clear sky and falls in widening veils.

Merlin wanders the construction site of Camelot in a mist of sunlight falling with the soft rain and does not sense the angel that accompanies him. This is the fifteenth summer that he has overseen the craftsmen and laborers toiling on the high plateaus and slopes above the verdant gorge of the River Amnis, and he is well pleased with the curtain walls, ramparts, and towers that now stand upon the emerald turf of the downs.

The city-fortress of his vision is nearly complete. It sprawls within a mountain cleft overhanging the river plain, protected by lordly crags to the west and north and open to a commanding view of the strewed forests and alluvial fields in the southeastern lowlands. Red pantile roofs from the river hamlet of Cold Kitchen gleam like pieces of coral far below, where the old Roman highway meets the Amnis, but otherwise, the modern citadel hovers alone among the green and rocky tumult of creation.

Workers sitting on benches and stools under canvas awnings and thatched canopies eating their midday meal of black bread, cheese, and leeks do not notice the shadowy blur in the sunny drizzle as Merlin strolls past. The wizard has made himself invisible to their eyes for this tour, the better to scrutinize their handiwork and oversee the intimate details of construction.

Ranks of Irish yews stand dwarfed before the imposing palisade wall. Atop the wall, archery platforms with lateral windows for enfilading fire are under construction, assuring that these defenses will forever remain unbreachable. The wizard believes that if his vision is fulfilled and the rightful king installed within these ramparts, no assault can ever be gathered against Camelot. Yet he has painfully learned that in this volatile world, no vision is certain, and he has made careful preparations to assure that this capital remains impregnable.

At the masons' work sheds, he lingers, admiring the precision of the stonecutters' work: Most of the funds that Merlin has collected for building Camelot have gone to hiring the finest sculptors from Ravenna, where the last practitioners of the dying art of stonemasonry reside. They alone possess the arcane knowledge to construct Roman archways, domes, and vaults. Even the seemingly simple production of cement and squared stones has been forgotten in Europe by all save these few artisans. Under their expert direction, the elegant spires of Camelot arise from a clutter of wood scaffolds and hempen cables.

Merlin blinks up through the sun-shower at the truncated towers. Soon enough, in a few more summers, there will be balconies, bartizans, and belvederes atop this mighty edifice, and pennants and banderoles will fly regnant in the wind, displaying the royal colors of this land's true king.

That hope, which has consumed Merlin his whole life, spurs him to continue his supervisory tour. He boldly paces the flagstones of the spacious courtyard that someday will ring with the hooves of the king's cavalry. For the countless time, he surveys the surrounding bulwarks, their thick bases tapering to elegant parapets, and he envisions the stables, barracks, and shops that will occupy the perimeter of this outer ward.

Already the carpenters have sunk the foundation posts for most of these structures. And there, discreetly recessed in the vallation, is the water main of concrete-enclosed tile pipes that feeds a sewer system of manholes and conduits. Merlin is proudest of this arrangement of pipes that he himself designed, which funnels water from the mountains to the living quarters upstairs with enough of an overflow for flushing latrines. Even the barracks and the stables will have running water and self-cleaning commodes.

Satisfied that his architectural plans are being fulfilled, the wizard directs himself toward the great hall, where the king will reside and conduct his court. For now, it is merely a wide circular wall of massive stones, roofless and empty within but for the workers' platforms and sheds. But by summer's end the huge cedar timbers imported from Lebanon will be raised as roof beams, and the large elliptical windows will be fitted with translucent glass discs filling the enormous chamber with radiant shafts of filtered gold.

Merlin stands at the spot to be occupied by the dais, admiring the luminous and secure space he has designed for his king. As he reviews the numerous alcoves and arched niches in the walls where counsel-studios and scribes' chambers will be outfitted, a ghostly twist of light suddenly appears in the shadows of the masons' scaffolds. At once, he senses the identity of this specter, and fright sparks along the knuckles of his spine. Morgeu! Though he has not seen this witch in fifteen years, he remembers with a groan her vehement magic. He intones a spell that inspires the remaining workers in the great hall to leave, each of them believing he is summoned away by the lure of vendors hawking baked goods and fruit outside.

Then, making himself visible, Merlin strikes his staff against a stone flag and speaks. "I see you, Morgeu. Come into the light and declare to my face why you dare disturb my work."

The vaporous figure edges closer, and when it touches sunlight it begins to shrink to firepoints clear as dewdrops. The starglints tighten to the apparition of a tall, broad-shouldered woman in regal scarlet raiment. A halo of crinkled red hair flares about a lunar-pale and round face, whose small, dark eyes gaze with a vibrant malevolence at the narrow wizard.

"I am come to tell you simply this, proud Merlin: that what you build you build for me and the honor of my womb alone. No stooge of your choosing will occupy this great hall, for I shall assure that crows eat your eyes and dogs gnaw your bones before any king but my own sons Gawain and Gareth rule from this palace."

Merlin pretends to stifle a yawn and turns away, attempting to hide his fright. Nothing he can say will ever dissuade Morgeu from believing that he was responsible for the death of her father, Gorlois, duke of the Saxon Coast. Since the duke's violent death, she has passionately devoted her life to mastering the sorcery necessary to avenge herself against the wizard. At one time she went so far as to give herself over to the demons themselves, risking both sanity and her very life to acquire the supernatural powers to match Merlin's magic.

"You needn't have troubled yourself to come all this way after fifteen years to tell me that, Morgeu." Merlin feigns disinterest by fully turning his back on her and pretending to study the master builder's plans on the easel that stands where someday the king's throne will sit. Surreptitiously, he watches the reflection of her apparition in the shiny surface of the builder's bronze ruler. "I have not forgotten the great love you cherish for my demise. I thought perhaps you carried some news worthy of distracting me from my work. Now begone and trouble me no more with your wearisome ire."

Creeping closer, the enchantress intones hatefully, "When next we meet in the flesh, Merlin, I will make you despair that you ever dared assume a human guise."

"Morgeu, you are wrong to fight me." Merlin turns slowly about to face the wraith, and the timbre of his voice reaches out compassionately. "Our king needs you and your sons at his side. Can't you see? This is the time of legend. Our lives and deeds will shape myth itself and survive the dark age to come. Be with us, not against us. Dare to touch the future."

Morgeu finds herself nearly entranced by the wizard's eyebrows. The gray tufts bend ever more sadly as he speaks. She waves her hands before her face to break the spell. "Enough! You think I am yet a child to be enraptured by your clever words and your will alone?" She pulls her scarlet robes tighter about her, and her image shimmers like a flame. "I have not come here to partake of your madness, demon. I come to astonish you with my hatred and to taunt you with this promise: The son of Uther Pendragon will suffer before I kill him."

"No!" Provoked by this threat to his ward, Merlin lunges toward the apparition, his staff swinging in a wide arc. Insubstantial as a mirage, the sorceress retreats before him, becoming again lunar mist, an ectoplasmic wisp, and then nothing. The wizard's staff slices through empty air and leaves him gasping as much with fright as exertion. His mesmeric spells had no effect on her. *No effect at all!* he mulls, and experiences a distress so sharp and strange it seems to be happening outside of himself, as though this event has been a dream.

Merlin sags, lowering himself onto a worker's bench, yet the fright in him does not relent, and the knuckles of his hand gripping the staff whiten. Morgeu has acquired the magical skills to fulfill her threat. She shares with the king their mother's blood, and sooner or later that blood bond will draw her to her unsuspecting brother, no matter the wizard's obscuring spells.

He looks about at the vast, round hall with its incomplete walls and empty windows, and wonders if the fifteen years of continuous planning and building have vainly raised a monument to his bitter strength alone. *Am I arrogant to believe that justice can reign in a world of fury? Am I mad?*

Pressing his brow against the upright staff, Merlin remembers his mother, the good saint Optima, in whose womb this grand vision began. The love he knew then persists as an ember of hope far back in his soul, the memory of his mother's love. *I cannot be wrong about that,* he thinks, recalling how Optima's pure and abiding faith in the goodness of God had countered the aeons of torment he had lived as a demon.

The sun-shower pelts harder through the unfinished roof, the golden drops drumming against the scaffolds, worktables, and the brim of Merlin's hat. For an instant, the angel draws closer to the wizard and stands in the place beside him that no one sees. And for that one fleeting moment, the hinge of Merlin's heart swivels the door of his mind open on the invisible world.

Merlin sees far off his mother in red raiment rising among columnar sunlight toward the blazing throne of heaven. He blinks, and what he thought was Optima flying in scarlet robes is merely a bloody scrap of vermin hoisted among the sun shafts in the beak of a voracious raven.

"Bah!" He dismisses the illusion with a scowl and pulls himself upright by his staff. The glimpse of his mother in a scrap of offal is enough to remind him of his destinal work. He turns his thoughts away from the fearful questions of purpose that Morgeu's wraith had inspired and returns with renewed determination to the chores at hand.

Satisfied that Merlin's grace has been restored, the angel drifts away on the nectared breeze and becomes again the summer rain that falls over Camelot like cool news from the lips of heaven.

BOOK ONE

EAGLE OF THOR

Chapter One

Dune grass flattens under the wind, and the fishermen of the cove village of Mousehole turn over their boats on the curving strand. Purple fists of storm clouds rise in the south above a choppy sea, and lightning casts its nets across the flat horizon. The fishermen hurry to secure their seines under their boats. The day's catch writhes in wooden tubs, a silver-gray mass of cod, sea bass, and eels tangled in amber kelp and broken rainbows.

In pairs, the men slowly haul the tubs up the beach, their wood-soled shoes crunching the sea's scattered jewelry of periwinkles, black mussels, and starfish. The sandy path through the salt grass climbs toward a shale ledge, where a priest awaits them to bless their day's catch. His brown cassock pulls tight against his scrawny body in the press of the wind, and the wide sleeves of his outstretched arms flutter like wings.

Beyond the priest, the tidal plain rises gradually toward a sandstone bluff cluttered with thatch-roofed cottages. For three centuries, this seacoast town served a Roman villa situated farther in, on the headlands among the wind-thrown oaks and elder woods. The vine-tangled walls of the villa still stand on the terraced bluffs above the cove, though the Romans abandoned it a hundred years before. Over time, its fine water gardens of reflecting pools and fountains have grown clogged with silt, and the oil presses, bakery, and stables long since burned by looters. A humble monastery established twenty years ago by Saint Piran now occupies its roofless colonnade, whose improvised walls of wattle and daub presently house a broken millstone that serves as its crude altar.

Before a stone Celtic cross erected on the shale ledge, the fishermen stop and place their half-filled tubs of fish on the ground. They kneel perfunctorily, eager for their blessing so they can hurry back to their families before the storm strikes. Impatiently, they gaze up at the priest, but he does not move. His gaze has locked on the horizon of bruised clouds, and a tremor of fear suddenly twitches his beardless face.

"Lord God have mercy on us—I see raiders!" the priest cries out, and crosses himself hastily. "Storm raiders!"

At the dread sound of that name, the fishermen leap to their feet and stare horrified at the purple horizon. Low as driftwood in the water, a score of shallow boats begins to emerge from the haze of spindrift and windy spume. Squinting, the fishermen can just make out the bristly shape of lances as the boats dip and rise on the turbulent sea. Their jaws swing loose as human bodies gradually take shape riding the thunder swells, scrawls of lightning in the air above them like the fiery signatures of demons.

Panic-stricken, the men abandon their fish tubs and flee. They know that storm raiders have recently sacked other hamlets along the coast, reducing Neptune, Landsfall, and Bluerock to charred scars on the beach. The denizens of those fishing towns had all been murdered, women and children alike, their scalps woven into cloaks, their very flesh flayed from their bodies to fashion drumskins.

The throb of those horrid drums looms closer on the thunder itself as the fishermen bolt toward their homes. By the time the men have reached their cottages and alerted their families, the first curtains of rain drape the beach, and the raiders, propelled by the incoming tide and the rush of the squall, sail atop the breakers.

Flight is impossible. The cove holds the village as if in a giant's hand. The villagers scramble on the footpaths that climb toward the elder woods. Above them, the monks emerge from their prayer huts bearing a wooden cross, relying on their faith to drive off the barbarian warriors or, failing that, to lead them into proud martyrdom.

Casting terrified looks over their shoulders, the villagers see the scows of the storm raiders shooting out of the combers. The shallow-draft boats slide onto the beach, sizzling on the sand like lightning. War cries flap in the blustery wind as the raiders, brandishing long swords and spears, jump from their vessels.

Desperate to buy time for their families with their lives, many of the fishermen halt in their flight. They wield staves and flensing knives and stand fast on the steep paths, hoping to hold off the barbarians long enough for the women and children to reach the monastery and the open fields beyond. But when they see the raiders charging up the beach, the village men realize that their sacrifices will be futile: There are too many of them.

Through the driving rain, the terrible visages of the storm raiders come into view. Most of the bearded, screaming men are half-naked, their loins wrapped in wolf fur and bearskins. Some wear helmets of human skulls bound together with scalp hair. Others brandish clubs of femur bones and beat drums that dangle the leather of shriveled human faces. All display garish tattoos on their burly bodies—dragon-eyes and fang-faces.

Screeching in their barbarous tongue, the savage storm raiders fly up the beach clothed in rainsmoke, a company of shrieking devils loosed from the Christians' hell. Before this gruesome horde, the priest and the monks fall submissively to their knees. Unhampered by such encumbrances of devotion, however, the fishermen immediately turn and dart gibbering up the footpaths, not far behind their fleeing women and children.

Out of the gathering night, a clarion peal sounds thinly above the din of the pernicious drums, above the thunder and the screaming. The monks do not look up from their prayers, but the puzzled fishermen hesitate, gawking into the slashing rain to seek the source of the silver tantara that sounds again, louder and closer. Terror, once boiling to sobs inside them, suddenly explodes in a hopeful cry at the sight of misty shadows looming through the elder woods above.

"Salvation!" one keen-eyed fisherman bawls out. "Christ's soldiers are here! We are saved!"

From out of the misty woods, a small troop of mounted warriors takes form under a white pennant emblazoned with a scarlet cross. They gather atop the bluff—a steady line of lancers and archers bedecked in bronze face masks and plumed rawhide helmets, their Roman breastplates embossed with Christian emblems of the fish, the lamb, the chi-rho. The sight of their chain-mail armor and their powerful warhorses causes first disbelief, then screams of fright transform into cries of joy among the villagers as they fall to their knees in amazement.

A clattering drove of arrows flies over the heads of the stunned villagers and totters the furious assault of the storm raiders. The horn blast sounds again, an aggressive blare that lifts a mighty cry from the gathered horsemen and sends the cavalry plunging downslope at a full gallop. As the warriors fly past, the astonished villagers throw their hands up in praise, and cheer.

"Lord Kyner!" one of the monks cries out exultantly, recognizing the curved Bulgar saber of the warband's leader. Swiftly, word spreads among the huddled folk that ferocious Kyner, the famed Christian chief among the Celts, has come to their rescue.

But the storm raiders do not falter. Mad with blood rage, they charge over the bodies of their fallen comrades toward the stone cross, the emblem of all they hate. The Christian horsemen ride hard upon them with axes and swords flailing. Through the veils of rain smoking across the strand, more barbarian scows slide out of the storm-driven swells, and soon the beach is crowded with war-fevered men clashing against the headlong steeds.

The jubilant hurrahs of the village folk choke in their throats at the terrible sight of horses collapsing and the nightmarish Saxons spearing and clubbing the unhorsed soldiers. Whirlwinds of rain seem to carry the barbarians slathered in gore among the mounts, and the pounding charge falters and staggers to a halt. Milling in brutal confusion, the armies hack at each other, and the screams of horses shrill among the boom of thunder and drums and the incessant cries of human battle fury.

The monks stand, uplifted by their fervent prayers for victory. Chanting in unison, they watch horrified as Kyner's horsemen whirl and lunge among the seething pagans who encircle them. Kyner, broad saber hacking, and his huge son, Cei, with his famous battle-ax whirling, fight back to back. Even in the driving rain, their red-plumed helmets stand out and draw upon themselves the hottest fury of the battle.

The brutal frieze of clashing enemies lurches higher up the beach, and the stunned villagers begin to back away, once again moaning with despair. Too many of the horsemen have fallen. The ferocity of the storm raiders draws strength from out of the black air, and they fight more fiercely standing atop corpses and felled beasts. None among the fisherfolk want to see the renowned Kyner and his proud son destroyed—but, surrounded on all sides, they seem doomed. Even the monks have dropped again to their knees, pleading for divine intervention.

As if in answer to their fervid cries, a remarkable apparition suddenly appears down the beach, emerging through smoking sheets of the torrential rainfall. Riding a blood-slaked gray palfrey, a lone cavalryman bounds among the frantic pagans, his sword a blur of blood-arcs and strewn flesh. His shield bears the ichor-splattered image of a woman. Peering through the torrent and battle frenzy, the monks discern on the shield-image the improbable likeness, the blue robes, golden halo, and serene features of the Virgin Mother.

Mary's unknown champion rides like a winged warrior, his steed dancing across the shale with an eerie, fluid grace, rearing and prancing backward on its hind legs while its rider chops and stabs, clearing the beach around him. Among the monks are men who have seen battles before and some who themselves have fought and found their faith on the killing plains clashing with Picts and Jutes. But none has ever seen such a display of lethal horsemanship.

Again, the monks are on their feet, the better to behold Blessed Mary's warrior cutting a swath through the barbarians. Nimble as a ferret among snakes, the bronze-masked rider drives his mount as though it were a weapon in itself. It curvets directly into the thickest knot of the melee, striking with both front and rear hooves even as the relentless blade cleaves bone and flesh. Then it volts around the fallen raiders and pierces deeper into the fray.

The holy shield twists to deflect a spear, and the palfrey tramples the lancer and hurtles among the crowd that is eager to kill Kyner and his son. Drawing the battle onto himself, Mary's champion spins a deadly circle, exposing himself on every side to the enemy's blows yet deftly parrying spear thrusts and spinning axes with his battered shield. Leaning down with his masked face against the horse's shoulder, he barges toward his chief and opens a path for Kyner and Cei to free themselves from the slaughterous throng.

Together, the three horsemen drive the barbarians back from the Celtic cross and down onto the flat strand. The monks follow, and the villagers behind them, emboldened by the abrupt turn in the battle. Rain sweeps over the beach of sprawled dead like folds of drapery, and the onlookers stare in amazement as the raiders hurry toward the sea like playactors retreating behind drawn curtains.

In minutes, the fighting ends, and the slaughter begins. Kyner and Cei withdraw, and the surviving cavalrymen run down the isolated clusters of barbarians, who still stand defiant among their maimed and slain comrades. The Blessed Virgin's champion flies remorselessly among the enemy, throwing himself into the struggle as if eager to cast his own life away. Yet time and again, his sacred shield protects him and his palfrey from ax blows and sword thrusts, and his blade unerringly pierces the naked warriors with rapid, expert violence, leaving a wake of carcasses on the misty beach.

"Who is that warrior who carries before him the likeness of our Blessed Mother?" the amazed and incredulous priest asks, as Kyner and Cei wearily dismount among the monks.

The two men remove their helmets and shake loose long hair lanky with sweat. Kyner's arctic-wolf eyes regard the holy men with the indifference of a powerful beast. Ice-blue in the torchlight, they gaze out from an inflamed mass of jutting bones—brow, cheek, and jaw—flushed with battle rage. The younger man is still ghostly pale from their frightful entrapment in the homicidal crowd. His broad, thick, and beardless face gasps for air more out of contained fear than exhaustion. He is the younger version of his father except that he lacks the elder's heavy, drooping mustache. "He is my father's ward," he manages with a hint of disdain, and accepts a flagon from a grateful villager. "Aquila Regalis Thor."

"The Royal Eagle of Thor," the priest translates the name. "A Roman Saxon?" He stares even more intently at the brutish warrior still charging hellishly up and down the beach, slaying the last desperate storm raiders.

"Saxon blood sanctified by the Holy Spirit," Kyner huffs, and lifts his leathery face to the cool rain, grateful to be alive. "A rape-child redeemed by Christ. We call him Arthor."

Cei blinks into the downpour, and says grouchily, "We've wounded men on the beach. Get your monks down there, priest."

The dazed monks hurry to comply, and the priest looks to the old chieftain. "Lord Kyner, Mousehole is remote from any of your strongholds. How did you know of our plight?"

"Never mind that, Father. My son is right. There are good Christian souls down there desperate for their last rites and others to be saved by timely care. Make haste and prove yourself worthy of their great sacrifice."

When the priest has departed, Kyner fixes a tight stare on his son, and speaks slowly to contain his anger, "You should have held the left flank." And, silently, to himself he says, *Seventeen years old and the man is yet a boy! What have I done wrong?*

Cei squints with incredulity. "You were in danger. I broke the flank to save you."

"And you nearly killed us both! Good men died this night because you cared more for me than our company. Is this how I've trained you?" He meshes his teeth and directs his anger through his jaws into one hurtfully cramped thought in his brain, *When will he learn? There is no compassion before the sword!* "You should have held the flank."

"And have you overrun?" Cei swipes the rain from his eyes and stares with a shrill anguish. "You are my father—and our chief."

Kyner puffs out his hollow cheeks with a heavy sigh. "I am an old man, Cei. I shouldn't be here at all. Arthor is right. I belong in White Thorn with the women."

Cei's face tightens like a fist. "Arthor is an arrogant bastard."

"Who saved our lives yet again this night." Kyner nods to his son. "I want you to show him more love, Cei."

"Is that an order, Father?"

"Must I so order?" Kyner sadly shakes his drenched head. "Have you no respect for your own brother?"

"Respect for that foulmouthed ingrate?" Cei shakes the rain from his face with an irate jerk. "I don't understand why you hold him to your heart and call him my brother. He scorns you as much as me. He's bad blood."

"But look at him, Cei." Kyner gazes with blatant admiration at the strand where Arthor has backed the last of the raiders into the waves. In the violet, falling light, he and his horse move like elusive shadows before the glowing breakers, charging at the howling barbarians and leaving their corpses adrift in the foaming water. "While we stand here in the rain amazed to be alive, when by all rights the blood of our lives should be running in the sand with the others who fell this gruesome night, still he fights. Look at him! By God, look at him. He kills with the grace of God's own avenging angel."

Cei gnaws his lower lip. "Is that why you love him more than me?"

"Not that foolishness again!" Kyner replies with swift anger. "Love. You speak of it as if love were some kind of money to be doled out at whim. You are my *son*. I care for you beyond love. And though he is a great warrior, you will be chief, not him. You would be chief this very night had you not broken flank."

"I don't want to be chief, Father."

"Not chief?" Kyner casts a dire look at his son. "For what then have I been grooming you all these years? Why do you think I am so angry with you when you falter on the battlefield? Someday you *will* rule our clan, and love will prove far less valuable to you then, far less important than experience. That is why I am here on this malignant beach instead of home with the women shucking nuts for the winter. And you say you don't want to be chief? In the name of God, son, what do you want?"

"I want you to look at me the way you look at him."

"Fah!" Kyner turns away in disgust. "I look at him with the admiration I would have for a marvelous hunting dog. Is that what you want, Cei? Then get down there and fight with all his brutal cunning."

Cei remains silent, struggling with himself. *I am a good warrior. I know it. I have been tried in battle and not found wanting. Yet beside that blood-crazed Arthor, I seem a blundering fool. He loves killing. He is the very devil himself when it comes to killing. How can I compare?*

"Get out of the rain, Father," Cei says, mounting his horse. "It's bad for your bones."

"Where are you going?"

"I'll see to our men. Take shelter. Arthor did not save us from the Saxon to lose you to the ague." He pulls his steed abruptly away and trots toward the beach, where night smothers the dead, and the living stir like detached pieces of darkness.

Kyner watches after him briefly, then turns about and trudges up the path toward the winking hearthfires of the hamlet. Old age has set its claws in him years ago, and now they flex, as they always do lately after any strenuous effort. He should have died this night, he knows. He should be among the corpses on the beach, his soul flown from this sour flesh and gone to its place in Purgatory to await Judgment. Instead, Arthor has preserved him—and Cei.

The chieftain bows his head humbly under the pelting rain. *Cei is a good warrior but not bold. And that is as it should be, for though he is strong, he is not clever. Yet, he is my son—he is my only son.*

From ahead, he sees torches flapping in the wet wind and the villagers in a throng singing their jubilant song in praise of sweet Jesus. Kyner is reminded how grateful he should be even to witness such a scene. Tonight, victory belongs to the Lord, and the chieftain's personal concerns gradually evaporate in the presence of such divine joy that redeems all suffering.

Chapter Two

The best fish of that day's catch arrive on pewter and wood plates. The monks place them atop their broken millstone altar, before an oaken crucifix carved by Saint Piran himself. The church, a squat structure with walls of woven sticks and packed dung, is the only structure in Mousehole large enough to host Kyner and his men. Even so, most of the villagers can find no place to sit down inside its crowded interior. They stand outside in the torrential night, squeezed together under makeshift canopies of hawthorn branches whose waxy leaves shed the rain. Happily, they tend the fires in the stone ovens and pass the plates of steaming fish into the church through the empty windows. And with the smoking eels aswirl in butter, the cod and bass smothered in hazels and berry sauce, come baskets of honey dumplings and barley loaves, bowls of dandelion soup sprinkled with hard-boiled egg yolks and blue cheese, mugs of blackberry pudding, and flagons of raspberry cider and whortleberry wine. The villagers spare nothing of their summer bounty for the honor of their rescuers.

Behind the altar, the priest and the monks bless the food and serve the warriors. Kyner presides at the altar in the hamlet's one chair, the ecclesiastic seat that the priest occupies during the daily celebration of the Eucharist. At his side, perched on a settle behind the altar, are Cei, the cavalry's officers, and the hamlet's elder, a local clan leader with a full mustache and braided, cloud white hair. The other cavalrymen sit on rushes covering the stamped-earth floor and use benches as tables. Seven of their number died in the fighting on the beach, and their helmets lie at the foot of the crucifix. The three most severely wounded have propped their helmets in the candlelit niche behind the altar so that they may receive the monks' healing prayers. Kyner's surgeon and Mousehole's leech tend those men in separate huts, where the festivities will not disturb their recovery.

No sooner has the food been served when a monk, soaked and trembling, bursts into the jammed assembly and shoulders through the village elders to the altar. "Father, he's killing them!" he blurts, seizing the priest's cassock.

"Be calm, brother. Who is killing whom?"

"The Eagle of Thor—killing the wounded Saxons! Even the ones who wish to convert! He's killing them all! And even as they kneel in prayer! You must stop him!"

"Hah!" Kyner laughs coldly. "None can stop Arthor. He won't stop until he's killed every one."

"But it's unchristian, Father," the monk protests. "These are men whose souls can be saved for Christ."

The priest turns a supplicating look to the chieftain.

"This brother is right, my lord. Our Savior insists we forgive our enemies. What your man is doing is wrong. Even if their souls cannot be won at once, surely you can press these heathens into thralldom and grant them time for the Savior's teachings to change their souls."

Kyner reaches for a honey dumpling and shakes his large, brutish head. "Arthor knows nothing of mercy."

"But he carries the image of the Blessed Virgin," the priest persists. "She is the mother of mercy."

"And Arthor leaves mercy to her alone." Kyner speaks around a mouthful of food. "For him, there is only the sword. And tell your brothers to stay clear of him. He'll send them to heaven if they try to protect the pagans."

"No!" The priest cannot accept this. "You would let him slay holy men?"

"Let him?" Kyner chokes on his food and flushes scarlet.

Cei pounds his father's back and frowns at the priest. "Arthor once beheaded a priest in Trier for trying to protect an old Saxon grandmother clutching the Bible! I tell you, he's the devil's own spawn."

"Aye—" Kyner coughs, freeing his throat and reaching for his goblet. "He's my iron hammer. But tell the whole story, Cei. That crone's Bible was hollow and held a treacherous blade meant for my heart."

"But . . . a priest!" the holy man says, aghast.

The chieftain quaffs the cider and dismisses the murder with a wave of his free hand. "He was an

Arian priest—a Christian polytheist. And empty-headed, to boot, for bringing such a viper into my presence. If not for Arthor, I'd have been slain in Trier, and at this moment Mousehole would be in flames."

The priest ponders this a moment and thinks to ask again, "My lord, how did you know the Saxons would raid us this night?"

Kyner wipes crumbs from his stupendous mustache. "Never mind that now—the killing has already been accomplished," he says, pointing to the open portal.

Arthor, tall and fearsome, stands in the church doorway in full chain armor. Gore-slick sword and shield in hand, his head covered in a rawhide helmet crested by scarlet boar bristles, he fills the portal like a silent effigy of death. His face remains hidden behind a bronze vizard impressed with a Gorgon's viperous grimace.

The festive animation of the room falls at once to silence, and the rescuers pass sullen, apprehensive looks among themselves. All but Kyner seem anxious. Indeed, a flush of admiration brightens the chieftain's heavy features at the sight of the stark warrior. But neither Cei nor any of the other officers seem to share the old warrior's affection, and this further arouses the priest's curiosity. Stepping past a monk who has moved aside to let Arthor in, he moves hurriedly to the door to greet the champion himself.

"Come into the house of the Lord of Peace and be refreshed, soldier of Christ. You fought zealously for your Lord. Perhaps too zealously, my son. There was no need to kill the wounded. We would have tended them."

"The Lord has said that those who live by the sword shall die by the sword," a voice replies, darkly muffled by the vizard. "I have fulfilled the law."

Gently, the priest lays a hand on the leather fist gripping the bloody sword. "Yes, my son. You and your comrades have saved us from the sword of our enemies. Now the killing is done. Come into the house of your Lord with your hands empty, a worthy Christian."

Arthor's hand opens, and the priest takes the sword and hands it to the monk behind him. "Cleanse and sanctify this blade, brother, for this night it has served our Savior. The shield as well."

"No." Arthor lifts the blood-streaked shield with its image of Jesus' mother, her hands clasped in prayer, her lovely, radiant head bowed. "The Virgin stands by her son."

The priest nods and smiles proudly, understanding. He reverently takes the shield in both hands. "I will place her there myself. Come. Share our joy at our salvation. Join us in this feast of our happy gratitude. Honor us with your presence."

"Bare your head, Arthor!" Cei shouts from across the crowded room. "The fighting's over. Now show some civility to these good people. This is a house of God, after all."

Kyner stands, goblet of raspberry cider in hand. "I drink to Arthor before our Lord and Savior and before this company. All of you are witness to his battle prowess in the face of our enemies. All of you saw

how he risked his life to save my own—and my son's."
The chieftain casts a pointed look at Cei, who grudgingly nods and lifts his goblet in the air. "To Arthor!"

A respectful chorus of voices echo. Unmoved,
Arthor unstraps his helmet. Short, sweat-spiked
hackles of badger hair stick out around a blond face
too young for whiskers. A murmur of astonishment
seeps from the monks, who had not expected a boy to
fill so large a frame let alone display the killing ardor
and lethal horsemanship they had witnessed on the
stormy beach. Jaws loosen at the sight of the youth's
callow features: rose-tinged cheeks in a milk-pale
countenance glossy and downed with adolescence.

The priest steps back a pace and his hands tighten
on the shield in momentary disbelief. A child! Yet
indeed, something wicked about the lad's cold eyes,
aslant and acid yellow, and his taut, angry mouth,
clamped as if perpetually ready to take or give a blow,
hints at an embittered soul. A cruel child, he thinks to
himself.

"Come, young warrior," the priest gathers his
wits to say. "Come and sit at the table with your comrades."

"Fah!" Cei shouts in cold mockery. "Arthor is no
comrade. Nor is he even a Celt. He'll sit at the back
with the new men, as he always does."

"Now, Cei," Kyner admonishes, "show some charity. The boy has saved our lives. Tonight he'll sit at table
with us. Come, Arthor. Place yourself beside me."

But Arthor ignores him and goes directly to the
crucifix, not even glancing at the altar-table laden
with its sumptuous piles of food. He kneels before the

helmets of those seven fallen in battle and closes his eyes. The priest follows and stands the shield before the base of the crucifix so that its top rests against the solitary nail that pierces Christ's feet, and he barely grasps the boy's whisper: "Mother Mary blesses you courageous men, who have paid with the sanctity of blood for her Son's glory . . ."

The resuming festivities mute the rest of his prayer, yet the priest, bending closer as if to steady the shield, sees sincerity in the flutter of the boy's closed lids. For a moment, his face loses its complex gloom and seems fixed by no more than a child's prayerful inwardness.

And then, abruptly, Arthor rises. His face sets angrily, eyes amber wasps. He ignores the entreaty of Kyner, "Arthor—stay! Feast with us. Ignore proud Cei, who wears humility poorly. Come, lad. Eat and drink at my side."

Through the length of the packed church Arthor stalks, meeting no man's gaze, his bristly brown hair brushed back as if by the wind of his passing as he returns to the storm-wrung night. The rain slashes against him, and he bends into it and hurries past the smoking ovens and the gawking villagers. Quickly, he leaves the hamlet and descends the dark paths toward the pounding sea.

At his command, the fishermen have stacked the Saxon's warboats, set them ablaze, and heaved the heathen corpses atop the pyre. Arthor walks away from those shadowy fires and their wet reflections in the black sea and follows the long, pale combers to the far end of the cove. There, the slurs of fire and torchlight from the hamlet cast meaty streaks of fire in the downpour.

Climbing a dune of witchgrass, he finds shelter in a shallow cave above the booming surf. He sits hunched, hugging his knees. Raindrops stand like tears on his cheeks, but he does not cry, though his breath stirs hugely in his chest, in distress. His heart kneads an old rage. He will not sit at Kyner's side like a faithful dog.

Smoldering for what he might be if he had been born to the chieftain rather than merely found by him, he plays for himself tedious fictions of greatness. His muscles ache with the killing frenzy that possessed him in battle, and he imagines that this strength is the might of a warlord, a king, spent building an empire. The ringing hammer-voices of the enemy clang in his skull, forging the victories of his kingdom.

But these are fictions, and they fall quickly away, no longer able to sustain him as they did when he was a child, before he learned his talent for killing. The bare truth remains, he is a foundling and nothing more, useful only because of his murderous cunning. He wishes he had never been found in that ditch in the woods where his shamed mother left him to die. *Better to be dead,* he thinks. *Better to be dead than nameless and with no destiny, no destiny but to be the strength of other men's destiny. Better to be dead.*

All night, he stays in the cave. Eventually, the song of the rain sifts through his tightly woven anger and soothes him to sleep. When he startles awake from a battle-dream, clutching for the sword he does not have, the storm has moved on. Clustered stars blaze over the black face of the sea. By their trifling light, he watches breakers rise and fall and phosphorescent crabs scuttling before them along the littered tide line.

Loneliness pervades him, and he prays again to Mary, the same prayer he has offered all his young life to the only mother he has ever known, "Mother Mary, let me be for you the Son you lost. Give me the strength to defend Him now that He has left us alone in the devil's world. Give me the strength to fight for Him until He returns."

And as always before, the same sweet voice opens from far inside him, so faint and still he must hold his breath to hear her say the same words she says each time he calls her: *Love is first, Arthor. Never abandon. Never abandon.*

At dawn, he bathes in the sea, then climbs the path among the black rocks and returns to Mousehole. The company, heavy-lidded from a night of drinking, sit heavily in their saddles. Kyner ignores him for shaming him in front of the company by spurning him at the feast. The boy-warrior will have to be punished. Cei orders him to saddle his horse, knowing Arthor cannot refuse, hoping he will, so that Kyner's hand will be forced to act more harshly.

Arthor complies silently, and when he is done, Kyner leads the company into the mist-strewn woods, not waiting for the disrespectful youth. The monks, stung with pity, help him prepare his palfrey. After he mounts, a monk returns his helmet, and the priest comes forward with sword and shield. They have been meticulously cleaned.

"Remember," the priest counsels, "our Savior served. Prince of Heaven, he served humbly. Go and do likewise, young warrior."

Arthor's hard mouth flinches with disdain, and the cold in his stare freezes the priest's heart. "Yes, Jesus served humbly, Father. But he knew he was a prince and born of God's love. I am but born of lust and violence. I will not serve humbly. I will serve with the sword."

The priest shakes his head sadly. "Then, my son, I ask you to contemplate what you told me last night. He who lives by the sword shall perish by the sword."

"I expect no less." The youth smiles grimly. "Am I not God's warrior?"

At those words, the sun rises all at once behind him, and the holy men, wincing before the sudden brightness, bow their heads in unison as though in the presence of majesty.

---✂︎---

Chapter Three

Melania of Aquitania, renowned in her province for her classical beauty and erudition, remained hidden in a tower for a year while warbands of Salian Franks ranged through the countryside stealing crops, murdering Roman landowners, and enslaving their wives and children. Melania's father and brothers died defending the vast Gallic estate that had been in their family for over five hundred years, and her mother shriveled away soon after, of melancholia. Her once noble and proud family teetered on extinction, surviving only in herself and her father's grandmother, a one-eyed hag who knew all the secrets of the ancient estate.

Great-grandmother connived with Melania as intimately and cunningly as a sister. Even before the mourning for their dead ended, they scrutinized their options. The Salian Franks, who had suffered under the iron fist of the last Roman general in northern Gaul, loathed everything Roman; so, there was no hope of marrying Melania to a Frankish chieftain to preserve the estate. Flight, too, was impossible. In Italy, the Ostrogoths and the kingdom of Odovacar were at war, while in the Eastern Empire, the most that a beautiful young woman of learning such as Melania could hope for—one without lands of her own—was the life of a high-class prostitute. Saint Helena, the mother of Constantine, the first Christian emperor, had begun her illustrious life as such a prostitute, and Great-grandmother offered her as an example. But Melania would not have it. Selling her favors to wealthy noblemen did not disturb her half as much as the misery of losing her family's ancient lands. She would do anything to preserve her ancestral estate.

"Anything?" the crone asked when she heard this. She stared intently at her great-granddaughter with her one good eye.

"We have already pondered a life of prostitution," Melania replied. "What could be worse?"

The crisscross of wrinkles in the old face netted a darkness from within, a shadow that seemed to leak from inside the old woman. "There is an unchristian way to save us. Would you have it, then?"

Melania arched her dark and delicate eyebrows. "What are you keeping from me, old mother?"

The hag cackled and led Melania to the tower. The spire of black granite was the oldest edifice in the province, erected by the estate's Roman founders in the century before Christ to serve as a watchtower. In the 180 years since the empire had become Christian, the tower had been used by the family as the bell turret of their church. Great-grandmother knew the hidden passageways that led first into labyrinthine cellars, then farther down into extensive catacombs that connected with the grottoes and caverns of a subterranean stream.

Accompanied by the wavery shadows of the oil lamp and the sibilant echoes of the blind current, the crone led the stately Melania past rock-hewn chambers crowded with lichenous kegs, cobwebbed amphorae, stacks of tablets, and bins of moldering scrolls. At last, the stone pathway meandering among the innumerable stalagmites delivered them to a crypt etched with inscriptions from the reign of Emperor Augustus. Into the anonymous dark of that recess, Great-grandmother thrust her oil lamp and exposed a profusion of long, thin-necked pots depicting animal-headed gods—the beakers and primitive retorts of desert alchemists—and a clutter of magical instruments: calipers with cuneiform markings, jackal-headed wands, wave-curved daggers, a necklace of ivory leviathan teeth, crystal spheres with bloodlike webworks at their cores, and mirror-glass discs that broke the lamplight into a delirium of rainbows.

In her gnarled hand, the old woman retrieved a small, intricately embossed urn of black silver. The wings of bearded sphinxes served as handles, and the urn itself embodied an orphic egg entwined by twin vipers whose gnashed fangs interlocked to clasp the hermetic lid.

"Do not open this," Great-grandmother warned before handing the urn to Melania; then, she reached again into the crypt and removed a silver throat band tooled with a reptileskin motif and twin serpent-heads with exposed fangs. She fitted the band about Melania's long, pale throat, and a magnetic chill sparked through the girl. "This will protect you from them."

"From whom, old mother?"

The crone did not answer but reached a third time into the crypt and came out with a knife, its blade of speckled lodestone and haft of quartz bound with bands of blackened silver. "And this, if needs be, will kill them."

"Who?"

"The lamia."

Melania's long, ebony hair fluffed with fright like a cat's. Lamia—a lovely Greek word that meant "devouring monsters." Since her earliest childhood, she had heard frightful tales of the lamia, shapeshifting wraiths that could thread through keyholes in their most tenuous form and then solidify to taloned beasts muscular enough to rip free a man's lungs and squeeze his throbbing heart before his startled face.

"I thought those were stories for scaring naughty children," Melania mumbled, gazing fitfully at the exquisite urn in her hands.

"Oh dear, no—those stories of the old Romans who founded this estate are all true, child," the crone says with a toothless smile. "Our forefathers did bargain with Phoenician traders for all these pagan objects, just as we heard in the stories when we were children. They had aspirations of sorcery, those first settlers who came here when this land was wilderness. They purchased magical amulets, necromantic potions, effigies of power whose use we've long forgotten. Most, truth be told, lost their efficacy centuries ago. But the urn you hold in your hands, the band about your throat, and this lode-knife—oh, they are yet potent, child, they are yet potent indeed—as you shall see."

In the daylight of the courtyard before the tower, the urn looked far less awe-inspiring than it had in the cryptic underground darkness. It seemed no more than an antique and outlandishly ornate jewel box, not large enough to contain anything of threat. But when the crone opened it, spiritous fumes hissed outward so violently that the air quaked with heat. Two fiery figures untangled and slithered translucently before them—bright muscles of flame in sinuous viper-shapes, with outspreading hair like the dust of sundown and features like firelight on faces of bone.

Great-grandmother danced around them, laughing, jabbing at them with the lode-knife, making their giant shapes skitter and twitch before her, making them slide away like haze in shimmering layers of sunbeams, then withdrawing the blade and pulling their radiant and vibrant plumes closer to her. "They fear the knife!" she shouted. "One stab of it, and they die!"

Melania backed away from their rasping drone of mad hornets, their sticky reek of dead things, and their cold aura, thick and weighty as the ocean's winter breath.

"Be not afraid, child," the crone assured her. "You wear the guardian band about your throat. They cannot harm you so long as you wear it. Come! Dance with us!"

Melania did not dance with them. She watched

appalled as the fireshapes with their skullfaces swirled around her great-grandmother. Phantom snakes, they coiled around her, and she spun with the lode-knife grasped in both hands until they retreated. Then, they condensed in the brash sunlight to a pool of green fog, an eerie phosphor that gathered upright, and hardened to a figure of a sable-haired man in a blue tunic—and beside him, another figure in a white gown, a lean woman with masses of chestnut hair and a lusty mole on her upper lip.

Melania recognized her grandparents even as the crone eked a hurt cry to see again her lost son and his dead wife.

The chimerical figures blurred and transformed themselves again, assuming the angular posture of Melania's father and the slender, hollow-cheeked mirage of her fragile mother.

"Make them stop, Great-grandmother!" Melania shouted.

The old woman jabbed at them, and the lamia hazed into the raw boy of the grown man who had been her grandson and Melania's father. The other curled into the cherished infant of the crone's first-born, birth chrism glistening like fur, eyes not yet unstuck, arms clenching at emptiness, naked and crying.

Weary of these apparitions, the old woman danced the lamia back into their urn and snapped shut the fang-meshed lid. Melania dropped to her knees and crossed herself. "It is as you say, old mother—an unchristian thing."

The hag sucked air through her wrinkled mouth

hole, winded by her perfidious dance, and smiled knowingly. "Unchristian they may be, but they are ours to use as we will—if we are cautious."

"How will we hold them?" Melania asked. "Will they not escape us and haunt the countryside?"

"Don't you remember the stories?" the old woman snickered. "They are bound to the urn. They cannot escape so long as the urn remains intact. And they will destroy any who enter their presence unprotected. Be aware of these simple truths, and they can do you no harm. Even I, a withered hag, can make them dance to my tune. Think how easy it will be for the spry young woman you are."

Yet weeks would pass before Melania mustered the courage to open the urn herself and more weeks again before her legs found the strength to dance with the lamia and control them with the lode-knife. By then, Great-grandmother had identified the underground passageway that led to the archaic map vaults. Somewhere in that extensive catacomb, an ancestor from the reign of Emperor Nerva had stored a chart identifying the location of a rich trove of gold coins. They had been buried somewhere in the hinterlands of Britannia against such a dire time as this, when only gold could buy salvation. With that huge treasure in hand, Melania could purchase a treaty with the Salian Franks or, if necessary, hire mercenaries from rival tribes to drive them out of Aquitania and assure that her ancestral estate would be restored and remain unmolested for the remainder of her life.

For a year, the women searched the map vaults

under the tower before they found what they sought. During that time, they lived off stores of grain, cheese, olives, and wine and kept a small garden and a few animals. When marauders encroached, they secured the barn, released the lamia, and hid in the tower, where the old woman giggled and the young woman shuddered to hear the terrible cries that followed. Packs of wild dogs and crows came regularly to feast on the torn bodies of the slaughtered. On the spring day when, with map in hand, Melania bid tearful adieu to her great-grandmother, the estate gleamed with the scattered bones of the lamia's victims.

With the urn secured tightly before her on the saddle of her draft horse, Melania rode north. She kept to forest trails and avoided the Roman roads. At night, she slept with the guardian band about her throat. Sometimes in the morning when she woke, she found her great-grandmother squatting beside her or her parents and a few times even a mirror copy of herself. But the lamia could do nothing more than startle her. They never spoke. They never touched her. She had become adept at using the lode-knife to return them to the urn, and before long she worried less about controlling them and more about how she would use her treasure to redeem her ancestral home. She imagined the noble men from Arles and Toulouse that she would consider for her husband, and in the mornings she began to wake to apparitions of handsome, virile swains.

The first few times that brigands accosted her in the forests, she never even bothered to dismount, simply tilted the urn away from her and opened it. After the lamia would do their gruesome work, she would ride on a short way and wait for their return. But eventually the landscape began to change. The oak forests, the olive groves and draperies of vine on Aquitania's plains thinned out and gave way to birch, pine, and dwarfed cedar as the land rose and folded into rugged terrain.

Now she walks ahead of her horse, leading it by the reins along the narrow trails above rock slides, where mists swirl and the whistle of a falcon startles green finches among the shining pines.

From an overhanging ledge a net falls without warning, its rock-weighted hem knocking her off her feet and nearly toppling her over the ledge onto the treacherous gray scree. Her horse whinnies with fright. Above her loom several brutish men with crow black hair. A boulder splashed with golden moss releases several more from their hiding place. They stand over her, laughing, bearded men in red-and-green rags—brigands—and she sees beyond them to where the trail rises toward heather blue peaks and clouds.

They remove the net, and she tries to rise but is shoved back by a gruff hand that rips the guardian band from her throat. "No!" is all she can shout before the men around her horse find the urn and snap open its lid.

The scream of an arctic blast reverberates off the rocky slopes, and the brigands gawk about, startled. Melania lunges to her feet and grasps for the guardian band—but too late. The face of the laughing man holding the band shrivels to a scream as silver flames engulf him and he collapses, flesh boiling off his bones.

Melania's hand clasps the throat band in the same instant that the spectral bone face of a lamia veers toward her, its spidery fingers already finding agonizing entrances into the smallest parts of her life.

---❦---

Chapter Four

Aelle, Saxon chieftain in the clan of Thunderers, is a destroyer of cities. A true Northman, he is a son of the eternal green-mountain forests, his eyes cut from blue lamps of glacial ice and his soul shaped from winter's polar lights. Fervently, he believes that cities are an abomination. They trap the human spirit. No one can be free in a city. They are cages, whose walls enclose and confine. In nature, there are no walls. There are heights and depths, yet always with crevices and pathways of rivers and streams, always offering options. Not so in cities, where walls meet each other at tyrannical right angles, offering no choice, only submission. Streets, too, are walls, except laid flat, denying freedom, enslaving the very direction people may walk. And the houses that the Christian city-dwellers occupy are not the collapsible, transportable tents of the nomadic Saxons but permanent abodes made of walls trapping the very land under them and the people inside them—traps, really, with right-angle walls built atop right-angle streets inside right-angle ramparts, everything in a grid, snared in the Christian net, like their god, who is caught, nailed to his right-angle cross. No wonder they call him the Man of Sorrows. Who but the mad could worship such a one? Even the Christian dead are trapped: Instead of the freedom of the pyre, they bury their dead in boxes. From birth through death, the evil ones live in cages.

Dedicated to the destruction of such evil, Aelle burns cities and frees the land under them. He slaughters Christians and spares the tribes the contagion of their sick religion, a truly mad religion that fervently seeks to convert all others to the insane faith that people are born evil, marked by the divine for eternal damnation unless they embrace the Man of Sorrows and share his terrible grief. No joy in this life, they claim, only suffering. Yet, what of the joy of the wild hunt that even the gods revere? And what of the splendor of spring after the fiery dark of winter? And what of woman, the joy of man? And what of the sun itself, so noble even as it crosses the immense snow plains? And the moon and the stars, the jewelry of night? And the privilege of silence when walking through snowy woods and the wind dies down with a hush among the slender trees and the small animals are asleep in their homes? Is not life itself joy? When one hears the laughter of children, is not the woman glad for childbirth no matter the agony, and is not the warrior happy for his wounds no matter their nagging aches?

Aelle is a proud destroyer of cities. Unlike other clans—Death's Angels, the Ravagers, Sons of Freeze—Thunderers do not sneak upon their enemies under the cowl of night and storm. They attack with the rising sun at their backs, and the thunder of their war

drums shakes the blue sky. The clan of Aelle is dedicated to the north god Thunder Red Hair and attacks
as he would, boldly. When the fortress town of
Regnum fell to such an assault, the Thunderers came
away with over three hundred scalps and enough
flayed flesh to make a hundred thunder drums. Aelle
himself shucked the scalps of the priests while the holy
men yet lived, honoring those worshipers of suffering
by not sparing them the pain their god so adores.
Later, when his men pulled down the city walls, he
stood on the backs of the priests, their peeled skulls
pink as melons at his feet.

The other Saxon clans fear the Thunderers, for
they know that Aelle is faithful only to Thunder Red
Hair. He despises Death's Angels and Sons of Freeze
for joining the Foederatus, the alliance of north
tribes, because they must obey foreign commanders
such as Cruithni, the Pictish king, and the Jutish
king, Wesc. Aelle will obey no king but himself, and
his clan goes its own way. He fears no one and is
bound by no obligations of loyalty to any of the other
Saxon clans.

Such independence he attributes to the special
favor of his god Thunder Red Hair, who took him
for his own thirty-five summers ago during the battle
at Aegelsthrep, when a British arrow pierced Aelle
between the eyes. The blow, with all its possible
grief, opened the eyes of infinity in him, and he saw
the gods themselves in the blue zenith—the great
warrior Bright Shining Blood with arms massive as
the turned wood of ships' masts, and beautiful Lady
Unique in a sleek gown dazzling as the coins on a

carp's back, and the one-eyed chieftain of the gods, the Furor, with his storm-beard and flowing mane of summer clouds standing beside his beloved son Thunder Red Hair. Thunder Red Hair's face, clear-cut as a garnet, smiled down at Aelle. That smile suffused the young warrior with such strength that pain fell from him like petals from a flower. He rose with the arrow still standing straight out from his brow and surged back into the battle. That glorious day, his sword Skidblade sent many Britons into the earth to await the mournful judgment of their Man of Sorrows.

A year later, this time as chief of the Thunderers, he fought alongside the Destroyers and the Green Blades, slaughtering many Britons at Crecganford and dancing in a bishop's robes like a red-winged bird. Each summer after that, he led his clan through the season's towering rains, calling on Thunder Red Hair to help him purge the land of the cities—the Roman vici—that would smother the land under them and poison the rivers beside them. And though he has never again seen through the infinite sunlight to the very forms of the gods, he feels them always near him when steel strikes steel, and he hears their satisfied sighs when he bends over his fallen foes and lifts their heads by their hanks of hair for the ritual cut above the eyes and feels the night weight of death in them.

Aelle does not see the gods anymore, though occasionally the scar between his eyes where the arrow pierced will throb with a cold hurt. And by that he knows that one of the Great Ones of the

Wild Hunt stands near him—Thunder Red Hair or that god's father, the Furor. Usually they come at propitious times, to lead him into an important battle or away from a place where his enemies lurk, or they come to make him aware of the greatness of an event, as when his son Cissa entered this world. Aelle has had many children without the gods in attendance, but when Cissa was born, twenty-six winters ago, the arrow scar throbbed with a ruby-cut pain. That night, the polar lights flowed free as living water. A white elk appeared from out of the forest's ice caverns, its great horns sparkling with bits of broken fire. A sweetly exotic perfume of summer settled over the frozen camp, full of the promise of legend, and the clan's Lawspeaker announced that Keeper of the Golden Apples, the Furor's mistress, had arrived to bless the birth of a seer.

As ever, the Lawspeaker declared the truth, for Cissa grew to manhood full of trance strength and prophecy. Lithe and muscular as his father, he excelled in the hunt and in the arts of war. But, unlike Aelle, Cissa's eyes of glacial ice see the invisibles as clearly as the sunrise and the dusk where they touch. From early adolescence, he has shaved his body and worn only tattoo runes, snakeskin thongs, and leggings sewn from the hide and hair of the clan's enemies, because this pleases the Furor, his spirit father. With Cissa at his side, Aelle has led his warband deep into the British countryside, where even Foederatus armies have dreaded to venture, and he has burned numerous vici—Banavem, Venta, and

Anderida—slaughtering all the inhabitants, compounding his respect among the north tribes and winning an audience with the chieftain of the gods, the Furor himself.

"Leave me behind," Aelle demurs when his son announces the heavenly summons. They stand together in a field not far from Anderida, where a farmer's barley had grown the previous summer and now pale lavender asters glow in the wild grass. "Who am I to stand before a god? I do not have your deep sight."

"You will not need deep sight, brave Aelle—not when you are in the god's presence." Cissa gestures to the green-and-purple sky lowering over the ragged tops of the forest. "You have been invited into the Storm Tree, and we will ascend as spirits and see with spirit eyes. To refuse to go would be an unhappiness for all who love your courage."

"Have I refused?" Aelle glares at his son. "I but question my worthiness. I am a warrior chief, not a seer."

"Mighty yet humble Aelle, we are each of us no more than a drop of the ocean that made us—yet in each drop turn vast oceans. Question your worthiness no more." Cissa points across the field to where thunder moves like a ghost through the big woods and the clan sits hunched under barberry canopies waiting for the rain. "The Thunderers do not know why I asked you to walk with me through this field. Let us return among them and say we came to taste the lightning and found it good."

Aelle shakes his head. "No. The strength in your

words has already opened the way for me. We have walked the paths of Middle Earth fearlessly though many have set their swords against us. Always, we prevailed. So, if the gods summon, why should we not walk the paths of the Storm Tree as well?"

Cissa smiles proudly and places his large, tattooed hands on his father's scarred shoulders. "Sit, strong Aelle, and we will rise together into the World Tree, where the gods await us."

Their knees bend, the tall grass rises above their heads, and a bolt of lightning explodes atop them in a glare of white fire. The blast shivers the marrows in their bones and blinds them with brightness. When they can see again, they blink at a rainbow land of which the summer of their earthly memory is but a dim echo. Zany green meadows tilt in all directions, crested with prismatic groves of immense trees above onyx boulders that spill tassels of waterfalls into iridescent pools. Breezes full of ripe apricot fragrances waft dragonflies and emerald birds through a sky-ocean of indolent clouds.

Startled, their breaths quickening, they stand, the light between them velvet with soft energies. Before they can speak, they see him striding toward them across the fiery green meadow, the opalescent wind in his stormy beard, his one eye fierce as a diamond, staring at them from under the falcon's hat he wears cocked over his empty socket.

"All-Father!" Aelle cries, and he and his son throw themselves to the ground.

"Stand, my children," his vibrant voice shivers the small bones in their ears. "I have called you here to give you honor, and there is no honor with your face in the dirt."

Yet, what dirt! The land of the Storm Tree smells like the fresh-bathed bosom of a young woman. Lifted by the good-hearted laughter of the All-Father, they rise. He stands before them, no larger than a very large man but with unknowable wisdom pleating the air around him.

"Come, walk with me, my children," he says in his cavernous voice. "Let me show you this lovely branch of the World Tree." He motions toward a horizon slippery as gold, and suddenly they are pacing with the towering god above the sunset curtains of the earth. Below, they see the oceans like fish pools, the continents' brown faces gazing serenely through spider nets of rivers. The Furor points to where the night winds blow back in auroral veils from the solar tide of dawn and sweeps his thick arm upward, exposing the celestial darkness with its clouds of stars and pinwheel fires. Then he motions them back toward the Storm Tree, and they are once more among the spectral beauty of trees like fountains of colors and water birds trailing thin lines of music through the azure spume of an immense sky.

The Furor sits on a cinnamon boulder and signs for his guests to make themselves comfortable on the verdant sward before him. At his back, the full moon bulges hugely, a plate of cracked ice in the tropical atmosphere.

"Aelle, you are the greatest living warrior among my children of Middle Earth," the Furor declares. "You are strong and wily enough to stand on your

own. You owe allegiance to no man, and you serve
me well in your conquests—for I have sworn before
all the gods that I would have the West Isles for my
own. And you—you are the living truth of my oath."

Aelle timidly lowers his head, and inquires, "All-
Father—dare I speak before you?"

"Speak—yes! You are my favored child. I will listen to you with my heart."

"All-Father, I am exalted to be here among these
wonders, here in the land of the gods, in the fabled
Storm Tree that holds up the worlds. You have
shown us many glories. My heart is full. Yet, I am
chief from the clan of the Thunderers, and when I
return to my people, they will ask if I have seen your
beloved son, our champion among the gods—
Thunder Red Hair."

The Furor looks sad. "You would see my son?
Then give me your hands."

Aelle and Cissa exchange astonished looks as the
Furor extends his powerful, square hands toward
them. Dare they touch a god? Cissa nods in awe, and
they reach out. Instantly, the beauty around them
shrivels away, and they find themselves in a wasteland
of sulfur sands and shattered rocks beneath a night sky
with gigantic evil stars that flare like cactus flowers.

"What is this frightful place?" Aelle whispers to
his son.

"This is the Raven's Branch, noble Aelle," Cissa
answers, "the topmost bough of the Storm Tree.
Above us is the Gulf of eternal night, the abyss in
which all creation floats as a bubble in a froth."

"Cissa knows," the Furor acknowledges, and

releases their hands. They stand among red dust and cracked tusks of stone. "And now I will show you a truth that even your clear-eyed seer knows not. Behold the gods who cherish me, who love me more than all the other gods."

A dune of ash fans away in a sudden polar gust exposing a cobra-hooded cavern. Inside, lanterns dull red as hung hearts shed a mute glow on eight prone bodies whose marmoreal shapes have the colorless, slippery look of statues. Cissa advances eagerly, recognizing these figures as gods revered in tribal lore, and Aelle follows more apprehensively, unhappy that he has been carried so far from the earthly senses he has trusted all his life.

"Sister Mint," Cissa breathes in a hush of awe above the husk of a large woman in floral cape and tunic of stitched leaves. "The wife of the Brewer, mother of healing! And here is Blue, the sea god—" His eyes widen to take in the god's proud features, his nakedness sleek as a dolphin's.

"And this," Aelle speaks standing before a figure wrapped in a cocoon tightness of robes that reveal only a portion of her hawkish face, "this must be the Ravager, the storm-rider, sorceress of the gods."

"Yes," the Furor concurs, his volcanic voice growing softer. "Beside her lies my heart's weakness." He nods to a young woman so lovely that staring at her stops their breaths and hurts their chests. "My daughter Beauty. And beside her, her dear friend, Silver Heart."

After beholding the phantasmal loveliness of Beauty, they stagger backward like men whose heartbeats have forgotten to go. They can look closely no more, and their eyes skim over lordly shapes blue-gray as dawn while the Furor recites their names, "The Dragon Witch, Wonder Smith, and my son, Thunder Red Hair—"

Neither Aelle nor visionary Cissa have any strength left to see the god of their clan in this morbid state, and they avert their eyes. "All-Father! Are they dead?" Cissa asks.

"Not dead, child—asleep." The Furor's one eye swirls with moon-pale watercolors of withheld tears. "They have given me their life strength that I might work the magic to fight for the West Isles and all the north lands."

"Fight?" Aelle asks, stunned free of the loveliness that numbed him. "Who would dare fight against you?"

The Furor laughs, bursting with affection for these devoted ones. "Tell him, seer. Tell him of our enemies."

"You know them, fierce Aelle. The rabid souls that must infest others with their worship of death."

"The Christians?" Aelle gasps, not comprehending how those demented souls could challenge so noble a being. "The Man of Sorrows fights you?"

"Not the Man of Sorrows, child. He is merely the latest apparition of my true enemies—the Fire Lords." The one eye squints, sending radial creases upward to his furrowed brow. "Do you know of them?"

"No, All-Father," Aelle says. "Are they the gods of the Christians?"

"They do not call themselves gods," the Furor states, his voice a rumble of disdain. "They say there is one God and each of them believes he is a messenger, an *angelos* in the language of the Greeks. But they are older than the Greeks. They came from the Gulf several thousand years ago, long before the Greeks built their temples. They are the radiant ones worshiped in the ancient river kingdoms of Persia and Ægypt. They are the fiery beings who brought the sorcery of numbers and letters to the desert tribes. They caught eternity in a circle, chopped it into sixty parts, and called it time. They worship the Word and enslave people with spells, written magic that lives beyond individuals and binds whole nations to their insanity. The Fire Lords are the ones who taught people how to build the first cities and how to tame animals and cut the land into the straight lines and boundaries of fields. They erected the first fences, and they are the ones who want to build walls across all of Middle Earth. The Fire Lords are my enemy. The Man of Sorrows is just their latest ploy to enslave the lives of the people with words written in his name."

Aelle raises both fists in pledge. "Then the Fire Lords are my enemies, All-Father."

The Furor nods with satisfaction. "You are as strong an ally to me as these gods who gave me their strength to fight the Fire Lords, to keep these evil beings out of the north lands."

"When will these gods awake?" Cissa asks.

"Soon in the time of the gods—but centuries will pass on Middle Earth before Thunder Red Hair descends again to lead his raiders—his *vikingr*—

against the minions of the Fire Lords." The Furor bends closer, and with him comes the smell of lightning. "For now, I need your help."

"Anything, All-Father," Aelle swears fervently. "How may we serve you?"

"The Fire Lords stole my sword Lightning."

Aelle looks to his son for understanding, and the seer answers his father by saying to the Furor, "The legendary blade fashioned for you by the dwarfs. It is famous in the Lawspeaker's tales of origin. The dwarfs gave it to you when you were forced to disguise yourself as a man and hide in Middle Earth from the wrath of the Old Ones."

"Yes, dear Cissa, that very blade that once protected me now is turned against me." The god's beard tucks in at his mouth as if tasting something bitter. "The Fire Lords stole it from my arsenal, from Brokk, the very dwarf who crafted the blade for me. They have given it to the Christian wizard Merlin. Do you know of him?"

Aelle's eyes widen. "Who on Middle Earth does not, All-Father? He is the wizard who plied his sorcery against the great chieftains Hengist and Horsa and destroyed them for the Dragon Lord of the Christians. He is an evil creature."

"He is not even a creature," Cissa adds, angrily. "The Lawspeaker says that Merlin is a Dark Dweller from the House of Fog—what the Christians call a demon. They claim that one of their saints tamed him to human form, and he serves now the Man of Sorrows."

"In truth, he is a Dark Dweller named Lailoken,"

the Furor says. "He has all the powers of a Dark Dweller but in human guise, and so he is very dangerous to us. All the more so now that he possesses my sword Lightning."

"Tell us where it is, All-Father," Aelle states boldly, "and we will retrieve it for you."

"If any of my children had such power," the chief of the gods says with a pleased glint in his eye, "it would be you. But the sword Lightning is guarded by the Dragon."

Aelle feels his heart shrivel at the mention of the Dragon, the vast planetary beast that dwells underground and devours the lives of men and gods alike.

"But the Dragon is asleep, All-Father," Cissa says. "No seer has seen it in fifteen years, and it is not expected to awaken again for a thousand years."

"Perhaps—" the Furor says, frowning contemplatively, "or perhaps this is merely a deception of the Dark Dweller Lailoken, who wants to lure me within striking distance of the Dragon's claws. I must be wary, for the Fire Lords are intent on destroying me—and then what will become of my children?"

"If we cannot retrieve the sword Lightning," Aelle asks, puzzled, "then what can we do for you?"

"Brokk lost my sword, and he will recover it," the Furor declares. "What I ask of you is to distract the gathering of Celts and Britons who guard the sword. Merlin has installed the weapon on a knoll called Mons Caliburnus. It lies near a fortress-city that he is constructing and has named Camelot. Every fifth summer, the Celtic chieftains and British warlords gather at Camelot to feast and plan their war strategies.

This summer is the third such gathering of our enemies in this hateful place. You are to attack them. While they contend with you, Brokk will take back my sword."

Aelle and Cissa stand stunned by the realization that the Furor's request is nothing less than a command to forfeit their earthly lives. But barely a heartbeat of shocked silence lapses before Aelle, his mind racing, swears, "What you ask is already accomplished in my heart, All-Father," and then humbly bows his head, "but the Thunderers and myself, we are only men. How can we fight a Dark Dweller from the House of Fog?"

"I will be with you," the Furor promises. "I will deal directly with Lailoken myself."

"Then happily do we sacrifice our lives against the gathered forces of Celt and Briton," Aelle speaks earnestly, mentally shaping a new stratagem to save himself and his son even as he speaks, "but is this not a task better suited to your berserkers who yearn to die in battle—for surely none may go against such a formidable host of our enemies and expect to survive? Do the Thunderers not serve you better as destroyers of the cities that blight the West Isles?"

A benign smile nests in the Furor's grandiose beard. "I ask much of you, I know this, my children. Berserkers *would* serve me better, for they are faithless to Middle Earth and love not terrestrial life with your passion. But there are no berserkers in the region where you are. They are all to the east, while you are already in Cymru, the kingdom of the Celts."

"Yes, All-Father," Aelle admits, allowing a tone

of contrition to soften his voice, already seeking a new rationale for his survival. "So now I must tell you the shameful reason why we are in Cymru."

"I know already, my child. My one eye sees much." That fearsome eye screws tighter in his craggy face. "Do not lower your head like a sheep. Your youngest son, Fen, is a captive of a Celtic chieftain— Kyner the Christian. To assure Fen's return to the Thunderers, you have been informing Kyner of the raiding plans of Death's Angels and Sons of Freeze, have you not?"

Aelle looks up at the god with his mouth down-turned, eyes pleading. "All-Father, forgive me! Sons of Freeze and Death's Angels squander their Saxon freedom by serving the kings of Picts and Jutes—!"

"Silence, child," he admonishes with profound gentleness. "You have no love of the Foederatus. I know this. But they are my children, too. And as I feel kinship and caring for them, so do you feel the same for your young son Fen. I understand you, child. I hold no ire against you, and I assure you that when you die in battle for me, you and your Thunderers will feast in the Hall of Light among all the heroes of legend from times past and to come."

Aelle bows contritely. All appeals are spent, and he accepts this with the same bravery that first led him into battle. "All-Father, the Thunderers will attack Camelot then, as you say."

"As you say," Cissa echoes, staring unbowed and radiant with devotion at his god.

The Furor smiles with satisfaction, and the air goes bright as lightning. The warriors wince and cover their faces, and when they look again, they are once more in their mortal bodies in a field of wild grass and pale lavender asters. Thunder shakes the air, and rain sweeps over the forest in sheets and crosses the field toward them like fragrant, translucent beings swimming down from the sky.

Aelle and Cissa look at each other and laugh and cry at once as the gray veils of rain wrap around them—for they are dead men now, dead men who must yet bear the burden of their lives.

---◈◈◈---

Chapter Five

Merlin casts a lingering look over his shoulder at Camelot, its skeletal derrick towers and scaffolds holding the empty iris blue of the sky where someday soon, he hopes, there will be spires and parapets. He hates to leave the construction unattended, especially now that the workers are dressing the stones that will secure the secret passageways. A forgetting spell will easily wipe the memory from the minds of the builders, he decides. But before that, he must make certain that the portal stones will fit with the necessary precision. And then, there is the matter of the roof beams, whose raising he must supervise to see that they are properly anchored to the foundation posts.

He pinches the bridge of his nose to relieve the tension between his eyes and turns his attention to the low sun among the western mountains. If he is to make the journey into the hollow hills, he must abandon all these problems and depart at once. He sighs, puts his weight on his tall staff, and steps off the gravel path into the sedge that climbs the sloping terrain toward the sunset. He munches a wizened apple as he walks, lulled by river sounds from the gorge below. Briefly, he glimpses at the far end of the valley the hamlet of Cold Kitchen, with its narrow lanes and red-brown rooftops. Then, the tree-crowned hills close around him, and only the weak colors of twilight distinguish the pathways of the forest.

By that dusty light, the wizard advances slowly toward the creaturely shapes among the shadows, which he is able to discern only with his strong eye. The faerïe live among the shadows, and once his eyes adjust to the dim shine of the night forest, he sees them. They are pieces of moonlight, though no moon shines. Quietly, they guide Merlin through the nocturnal distances, sometimes flitting so close that he can see their nightgowns of fog, their glowworm bodies and sticky halos. The wizard knows they have no faces, no bodies either; they are purely designs of energy, tiny sentient waveforms that sometimes migrate into animal bodies. As a demon, he used to smash them like flies because of their mindless joy. Now he is grateful for their help in finding his way into the underworld.

Merlin seeks the roots of the World Tree, the Storm Tree, the Cosmic Tree that the north tribes call Yggdrasil. It is actually the vast magnetic field of the planet. Its lines of force arc like immense boughs high over the earth, and there, giant electrical beings exist—the gods of human lore. The Celtic gods, known as the Daoine Síd, once dwelt there, too, in ages past when they and the Celts were the dominant powers of Europe. But, a millennium ago, the Fauni, as the Greek and Roman gods are known, drove them out of the Tree and into the subterranean regions where the planet's magnetic field coils like mighty roots. Down there in the netherworld, in the presence of the terrifying electrical Dragon that dwells at the core of the earth, the Síd struggle to survive. What is worse, to keep the Dragon from devouring them during its restless wakeful spells, they must on occasion feed it the radiant bodies of other gods, giants, trolls, dwarfs, and even humans. Thus, to be lured into the hollow hills by the pale people is a doomful fate. But Merlin is not concerned. He knows that the Dragon has recently succumbed to a long slumber from which it will not rouse for another thousand years. The wizard's only anxiety is finding his way among the intricate and immense rootcoils of the World Tree, and he is grateful that the Síd have sent the faerïe to direct him.

Like jittery fireflies, they lead Merlin onward through the grainy darkness, toward a streak of sunset that eventually expands to a flame-woven horizon. An incandescent palace of slender butyl blue columns and fireball domes rises from its midst. This is the court of the Daoine Síd's king, Someone Knows the Truth. Merlin has been here before, and he walks without hesitation into the blazing hall and toward the flaring throne, upon which sits the massive monarch with the head of an elk.

The wizard is unfazed by the splendor of the palace and the bestial appearance of its lord. Everything in the branches and roots of the Great Tree is illusory—electrical weavings in the brain of the perceiver. But the power displayed here is entirely real, and before it Merlin sinks to one knee and, with sincere reverence, removes his conical hat.

"Majesty," he begins, "I have come here before you with an urgent plea . . ."

"Don't blow empty words in my face, Lailoken," the king responds gruffly, his voice rumbling like surf. "Uther Pendragon belongs to me yet. Even as we speak, he prances blithely in the Happy Woods, not a Christian thought in his soul, I assure you. The Piper's music has purged him of all dread of sin and damnation, and he is as giddy now as any Celtic sprite that ever drank starlight and danced on moonbeams."

"My lord, I have not come before you to plead for Uther Pendragon but for his son, Arthor."

"Arthor? The youth has the soul of Cuchulain," the elk-headed god reminds him with annoyance. "What greater gift could I have given him? What more dare you ask of me?"

"Protection for him," the wizard speaks, eyes downcast. "His half sister Morgeu covets for her children Arthor's high status and intends to murder him. My woe is this—Morgeu's sorcery is capable of what she threatens."

King Someone Knows the Truth waves him away dismissively. "You are a wizard, Lailoken. Surely, you have the power to guard him."

"My power is less than I would like, lord. I have invested all that I can command into building Camelot, into creating a kingdom that will endure."

The elk face mutates with anger to a predatory snarl. "A *Christian* kingdom, Lailoken, which brands *me* a devil and keeps the Daoine Síd underground."

"This is true, my lord," the wizard accedes, face lowered as he stares up from under his hoary brow. "History defeats you. But this has been so for centuries now. The Christians are not your enemies."

The king of the Celtic gods stands, and the seams of his buckskin vest and leggings burst with a swollen rage that distorts his deer visage to a wolf's snarl. "They say I am a devil. Look at me! Once I was the supreme god of all the tribes. My image adorned the cavern walls in the sacred places. And now I am a devil. And you want my help with your Christian kingdom?" His voice sneers: "What is the curse the Christians use? 'Go to hell!'"

Merlin rises and leans on his staff, hat in hand. "It was the Fauni drove you underground, my lord, not the Christians. The Furor has destroyed the Fauni. Now he will destroy the Christians—both Britons and Celts. And he won't stop there. You know, he will slay you if he can. Once he fully realizes that the Dragon is asleep, what will keep him and his Rovers of the Wild Hunt from swarming underground and slaughtering all the Daoine Síd? The Christians alone can protect you. They will drive the Furor from these islands. But you must help them. You must help Arthor."

The king's features recompose themselves as he contemplates what the demon-wizard has said. "Arthor bears the soul of the Celts' most fierce warrior," he says at last, his voice tamed. "I will not have him squandered to some jealous sorceress. By my word, he will live to fight the Furor. Return to the dayheld world, Lailoken. I will send the elf-prince

Bright Night to meet you. With him to watch over Arthor, you may work unhindered on your city-fortress for the future king."

Merlin bows gratefully and backs away, eager to remove his fragile mortal form from this illusory domain of shifting energies.

"But mind you, Lailoken," the god calls after him, his orotund voice echoing from all sides, "I want respect for the Daoine Síd in Camelot. Among your Christian icons, be certain that there are included Celtic emblems that honor us who have enabled you."

"You have my word—" Merlin begins to promise. But before the wizard can finish, he finds himself flying backward among windblown soot, the palace shaped like fire diminishing to a gaseous, swirly glare and then to a mere splinter of twilight before darkness overcomes him.

Quickly, the wizard chants a vigorous spell to liberate himself from the subterranean god's grasp, and he is sent sprawling, robes flapping, through a tumult of leaves to the floor of the forest. Sunset colors—scarlets, maroons, luminescent greens—fill the atmosphere between the dense trunks and boughs, while overhead, the first throw of stars glints in the purple zenith.

Animal sounds sift back after the crash of Merlin's expulsion from the hollow hills fades. He rubs a knot on the back of his head where a rock has kissed his skull and staggers upright.

"You're a bold one, Lailoken," a gleaming voice speaks from among the smoke of twilight.

"Bright Night?" the wizard recognizes. "Show yourself."

"But I *am* right before you, man." A laugh glitters nearby.

Merlin retrieves his staff and waves it around. With its revealing power, it discloses directly in front of him a bareheaded figure with long hair so red it glows and flamboyant green eyes aslant as a donkey's. He wears a suede vest, blue tunic, fawnskin trousers, and yellow boots, and his beardless face grins cockily. "Well, I must say, I feel as happy as a dog's tail to see you again, Lailoken."

"My name is Merlin now, Bright Night," the wizard says, casting about for his hat.

"Is this what you're looking for?" Bright Night asks, offering the wide-brimmed hat with the conical, bent peak. "A fancy piece of work, this—and your robe as well. From the looks of you, I'd say the business of wizardry very much agrees with you—Merlin."

Ignoring the remark, the wizard brushes back his disheveled hair and fits the hat to his head. "I need your help, Bright Night. Arthor is in trouble."

"It's been fifteen busy years, Merlin," the prince complains, looking transparent among the dark trees and the luminous sky. "Fifteen years, and you've not come to the hollow hills once or even sent a raven with news of your grand project. Tsk. I cherished the faith that we were friends."

Merlin huffs with surprise. "Enemies keep close, Bright Night. Only true friends can keep their distance."

"I thought perhaps you were unhappy with me," the elf says, "because it was I who came to take Uther Pendragon to the Happy Woods."

Merlin scowls. "No, no—not at all. I haven't held that against you for a moment. Uther made the pact with your king: his soul for the warrior Cuchulain's. Now the Celtic warrior is reborn as Arthor, and Uther dances to the Piper in the Happy Woods. That was Uther's intent, and it is fulfilled. How could I spite you for that?"

"Good. Silence is a text easy to misread."

"I've been hard at work these many years, Bright Night. With Uther dead, the British warlords have been squabbling among themselves for the title of high king. You don't know—it has taken all my powers to prevent chaos, total war. I admit, I wanted to summon you earlier, to serve my cause. But in truth, I did not think that an elf-prince should be pressed into the service of *my* hopes and aspirations."

"And now?" Bright Night's eyes betray a look of resentment. "So why now have you gone to my king to command my service?"

"Because Arthor is in danger. Quite simply, I cannot help him without abandoning Camelot— and if I do, there will be hell itself to pay without me there to mediate between the Celts and Britons." Merlin intently fixes his frost gray eyes on Bright Night, wanting to bring to bear all the magical charm he can muster, but darkness leans through the elf, blurring his image. "Anyway, I thought you were happy as a dog's tail to see me."

"Oh, I am," Bright Night agrees, his voice softening. "It's just the lowliness of the task that irks me. I'd rather fight the Furor and his storm raiders than stand guard, which is menial work that can be done just as well by faeries."

"Aye, but it's Cuchulain's soul you'll be guarding," Merlin reminds him. "The future king of Britain."

Bright Night nods reluctantly.

"Then you will help me?" Merlin presses.

"No," the elf says, then breaks into a playful grin. "But if you let me wear your hat, I'll consider it more closely."

"My hat? Whatever for?"

"I want to feel what you've been thinking all these years."

Merlin shrugs, removes his hat, and affixes it atop the elf-prince's head. "Now take me to Arthor."

Bright Night sweeps his arm through the hyacinth-colored air, and a flurry of faerïe lights swarms off against the grain of the wind. As they hurry after the gust of sparks, the prince chuckles, tickled by all he feels within the demon-man's cap: a full heart's frenzy, dazzling with ambitious expectations and undertremors of anxiety. "You dream big dreams, wizard," he says hurrying among the trees. "When your mother birthed you, do you think she ever had anything as grandiose as Camelot in mind?"

"Fragile hopes require strong vehicles," Merlin says, breathing hard to keep up with the cold motes of light spinning through the gathering darkness.

"Yet, you must admit," the elf-prince challenges,

"if you fail, Camelot will persist only as a monument to our stillborn dreams and our broken lives."

"Then," Merlin gasps, "we must—not fail."

Through the arched boughs of dark trees, the faerie lead the wizard and the elf-prince past peaty ponds, where herons stand like phantoms in the frail light. Wild ducks burst loudly into the gloaming, while a crow flies on furtive wings toward the night. Sedges fall away into the rank grass of a lush pasture where a bridleway climbs toward a Roman road. Before them, a company of riders stands silhouetted among the sprawling sycamores, erecting tents for a camp.

Merlin stops, and says in a hush, "That is Kyner's company. Arthor will be among them. I dare not show myself. I have already drawn too close."

"My king tells me you fear Ygrane's daughter, Morgeu," the elf-prince says, returning the wizard's hat. "I have not seen her these past fifteen years. At that time, she had no fearsome powers of her own. The demons were her strength."

"She has since found her own wicked powers, good prince. Beware of her. If she approaches Arthor, you must summon me at once. Do not reveal yourself. I believe she has the magic to destroy even radiant beings such as yourself."

"I need no warning of Morgeu the Fey," the prince states, "for I shall not be staying here—or anywhere near your beloved Arthor."

"But you told me—"

"That I would consider your request more closely," the elf reminds him. "And I have. Though

my king, Someone Knows the Truth, is old and oft
makes weak decisions these days, he is yet my king
and I dare not wholly disobey him. So——" From a
small pocket in his suede vest, he produces a mirror
tiny as a thumbnail, with a miniature blue rose
pressed between its clear and silvered lenses. "I shall
give you this summoning glass. When you burst it
and the blue rose that comes from the Happy Woods
is touched by the harsh light of this world it shrivels
with a shriek I could hear in Cathay. I shall come to
that call and exert my powers to help you—or any of
your minions—to accomplish one worthy task." He
grins close-lipped and merry-eyed, like a gypsy.
"Does that satisfy you, Merlin?"

"No," the wizard answers flatly. "What of
Morgeu's threat? Who shall watch over Arthor?"

"Leave that to the faeries," the elf suggests.
"They'll fly to you swifter than wind if he's in jeopardy. Trust them."

Bright Night hands him the summoning glass,
and Merlin accepts with an unhappy frown. "I am
disappointed in you, prince."

"And I in you, wizard. I had cherished such lofty
hopes of your devotion to the Daoine Síd. After all,
you are a demon in human flesh. I thought you
would fight more virulently against the Furor."

"The Furor has come to fulfill the old prophecies," Merlin says grimly. "Not even the Fire Lords—
the Celts' famed Annwn—can stop him. Do not
cherish false hopes, bold friend."

The prince receives this warning with a dour jut
of his lower lip. "So then, you are back to Camelot?"

"Yes. The roof of the great hall is to be raised, and it is a task that may require my magic." Merlin claps a gnarly hand on the elf's shoulder and feels his chill heat vibrant and insubstantial as a prayer. "Thank you for the summoning glass. I shall not burst it until dire need is upon me."

"Go, then," the prince says in the dark with a starglint of smile. "Our friendship will hold the distance."

Merlin slips into the night, his beard and long hair glowing briefly like wisps of fog before he vanishes entirely. Prince Bright Night stares with a morose frown into the darkness after he has gone and bemoans his fate, reciting the same internal incantation of his past that he has been repeating to himself for the thousand years of their exile:

He alone of the Síd cherishes the rageful hope of storming heaven and reclaiming a place in the upper world. The others—Old Elk-Head, the faerïe, and the other elves of the Daoine Síd—have succumbed to their earthly fates inside the hollow hills.

Before the Dragon began its most recent slumber, Bright Night earned his fame among the Síd by his skill at bringing oblations to the cosmic beast. Reckless of his own life, he faced down trolls, shapeshifters, giants, even gods, tricking each of these electrical beings into the Dragon's snares. The gods Tonans, Pluvius, Orcus, Ull, and Vali all have surged from the Great Tree, provoked by his taunts, and plunged howling into the subterranean maw of the Dragon. Brutal satyrs and gnomes, too, have dared stalk him, barbed by his insults, and come within

inches of breaking his life before the claws of the
Dragon broke theirs.

Death holds no terror for Bright Night. Life is his
suffering, for he too well remembers the glories of
the Síd's lost home atop the Sky Tree. In the night
pastures of the Tree, with the stars big as snowdrops,
he sat enraptured, blank with bliss, shining inside
with the aura of the earth. By day, the sun's wind, full
of horizons, polished his soul so shiny it seemed to
reflect all the world in itself. He lived happy as grass.
Love and destiny for him in those days were the same
word.

Now and for the last thousand years since heaven
was lost, Bright Night and the other Síd live in the
long sunset, in the cavernous burrows and vast sub-
terranes of stalactite dells lit by the moody hues of
fulgurant lava. He hates it. The confinement, the
grinding noises and drippings, the hot stinks—all this
offends him. He would rather die in an ogre's slob-
bering jaws, wounds open to the sun, than dwell
safely another day among the red shadows in the hollow hills.

Yet, much as it pleases him to strive for freedom
in the dayheld world, he does not want to watch over
young Arthor. He has seen the coming darkness, and
he knows that Arthor, for all the strength of
Cuchulain and all the love of the angels, cannot hold
back such a dark tide.

For the sake of Someone Knows the Truth, Old
Elk-Head, who has ruled these lands since even
before the ice mountains came and went, he
approaches Kyner's camp. Woven into the night, he is

invisible. Through the golden haze of firelight, he strolls, looking for Arthor among the low-lying field tents.

"He should have been back with the victuals by now," Kyner grouses, returning from the vesper prayers he has conducted under the sycamores with most of the company. "Stirpot flummery is well enough for us, but the wounded deserve eggs and fresh milk. Go on, Cei, and find out what's keeping him."

"Why me, Father?" Cei grumbles from where he sits roasting an apple in the campfire. "Arthor hates me. Send one of the men."

"He is your foster brother, Cei. Now go."

Kyner's stern look sends Cei lumbering into the dark. He follows a footpath through the tasseled pasture grass toward the yellow lights spilling from the farm huts on a nearby knoll. Bright Night hurries ahead and finds Arthor at the curve of the hill entangled with a young peasant woman. Her giggling reaches Cei, who comes running, shouting, "Arthor! You pizzle-brain! Father will flay your hide!"

The maiden shoves Arthor away, tweaks his nose, and rushes off laughing, her yellow dog bounding behind her like a bright smudge in the night field.

Cei rushes up and cuffs his younger brother behind the head. "You're disgusting, boy! You behave like an animal!"

Arthor whirls about, his eyes flashing in the dark.

"Go ahead, cur, hit me," Cei challenges. "Show me again I'm right. You're just an animal—a Saxon animal pretending to be a Celt."

Arthor shoves him away. "At least I like women," he mutters, and swoops up the basket of foods he has just purchased from the farmers.

"All right, insult me, then," Cei calls angrily, following Arthor's big strides back toward the camp. "Mock my faith. But my faith will not have me ravish any woman in the night."

"I did not ravish her," Arthor protests. "She was ravishing me!"

"Hah! Tell that to Father!"

Kyner already stands at the camp's edge, glowering at the two young men as they march into camp shouting at each other. Prince Bright Night lingers in the moonless field, wanting no part of the endless bickering of men. He watches the white fires in the sky until the campfire is dampened and the Celts sleep. Then he slips out of the night and hovers over Arthor's slumbering form. The faeries prance upon his bristly hair, sit on his nose, and crawl over his inert face.

The elf-prince lies down beside Arthor, so that their heads touch, and he feels into the young man's memories, feels everything that he has experienced in his fifteen angry years. Despite Kyner's heartfelt love, the boy has grown up a thrall, always aware he did not belong. Indeed, though, he traveled with the chieftain on his diplomatic tours among all the Christian strongholds in Britain and Gaul—as his stepbrother Cei's lackey, a humbly dressed servant for the chieftain's brightly garbed son. By token of Kyner's Christian charity, they shared the same tutors in Latin, history, and mathematics and learned at Kyner's

knee the books of the Bible, though none pressed
Arthor for his understanding, for none cared.

The boy was well fed, housed comfortably with
the other servants, and expected to be grateful. Yet he
was never grateful. He resented his role as a servant,
and his bitterness curdled early in life to cruelty: He
tortured animals—drowned weasels, blinded rats,
hobbled dogs—and the other servants, appalled,
would report him regularly to Kyner, who put him to
work with the butchers. There, he perfected his
killing skills with knives and hammers as he slaughtered beasts with a fervor that frightened the meat-
men.

But even at that callow age, he had other talents
that better pleased his patron. Where Cei has always
been clumsy and slow, the boy they call the Royal
Eagle of Thor was as agile and swift as his Saxon
name implied, though he was tall and big-boned for
his few years. Kyner admired the lad's acrobatic skills
and pony tricks and forced him to entertain their
hosts wherever they traveled. Juggling on horseback,
leaping between saddles, winning every obstacle
horse race he entered no matter the steed, Arthor
garnered accolades from kings and dignitaries in
every land they visited, and thus he earned the
respect of the warlord who had reared him.

That respect expanded to Kyner's outright admiration when Arthor's entertaining abilities proved
useful on the battlefield. As a twelve-year-old, he
rode and fought in his first military campaign,
accompanying Kyner on a policing tour of the chieftain's domain. Expected to tend and groom the

horses and to make the arduous journey more comfortable for Cei, who came along to observe and learn, Arthor rushed into the fray on foot during the first engagement against a band of maniacal Pictish raiders. Swinging a fallen battle-ax and wearing no armor, he slew four tattooed warriors before Kyner could pull him out of the battle.

After that, Arthor asked for and received permission to wear chain mail and ride on horseback at Kyner's side. To save face, Cei forced himself to join them, overriding his fears and unreadiness. For the last three years, Arthor has continued to amaze Kyner—and not only by his martial powers. There were other, more unsuspected facets to him as well. From the first, for instance, the young warrior requested that his shield bear the likeness of the Savior's mother.

"Why?" Kyner demanded to know, astonished that the boy who had grown into a cold-hearted killer of animals and men desired so gentle an image on his armor.

"As I have the blood-thirst of my Saxon forebears," he answered in his surly way, "I shall need her at my side to remind me of mercy."

The reply pleased Kyner, and he inquired no further. But the elf-prince lying beside Arthor in the night field feels the young man's soul and knows the true reason for his devotion. The cruel boy has turned his rage outward to slay beasts and warriors because otherwise that fury would kill him. He hates himself. He is not like the others—not a Celt, not a mother and father's son, no, nor even a soul with a

Christian birthright. He loathes what he is—a creature born from a carnal spasm of violence and abandoned for what he is, horrid and unlovable even to his own mother. And so he has turned to the one mother who can love him, the mother of pity who understands all sorrows, even his: the *mater dolorosa,* the Mother of God.

Prince Bright Night sits up with this revelation. *Merlin has served you poorly,* the elf thinks, gazing with desperate concern at the blond young man and the mighty soul within him trapped in its ignorance. *You have been poorly served in this bid for glory, young king.* Then, the elf rises, faerïes swirling around him in cold sparks, and strides angrily into the night, wondering what destiny could be worthy of this mortal misery.

_____ ⌘ _____

Chapter Six

The sea rocks in its cage, its white fingers grasping the black boulders of the jagged cliffs, sliding away and then grasping again as if mounting the strength to climb out of its pit. Above it loom the majestic white stone towers and tiered turrets of castle Tintagel, stronghold of the Celtic queen, Ygrane. Once, this citadel served the queen's first husband, Gorlois, duke of the Saxon Coast, and housed his soldiers. But now it acts as a cloister for the Christian queen and the white-robed nuns who minister to the surrounding countryside as Holy Sisters of the Graal.

Each day Ygrane, as abbess, conducts the synagogal service of scripture reading, psalm singing, and homiletic sermonizing that comprises the Mass, sharing with the other nuns the opportunity to serve as Christ's surrogate, so that eventually all may have the chance to administer the Eucharist. Then she leads the Holy Sisters into the outlying communities to do the work Jesus himself would have done if he were in their place. By late afternoon, after a long day of tending the sick and indigent of the outlying hamlets, they return to Tintagel, eat a humble meal prepared by the castle's acolytes, and retire to their individual chambers for solitary prayer and meditation.

From a parapet balcony on the western face of Tintagel, Ygrane, queen of the Celts, stands at a balustrade of coiled marble serpents and watches the colors of the sea change. With the ocean as her altar, she prays to *Stella Maris,* Star of the Sea, the Mother of God. As she does every evening, she prays for the salvation of her people and the preservation of her child, Arthor, whom she has not seen in fifteen years, since he was an infant and the wizard Merlin took him from her breast.

Behind her is the round table, the large wheel of Merlin's creation, which she and Uther, her second husband, rolled among the cities of Britain as they toured their kingdom. At each city, it would lie on its side atop marble posts and offer a gathering point of political equity for the various rulers of the land to meet. Even now, in disuse, its smoky gray laminar surface polished to a mirror clarity still reflects the world in dusky inversion. At its center sits the Graal, a slender goblet of gold-laced chrome.

This Graal is Ygrane's most prized treasure. It is no ordinary goblet but in fact an antenna that receives and redirects the energies of the Fire Lords, who are the radiant beings that the Celts call *Annwn* and the Christians revere as angels. On occasion, these supernal beings visit the Graal themselves. Ygrane thinks how many times she has stood before them in the years since the good Sisters of Arimathea delivered the holy vessel to her castle on the snowbound Christmas morning of 474 A.D. Whenever the

Annwn came, they would appear before her in sacred vestments of iridescent gold—tall, beardless men with silver hairs of sunlight. She would look through them, and they would speak soundlessly to her, their huge, lustrous eyes reading her thoughts even before she could voice her questions. Once, she thought to ask about the nine mysterious women who brought the Graal to her all those years ago.

They are the Nine Queens of times past, the Annwn answered, *one selected from each span of ten thousand years that the human race has dwelled on earth. Nine women for the ninety thousand years that humanity has been ruled by queens. They dwell as spirit beings now, Ygrane—on Avalon, experiencing all the troubles and triumphs of your race. We use them to help change humanity. They are the great ones of the past whom we keep alive to witness the present, so that they may help change the collective soul of the future.*

And before Ygrane's next thought could even form itself in her mind, they anticipated it, and replied, *Know this, Ygrane—your son Arthor will be the first man to take his place among the Nine when the eldest of the Queens is released from the group, her spirit allowed to return to the rhythmic duration of death and rebirth. Arthor will take her place, and he will represent the past ten thousand years that kings have ruled on earth.*

"My son—" Ygrane's hands groped forward, to touch the vaporous angels, and felt the benediction of their lustrous, ungraspable energy. Implacable pleasure jolted through her, so fierce her head tilted back and she rose to her toetips. "My son will serve the angels," she said aloud, her joy a fence from despair and bitter fear.

So now, once again, Ygrane prays for her son. Since their last encounter long ago, she has asked no further questions of the *Annwn*. She does not want to know what will happen on Avalon over the aeon that her son must serve the radiant beings. She is afraid for him. The angels, during their visits, stand before the Graal, their huge bodies fiery blue, cyanic and empty as pieces of the sky, and in their presence she prays for a world without war and is glad when the luminous beings, with their wings of muscular lightning, do not speak.

Most days, Ygrane is left in solitude after the long day of mission work. When she can pray no more at the altar of the sea, the queen turns and sits at the round table in one of the high-backed ebony chairs delicately carved with dragons and unicorns. Resting her arms on the table, she extends her hands toward the Graal. She does not need to touch the holy vessel to feel its power. Invisible energies spill out their color and fragrance in her mind—a blue dazzle of amaryllis scent that fills her with longing for times past. She thinks of her second husband, the only man she truly loved, Uther Pendragon, and she wishes she had the magic she once possessed so that she could see him now in the joyful netherworld, to see if he is happy dancing to the Piper's passionate music.

"I assure you, my lady, he is happy as any soul could be."

Startled, Ygrane sits up taller but sees no one in the chamber or on the balcony behind her. "Who is there?"

"Surely, you recognize me, my lady," the darkly gleaming voice says. "Use the power of the Graal to see me."

She leans forward to reach the silver-gold goblet and notices in the table's gray mirror the reflection of a lynx-eyed man with a mischievous grin. "Bright Night!" When she looks up, she cannot see him, and when she peers again into the tabletop he is gone. Only after she stands and takes the Graal in her hands does his apparition waver into view, an image of pollen dust aloft in the silver aura of the ocean that shines through the balcony's open doors.

"Once you could see me clearly by daylight," the elf says, shaking his head sadly. "You spent all your magic taming a unicorn—and where is that beast now? Flown to heaven. Don't you feel the fool?"

"God's fool, perhaps." Ygrane, a tall woman with slant green eyes and a tawny complexion ruddied by her years of devotional service in the countryside, gazes levelly into the elf's transparent face. "You have not come here after so many years to taunt me, have you, Bright Night? My faith in the Christian truth will not falter."

"I am not here to taunt but to warn," the prince says, sitting casually on the edge of the table. "You must know how much the elves and the faeries still trust you. Once you were their queen. But for years now you have been converting them. Don't deny it."

Ygrane smiles, a slim, knowing smile, and sits down, placing the Graal on the table between them. "So, the old elk-king has sent you to warn me to stop converting the elves—or else?"

Bright Night thumbs his dented chin reflectively. "Do you know what happens to an elf or a faerïe who is converted?"

Ygrane nods. She knows very well that when such beings relent their alliance to the netherworld among the vast coils of the World Tree that sustain them, they lose their form and resonance with the Daoine Síd and flow into the wider cascade of energy that pours into all organic life-forms—human, animal, and vegetative alike. "Their souls become living things."

"They lose their immortality," Bright Night says sternly. "They are reborn as physical creatures that must endure all the limitations and indignities of life in the dayheld world—including disease and death. Why do you inflict this on us?"

"I inflict nothing," the queen asserts calmly. "I trust in the teachings of my Savior. The kingdom of heaven is spread all around us, for those with eyes to see. Why not give the faerïes and the elves the chance to partake of God's creation?"

"Our lives in the hollow hills are part of creation already," Bright Night says with a brittle edge to his voice.

"No, Bright Night," Ygrane responds softly, with a gentle shake of her head. "I myself thought so, too, once, but not anymore. Look at how you live, underground, where time has stopped for you. You have lost touch with your own faith. The ancient Celts speak of the two worlds: the Godhead of the Annwn in the life of the sun—and Cythrawl, destruction and blackness. I offer you the chance to return to the life of the sun through the Son."

"You're a true Celt in your love of riddles, Ygrane," Bright Night replies with a sly smile. "But you'll not be converting me with your devious words."

"In fact, shrewd prince, I do not convert anyone," Ygrane claims earnestly. "The faith of the Celts and the Christians are the same. Jesus is Yesu of the mistletoe, the All-Heal our prophets have long predicted. He and they agree that the soul, being immortal, does not die, but travels through the kingdom of heaven, through the Godhead of the Annwn, which is spread all around us, as Jesus himself teaches. I simply call the faërie and the elves out of the darkness of the underworld to live their lives in the radiant world of the sun."

"Call it what you will, Ygrane, but King Someone Knows the Truth is unhappy that you have taken from him many of his followers. He has sent me to warn you to stop."

Ygrane lowers her gaze, glimpsing her worried scowl reflected in the tabletop. "Or else—"

"King Someone Knows the Truth has ordered me to watch over Arthor," the elf says. "I will say no more."

Ygrane looks up with a flash of ire. "You would not harm him!"

"Of course not, my lady." Bright Night pushes to his feet and begins to move away, fading to points of light, like snow crystals melting. "Yet if my king so commands, I will have to withdraw. And, Merlin assures me, your daughter intends to murder her half brother . . ."

"Bright Night!" the queen calls after him. She

seizes the Graal and stands, searching for the elf-prince. But he is gone. Looking behind, she sees only the ocean reflecting orange-and-red coins of water and the green air above, empty of all elves and faerïes.

In the following days, when the pale people do show themselves before her, she ignores them. Her mission is not to convert the dwellers in the hollow hills, like some saint sent to redeem the primeval souls of the Celtic underworld. Instead, she wants to live as Jesus himself would have lived here on the Saxon Coast, attentive to the suffering of the poorest people, mindful to the end of the needs of the neediest.

One drizzly day, with fog along the shore and the sky an audacious velvet of gray, the faerïe rise up in alarming numbers and flurry like fiery moths in the rain. Even some of the Holy Sisters notice them sparkling in the ditchwater and think them perhaps the hem of some wandering angel's garment. Ygrane knows better and pays them no heed. She has no idea that they have come to warn her that King Lot of the North Isles and his small entourage are milling in the great hall, waiting for her. With him are his thirteen- and twelve-year-old sons, Gawain and Gareth, and his wife, Morgeu, Ygrane's daughter.

At the sight of them, Ygrane can only stand at the doorway stunned, wordless. She has not seen her daughter since the marriage. Between herself and Lot, who was her staunchest of allies during her reign as queen, little affection remains. He is an old-fashioned Celt and passionately antagonistic to Christians. But

Morgeu looks so much harder and stronger now than Ygrane remembers. Still, she wears the traditional tribal *gwn,* a sea-green garment that falls to her ankles from a high-waisted brocade of gold and gems beneath breasts covered by plaited tresses of her long, crinkly red hair. Her round, pale face stares out impassively at her mother, and her small, dark eyes shine with a haunted darkness.

King Lot comes forward, gray-haired but unstooped by age, his pale eyes watching coldly from their dark caves. He wears Celtic battle attire, buckskin leggings and boots, his chest bare but for the slanting sword strap that secures his weapon to his muscular back. The fair, long-haired boys are dressed as warriors as well, in soft leather trousers and cross-laced suede boots with daggers in the cuffs, their lithe bodies naked from the waist up.

"Lot—Morgeu—" Ygrane falters and opens her arms to them. "You sent no word, or I would have prepared a formal reception."

"Tintagel stands as a Christian hostel, so I'm told," King Lot says in his gruff voice. "What point for us to announce our coming when all are welcome here."

"Yes, of course," Ygrane agrees, and when she sees that neither Lot nor Morgeu will accept her embrace, she lowers her arms awkwardly. Even her grandchildren, whom she has never seen before, gawk at her, appalled to see a relative of theirs—a grandmother, no less—with cropped hair and heavy ecclesiastic robes, the white bodice stitched with the scarlet cross of the Christian cult. "You are welcome to Tintagel as are all travelers on the path of righteousness," she adds softly.

"We have come to show our sons where their mother was born and reared," Morgeu says, looking around at the high colonnades and vaulted ceiling of the main hall. "We'll not stay long. Tomorrow we continue on our way to Camelot for the fifth-year festival."

"Is that this summer?" Ygrane asks, approaching her grandsons. "Heavens, I've lost track of time. But I should know by looking at the two of you—young men already. Will you be entering the contests, then?"

They look to their father, who gives a barely perceptible nod before the eldest answers brightly, "Yes, Grandmother. Gareth will be riding in the races, and I'm to enter both the lance run and the ax throw."

Ygrane smiles proudly at her strong grandsons. "Before you leave tomorrow I'll see if we can find some of your grandfather's armor. Would you like that? A Roman shield, or perhaps a spear?"

"Very much, Grandmother!" the youngest blurts before his brother nudges him to silence.

"My sons will not have Roman gear," King Lot interrupts brusquely. "Celtic weapons serve them well enough."

"Of course." She smiles at them. "You are young Celts and should know well the weapons of the clan. If there is time, I will tell you war tales of my travels with the fiana, the roving warriors who served me when I was their queen—before I came to serve Yesu, the All-Heal of our salvation."

"Boys," Morgeu summons. "Go with your father now. He'll show you the castle. I would like a word with your grandmother, alone."

The boys bow courteously to their grandmother, less disturbed by her strange appearance now that she has referred, even in passing, to her Celtic past. As they follow King Lot and his entourage through the main hall toward the eastern portico, where the acolytes have prepared a long table set with a summer's feast, Ygrane takes Morgeu up a winding staircase to her chambers in a western tower. They sit together at the round table, in the presence of the Graal, while the gray sky darkens and the sound of the rain brightens.

"We have been apart as many years as we were together," Ygrane observes, her green eyes bright with curiosity as they play over the familiar yet new features of her daughter.

"The North Isles are far, Mother," Morgeu answers, running her fingers over the lustrous rim of the table—this emblem made by Merlin. She removes her hand and folds it with the other in her lap.

"But distance is not why you have stayed away," Ygrane states sadly.

"My husband keeps the old ways for his family and his clan." Morgeu shrugs. "Your Christian faith threatens him."

"You were Christian in your time here in Tintagel," the queen remembers, a mischievous glint to her searching stare. "Your father insisted on it."

"And when I visited with you in Cymru, you insisted I learn the ancient Celtic faith," Morgeu counters. "How ironic that having tasted both I chose your religion even as you abandoned it."

"Had your father loved Jesus as much as Uther did, perhaps I would have become Christian sooner."

Morgeu curls her lip with disgust. "My father was a good Christian soldier."

"More soldier than Christian, you must admit, Morgeu. That was his demise."

Morgeu's small, dark eyes spark with rage. "The demon Lailoken killed my father. I was there. I saw him."

"Might you not have misread what you saw?"

"No," she answers with sharp certainty.

Ygrane shakes her head. In the dim rainlight, her features appear as serene as an icon. "Child, you cannot bear this terrible hatred your whole life long."

"I shall bear it until Duke Gorlois is avenged."

"And how will you avenge his death? With more death? Evil cannot make merit of evil. You should know that by now, Morgeu."

Morgeu's voice tightens with threat: "What I know is that Merlin intends to make your son by Uther the high king of Britain. I cannot allow that."

"You hate me that much, Morgeu?"

The crinkled red tresses tremble as she shakes her head. "Not you, mother—Merlin."

"Don't lie to me, Morgeu." Ygrane bends forward, her calm face emerging from the dimness concrete and still. "I am the one you hate. Because I am the one who took Lailoken into my service all those years ago. I am the very one who gave him his name. Myrddin, Merlinus, Merlin—the man from Maridunum. In service to me, he used his magic to transform Theodosius Aurelianus into Uther Pendragon. And in doing my work, your father was killed. Accidentally—yet dead, nonetheless. So, it is me you hate, Morgeu. Admit it."

Morgeu draws away as from a dizzying precipice. "You are a witch."

"I was such a one," Ygrane admits, and sits back in her chair. "We spoke with the pale people, you and I together. And we rode the unicorn. Surely, you remember."

"You are yet a witch," Morgeu says in a small voice. "You fill me with such hate."

Ygrane lifts her long-fingered hands. "I do not give you this hate, Morgeu. That comes from your own stubborn heart, which has much to learn of mercy and love. But I do insist you direct your hatred at its true target, which is myself—not Merlin. And not my son." She places her hands on her breasts. "Hate me if you must. I could have been a better mother."

Morgeu's pale face seems to float in the dark. "What is his name, this son of yours?"

Ygrane looks away, at night standing in the window, afraid to betray what she loves by a stray word or loud thought. "I will tell you nothing of him, Morgeu. He is in Merlin's care, and when the time is right, he will come forward and rule this land righteously—as a Christian king."

"Merlin tells the Celts that the future king bears the soul of Cuchulain." A mocking smile lights up in the gloaming. "How Christian can he be?"

"That will be his choice," Ygrane replies, and

meets her daughter's taunting stare. "Like yourself, he will know a Christian upbringing. What he does with that is between him and God."

Morgeu sighs angrily. "You are no less stubborn than I, Mother."

"Perhaps. Yet there is a great difference in our stubbornness, daughter—for what I want, I leave to love and God, while you strive for your desires with hatred and your own implacable will."

"Ah, Ygrane—Ygrane—" Morgeu struggles to keep from shrieking her rage. "You are so full of your own goodness there is no room in you anymore for others. No one can get close to you except strangers—the sick and the poor—and then only for a little while. That is why you have no man, no family. Your goodness leaves no room even for your own son. Others must rear him for you. I pity you, Ygrane."

Ygrane stiffens, stung by this hurtful truth. Under her breath, she works a little prayer to Jesus through her heart, and when gentleness returns, she says, "Let us not talk of me. Tell me about my grandsons."

Morgeu exhales hotly. "What do you care of your grandsons?"

"Morgeu—you will not come to me again. This we both know. Tell me about my grandsons before you go. Tell what it was like to give birth to them, to suckle them, and to watch them grow. Tell me their stories. I ask nothing more of you."

Reluctantly at first, Morgeu talks of her children. But then, an opportunity comes clear to her. She realizes as they speak in the offhanded manner of mother and daughter that this request to review her past is a chance to seize her future. Here in the silken dark, with the terrific sound of the ocean thrashing below on the rocks, and the rain whispering, filling the air with a drowsiness akin to pleasure, she decides to use her magic on her mother. While they talk about Morgeu's pregnancies and the self-forgetful first days with her babies, the enchantress laces her accounts with secret magical spells. Her intent is to work her sorcery on her mother and draw from her the name and hiding place of Ygrane's son, so that she may find him and kill him.

The younger woman's magic is strong, and Ygrane has no defense against it—indeed does not even realize that magic plies its corrupting strength against her. Yet, in the silvered darkness of dusk, the Graal shines with a bruised blue light, and its power dissolves all of Morgeu's attempts to trance her mother. And more than that, the noctilucent aura of the Annwn's vessel reflects the sorceress's magic back on herself and mesmerizes her instead.

Morgeu straightens in her seat, suddenly wordless, and remains unmoving and unblinking.

Ygrane sits with her silent, staring daughter and prays for her, believing the spell is some self-induced trance, a curious occurrence but hardly uncommon for Morgeu the Fey. An angel sweeps through the room, smoky as an underwater flame, filling the chamber with a sun-baked fragrance of desert juniper and thistledown before disappearing in a shimmer of aqueous shadows.

And within her trance, Morgeu dreams that she is cuddling her half brother, and he is suckling her teat like a teenage son shocked back to wanton infancy by battle madness. She cossets his curly hair and strokes the worry from his clenched brow—and all the hate nesting in her heart hatches an unassuaged and newly fledged love.

This is the influence of the angel married to the magic that Ygrane wields unawares. Blood magic this is. Morgeu's shared blood with Arthor sings with his adolescent yearnings and stirs in her the same desire that haunts him—the tragic beauty of love hunger.

The old voice of the sea calls from the seacliffs, and Morgeu hears it from far back in her mind. Gulls wheel over the skerries, cormorants roost upon the salt grass of the headlands, and pelicans wade in the tide pools where her wraith flits like a girl dancing on the seashore, dreaming of lovers. Not a married woman, not a mother, but a maiden again, with fancies of love, she drifts among the beach wildflowers and the strewn litter of the sea.

Slowly, as she fades back into her tranced body, Morgeu carries the love she has found under the influence of the Graal's magic and the angel's dream—and this passion warms the coldness of life. Murder is impossible now. Though she retains the need for vengeance, which has shaped her soul and with it her life, she cannot slay her brother, her own blood. Anguish and tenderness have fused. Magic has made them one.

At midnight, King Lot enters Ygrane's tower chamber and finds Morgeu asleep, the queen praying in the dark beside her. He carries his wife to their room, and she slumbers remorselessly until a wing of sunlight pushes through the curtains.

As they leave Tintagel for Camelot, a blue sky deep as a jewel covers the Celts, and Morgeu embraces her mother with heartfelt longing she has not felt in years. Mother and daughter kiss, and then Morgeu rides off with her husband and sons serene as a swan—for in her heart the frightful hatred she has always felt for the son of Uther and Ygrane has transformed somehow, almost miraculously.

She will not murder her half brother, she consciously decides. Rather, she will love him—and she will use love as a weapon. With a tantric magic of carnal love, she will exact her vengeance by employing a sorcery ancient as Ægypt, where royal brother and sister coupled to birth the land's true ruler. And in this way, her father Gorlois will reach past death through her body to seize Uther's son and squeeze from him a poetic justice beyond the grave.

Chapter Seven

Merlin sits on the sun-washed turf of Mons Caliburnus with his long blue robes puddled darkly around him, hat in his lap, and the summer wind careless in his long silver locks. Below a precipice of green-black ivy and bosky willows, the River Amnis, mottled with cloudlight and beech-wood reflections, ripples like a snake in its new skin as it winds among water meadows and disappears into dense groves of evergreen magnolias, walnut trees, and oaks.

On the backbone of the hill, just above the wizard, the star stone squats: a flattopped boulder, not unlike in appearance to a giant anvil, cleaved down its middle by a blade of blue-white steel wedged between its black lobes. Closer, the aerolite displays orange freckles of rust, but from where Merlin sits, the ferric slag appears silver-black, a chunk ripped from the night sky.

His attention is on the sword, the emblem of power that will be drawn from the stone this summer to initiate a kingdom. He admires its gold haft roweled with elfishly intricate circlets, its long, slender handguard simple as a Hebrew yod. He runs his fin-

ger along its beveled blade, the steel polished so clear
it mirrors the bright day's towering clouds. This
sword holds all history in its elegant form. Shaped for
the Furor by his clever dwarfs long before those
whose days built Rome, the sword Lightning has
fought elder gods, giants, trolls, battle-lords, and
their minions—and Merlin ponders how well it will
serve its new master.

The irony of stealing this sword for the king from
the hand of his enemy sharpens with the understanding of all that the wizard expects of it. Not only must
it defend against its former possessor, the Furor and
his frenzied tribes, whose only rule of law is might, it
must conquer the civil strife between Briton and Celt
and defeat the iniquity of the people who have
adopted it. Uniting the kingdom against its internal
turmoil of despair and corruption, it will serve the
virtues of Christendom—protection of the weak,
defense of family and society—and become a symbol
of righteousness, the father of the courage the king
requires not to fail.

Already the sword Lightning's reputation
resounds through the islands, and bards and court
musicians sing of it, declaring Merlin's promise that
the next hand to hold this sword will be the king's.
Its former name is almost forgotten, supplanted by
the name of the Roman place that holds it—*from
Caliburnus:* Excalibur.

But before the sword Lightning can strike out
from Caliburnus against wickedness and injustice,
young Arthor must survive to become king. A sober-
ing thought, Merlin realizes. In the wizard's lap,

under his hat, he holds a letter from Ygrane arrived by carrier pigeon just this morning. The letter, warning of Prince Bright Night's threat to abandon Arthor, troubles him profoundly, for he can well imagine betrayal by the elves. Their monarch, Someone Knows the Truth, is—as his name implies— a god for whom the truth is uncertain: He has endured since before the ages of ice by using whatever truth enables him to survive. And by living for longevity, his word has become only as good as he needs for it to be.

Merlin nods his head resignedly. As reluctant as he is to acknowledge it, he knows what he must do: At this critical time, he must be with Arthor. Ygrane's letter assures him that the wizard cannot trust half-seen and unseen beings to accomplish what he must do for himself and for all people. Yes, he must be with Arthor. All the arrangements at Camelot are in readiness for the coming festival: The tournament grounds have been prepared for the contestants, and the people of Cold Kitchen have the provisions well in hand for the gala fete. But who will manage the arrival of the dignitaries and keep the antagonistic warlords and chieftains from attacking one another? Only by using his magic has Merlin managed to avert outright warfare during the two previous gatherings.

A rustle in the bee-haunted lime shrubs at the spur of the knoll pulls Merlin from his contemplation. The brails of his heart—the cords of energy that reach out from his center to touch the world—feel that it is not animal, not some stag or bear, but a human. Someone approaches, and the wizard quickly fits his hat upon his head and rises. He crumples Ygrane's letter in his fist and, with a muttered fire-spell, ignites it and tosses its flaring ashes into the air.

"Wizard!" a man's voice calls from below, and an old man spindly as a scarecrow slips through the lime shrubs and hobbles up the knoll, his hatless head bald and splotched with sun blisters. "Wizard! Do you remember me? Hannes—the master builder—from Hartland."

"Hannes?" Merlin does not recall the name, but he does vaguely recognize the fellow, older now than the lanky monkey of a man who constructed the round table for the wizard sixteen summers ago. His ginger whiskers have turned gray, yet the blue opals of his eyes glitter as brightly as the day he proudly unveiled to Merlin his finished masterpiece and then refused money for it. Merlin's palms go damp at the recollection. Now it all comes back: in lieu of pay-ment, this man with his comically large ears and apish features, had instead insisted on another form of remuneration for his labor: He wanted one wish, to be collected at some future date. And Merlin, eager to return to his king and queen, had agreed.

"You've come for your wish then, master builder?" Merlin asks apprehensively as the aged man limps closer, his tired bones clearly struggling with the climb. He wears a threadbare dun jerkin, green trousers stained gray with dust, and frayed sandals knotted with bine.

"Please—Hannes, call me Hannes, wizard," the man huffs and stops several paces away, clutching the ache in his sides. "I'm not a builder anymore, master or otherwise." He holds up his hands and shows off his twisted fingers and knobby knuckles. "I can no longer hold the tools."

"Ah, well, I can help you with that." Merlin sighs with relief, reaching for the carpenter's warped hands. But the spindly man tucks them away against his gaunt chest.

"Oh, no, wizard. 'Tis not for them I've come." His round face wrinkles to a broad smile. "I've another wish entirely in mind. Another wish entirely. But first, let me ask after my handiwork: Are you pleased with the table I made for you?"

"Of course, very pleased," Merlin avows. "It proved most useful and will again someday. It has the stature of legend, that the king should have a headless table that he is able to roll with him wherever he travels."

"Aye—but it could not roll to heaven, could it?" Hannes notes lugubriously. "I was saddened to hear of good King Uther's demise."

"Quite so. But the round table stays intact at Tintagel," Merlin replies, "and will serve our next king."

"The noble hand that draws this sword from the stone, eh?" Hannes squints at Excalibur and pokes his tongue against the inside of his cheek as he assesses the weapon. "A supernatural blade it is, for sure, just as the bards say. On my word, I've never seen the likes of it. Look at it all agleam, so stubborn with light. May I touch it?"

Merlin stands aside, and the carpenter clambers

to the star stone and puts his gnarled hands on the gold helve.

"It has magic within it, all right," Hannes murmurs, whistling through his crooked orange teeth. "Why, it makes the salt sing in my blood!" He presses his brow to the flat of the blade and slowly sinks to his knees. After a moment, he turns about and sits in the grass with his back against the stone, an almost conspiratorial smile on his wizened face. "I'm sure I don't need to tell *you*, Master Merlin, how happy one feels with magic in one's blood. Isn't that so?"

Merlin approaches impatiently, wondering, *What does this tired old goat want if not his health?*

"You know, wizard, when you came to Hartland all those years ago and rolled away your wheel table, I'd never seen the likes of such magic before. Nor have I since—though I've heard the bards singing of you, Merlin. I've heard them sing of how you rode the unicorn to Avalon to bring back this sword, Excalibur, and how you set it in stone for the coming king. I heard them sing how you tamed the Dragon for Uther, and how you journeyed into the hollow hills with him to meet the lord of the elves. And I knew it was all true. I knew because they also sang of the round table that I helped you fashion, and I'd seen that with my own eyes, how you rolled it out of the forest with your chants. I knew they sang the truth of you."

No shortage of breath in those old bellows, the wizard thinks, and nods testily.

"I'd have come sooner to you for my wish," Hannes admits, "but holding the wish felt so much more powerful than using it. I thought I'd need it one day when my wife or children fell ill or the sea wolves swarmed down upon us. But the Saxons never came. My children, bless them, have suffered no hardships and live this day with children and grandchildren of their own, expanding the ship-building yards I founded in my youth. And my wife—" He shrugs haplessly. "She got old like me and wanted to find her way to heaven not back to earth. So the years have sped away, and now I find myself at the end of my life. At the end of my life but with one wish on my hands."

"Surely you have decided what you want for your wish," Merlin states, "or you would not be before me now. What is it, then, Hannes? If not health, then is it wealth?"

"No." He brushes the air with a noncommittal gesture. "I want what cannot be taken away from me. I want knowledge."

"Knowledge, is it?" Merlin chuckles and nods approvingly. "And what knowledge would that be, Hannes?"

The carpenter answers proudly, "The knowledge you have, Merlin. I want to be a wizard—just as you are."

A surprised hole opens in Merlin's beard. "Surely you're joking! Wish for anything else, man. Anything else at all would be better than what you ask."

Hannes juts his whiskered jaw adamantly. "But that's all I want. I want magic, Merlin. I want the magic you have."

Merlin thrusts to his feet and waves the request

aside. "That cannot be, Hannes. I am not wholly a man. I am a demon."

"Yes, so I have heard the bards sing." He gazes up at the wizard with an expression of impish solicitude. "Lailoken, they say, is your demon name. You fathered yourself on your own mother when you were an incubus. But you have redeemed that abomination by serving the good. And by that I know you will keep your word and fulfill my wish."

"You are mistaken, poor fellow. I cannot make you a demon."

"But you can make me a wizard—can you not?"

Merlin studies the carpenter, noting the man's childlike sincerity, an enthusiasm that defies the weariness of his own flesh. *Is it possible he is a gift?* the wizard asks himself, *a gift of chance—of God?* He scratches his chin whiskers ruminatively. And then an idea dawns on him. "All right," he says at last. "I can make you a wizard, Hannes, but only to the full extent of your own endowment."

"What does that mean?" Hannes's face shines with hopeful expectation.

"That means, you shall not have my powers but your own. Each of us lives out our fate, after all—separately, individually."

"But I will have magic?"

"Oh, yes," Merlin answers, with a skeptical, sidelong glance, "though that is not in itself a happiness, you should know. To be a wizard, you must give me a part of your life you don't have."

"You speak in riddles, Merlin."

"Aha. But that is the nature of magic, Hannes.

Don't you see? To be a wizard, you must give me the secret part of yourself, your destiny. You have lived a good life—till now. Do not seek magic. Trust me. It is an unending mystery, a longing that goes on even after the heart gives out. Wish for anything else."

"No, Merlin. I stand by my one wish. I wish to be a wizard like you. You must fulfill that wish for me."

"Do you know what you are asking?"

"I want to be like you."

This is your chance, Lailoken. Merlin spurs himself to a decision. *Seize it for the sake of your king. Seize it!* He forces himself to frown doubtfully and pluck at his chin hairs as if struggling toward a decision. At last, he accedes with a heavy sigh. "Then, I welcome your wish, Hannes, and I will fulfill it to the best of my ability."

Hannes struggles to his feet, wrinkled features bright as a child's. "Wonders! I knew you were a generous man. So! How do we begin?"

"First, you must understand that magic carries a profound responsibility." Merlin stares him squarely in the eyes, glad for his own ulterior designs that they share almost the same height. "I cannot simply empower you and send you off into the world, you know. You must prove your worthiness, Hannes. Are you prepared to do that?"

"Yes, of course." The carpenter forces himself against the creak of his brittle bones to stand taller. "What must I do, Merlin?"

"I want you to walk in my shoes for a while—literally." He takes off his hat and puts it on Hannes's head, where it instantly sinks to the level of his curly eyebrows and rests on his ears. The wizard tightens the headband so that it sits on the smaller head more authoritatively. "I want you to wear my clothes, to carry my staff, and to bear my very name."

Hannes blinks with puzzlement. "You would have me pretend to . . . to be you?"

"Not pretend, Hannes." Merlin wags his finger. "You are to *be* me, in word and deed. You will have magic, but you must use it in the manner that I would—with primary concern for the well-being of others. If you succeed, you may keep the magic and depart from here as yourself, Hannes the wizard."

"Otherwise—" Hannes's round eyes narrow apprehensively.

"There is no otherwise," Merlin answers gruffly. "If you fail, you will lose everything—your sanity, your life, and probably the sanctity of your soul."

Hannes staggers back a pace. "But surely you will guard over me?"

"Not at all. I will not even be here. I must depart this very day on a mission of the highest importance. You will remain here at Camelot as me, Merlin—the wizard of Britain."

"But . . . but with your powers?"

"Yes."

"By God's whiskers! How long will you be away?"

"Days only. I go to escort the future king to Camelot. If I am successful, I shall return with him by the start of the five-year festival."

Hannes looks relieved. "Oh, thank goodness. That is only days away."

"But dangerous days for you, Hannes. The warlords and chieftains will soon arrive, and you must keep the peace. They'll murder each other given half the chance."

"I?" Hannes clutches at his chest. "They will spot the ruse at once."

"Not if you are cunning—as a wizard must be. Few of them actually know me well enough to see that you are not me. My robes, my hat, and my staff will be sufficient evidence of my identity." The wizard scrutinizes the carpenter head to toe. "Hmm. We will definitely have to do something about your beard, however. It's not nearly long enough. And your hands. You'll have to be far more limber to do what must be done. Hold still."

Leaning his staff against the star stone, Merlin splays his large hands over Hannes's face. Suddenly, he presses close and expels a massive shout into the carpenter's face. The poor man startles but cannot move. Paralyzed, unable to fly outward, his fright implodes instead, cracking the rust in his joints and then hurrying swiftly through his whiskers, lengthening the silver filaments of his beard down to his waist before the wizard releases him and drops him to his knees.

Hannes huffs the shock from his lungs, flexes his limber hands and shrugs his newly liberated shoulders. Filled with lightness and awe, he rises, and laughter feathers from him. "I am changed, Merlin!"

"Not yet. Not really. The magic is yet to come." Merlin peers at him closely. "But you must consent to what I ask of you."

The carpenter hesitates. He moves each finger independently, letting his amazement seep into the smallest crevices of his bones; then, he speaks as if to his hands, "How can I consent? I don't honestly know what you're asking of me." He lifts his tear-bright eyes to the wizard. "I don't know the first thing about your—my responsibilities at Camelot."

Merlin straightens the hat on Hannes's head again and regards him sternly. "Just this: You *must* keep the warlords and chieftains from each other's throats."

"But how?"

The wizard's eyes widen. "You are Merlin now. Merlin himself! Show your presence, man. Act with authority. Remind one and all that they serve a higher good than avarice. Tell them, again and again if you must, that they are subjects of the true king, who shall soon draw the sword from the stone by his own hand. That always works. Excalibur is an emblem of God's authority. You felt the power in the sword yourself. It is *real*. Trust in it."

"I will try," the carpenter promises weakly.

"You will do more than try, Hannes, or we shall not even begin." He seizes the man's shoulders. "You must succeed! You must be me—just as you have wished. You can do it. The future king of Britain depends on you."

"You ask a great deal, wizard," the carpenter mutters, "even though 'twas I who desired it."

"Indeed I do, master builder—but only for a few days."

"And afterward, the magic is mine forever, to do with as I please?"

"It is the magic that will do with *you* as it pleases," Merlin corrects him. "It is always thus."

"I will be Hannes the wizard?"

"If you stand in my stead until I return—then, yes, you may leave from here as Hannes the wizard." Merlin cocks a hopeful eyebrow. "Are we agreed?"

"Yes."

"Good. Then put your left hand on the sword and take the stave in your right hand."

Hannes complies, and Merlin clasps both of his hands on the Stave of the Storm Tree and directs his heart's brails into the carpenter. Carefully but decisively, the wizard begins to open the gates of power in the man's body. When the first gate swings wide, summer enters Hannes—the enormous company of the sky's cloud giants, the horizon's rising birds, the shadows' painted spiders, and the dreamclothes of all the trees.

Hannes reels as if punched. The forests billow like sheets in the wind, and the very stones seem to breathe.

"Hold tight to the stave and the sword!" Merlin commands, unlocking the second gate. Suddenly, the auras Hannes sees around things do not waver like hallucinations anymore but steady into something similar to a glow of sunset, infusing all he looks at. And he realizes that he can see the truth of all that is before him. He can see in the blades of grass all their soft powers, weaving sunbeams, air, and water into their green fabric. When his gaze shifts to a stone, he can detect its icy truth, seeing the cold core from where, in winter, frost aims its rays. And, staring straight at Merlin, he can see the demon's night-deep eyes stare back, baleful and sleepless yet simultaneously warm, comforting, and full of undying love.

When the wizard unlocks the third gate inside Hannes's body, the master builder swells with power. The ends of the world connect inside him. With a willful tug, he discovers he can budge clouds. With a cry, he knows that leaves will fly off trees. He feels this with a certainty, and he looks to Merlin for permission.

Merlin smiles and decides that Hannes now possesses enough magic to satisfy himself that he is in some sense a wizard. *Let him be spared the fourth gate, the heart's brails that can become knotted with expectations—and let him be spared the long sight into time that can blind him with memories of what is yet to be.*

Hannes releases the stave and the sword and reaches into the earth with his will. "I am changed!" he cries, twitching with laughter. "Behold!" He feels underground a stubborn bulk and pulls strongly at it until the loamy flesh of the sward peels back before a glacial boulder. Stunned at his newfound strength, Hannes releases his magical grip, and the giant rock tumbles down the knoll and crashes into the lime shrubs.

"Yes, you are changed, Hannes," the wizard agrees somberly. "This power has become yours—for good or ill. Now put on my robes."

Fingers aquiver with amazement, Hannes strips and accepts the wizard's robes. They slip on cool and silken as ice fog and fragrant as citrus.

"Now I am the wizard!" Hannes declares, and

spins about, his dark robes fluttering. His stomach tightens, and his magical will snatches his fallen hat and flips it back onto his head. "I am Merlin!" He gawks at the skinny, rib-slatted wizard donning the worn, dusty clothes Hannes has shed, and a troubling thought arises. "But what if something goes wrong?"

Merlin tightens the hempen cord of his trousers. "You must make it right."

"And if I fail—if the storm-warriors come with their one-eyed god—"

"Take this." Merlin presses into Hannes's palm the thumbnail-sized mirror that holds the blue rose of the Happy Woods. "It is a summoning glass given to me by the prince of the elves. If you are desperate, break it, and the elf-prince will come to aid you."

Hannes turns the dainty mirror between his fingers and squints at the solar reflections twisting inside it. "But, Merlin, what if this elf comes and cannot help? What if I am overwhelmed with unforeseen difficulties? How will I call for you?"

"Do *not* call for me!" Merlin scowls sternly. "That would put our king in jeopardy. You must not call for me. You must find all the solutions to your problems for yourself. Do you understand?" The wizard peers closely at Hannes, and speaks sharply and with finality, "You are a wizard now. The power—all the power—is in your hands. Do not look anywhere else. There is nowhere else to look."

Chapter Eight

Arthor stands in White Thorn, the hill fortress of the Christian Celts, where he grew up. All around him—stacked in corners and strewn across the polished maple-wood floor of the great hall—the traveling satchels of the chieftain's household lie waiting to be gathered by the servants and secured to the pack animals for the long trek to Camelot. Everyone in the clan is to go, and the stronghold will remain occupied by only a skeleton force of novice warriors left behind to prove their worthiness. Excited voices echo from the corridors that lead to the living quarters of the noble families—the chieftain's kin and their thralls, who are gathering garments and bedding for the month-long holiday.

As the chieftain's ward, Arthor, who resides in the thralls' barracks with the other servants, may enter the great hall whenever he pleases, though he has never come unless invited.

Moving in a slow turn, the young man looks up at the arched ceiling looming two stories above him, its great crossbeams bearing the clan's trophies: stag antlers, Roman shields, lances, and battle-axes. Once, in the pre-Christian time, human skulls adorned these timbers. From those pegs now dangle animal pelts.

The cloud gray hide of the dire wolf is Arthor's trophy, and it pains him yet to see it displayed in Kyner's hall. He killed the animal with a spear when he was twelve. He had been hunting deer with Cei when the beast emerged snarling from the under-brush. At its charge, Cei had yelped and fled, while Arthor had instantly seen the futility of flight. He stood his ground and did not throw until he was sure of his target. Later, he claimed that Cei had slain the wolf—not out of regard for Cei but because, if he had told the truth, the magnificent skin would have dec-orated a lowly wall in the servants' barracks.

Now the wolf's pelage, empty of eyes and gullet, only inspires shame in him, for Cei admitted the truth that first Sunday after, at the sight of Jesus nailed to His boards. Soundly thrashed by Kyner, Cei resented Arthor's lie, and nothing has gone right between them since.

"What are you here for?" the familiar gruff voice of his stepbrother asks. Large as his father and even more muscular, he walks down the corridor from his chambers with the gait of a giant; the servant behind him hurries after, almost entirely hidden by the mounds of garment satchels he carries. Cei motions brusquely for the servant to go on, and the thrall stag-gers across the great hall and into the blue light of early morning.

"I was sent for." Arthor meets Cei's hard stare. "Is he here?"

The chief's son looks Arthor over from head to toe, noting the younger boy's best clothes—a cowled green tunic, tawed leather vest, cordovan trousers, and cuffed riding boots—and he smiles with a hint of malice. "I see you're ready early. Looking forward to Camelot, aren't you? A chance to show off your pony tricks to the young ladies. Rutting and killing—it's in your blood, isn't it?"

"Is he here?" Arthor repeats levelly, refusing to be baited.

"He's in church with the elders. He left me to supervise the lading, and look at me, I'm not even dressed yet." He plucks at his baize nightshirt, then points to the satchels mounded on the floor. "See that those are properly packed up, Arthor. I'm going to ready myself for the journey."

"Pack your own satchels, Cei," Arthor replies, and turns to go.

"You forget your place," Cei calls after him.

Arthor stops and turns. "No, I believe you forget. I'm not your servant."

"Did I call you a servant?" He shakes his square head with mock pity. "You are my *younger* brother. Remember? Your place is to serve."

"I'm not your brother either."

Cei curls his lip in disgust and waves him away, dismissing him. "Get out of here, Arthor. You are hopelessly arrogant. So full of yourself. Well, Father has a good punishment for you, Royal Eagle of Thor."

"Punishment?"

Cei fills his large face with disdainful surprise at

his stepbrother for forgetting his offense. "You shamed Father at Mousehole. You forget, but he hasn't. Now you're not going to Camelot."

"So you say." Arthor turns away sharply.

"And I would know, wouldn't I?" Cei calls to his back. "I live here—not in the servants' barracks."

Without a word, Arthor stalks out of the great hall angrily, shoves aside the thrall returning for the other satchels, and stomps across the packed-dirt range of the fortress. Horses milling in the ward awaiting their riders shy from him, and he punches the haunch of a sumpter mule in his way and sends it scampering with a hurt bray. Servants preparing the baggage train move aside and look nervously away from him. Even the guards on the timber pilings that enclose the settlement notice the commotion but divert their attention as soon as they recognize Arthor.

Emerging from a stockade of raw lumber, several bare-chested soldiers pause as they escort a prisoner—the Saxon hostage Fen—toward the great hall. Arthor is too angry to wonder why. Distractedly, he watches from across the range as the Saxon brusquely shoulders past his guards into the light. Draped in a monk's brown cassock, his arms fettered, the warrior shakes his silver-blond hair from his eyes and fixes his stare on Arthor. This slender man with a solitary face of angular cheekbones and thick, muscled jaw gazes at him as if expecting a sign of recognition, but the boy pays him no heed.

The first time Arthor set eyes on him was winter. Fen had just been captured during a Saxon raid on the farmers of a narrow valley when a sudden squall blew over them and trapped the raiding party in the dell. Kyner, alerted by alarm fires on the hillsides, arrived in the midst of the storm, and recognizing the thunderbolt scar that jags across Fen's chest as a royal emblem among the Saxons, the Celt leader ordered him taken alive. Fen's status as a chieftain's son denied him the battle death all storm-warriors crave.

Since then, Fen has sat mute in the stockade, eating whatever his captors have put before him, staring sleepy-eyed at the priests who alone have permission to talk with him. Now and then, Kyner has paraded him naked in the great hall and the barracks, simply to amuse the women and to show the men that the dreaded Saxon storm raiders are men like any others. On each of those few occasions, Fen has looked to Arthor as intently as he stares now, as if some unspoken secret shares itself between them.

Arthor ignores the prisoner. Fists swinging at his side, he steers himself directly toward the wooden church, White Thorn's most ornately carved building, determined to burst into the gloomy interior and confront Kyner in front of the elders. But as he nears the arch-roofed building, he hears music and the elders and clan warriors singing jubilation to the Savior in voices like an effulgence from thunderheads.

He stops. The music holds him. Summer air thickens in his lungs as his furious breathing slows. The singing enters him with a thrill and an ache, momentary as smoke, filling him with a sorrowful glory—and his anger shrivels. For as long as the congregation sings, he stands outside the oaken doors, staring at the engraved cross in its Celtic circle, his body wavering gently as a flame's interior.

The beauty and mystery of the music lift him toward a clarity he has not felt in many months, and when the decision settles upon him, he feels light as a blossom: He will not stay with the clan any longer. He will go his own way, and in doing so will take what risks befall him, a true orphan, carried only by the horizon.

When the music stops and the doors open, he stands aside and waits as the priest, monks, and holy sisters exit first. Kyner follows, commander's thong about his brow, white tunic emblazoned with a scarlet cross, accompanied by his warriors and the clan's elders. At the sight of Arthor, he nods, then turns and speaks reverently to the elders, the old men and women in their traditional hempen robes with bines of summer flowers in their gray hair, and sends them off to the wagons that will carry them to Camelot. Then, with a curt hand signal, he dispatches the mustached warriors in their riding leathers to escort them.

"I trust you have been shriven by the barracks priest this morning?" Kyner asks, stepping closer.

When Arthor affirms by lowering his chin, the grizzled chieftain slaps a thick hand on the young man's shoulder. "Good. You'll need God's protection for what must be done."

A heartstring twangs apprehensively in Arthor. *Is Cei right?* he wonders. *Am I to be punished?* "Lord?"

Kyner sighs softly, disappointed that Arthor

won't call him father, hasn't called him father since he began wearing armor. "Arthor, I want you to return the Saxon hostage to his tribe. They are——"

"Me?" Arthor's heartstring snaps painfully in his chest. "Why do you send me?"

Kyner's weathered brow flexes with anger at the youth's insolence. He takes the boy's arm in a firm grip and sternly leads him into the church, out of hearing and sight of the community. Only the carved figurine of Christ in his agony is witness among the incense-smoldering shadows. The chieftain begins in his gravelly voice, "I am sending *you,* Arthor."

"Why?" Arthor's slant yellow eyes tighten. "Because I am expendable, and Cei is too beloved for you to send into a Saxon camp?"

Kyner's whole body flinches to hear Arthor speak like this. Rageful looks and defiant smirks have been the extent of the boy's contemptuous conduct until now, and each of those has been answered with a sound thwacking. But the chieftain restrains the impulse to lash out at the youth. *I need for him to do this willingly,* he tells himself to quell his ire; then he says simply, "I want you to go. I ask it *of* you to go."

"Why did you not tell me sooner?" Arthor cocks his head suspiciously. "I thought I was to go with you to Camelot for the festival."

Kyner blinks with perplexity at Arthor's wrathful tone. "You will meet us there after returning the hostage."

"You mean if the Saxons do not kill me."

"I mean what I tell you," Kyner replies, losing patience. "I am entrusting you——"

"Entrusting or punishing?" Arthor thrusts his face closer, challenging the older man. "Why didn't you tell me sooner?"

"Punishing?" Kyner clasps his hands on his hips to keep from shaking sense into the youth. "You think I am punishing you? For what? For what happened at Mousehole? I have forgiven you for behaving so shamefully. You fought brave and well that night. No, I'm not punishing you. I am entrusting you with a dangerous and important mission."

"If this is so important, then why didn't you tell me sooner?"

"The word came at dawn by herald," the chieftain answers, edging his voice angrily. "The acknowledgment was sent before you came from the barracks."

"You could have sent for me."

"I am the chieftain, Arthor, and I am telling you now, you will return the Saxon to his tribe."

"Why did you have to send for me?" Arthor asks, veins ticking at the sides of his neck. "Why couldn't I have been with you, like Cei, like the others? Why must I live in the barracks?"

"You know why."

"Because I am a son of war, a mongrel, a bastard half-breed."

Kyner's heavy mustache blows outward with a ponderous sigh. "Arthor, you shame me with your anger, your bitterness. Be who God made you."

Arthor's face mottles with the heat of his emotion. "God made me a mongrel. Why should I not behave like one? The war of Saxons and Celts goes on inside my own body. I cannot be one or the other. What am I then?"

Kyner answers flatly, "You are a soul—a Christian soul, Arthor. Your anger disgraces God."

"Why has God done this to me?" He opens his arms to the crucifix. "Why?"

"You ask why of God—you ask why of me." Kyner jabs a blunt finger at the infuriated adolescent. "You are insolent, Arthor. Accept your place in the world, where God has put you. Stop this foolish rebellion against yourself."

"How am I to accept my place when you have taken that from me?"

"I?" Kyner's pale eyes widen with surprise. "Your anger puts nonsense in your mouth, boy."

"You found me in the forest. You took me from where my mother left me to die."

"So?" A frown clenches the chieftain's brows. "Was I supposed to have left you there?"

"Yes! My mother intended for me to die. Why did you deny me that?"

Kyner shakes his head, stunned. "I—I am a Christian. Each soul is precious to me. I saved you for Jesus."

"Jesus!" Arthor spins away and comes back, nostrils flaring. "Then you should have given me to one of your Christian thralls to rear. I'd have known no better. Why did you keep me for yourself?"

Kyner stares mutely, confused. "I found you. God placed you in my care."

"Then why don't you care for me?"

Softly he answers, "I do."

"By having me eat and sleep in the servants' barracks? By making me serve Cei?"

Kyner shakes off his bewilderment and declares, "You lack all humility. That is your sin, Arthor."

"Humility? I should be grateful to fight for you in battle and serve you and your household at home?"

"Yes!"

"But you reared me as a chieftain's son," he rejoins with an almost pleadful whine. "The same tutors who taught Cei his Latin lessons taught me. The same priests who led Cei to Our Savior, led me. We visited the same courts with you. We prayed at the same shrines, conversed with the same philosophers. I am as well learned as any chieftain's son. Yet you and the others treat me like a vassal."

"Enough!" The chieftain slashes his hands between them and speaks in a loud voice: "Cei is my born son and a Celt. You are my found son and lucky to be alive at all. You should be grateful for the life you have instead of whining because you are unhappy with your station in life. I won't have it, do you hear me?"

Arthor steps back a pace, and his shoulders slump. "I have kept my silence in the past."

Kyner nods. "You have. I am disappointed now to learn that these are the thoughts you brood upon. You are an arrogant ingrate, Arthor. I am ashamed of you. But I am a Christian, and I believe in forgiveness."

Arthor hangs his head and glowers. "I do not ask your forgiveness."

"You do not need to," Kyner says in a strict voice.
"I forgive you anyway. You *are* my found son.
Nothing can change that. God has bound us, and
your bitterness cannot separate us."

Arthor peers up at the latticed shadows among
the rafters. When he lowers his gaze, his broad face
stares quietly, almost drowsily, at his stepfather. "You
have treated me well, Kyner, for what I am. I will do
as you say and return the hostage to his tribe."

"Good." The chieftain huffs with relief. "This is
important to me, to the whole clan. You know who
that hostage is. He has served us well by forcing his
deadly father to inform on the other Saxon tribes.
Many of our people's lives have been spared because
we used this murderer wisely. But now, it is midsummer, and we must return him as we agreed. He must
be returned—whole—before Aelle leaves our kingdom. That is why I need *you* to do this. I know you
will get him to Aelle safely. I cannot say the same for
Cei. Much as I love him, he is not half the warrior
you are. And if we fail to return Aelle's son—if he is
hurt or killed—Aelle's fury will be rabid. Do you
understand? This mission is vital to the well-being of
our people. Many lives are at risk. You must not fail."

The outpouring of a lifetime of rage has left
Arthor feeling as soaked in solitude as a stone, and he
speaks numbly, "Perhaps, then, you should return
him yourself."

Kyner's deeply seamed face darkens. "If I did not
have the entire clan in my care on the journey
ahead, I would. Aelle is not to be misjudged, and I
am wary about sending even you. But you are my

iron hammer, Arthor. For all your wrath and cruelty, I have learned to rely on you in the fury of battle when a man's mettle most clearly reveals itself. You can be trusted."

"I will do as you say, lord." Arthor speaks woodenly. "I will return the hostage to his tribe. But I will not meet you at Camelot. And I will not return to White Thorn—or ever again to the clan."

Kyner shakes his head with such adamancy it barely moves. "You will return."

"No. I will make my own way in the world. I will be my own master."

"You speak from impudence, Arthor."

"I speak from what I am."

Kyner practically snarls. "You are insolent. I say you will return. And you will."

Arthor's eyes stare shrilly. "I will not."

"I am commanding you, Arthor." Kyner's words glint like steel. "You will meet me at Camelot when your mission is complete."

"I will not be there."

Kyner puts his big hands on Arthor's shoulders, and a vehemence vibrates between them. "Yes—you will."

Arthor's voice rises and falls in a blur: "And how will you make me, old man?"

Unable to restrain himself anymore, Kyner shakes Arthor so hard that the boy's jaws clack.

Arthor's arms shoot up abruptly between them, knocking Kyner's wrathful hands away, and he shouts, "Go ahead, strike me! Hit me for not obeying you, old man! Thrash me like a common vassal!"

He pushes at Kyner's bulky mass but doesn't budge him. "Come on, old man! You want to hit me. Go ahead!" He shoves harder at the immense, squat, and deadly warrior.

Ringing a silver note from the scabbard, Kyner's sword emerges. "I will not strike you," he whispers, and turns the broad blade of the Bulgar saber between them.

Arthor's stare winces at the sight of Short-Life unsheathed before him, rays of reflected light like quartz vertices in the air. His jaw sags, and his legs feel like smoke. His sudden fear makes his anger flare even hotter, and he says in words that rise from far inside his burning chest, "Then kill me. I am ready to die! I have been ready a long time."

"I am not going to kill you," Kyner speaks gently. "Take this."

A rival heartbeat knocks from somewhere behind Arthor's eyes, so loud he is not sure he has heard the old man. "What?"

"Take it." Kyner grabs Arthor's limp hand and forcibly places Short-Life in his grip, squeezing his fist until the boy's grasp takes hold.

"What are you doing?" Confusion drains all his anger into sudden cold.

"I am giving you Short-Life," Kyner answers, "to protect you on your journey—and to assure that you return."

Arthor gives his stepfather a smoldering look. "I don't want your sword. I don't want anything more of yours."

"You are worthy of this blade," Kyner says,

removing his sword strap and scabbard and bending
to secure them around Arthor's waist.

The young man swipes the chieftain's hands
away. "Keep your sword, Kyner. I have my own."

"Not like this one," Kyner says, grabbing the
boy's arm and holding it up so that the broad blade is
close to their faces. "Look at it, boy. It has the heft to
cut through bone. You'll be alone out there in the
wild woods. Alone with the wolves and the roving
gangs. You'll want a strong sword, one that won't
break against any shield. Take it!"

Arthor stands still, numb with rage, as Kyner
secures the scabbard strap about his waist. "You'll
never see this sword again, old man."

Kyner snaps the clasp into place and straightens.
"I've had this sword since I was your age. I won it in
battle on the Catalaunian Plains in Gaul when the
Christian Celts fought with the Visigoths and the
Roman troops of Flavius Aetius against Attila and his
Huns. It is my battle-soul. It will protect you."

"I will protect myself." Arthor extends the sword
haft toward his stepfather. "Keep your battle-soul."

"I will keep it," Kyner says, "in your hands.
Return it to me at Camelot when your mission is
done."

Arthor grits his teeth so tightly his jaws pulse.
"So be it then." He glares at the sword in his hand,
the fire of the opal in its steel shining in his hard eyes,
and he slams the blade into its scabbard. "Short-Life
goes with me—and you'll not see this saber again."

"I will see it again," Kyner replies with certainty,
saying directly into the boy's golden eyes, slowly and

forcefully, "I will see it again, because you will return it to me at Camelot. You will obey me—because you are my son."

"I—I—" Arthor stammers, flaring with anger. "I am not your son, Kyner. Have you heard nothing I've said?"

"You rage against life." Kyner, veteran of fifty years of murderous battles, shrugs the pain away. "How can I blame you? You are right to want better for yourself. I want to give that to you. I want to give you peace. But this battle-sword is all I truly have."

Arthor feels all the angry words that he could say burgeoning inside him with a dull roar. He clamps his jaw tightly, determined to say no more. He will simply go—and not come back. That determination calms him down, and he turns and stalks out of the church into a summer morning's velvet air.

"Aelle awaits you in the oak forest north of Hammer's Throw," the chieftain instructs as easily as though no fury had passed between them. He describes the best routes across the countryside as they cross the range toward the waiting caravan. Cei has already mounted and waits at the head of the cortege, staring in smug satisfaction at Arthor's grim face—till he notices Short-Life at the foundling's side, and his features pale in surprise.

Fen also sits mounted, hands bound, staring up into the alders. The dark diamonds of his eyes watch bees swagger on the breeze and clouds traveling in silence on the paths of dream. Then he spies Arthor. Raptly, he observes the tall youth with the broad shoulders and the lion's breadth of bone between his long, amber eyes. When their gazes meet under the trees, shadows pause.

"Return his son to Aelle, and our agreement with him is complete," Kyner tells Arthor. "The Saxon warlord has sworn a blood oath that you will be respected and left unharmed. But be wary, Arthor. I do not need to tell you of the treacheries of our enemies."

Arthor looks away from the Saxon's blue stare, and the breeze stirs again, glimmering through the branches with emeralds and topazes.

Thralls bring the horses of the chieftain and his son. Hung from the saddle of Arthor's palfrey is his helmet, his shield with the Virgin's image, and his sword. He removes the sheathed weapon and passes it to Kyner. "Here. By this, remember I was once your ward." When Kyner takes the weapon, Arthor turns away quickly, mounts, and stares down coldly at the old warrior. "The hostage will be returned. I swear that before the Blessed Mother. I swear that—and nothing more."

Kyner steps back. "Go with God, Arthor. We will meet again in Camelot."

Arthor shakes his head ruefully and rides off, turning slightly only to be sure that Fen follows.

Kyner holds up Arthor's sword in its scabbard and watches sadly as the young man and his hostage ride out of White Thorn. "Go with God, Arthor," he says again, his breath unfolding softly as a prayer.

Chapter Nine

Melania feels as fluid as poured water. The lamia possess her—and she possesses them. Released from their black silver urn by the wildwood gang who have ambushed her, the lamia would have ripped her flesh from her skeleton had she not grasped the guardian band in the same instant that they seized her. A moment sooner and she could have driven them back into the urn.

Now, they circle her like particles of fire. They chew on her but they cannot eat her because of the guardian band. But those who get close enough, they shred, rip, tear into carrion.

She travels through the wild places, far from people. The lamia do not touch the animals. They prefer human flesh.

Even plagued by her demons, her brow wears a stamp of determination. She will find her ancestral treasure buried on the island of Britannia four centuries ago. And the gold will go back to Aquitania with her and buy the mercenaries she needs to save her estate. She will do this, no matter the lamia, no matter the pain.

The skin of her face shines with the gift of blood

that the lamia cannot touch. They circle her angrily, arms folded around and through each other. The purple velour of their manes, the wet leather of their snouts smears in the air with their mad circling. Firepoints glint where they are and stiffen to shadows where they are not.

How long can they live without eating?

She wonders this but never finds out, for no matter how careful she is to stay in the forests and on the high trails, people find her. Sometimes they are drovers searching for their cattle. She gallops from them, bends low over her horse's withers, and covers her ears—and still she hears their screams. Sometimes they are brigands stalking her. Then she stops her horse and simply watches as the lamia yank the leering faces from their skulls.

Many times she has tried to drive the lamia back into the urn. She has held the container by its sphinx handles and scooped the air where they glitter, but they swirl away. When she brandishes the lodestone knife that can kill them, they hide in her hair and lick the salt from her neck.

This hurts her, because it draws the salt from her blood. It makes her head pound and her flesh slick and feverish. To stop them, she bangs the knife against the silver serpents of the urn. Disturbed, they fly off a short way and glower at her. One sits in a tree branch, wings folded, furious-looking as an eagle or the bronze eidolon on a Roman consul's staff. The other writhes in the dirt, flat as a shadow but in dazzling hues—vermilion, gold, green, striped like a zebra, freckled like a leopard.

Melania lives off summer—eating berries and nuts, drinking stream water. With the ease of smoke, she moves from day to day, always northward, seeking her treasure.

To cross the channel to Britannia, Melania rides along the bluffs above the rocky coast until she locates a fishing village. And she waits. She will not endanger the people. At night, she leaves her horse in exchange for a small boat and rows out under the star-wrinkled night before hoisting the craft's single sail.

Melania abandons the boat on a cliffside beach under dragon's-tail clouds, a fiery dawn. All she takes with her are her shabby clothes and the weapons she needs to control the lamia—the empty urn, the magnetic dagger, and the silver throat band that keeps the lamia, who have already penetrated her aura, from possessing her flesh.

The lamia beat at her eggskull. They want to kill her, but the guardian band dims their strength. All they can do is hurt her. To mute the pain, she chews willow bark and poplar roots as her great-grandmother taught her, and doggedly walks north and west toward the interfingering hills that hide her treasure.

Lithe as a flame, Melania scampers through the primordial forests of the remote island. The lamia, for all their hurting, charge her with a peculiar lightness. She partakes of their energy. When they kill, she is stronger. Yet, she despises this strength. She wants no innocent blood on her hands, and she ignores the sulfurous headaches and stays away from the hamlets and the wet, mulchy smell of turned earth.

When she reaches the place of hidden treasure in

an oak grove outside the black stone walls that enclose the City of the Legions, she is exhausted. The lamia have not eaten since she arrived on the island. Someone must die for her to carry the strength that will easily budge the stones and the black earth.

But she will not visit the City of the Legions. She will not walk the rutted dirt roads. Bewitched by the painful hungers of the lamia, she digs slowly with her bare hands. When sheep bells tinkle, she flees into the forest and waits for the shepherd to pass. The lamia seethe, but they are too weak to hurt her more than she can bear.

Five days later, Melania completes her digging and finds the treasure cache empty. Her heart's small immensity nearly explodes with grief.

She stares at the empty socket under the lisping oaks and stares and stares until the details take on a magical intensity: the tree roots flare like wicks. The stones are not dead.

The wizard Merlin took the gold coins from our grasp seventeen summers ago. The lamia make the stones speak in a voice like bending iron. *The gold bought greatness for the Aurelianus brothers. And with greatness came death. There is no more.*

The voice of the unsayable passes. Melania's hands clutch at the gold pieces of sunlight let down by the leafy canopy. The lamia laugh, hungry and sick.

Melania pulls the lode-knife from her belt, and the lamia press close to her skin, hot and prickly, and they beg her to stab at them. Her hand wavers. If she slays herself, the lamia will spurt free of the guardian band's hold. They will range across the countryside, ripping the hearts from young children, their favorite delicacy.

She puts the knife away and staggers into the forest, bound for nowhere. Sluggish as freezing water, her movements catch on everything around her—her hair and clothes snaggle among the brambles, and her mind glares blank as snow. In the night, she hunkers over the urn and watches it glow green. The braided snakes on the orphic egg slither, and the long wings of the bearded sphinxes flutter.

Then, one morning, the green doorways of the forest open upon a Saxon camp—Aelle and Cissa and their naked warriors dressed in scars and blue paint. Even clumsy as icy water, because the lamia have not eaten in weeks, Melania is still more swift and silent than any mortal, and surprises the warband.

The nearest Thunderer leaps up, a knife in each hand, and the voracious lamia seize him. In an instant, he is a ripped carcass hanging from a tree by his feet, his shocked face staring at itself in a mirror of puddling blood.

The Thunderers shriek with fright, their souls of blue lightning dimming with fear. Except for Cissa. He shoves his startled father behind him and beats his naked chest with his fists, sounding the drum of his body to summon the Furor.

The lamia swoop toward him but are pulled away with high tearing screams. Melania falls to her knees under the impact of their loud cries that seep like hot tar into her inner brightness, hardening to darkness within the light of what remains of her life.

She swoons. Fading, she sees the Furor. Colossal as a tree, with his beard and mane tangled in the clouds and his vacant socket empty as the black behind the sky, he holds the lamia in one hand like squirming eels. His single eye shadows forth such azure arctic loneliness, such impossible loss and grief, her breastbone groans, unable to lift to a cry the burden of such sorrow.

Cissa crouches over her. He has dealt with witches before. He has wrestled werebeasts, impaled vampyres, and bound lamia in the aboriginal forests of the Thunderers' wanderings. The Furor has trained him well. He snaps open the orphic urn, and the lamia are shoved yowling into the confining darkness. Then he takes the witch's smudged face in his tattooed hands and studies her southern features—the Greek nose, the full lips, the droopy dark eyes—and he nods.

"This one lives," he announces.

"She has killed our clansman," Aelle protests, and the other Thunderers murmur agreement. "Her blood must wash his."

Cissa holds the basket of her ribs and feels her fear scrabbling and knocking within. "You are not a witch," he says in the Latin tongue of his enemies. "You are a frightened woman."

Melania shakes the bleariness from her head. She looks about for the Furor but sees only the treecrowns screening the far furnace of the sun. The lamia's power has vanished, and she feels exhausted, hollowed. The man holding her has the frightful aspect of a serpent, for he is totally hairless, his flesh stenciled with scaly coils.

"This one lives," Cissa repeats. He plucks at her tangled, dark hair matted with burrs and twigs. "When she is cleaned up, she will be beautiful in the Roman way. Some use will come of her."

The Thunderers gather around their slain comrade and lower him from the tree. "And what of his blood?" Aelle inquires of his shaman son.

"His blood has paid for ours," Cissa answers, and releases Melania, done with her. He picks up the urn and turns it wisely in his stained hands. "Behold, noble Aelle, the shape of our salvation."

Aelle huffs impatiently. The scar between his eyes throbs from the strong presence of the Furor, who still stalks through these woods, somewhere nearby. "Tell me plainly, son, what you see."

Cissa's reptilian face cracks a smile. "I see that the Thunderers do not have to attack Camelot. I see that we do not have to die to distract our enemies while the Furor retrieves the sword Lightning."

Aelle tugs at his hay-nest beard, not comprehending. "The Furor has ordered us—"

A rustling in the underbrush puts swords again in the hands of the Thunderers. From among alabaster-pale poplars, a startling figure emerges—squat, immense, and fierce. A dwarf dressed in studded leather straps that crisscross an iridescent tunic of fire-snake skin.

"Put your swords away!" the creature orders. He is half as high as a man but twice as wide, with huge, muscular limbs, and a cubed head of tufty gold hair and red whiskers that swirl over pugnacious jowls. "I am the Furor's dwarf—Brokk."

Aelle goes to one knee before the agent of their god. The other Thunderers follow—except for Cissa. "Get up," the shaman calls. "He is but a minion of our Lord. And one who has lost the sword Lightning to our foes and put all our lives in jeopardy. He is no longer worthy of our respect until he has recovered the Furor's sword."

Brokk scowls at him and strides menacingly closer, but Cissa does not flinch.

The man's eyes stare cold as the icy heart of winter. "I am the priest of the Furor. I am the one you have been sent to obey."

"I obey none but the Furor himself." Brokk snarls, and shows his huge square teeth. "I am older than the children of Woman."

Cissa beats the drum of his body, and though the morning is cloudless, the sky darkens. Summer scatters itself before a boreal wind that burns with cold.

Brokk's square face bends woefully, and he admits, "The Furor has sent me to work with you, to recover the sword Lightning. I mean you no harm."

In the background, Melania curls more tightly against the wall of a mammoth oak. She does not understand what the snakeman or the dwarf are saying, but they hold the urn between them. In the sudden dimness, they unclasp the snake-fang lid, and the lamia, still weak from their long fast, seep out like cool flames of moonlight.

The dwarf's leather-bound hand with its metal knuckles shoves one of the ghostly creatures back into the urn. The other, the dwarf wraps about himself like a windy shawl. Instantly, he grows in stature and stands facing the viper-priest, precise as a mirror image.

Terrified at what she sees, Melania tries to scuttle away, but in moments she is snatched and dragged back before the hairless tattooed warrior and the dwarf, who now holds the lamia in one hand like a limp pelt of silver fur.

Then seizing a hank of her hair, the dwarf runs his blunt fingers over her quivering face. She jolts as his electricity runs across her flesh and tickles the frosty outlines of her organs. His small eyes thread a burning light.

"I will take this one for my pleasure," Brokk announces, and folds back his tunic to reveal a red pizzle the size of a man's forearm.

Melania scrambles backward crabwise, face wrenched with horror, and Cissa steps astride her.

"No, Brokk. You will not have this mortal woman. She is mine. The Furor has given her to me."

Brokk's grinding teeth brattle with a sound like falling rocks, but he steps back.

"Now, you shall go," Cissa orders, and points into the forest. "Camelot is in that direction. With the shapeshifter to wear, you will enter among our enemies and take back the sword Lightning. Then you will have won again our respect. Now, go."

With an embittered scowl, Brokk wraps the lamia about him and shimmers into the shape of Melania. In that guise, he walks off and does not look back. As soon as he departs, the siege of darkness lifts from the summer day.

Aelle bows his head in gratitude to the Furor for

bestowing upon him his able son. Then he signs for the others to prepare a pyre for their fallen comrade, and he regards the bedraggled Roman woman in her rags. "You should have given her to Brokk," he tells Cissa.

The Furor's priest shakes his head and lifts Melania to her feet. "No, worthy Aelle. This one has another destiny."

"You will take her for yourself?"

Cissa passes a disappointed look at his father. "You know me better. I take nothing for my own."

"Then, why?"

"Why is a word. What I want from her is beyond words."

"I do not understand you, my son. She is a Roman woman." He motions in disgust at where she stands bent and slovenly, peering at them through the twisted shag of her hair. "Look at her. She is weak, filthy, and she brought death into our camp. Look at her."

"One must not look through the eyes expecting to see."

Aelle shrugs and announces loudly for all the others to hear, "You are as much the Furor's son as mine, Cissa, so I cannot expect always to understand you. You may keep the Roman woman. She has killed one of ours but has liberated the rest of us from the Furor's command to attack Camelot. Let us go now to the oak grove outside Hammer's Throw, where the Celt Kyner shall free my son Fen. Then we will depart this island that is haunted by the ghosts of our enemies, and we shall winter in the reindeer forests beyond the rivers of the morning sun."

Melania understands nothing of what the heathens say until the viper-priest turns to her and speaks in her language. "We are the Thunderers," he begins. "We have burned your villages and the people in them. We have taken your magic for our own. Now your lamia serve us. Know this: I have saved you from the dwarf not for myself but for our god, the Furor. If you try to flee again, I will kill you slowly in his honor."

"Why must I stay?" Melania asks in a sodden voice. "What are you going to do to me?"

"How can I say?" He takes her chin in his hand and lifts her sooty face to his hungry gaze. "The gods alone know how lovely the unspeakable must be."

Chapter Ten

Sunset crosses the sky in red strokes as the west wind rises over the mountains and Camelot. King Lot and his entourage set up camp on the high meadows, where the Celtic chieftains situated themselves in the two prior festivals. The British warlords erect their tents on the fields at the far side of the champaign, so that the construction site of the fortress-city lies between them and the Celts.

Lot is the first of the Celtic chiefs to arrive, and he raises his pavilions close to the tree line so that there will be ample room in the meadows for the large companies of his Celtic peers, Lord Urien and Chief Kyner. The sun sinks while the tents go up, and when the work is done a line of green is all that remains of day in the cloud-streaked skies the night inherits. Lot insists that he and his sons seek out Merlin to pay their respects and formally announce their arrival, but Morgeu will not face her nemesis in person. As in years past, she goes into the wild woods to worship the arboreal gods and work sorcery for her people.

This does not trouble King Lot. He is old and well pleased with Morgeu, for her amorous spells and uxorious ministrations satisfy his manly desires, while her passionate devotion to the Celtic gods exalts his spiritual status among his clan. In the fourteen years they have been wed, she has not only awarded him with two able sons, she has expertly advised him in battle strategies against the Gaels, worked magic to dispel the mighty storms that usually thrash his kingdom of the North Isles, and, by eliciting the faeries' help, has delivered spectacular harvests for the domain's farmers and fisherfolk. Life has never been sweeter for King Lot.

Torches held in the grip of the king's guard light up the night with a liquid, bronze air, and Lot, Gareth, and Gawain march eagerly down the meadow lanes leading a long line of clansfolk. Ahead, the construction site towers in skeletal scaffolds against the scattered stars, and the friendly denizens of Cold Kitchen wait behind long tables laded with Celtic foods—braised salmon, quail stew, beef skewers, eel soup, hazelnut cakes, honey dumplings, black-currant pies, wheels of blue cheese, and raspberry puddings. Jugglers spinning firebrands, harpists, pipers, fiddlers, even ale-minstrels singing stories and bearing numerous horns of liquor are there to greet the Celts.

Inquiring after Merlin, Lot and his sons are directed through the gargantuan gates of Camelot. In the central hall, among building platforms and workbenches illuminated by fiery braziers, the figure of Hannes masquerading as Merlin paces among the dancing shadows, chuckling to himself. Since Merlin endowed him with magical powers three days ago, he has hardly slept at all, so enamored is he of his astonishing new strengths. Hour by hour, he learns more about the skills that can yank boulders from under the earth and numb water to ice, and he delights in his experiments.

"Merlin!" King Lot calls from the arched portal to the circular chamber.

Hannes whirls about, startled, and gaups at the tall, bare-chested warrior with the brindled braids, drooping mustache, and keen, eagle-browed stare. His half-naked boys, one on either side, have the feral air of young brutes, pugnacious jaws set defiantly, and their small eyes dark and threatening.

"What do you want?" Hannes asks apprehensively, waving his magical stave before him to be certain that no host of pale people accompanies this dangerous trio. "Who are you?"

"Who am I?" King Lot squints menacingly. "What do you mean, wizard? It is I!"

Hannes leans on his stave, edging back into the shadows. "Forgive me. I am a bit addled, you see. I— I have only recently come from a magical journey into the hollow hills, and I would not recognize my own mother, blessed Saint Optima, were she to arise before me this very moment."

"I am Lot!" the king announces, loud with impatience and incredulity. "And what has become of the dark thunder of your voice? You sound squeaky as a mouse!"

"The spirits—it was the spirits seized my throat pipes and bent them so they squeak so. Pay that no mind, Lot."

"Step into the light, wizard," the king commands.

"I would show you my worthy sons, Gawain and Gareth."

Hannes inches forward, head bowed. "Strapping youths, hale and strong-boned they look to my eye, Lot. They will make fine men, stout warriors, to be sure."

Hands on his hips, the king bends forward suspiciously. "It has been full five years since we walked together among these stones, yet you seem much changed in my eyes. Is that truly you, Merlin?"

"Truly me?" Hannes strives to load his piping voice with umbrage. "Truly me?" He waves his stave at the braziers, and the flames blaze green. With a hysterical laugh, he whacks a carpenter's stool, and it dances, sidling and whirling among the support tresses and dangling pulley cables. "Who else but Merlin could work such magic?"

Even as his words echo in the large and hollow chamber, the stool collides with a brazier, spilling the sickly green flames atop the wizard. Hannes yelps with fright and pain as the green fire bites the exposed flesh of his face and hands and ignites his beard in a gust of spinning sparks.

With terrified shouts, Gawain and Gareth leap out of the chamber, leaving their father standing alone and astonished in the emerald fireshadows.

"Enough, Merlin!" Lot kicks the animated stool into the air as it prances by, and it collapses to the floor inert.

Hannes drops his stave and beats at the snapping flames in his beard with his hat, striking puffs of blue smoke from his body and finally lifting his robe over

his face and hands and smothering the frenzied con-
flagration. The flesh of his rib-sharp torso looks
white as flour milled twenty times, yet when he lowers his robes, his singed and fuming features show
white only in his startled eyeballs.

"You have changed," Lot acknowledges. "I see
that plainly. You have changed in form and in manner. I struggle to believe that you are the very
demon-wizard my wife Morgeu despises. Perhaps I
should summon her from our camp to witness you in
this more giddy shape. You seem far less the terrible
figure of memory. You seem more a man to my eye,
Merlin—and a laughable man at that."

Hannes stops swatting at the last sparkling embers
crawling in his shriveled beard and asks tremulously,
"Morgeu—the sorceress? Morgeu the Fey? She is here?"

"Aye. But put your fear aside, wizard. I have
come to introduce you to my sons but also to tell you
this for certain: The years have not diminished my
wife's loathing for you, nor will beholding you in this
ridiculous state soften her heart. Know that she has
come not to see you or even Camelot. She is here to
stravage the countryside for crystal and herbal
medicaments. None of us will be seeing much of her
these days. A woe for me, who loves her dearly—but
a certain joy for you, eh, wizard?"

"Yes—yes—a certain joy for me." Hannes wipes
his scorched brow, picks up his stave, and, bent over
his pain, retreats into the shadows. Merlin had not
said that Hannes would have to confront others with
magical strength. But then—*Mother of Mercy!*—he
had not said such ones would not come, either.

As a perplexed King Lot departs, Hannes over-
hears the youngest of the boys declare, "He is not so
fearsome as mother says. He looks more a skinny and
foolish old man than a demon."

"A skinny and foolish old man who can make
stools skip and jump!" the eldest complains. "And did
you not see how he danced with fire? Let's have no
more to do with him, Father."

Hannes retreats deeper into the dark corridors of
the incomplete building and rubs his stave along the
walls, making the stones shine with a dull light that
enbrowns the air. By that vague light, he inspects his
burned hands and moans to see them laced with blisters. A few cooling chants, and the pain of his seared
body dims.

He must be far more careful with his magical displays, he realizes. In the coming days, the British warlords will arrive: Marcus Domnoni, who knew
Merlin at Tintagel when Hannes built the round
table, Severus Syrax, the oriental *magister militum* of
Londinium, who hosted the wizard in the governor's
palace, and the dread Bors Bona, who fought
remorselessly for him on battlefields across Britain.
How will he deceive those wily Romans who survive
by expecting treachery in every shadow? He must
behave in a more subdued and dignified manner. If
Morgeu the Fey had witnessed his blundering antics,
he could well be dead now.

Fear booms so loudly in Hannes's chest he wor-
ries that the sorceress will hear it. But perhaps
Morgeu is not as powerful an entity as the carpenter
dreads, he reasons to himself. Merely a mortal, she

must learn and relearn her magic—unlike her arch-foe, that demon-wizard Merlin, whose powers are not human at all.

The sorceress Morgeu the Fey does possess powerful magic—such as the ability to walk out of her body—but only after much arduous preparation. Her spells to bewitch and ensorcell depend on internal disciplines that require constant maintenance and attentiveness. The effort is exhausting. Only Morgeu's determination to avenge her father's death empowers her.

Squatting in the dark woods, she stares angrily through the tree awning at the phlegm of stars spewed across the sky. She wants to fly as her enemy Merlin flies. Then she could swoop through the night like an owl with the soul of a dead Celt caught in its throat. She would follow her inner sense, the inner calling of her half brother's blood. It calls to her as nimbly as her own passion. In trance, she hears that lustfulness most clearly—the adolescent urgings that thicken in his body.

The worm of blood that crawls in his veins has the same mother as her blood, and, by that common link, she can feel him with her magic. Desire in him seeks a naked joy, and in trance she feels it echo in the most glorious parts of her. By that resonance, she could easily find him—if she could fly. But she cannot. And on her journeys out of her body, she loses her way, because Merlin employs his demon powers to confuse her. He has cast a spell that scatters the echoes from her half brother's yearnings, scatters them across the horizon so they seem to come from every direction. If only she could fly, she could lift herself above the scattering and see their source.

Instead, she must sit in the dark and work hard on her trances. Like the good and bad powers of fire, trance helps and yet hurts. It helps her contain her rage—and it hurts when she is alone like this in the melancholy night and cannot reach with her anger beyond herself, cannot strike her enemies—the demon Merlin and the half brother seeded by murder in their mother's womb.

Spiders crawl through her heart whenever she thinks of her father's death, which had made way for Pendragon to wed her mother.

Father, I will avenge you, she swears to the ghost of Gorlois. *I will avenge you—not with murder, but with love.*

The light of her words brightens in her mind, serene and pitiless, and mingles with the carnal echoes of her half brother's life. From everywhere and so from nowhere, those ardent echoes circle around her, passing through the spaces and silences of her trance to feed her heart with bitterness.

Chapter Eleven

With a summery breeze at his back and morning sunlight running brightly across a landscape of quilted hedgerows and pastures, Merlin walks briskly on a road warped with shattered paving stones. He feels odd without his staff, his hat, and his robes, and he leaves behind the wooded mountains around Camelot not willingly, yet without pointless resistance. He must go to Arthor. Disguised, of course. The lad is not to know that he is king, not until the clans and the families have gathered at Camelot and Merlin has delivered him into their presence. Only then, with the sword Excalibur drawn from the stone before all eyes, including the boy's own incredulous gaze, will Arthor be in a position not only to confront his fate but to reveal it to all Britain. The revelation, Merlin knows, will go a long way to enabling the youth to accept his new station and the awful responsibilities that attend it.

With that resolve, Merlin determines to call himself by his alternate's name—Hannes. But disguising himself as a carpenter leaves him uneasy. Jesus was a carpenter, and the wizard, out of respect for his deceased mother's reverence for the Savior, wants to avoid any association with that holiest of men. *Then why not be His opposite, of sorts,* Merlin asks himself. He ponders a minute, then his beard opens to a wide grin. He will disguise himself as a gleeman—a vagabond joker!

"As the Lord raised the dead from the spirits of the grave, I will raise the spirits of the living by my humor," Merlin declares, well pleased. He stops and faces the banked conifers that rise like dark, steep flames at the roadside. "You shall be my first audience—you, the living board! And I promise, when I make you laugh, I shall not take a bough. Nor shall I be offended that everyone here leaves."

Vastly amused at himself, the wizard slaps his thigh. "You're not laughing," he notes, suddenly somber. "In truth, I get more zest from a *ghost.* At least a ghost thinks it's alive—but that's its *grave* mistake!" He pauses, then guffaws. "Why do you think they put locks on mausoleums and iron gates around churchyards? Because people are just *dying* to get in!"

Merlin grins broadly at the conifers before his foolishness congeals to disappointment. *Ach, I'm a poor gleeman,* he thinks sadly, *because I'm not wholly a man. That must be it. I'm a demon merely pretending to manhood.*

The wizard continues glumly on his way. The sun scalds his bare pate, and as he walks, he absent-mindedly fashions a hat from plaited grass and polished leaves of ivy. Gradually, the road breaks into cobbles and tufty grass golden with bees' desire. Suddenly, there in the middle of the road stands a small dog the color of cast iron scorched in a kiln, ashen black tinged with rusty powder, with a splash of white over one eye as if hit in the face with a snowball. Its tough, tightly compact body shows slats of ribs, and its bowed, ready legs wear badges of dried scabs and bristles of burrs and nettles. Clearly, the animal has known hardship.

When Merlin approaches, the eyes, large and humorous, turn wickedly long and devilish, and its tiny, comical ears lie back, drawing the loose folds of its snout to a fanged snarl. The wizard whispers a happy spell, and instantly the cur's face relaxes and its long tail shoots up and whips the air.

"Ha!" Merlin shouts with delight, and affectionately rubs the dog's hackles. "You're no wolfhound from the depths, are you? Just some mongrel like me, off on your own. Come along, little one. Let's clean and feed you and see what your opinions of this world are."

At a pond overgrown with duckweed and creeping mints, Merlin sits on the rock verges and gently washes the filthy animal. The wizard whispers soothing magic, and removing the bramble thistles and salving the open wounds with mallow and willow sap proves a comfort to the creature. The dog grins happily and shakes watery rhinestones from its bristly fur.

"You shall come with me," Merlin announces, and playfully wraps the dog's head in green ruches of duckweed so it seems to be wearing a pharaoh's turban. "You shall be my wise dog. And you will entertain the people in ways that I have not the wit to do. And because, with my magic, you shall seem wise enough to be your own master, wise even as an animal god of ancient Ægypt, you shall be known as . . . as . . . Master Sphenks!"

The dog shakes off the shirring of pondgrass and yaps merrily. Then, Merlin leads Master Sphenks through a woodsy field blue with flaring harebells to a glassy stream, and there calls up several trout. While the animal gnaws at its raw fish and the wizard braises his in a small fire, they talk about the dog's life.

There is not much to tell, as the dog has been wild since birth; only that the world is much improved now that the wizard has used his magic to drive off the lice and to provide food the likes of which Master Sphenks has never tasted. How eerie and beautiful to be here with this two-leg, whose kind have always before thrown rocks, the little dog says with its flurrying tail. It grins at its new friend, who smiles down at it from inside his flustery, white beard. Overhead, opulent clouds stream past, and Master Sphenks grins sweetly into life's everlasting flow.

Farther upstream, a league away, Arthor and Fen ride through a sapling forest that spins sunlight to threads like hot glass. In the sugared heat rising from carpets of daisies and violets, they ride bare-chested and hatless. Arthor has untied the hostage's hands, and they travel together, seemingly easy as comrades. Fen has spoken not a word, nor Arthor, since leaving White Thorn, yet the two understand each other. Fen is going back to his people, and soon Arthor will be at his mercy.

Along a stream hung with trees, the Saxon draws alongside Arthor, and says in guttural Latin, "You are of my people."

Arthor skims a thin smile across his broad face. "You talk your enemy's tongue."

"Aelle made all his children learn." Fen watches him with great intensity. "You speak the enemy's tongue—but do you speak your father's?"

"I don't have a father."

"Everyone has a father."

"I like it better when you don't talk." He kicks his palfrey to a faster trot and pulls ahead through the proliferant rivergrass and a mass of yellow butterflies.

For the remainder of the day, they ride in silence. In the hamlet of Telltale, they eat a meal of black bread, cheese, and dandelion greens, and Fen remains mute. All that afternoon, as they journey among the tilled fields under bosomy hills dark with forests, they say nothing. Coming to a wild orchard of ambering fruit, they pause beside an ancient sundial that served a villa now sunken in blowing grass and drizzles of pink blossoms. There, they sit eating apples with their backs to the sundial's stone post, its engraved satyrs worn to shadows by centuries of northern rain.

Then they ride again, past shepherds and farmers on their tilted pastures, past more remnants of Rome—a shattered row of columns that vines twirl upon, climbing above shards of mosaics with images exhausted by lichen. In the ephemeral dusk, they let the horses graze on the blue shadowland of a hillside

while they eat muffins and salt meat from Telltale
with apples from the wild orchard.

They tie the horses to evergreen ash atop the hill
and lie down to sleep in a nearby stand of birch
under a hectic moon. Moonlight searches the higher
branches. Fen's voice, disembodied in the dark,
seems to climb down from there, "I don't understand
the Celts. You are a great warrior, yet they make you
eat and sleep with their servants. That is why they are
weak. They do not reward greatness. Among the
Celts, you must be the son of a chief to become a
chief. But among my people, who your father is
makes no difference. Each person makes his own
destiny. You would be a chief among my people—
among your father's people."

"I don't have a father," Arthor grumbles. "Go to
sleep."

"Your father is a Saxon. Your blood is Saxon."

"Shut up."

"I have seen the way the Celts treat you. You are
little more than a dangerous dog to them. They let
you loose to kill their enemies. Otherwise, they keep
you in a kennel. Leave them. Join with a Saxon clan
who will accept you proudly for your bravery. Or
take your own freedom and hire your sword to chiefs
who will pay you well."

Arthor knows Fen is right, and that is why he is
determined to go his own way. As he glides toward
sleep, he holds Short-Life close. With this saber, he
will cut a path for himself through the world. Mother
Mary, on the shield that stands against a birch, smiles
softly over him as the moonlight makes her phosphor.

She will stand beside him. She is all he needs, he thinks, and falls asleep.

Morning comes with the color of pearls and acres of rain that run over the hilly land to the north, dousing the sleepers with cold droplets. The two travelers rise and ride to meet the rain through narrow trails among hedges of black hollyhock and into fields of blue larkspur. Hunched over in the wet wind, they peer ahead to where the sun slumps golden among shelving clouds above an ancient forest that ranges to the terminals of the sky.

A thorp of sod-roofed cottages occupies the elbow of a stream. One cottage has a red kine grazing atop it, and two others plait brown threads of cooking fires into the east wind. On the cow path that leads down to the thorp, the rain stops, and directly ahead of them a tall, angular old man and his small dog step from the hedges. He is wearing a long white beard and a ridiculous hat of plaited grass and ivy that makes him look very like a god of Roman times in disguise.

"Hail, travelers," the old man calls in a gravelly voice far bigger than his narrow body should hold. "I am Hannes the gleeman—and this is my wise dog, Master Sphenks."

The rusty black dog with the white-patched eye leaps in the air and twirls about with a happy yelp.

"We are bound for Hammer's Throw," the old fool continues, "and we seek the protection of Christian soldiers to guard us on our way."

"We are not Christian soldiers," Arthor replies. "God help you with your travels, old man."

"Yet, boy, I see you bear the image of Our

Savior's mother," the gleeman presses, and the dog at his side sits up, paws pressed together as if praying. "For the sake of she who knew love's labor best of all women, I ask your protection."

"I am a Christian," Arthor admits, "but this man beside me is the warrior son of the pagan chieftain Aelle. Best you find other companions for this journey, old fool."

Master Sphenks lays its face to the ground and covers its eyes in mock fear. "Aelle of the Thunderers—the destroyer of cities?" the gleeman asks, then scowls darkly and points an accusing finger at the Saxon. "Many thousands of Christians have died horrid deaths at Banavem, Venta, Anderida, Regnum—cities where every man, woman, and child were slain by Aelle and every house burned to ash. Why is this murderer alive at your side, boy, and you a Christian soldier?"

"Be on your way, fool," Arthor says, trying to ride past him, but the gleeman will not budge from the narrow cow track.

"Avenge those Aelle has killed and slay this heathen murderer," the old man insists. "Give me the sword to do the deed, boy."

When the gleeman steps closer to grab for the sword, Arthor puts his foot against the fool's chest and kicks him into the rocky bramble. Master Sphenks yaps angrily, stands on its hind legs, and punches the air like a pugilist.

Arthor ignores it and rides past, but Fen looks back, amused by the wise dog and the angry gleeman. If he had a sword, he would gut the fool just to see the little dog dance with grief.

The riders stop in the thorp and eat a puree of pulse thickened with barley flour. Arthor purchases hard-boiled eggs, several loaves of oat bread, a large wedge of green cheese, and a bag of chestnuts, and they ride out, headed for the immense forest. The trees move apart, and the gleeman and his wise dog are waiting for them yet again on the forest track.

"This is Crowland you're entering, Christian soldier," the old fool warns sternly. "There are brigands about—wildwood gangs. You'll do well to take me and Master Sphenks with you. I do not need to remind you that you'll get little help against your foes from the likes of that Saxon creature who rides at your side. And even a fool such as myself can see you're but a boy. You'll need the wisdom of my dog to correct your lack of years."

Arthor rides on as if he does not see the old man, his horse bumping into him and shoving him aside.

"Where is your Christian charity, lad?" the gleeman calls, and Master Sphenks shakes its head ruefully. "You shame the Lady of Grace whose image you bear."

Arthor does not listen. Mother Mary wants him to travel alone, to fulfill his last promise to Kyner. After that, he will be free to tend all the fools and their wise dogs she sends his way. He and Fen ride steadily into the forest, startling doves that flutter like ghosts into the vaulted darkness.

Chapter Twelve

Accompanied by three hundred infantry, eighty archers, and thirty lancers, Severus Syrax arrives at Camelot intending to crown himself high king of Britain. A gaunt, swart man with a forked beard, aquiline nose, and proud mouth, he affects the oriental manner of his Syrian ancestry by wearing a turbaned pith helmet and Persian-style silks beneath a gold-bossed Roman cuirass. His steed is a long-necked white stallion with slender legs lively as flames. It carries him haughtily on parade with his troops, along the handsome paved rose stone boulevard that leads from the Roman road through the red-roofed village of Cold Kitchen, and up the yew-cloistered slopes to Camelot.

For fifteen years, Severus has prepared himself for this regal event. While other warlords feuded with each other and skirmished with the Celtic clans, he managed to avoid all conflicts and meticulously built alliances with the small mercantile families of Britain's *coloniae*. He extended credit from the rich coffers of the Syrax family to those potential allies who needed capital, and he installed spies and agents in the powerful and independent households that did not need him. Over time, through a patient progression of selective poisonings, orchestrated marriages, and blatant coercion, he won influence within a majority of the island's great families.

Then, bolstered by the support of Britain's commercial leaders, Severus bid for the allegiance of Bors Bona, the fierce British warlord from the north possessed of a formidable army, and he won Bors over by promising him taxation rights on all the overland trade routes among the *coloniae*. Such rights virtually guaranteed a fabulous fortune, which the Syrax family were loath to deny themselves until they realized that without Bors Bona, they would have lacked the military might to intimidate the Celts.

As he rides into Camelot now, Severus Syrax is thinking very intently about the Celts. His wealth means nothing to them, they who worship freedom above possession; and his army, even with Bors Bona to back him, can only make them fear him, not acknowledge him as high king of all Britain. So, to win over their superstitious pagan souls, he calculates he must eventually have the cooperation of the one Briton they truly respect—the wizard Merlin. But first, he must get Merlin's attention.

Commandeering the palace grounds for his camp, Severus orders pavilion tents erected for his officers in the courtyard within the rampart walls of the fortress, and directs that his quarters shall be set up within the great hall itself, which has had its vast cedar roof raised into place only days earlier. He orders the workers' scaffolds and benches removed to make room for his furnishings, which include a canopy bed, elaborate mahogany wardrobes, even an ebony throne inlaid with mother-of-pearl and amethysts big as walnuts.

"Merlin will not stand for this," the foreman of the construction workers warns, when he sees the display. He is a stout, red-faced man with a loud voice that is used to being obeyed. "We've all heard him say it, time and again: *all* participants in the festival are to camp upon the meadows. *No one* is to occupy the fortress but the high king himself."

Severus stares down his beaky nose with dark, unblinking eyes, a flat, lizardlike stare that openly challenges the foreman's outraged frown. "Send Merlin to me," he orders with an unperturbed smile.

Two leagues away, in Cold Kitchen, Hannes has kept himself busy inspecting the bake shops, butchers, fishmongers, and grocers, doing little more than driving mice out of their larders, settling petty disputes, and helping repair leaky roofs and warped wagon axles—anything to keep away from Camelot.

For the two days before Severus Syrax's arrival, Hannes has delighted in amazing the merchants and farmers of the hamlet with his magical abilities. Anxious to avoid inspiring suspicions the way he had with King Lot, he has roamed the winding lanes and crooked streets, driving rats and street debris ahead of him, sending both tilting out of town in small, black whirlwinds.

But magic, still awkwardly unfamiliar to the carpenter, has failed him time and again. His sooty squalls disastrously collide with the crofters' wagons coming into town laden with vegetables. And then Hannes must douse each blackened farmer with a

cleansing spell, and that leaves them grimeless but
with their clothes shredded and their hair tangled in
tiny elves' knots. The rustics laugh at the wizard's
flustering antics. Merlin had always kept aloof from
them before. What a rare, festive mood the wizard is
in these days, the villagers marvel, relishing having
him dote on them, however mischievously.

To Hannes, though, working magic feels like the
blackest blunder of his life. Even so, it is for him a stu-
pidity capable of brightening abruptly to a brilliant
cleverness—sometimes so radiant it blinds him to
what will follow. Recently, faced with a toothache in
the jaw of the tailor's wife, Hannes was unsure how to
begin, but reaching into the cave of his chest where
Merlin compacted his magic—there it was—a fiery
energy shaped like geometry. He put his hands on the
woman's jaw, shut his eyes, and the barbarous words
came from that geometric blaze inside him, filling
him with a sudden and subtle strength that flexed
through his hand and kicked the woman's head back.
She spit out the rotted tooth, then laved him with
praise, her face absolutely beatific with relief.

In minutes, news of the bloodless defeat of her
suffering crossed the village, and since then the wizard has been swarmed by an unending line of the sick
and ailing. By day's end, Hannes no longer has the
strength left even to stand and must be carried to a
cot the villagers have prepared for him in the church.
Slumbering, he dreams of blisters, cankers, gumboils,
polyps, and chancres piled in his hands like gems. He
wakes nauseated at cockcrow and slips out the chan-
cel door to avoid those waiting at the font for healing.

To the further amazement of the townsfolk, Hannes spends that morning working with his hands, planing lumber in the carpenter's shed for delivery to the workers in Camelot. Blessedly, he has healed the villagers' chief ailments, and after relieving a neatherd of a sty and the smith of a bruised thumb, no one troubles him further. It feels good to work with wood again, and he is grateful to Merlin that the gnarled bones of his hands have been unlocked. Giddy with the perfume of sawdust, he sings a happy, if wistful, song to his dead wife, wishing she could see him now in Merlin's robes and hat.

At midday, when Severus Syrax parades through Cold Kitchen with his lancers, archers, and infantrymen, Hannes manages to avoid the scene entirely, finding work to do in the sheep meadow. In his tremulous voice, he bleats out a magical song that makes the ewes and their yeanlings come marching past the shepherd in a straight line, to separate more easily the animals to be sold at the mutton market. A day's work is done in an hour. Then, the wizard tries using his magic to pull raspberries from distant thorny vines. When the loudmouthed foreman and his gaffers finally arrive to collect Merlin, they find the wizard hunched over in the meadow, startled by his own magic as the red pellets of fruit hurtle about him like hail from the sky.

Informed that Severus has entered Camelot and has appropriated the great hall for himself, Hannes winces. He brushes the smashed raspberries from his hat and cloak. "Perhaps he's just inspecting our work?" he offers in a high, hopeful voice.

"My lord, he's set up a throne!" the foreman insists. "When the Celts get wind of that, blood will surely spill in Camelot. You must come at once and get that arrogator out of there!"

With ponderous reluctance, which the foreman and his men interpret as weighty rage, Hannes stalks across the meadow, staff in hand. He refuses to ride, wanting as much time as possible to prepare for the frightful confrontation. But all he can think to do is summon courage with a magical chant. By the time he reaches Camelot, he has sung it so many times that he is virtually drunk with bravery. He will make Syrax's throne dance out of Camelot, he thinks smugly to himself; and if the warlord so much as looks cross-eyed at him, he will shout spells that will tie his tongue to his toes. His face stern with resolve, he floats light as smoke past the glittery line of guardsmen that Syrax has posted at the main gate.

Severus Syrax sits in the circular central hall, pert upon his ebony chair, beringed hand twirling a curl of black hair at his temple. At the sight of him, so imperious and foreign in his shiny ringlets and kohl-rimmed almond eyes, his silk robes like vaporous layers of ether floating on his body, all valor suddenly wisps away from Hannes and leaves him cold with fright. "So at last you are here," the *magister militum* says sourly. "Why have you kept me waiting, Merlin?"

Relief floods Hannes at the warlord's acceptance of him as Merlin, and his mind goes airy and loses all chance of reclaiming its angry edges. Meekly, he replies, "I had work to do in Cold Kitchen."

"I marched through that miserable town," Severus says with a pained and irate expression. "You saw me. Everyone saw me. You should have come to greet me."

Hannes leans heavily on his staff to stay upright despite his trembling. Not knowing what to say, he finally blurts, "You can't stay here."

Severus's thin eyebrows arch sharply. "Really?"

"Only the high king may occupy Camelot." Hannes shrugs weakly as if he cannot help this immutable fact. "Everyone knows that."

"Yet, here I am." The warlord opens his arms in a graceful, feminine gesture. "Therefore, I must be the high king."

Hannes swallows hard and says aloud what Merlin has obliged him to say: "You will have to draw the sword from the stone."

"Bah!" His dark, Persian face sharpens spitefully. "We'll have none of that nonsense, Merlin. I have forged a coalition with most of the families. Only Marcus Domnoni has refused my entreaties. But at your command, he will fall into line."

"At my command?" Hannes speaks with genuine surprise, the warlord's anger making him forget for the moment who he is supposed to be.

"Don't play the fool with me, wizard. You've jerked the strings of these marionettes for fifteen years now, denying Britain a leader while you play your puppet games with warlords and chieftains alike. That's over now." He leans far forward, his eyes black flames. "I tell you, I have the allegiance of the families. Bors Bona has thrown in his lot with me. You will command

Marcus Domnoni to obey—and you will do the same for the Celtic chieftains."

Flustered, Hannes shakes his head with dismay. "I can't do that."

"If you refuse, there will be war."

"No—no war." His voice sounds dwarfed by the thunder of his heart. Again, he states Merlin's command. "Draw the sword from the stone. That is the challenge."

"That is your magic, sorcerer. You decide who pulls Excalibur. You are the maker of kings. You made Pendragon. You can make me." He sits back slowly, his anthracitic eyes lazy. "If not, there will be war."

Hannes feels that frightful word go through his robes into his bones, and the shudder of his fright stiffens to anger that Merlin has put him in this dangerous position where the lives of so many innocents hang in the balance. Emboldened by that anger, he begins again, "I can make you into a rat, too. Would you like that, Syrax?"

"Don't threaten me, wizard. Don't think I haven't thought how to handle a viper like *you*." He says the last word as though it is something truly revulsive. "If anything is to happen to me, Bors Bona will sweep over this land like a storm of fire, and your precious Camelot will be ruins before it's even finished."

Shivery fear drains Hannes's strength, and he sways with the weakness of his knees, his joints swiveling awkwardly so that he must put all his weight on the staff to remain upright. What would Merlin do? Magic? He considers for a split second putting the warlord to sleep, and his guards as well, and having them all hauled out to wake up in the fields where they belong. But what then of Bors Bona? If there is war, it will be on Hannes's head. The very thought leaves his bones feeling like rotten wood. In his fright, he is somehow reminded of his long years as a master builder and how he used to tame warlords who came to him with their brutal demands. And then a broad smile slowly pleats his bearded face. Of course! There was a special magic he learned on his own, a magic that could move the heaviest heart in mere minutes: flattery.

"I like your courage, Syrax—and your cunning," Hannes says. "You're a clever one, all right. You're the very man I've been waiting for. Indeed, if you can now behave with the grace and dignity becoming a monarch, you shall be high king of Britain."

Severus Syrax tilts his head suspiciously. "What are you saying, Merlin?"

"The legend, Syrax." His voice swells with new-found confidence. "You must fulfill the legend. You realize, of course, that you can't win the Celts and Duke Marcus by force. They are people with large-ness of heart. Why do you think I set the sword in the stone as a challenge? To capture men's hearts. Seize that, mighty lord, and you will not need force."

The warlord's dark eyes narrow. "You will arrange for me to draw Excalibur from the stone?"

"That is the only way to assert authority without resort to arms," Hannes says firmly. "You must fulfill the legend. And I will help you. But it must be done properly."

"What do you mean?"

"The festival has yet to begin." Hannes steps closer, his certainty brightening something deep inside his stare. "Marcus, Bors, Kyner, and Urien have yet to arrive. When they do, and the festivities have been enacted and fulfilled as they have been in the two previous gatherings, then you shall have the chance to draw Excalibur—and I will see that the legend is fulfilled."

"Good." Severus Syrax lifts his forked beard in approval. "You are a reasonable old wizard after all, Merlin."

"Britain needs a king," Hannes says, nodding complicitly. The hook baited with flattery is set; now, to pull him to where he belongs. "I have been waiting a long time for the right man. Now that he is here, the ascension must be done in the right way. You cannot stay here. You must take your place in the fields outside Camelot. Only after the sword is drawn may the high king enter this place."

"Of course," the warlord readily agrees, nodding his coiffed head. "We don't want to inspire suspicions of collusion between us, do we? The magic of the legend deserves respect if it is to be effective at the moment when I need it to assume the throne."

Hannes smiles, sealing their shared understanding. "We shall tell everyone that you have entered only to inspect the construction. I shall extend that right to the other lords, so there is no jealousy."

Syrax rises and steps toward Hannes. "Fine, Merlin, fine." He squints his hooded eyes. "You look less frightful than last we met. They say you are a shapeshifter. I only pray that your word does not shift—for then, many will suffer."

Hannes's wide smile does not flicker. "I assure you, Severus Syrax—Merlin will keep his word."

Chapter Thirteen

In the dark forest of Crowland, Merlin and Master Sphenks follow Arthor and Fen from a distance. The sun hangs its prisms in the rain-wet canopy so that the high branches glitter like a pelt of stars. On the forest floor, a dense labyrinth of root-buttresses and honeysuckle shrubs hold the lanes among the trees, slowing the travelers. Jackdaws holler from boughs above deepening drifts of slant sunlight, a scent of violets shoots past on a curl of wind, and milkweed tufts flow in a cloudy river through the leafshadows.

Ahead, an oak has collapsed, and the riders dismount to walk their steeds over it. At the moment Arthor and Fen begin clambering over the obstacle, frenzied screams explode from all sides, startling the horses. A half dozen maniacs—roving plunderers who ambush travelers for their coin and the thrill of killing—drop from the trees and fly out of the underbrush, rat-hair lashing, axes and daggers hacking.

Instantly, Fen leaps atop the log, hoping to mount his horse from there and fly from the killers, but his steed has jumped the fallen oak and clops away in a panic. Arthor's mount, too, has broken away, disappearing among the shrubs. The youth has no shield or helmet, but Short-Life sings from its scabbard.

"A knife!" Fen calls, signaling Arthor to throw him the dagger sheathed in his boot cuff. But Arthor pays him no heed, and the Saxon fetches about for a tree limb or a rock to defend himself. There is nothing, and he jumps down from the log and crouches, prepared to grapple bare-handed with the attackers.

Arthor whirls the Bulgar saber from hand to hand, cutting the shadows with a sound like the north wind. His boyish face has set to a smile of evil intent. He wants this. To drink blood with Kyner's saber flushes him with crazed desire, and he answers the shrieks of the brigands by releasing a wild war whoop that sets his bare-shouldered body dancing with the naked blade.

Blood flies like sparks, and the two nearest bandits collapse in a flurry of limbs and arterial spray. Arthor prances over them, ducks, leaps, skips, and— gyrating like a man gone mad—screeches a killing laugh as he exposes himself to the enemy's steel, luring them into the blunt range of his blurred weapon. With the hollow thump of meat, another plunderer strikes the earth, hands tangled in his bowels.

Fen has never seen such beautiful frenzy, such controlled annihilation, not even among the berserkers. This boy kills with a hideous ecstasy. The Saxon kneels in awe, breath stalled. Three ax-men, wild at the deaths of their comrades, converge on Arthor. The death-dancer spins, driving them back, then stops cold, the short broad blade limp in his slick hand, and waits. Chin tucked, he grins mirthlessly, a boy amused at their fear. His amusement infuriates them, and they lunge.

Arthor slashes. One bandit staggers back, vomiting blood, a second holds up the stumps of both wrists and sags under the twin geysers of his spilled life. The third and last of the killers flees. He leaps over a flat rock and dwindles into a cypress alley. With a defiant cry, Arthor hurls Short-Life so that it hits the flat rock whirling, caroms off it, and wings after the fleeing man. It strikes him between the shoulder blades and severs his spine.

The Saxon can only blow out his astonishment and empty his lungs in awe. How the boy's killing genius inspires him! He scrambles forward and, almost without thinking, seizes an ax from the spasmed hand of a dead brigand.

"Arthor," he calls out, wanting this remarkable youth to see his death, to know it and to know, too, that it is Fen of the Thunderers who slays him.

Arthor turns slowly, and his amber eyes lid heavily, recognizing his blunder.

"You are a great slayer of men," Fen tells him consolingly. "I will wear your hair on my sword belt with pride."

Expertly, Fen flings the ax at his foe with mortal force, so accurately that Arthor sees there is no merciful inch of escape or even hope of a glancing wound, that there is no alternative at all but to meet ravaging death with a raw grimace.

As if from nowhere, Master Sphenks spurts through the trees. The small animal leaps, cleverly catches the hurtling ax helve in its jaws, and rolls to a tumbling mass at Arthor's feet. Without blinking, the young warrior snatches the ax from the ground and rushes forward.

Furiously, Fen reels around in a desperate attempt to flee but collides with the old gleeman, who has come huffing behind his dog up the trail. Before Fen can struggle free of the man's bony grasp, Arthor seizes him by his hair and yanks him upright. The Saxon thrashes about briefly, intent on savaging the youth, but instead takes a blow between the eyes from the blunt end of the ax. The impact sits him down in a spray of hot stars.

"Kill him!" the gleeman cries. "Kill the heathen murderer!"

"No!" Arthor commands. "Get the horses."

"The horses?" The old man slaps the side of the Saxon's head. "Did you not see? This snake tried to kill you!"

Arthor levels a cold look at the stranger. "If you want to ride with me, old man, get the horses."

The gleeman blinks with disbelief. "And that's all the gratitude you have for the ones who saved your life? Just, get the horses?"

The young man does not answer. His pale flesh shines with the gloss of his exertion, and his roseate cheeks glow, flushed. Yet the soft contours of his fifteen-year-old face belie the hard stare in his grim eyes. "I have no gratitude for this life."

The gleeman steps back, stunned to realize that the boy is serious. Master Sphenks has come up beside him, and together they go off to find the horses. The old man shakes his head sadly as he wades through the gilly grass. As the wizard Merlin, he assiduously avoided having anything to do with the child, fearing that enemies—Morgeu the Fey, demons, the Furor—would find Arthor and kill him. Now he wonders with cold despair if his neglect has killed the boy's spirit.

Merlin avoids using magic to call the horses. Even at the crucial moment when Fen's flung ax threatened the future king, the wizard restricted his power to the wise dog. The radiance of magic throws long shadows that the dark entities will recognize. Until he reaches Camelot, the boy's best protection from the malefic forces dedicated to his destruction is his anonymity.

Merlin returns with the horses, with Master Sphenks standing atop one of the saddles, and they find Arthor laboriously breaking the axes and daggers of the dead brigands. Fen sits against the fallen oak, glowering morosely, his hands tied together by his boot cords.

When Arthor is done and stands sparkling with sweat and wrathful exhaustion, Merlin comes up beside him. "What is the name of the soul my impetuous wise dog has detained so unhappily in this world?" he asks softly.

Arthor pauses to retrieve his saber before answering. "Does it matter what my name is?" he asks wearily, then shrugs. "I am Aquila Regalis Thor— Arthor—ward of Chief Kyner." He hefts the Bulgar blade. "This is Kyner's sword, Short-Life, by which I am charged to return his hostage—this Saxon, named Fen—to Aelle, chief of the Thunderers."

"You are so young," the wizard says, and Master Sphenks leaps from the saddle with the strap of a water flagon in its jaws. "You can't have seen more than fifteen summers."

Arthor accepts the flagon from the wise dog with a tight smile and drinks. Then he stares closely at the old man, scrutinizing the long, sallow skull and the huge sockets, like the ossature of a great ape, holding mineral eyes cloudy as quartz. He wipes his mouth with the back of his hand, and replies, "I am old enough for Kyner to send away into the world—and young enough to have blundered and grown no older if your dog had not interfered." He passes the flagon to the gleeman. "I am certain that Kyner, who set me this mission to preserve the peace of his people, thanks you."

Merlin demurs with a mischievous slant to his eyes. "It is not I your chief must thank, young Arthor, but Master Sphenks."

Arthor bends down. "Then my master thanks you, wise dog, for saving the life of his dog."

Master Sphenks sits back and extends one leg straight out in salute.

"One dog to another." Arthor laughs and returns the salute. "You are welcome to journey with me to Hammer's Throw, old man—and your dog, too— though what lies ahead is dangerous."

"What lies here is no less dangerous," Merlin says, gesturing at the dead brigands hazed in flies. "We will travel in your protection."

With Fen and Master Sphenks on one horse and the other two following, the group sets off again.

Merlin rides behind Arthor on the palfrey and listens deeper into the youth, hearing all the sorrows that have shaped him. They are the oldest illusions among men—pride, shame, vanity, and anger: the pride of blood denied by the shame of a lowly birth, the vanity of nobility, and the angry bitterness of its lack.

If this furious soul were not himself Celtic elite, a proud warrior's soul, perhaps the boy could have been satisfied being the chief's beloved ward, his favored servant. Instead, he rankles at the commands of others, knowing in his pith a wider design to his destiny than the toil and demands of other people's ambitions.

That reluctance to serve disturbs the wizard. He wants to tell the boy that self-importance is a dangerous dream. When that delusion is broken, it makes one feel that the weight of the past smothers the future, when in truth the world lies waiting for anyone humble enough to separate the wish from the reality and serve what is. But this truth cannot be spoken. It must be lived to be understood.

"There is a trail in that direction," Merlin says, pointing through the congested trees. "It is a bypath that leads to the glades and the hamlet of Apple Garth. We can rest the horses and take supper there."

"You do not speak as gruffly as the common gleemen I've heard at the bean feasts," Arthor observes, guiding his horse in the direction the old man has shown. "You speak fair Latin."

"Oh, I have served kings," Merlin admits, telling Arthor of the king of Cos without mentioning that the man was, in fact, his grandfather, and other such tales of life in the court before Cos and his castle were destroyed by the Picts. In a merrier tone and caught up in a loquacious mood, Merlin then discourses on King Cole, the current monarch of the east coast at Camulodunum, who has held on to his throne not by fighting his enemies, the Angles, but by taming them with hemp pipes and bowls of mead, and organizing them into drunkenly happy orgies of fiddling and dancing.

"You served as jester for King Cole?" Arthor asks idly.

"Indeed. Would not that life appall this Saxon?" the gleeman responds, gesturing to their glowering prisoner. "I judge from his harsh silence that his people consider hemp, mead, and fiddle music no substitute for spilled blood and stolen land."

Later, as the riders enter the glades, the land itself answers for Fen, for Apple Garth has been destroyed. The charred husks of its houses stand in scaly black posts above weeds that hide the ashes. The scattered bones and skulls of the unburied dead bloom with wildflowers nourished by flesh gone to wormdirt. The small limbs of children and the seashell skulls of infants litter the glade that shimmers colorfully with goosefoot, purslane, panic grass, feverfew, phlox, and gory daylilies.

Arthor unties Fen's wrists and pushes him off the horse. "Bury them," he orders.

Fen stares up dazed from where he has fallen.

"Use your hands," Arthor tells him, "and cover all these bones with dirt. Do it, or I'll cut out your bowels."

While the horses graze, Arthor, Merlin, and Master Sphenks share the last of the provisions and watch Fen on his knees covering the bones with handfuls of sod. The wizard feels an elemental loyalty sitting beside the young man that he has helped to create, that he has god-fathered by his magic, and now must watch over in person, in the presence of their enemy, in this place of murder.

"Why are you looking at me like that, old man?" Arthor asks suspiciously, chewing his black crust of bread.

"You look familiar," Merlin answers truthfully, thinking of the boy's parents, golden-eyed Uther Pendragon and tawny-skinned Ygrane. "Forgive me. An old man sees familiarity everywhere."

Master Sphenks carries a bone to the Saxon and sits waiting for him to cover it. At this, Fen will abide no more.

"Go ahead, cut out my bowels," he challenges. "Kill me! I'll not honor these dead things."

Arthor shrugs and rises. Bare-chested and sandy-haired, he looks like Fen's clansman as he stands over him and ties the Saxon's wrists together. He helps Fen mount, and Master Sphenks hops onto the withers. They ride on, leaving the bones behind. The glade returns to the dark green corridors of the forest.

Presently, Merlin speaks from where he rides behind him: "Chief Kyner will be proud of you."

"I will not see Kyner again," Arthor answers coolly. "After Fen is returned to his people, I owe nothing more to the Celts. I will go my own way."

"Your own way?" Merlin speaks with thick

incredulity. "What hope for one so young in this ruthless world?"

"They have hope who have nothing else."

"You quote Thales," the wizard observes, impressed. "Surely, Chief Kyner educated you well. Why are you leaving him, then? What better lord could you find?"

"No lord at all, gleeman," Arthor answers flatly. "All earthly lords ape greatness. The history scrolls teach us to admire them—Alexander first of all and then the Roman conquerors. But are they great? I say their greatness is vulgar."

"You do, do you?" Merlin chuckles dryly. "What then, young Arthor, do you conceive as greatness?"

"For me, greatness is nature itself, God's creation. Balance that against history, I say. Beauty and goodness belong to God and to His creation. The Greeks knew that. They built the city, the *polis,* in nature, each city responsible for its own place—until Alexander, who conquered it all, imposed one law, his law, and made it an empire."

"Why is that wrong?" Merlin tests. "He united all the city-states to serve one another."

Arthor answers with disdain, "He built the State—the rule of men not *in* nature but *over* nature."

"But he did not ignore the Greeks," Merlin presses. "He was Aristotle's pupil."

"Who taught him reason—but he ignored the earlier Greeks, the beauty Socrates worshiped, the goodness Plato tried to define. In our quest for empire, we have forgotten that there is far more to life than reason, old man. We turn our back on nature. As

Pythagoras writes, 'We have forgotten that there is a beauty to nature that balances the music of numbers even with the tragedy of blood.'"

Merlin nods and smiles to himself, satisfied that this angry youth has framed his vexed soul in noble ideals. "Yes, Arthor. What you say is true. We love power, and we are ashamed of beauty."

"And so our lives become miserable tragedies," Arthor continues, hot with emotion, "vulgar efforts to pass greatness from father to son when greatness cannot be passed on at all. Each individual, each society, must make its own greatness."

"You speak like a Saxon," Fen mutters. "You despise the tradition of monarchs, even as you love the freedom of the strong man."

Arthor glares at him, and the Saxon nods knowingly.

Sunbursts of late afternoon flare in the tunnels of the forest, and they ride in silence toward the burning end of the day.

Chapter Fourteen

Brokk is the most clever of the Furor's dwarfs. He was made by the gods to know and to make. He knows how the world fits together in tiny pieces called atoms and how the atoms themselves are put together with tinier pieces yet, with little bits of lightning that the atoms share. He knows that things are solid, liquid, or gaseous because of how the atoms fit together, how they share their portions of lightning. He knows the atomic secrets behind the appearance of things. Reflectance, ductility, compression, color, and density have everything to do with how the atoms fit together, and in his workshop in the arctic north he and his dwarfs have the tools to rearrange atoms with heat, pressure, and lightning, in both subtle, hairraising static charges and stupendous thunderbolts. But out here in the summer woods, all that the dwarf has is his mind, and he is baffled by how the lamia, which has been given him by the Furor, shapeshifts.

The creature obviously is composed of a viscous kind of lightning, a plasma, as are the gods themselves. Wandering through the forest's green shadows, Brokk wraps the lamia around him in one shape after another, each time feeling like a coal breaking into flames. The heat rends through Brokk, feeds off the image of the thing the dwarf stares at, and burns him into that shape. He flares to a crow, flaps up into the forest canopy, and perches above the rumpled green world blinking at the sun and wondering how this can be, this total realignment of his atoms.

He unravels the lamia to the shape of mist and settles through the branches to the forest floor drifting on the summer breeze. He rolls himself into a mossy boulder, stretches into a svelte rowan hung with red pomes, collapses to a brown puddle reflecting the shattered sunlight of the forest ceiling.

A deer peers down at him, and he struggles to rise up into its nimble form—but he lacks the strength. Hard as he tries, fatigue defeats him. Then he rips himself free of the lamia, snaps it loose, and hangs it on a sun shaft. It looks grotesque. Withered gray as steam with lineaments streaked like coal soot outlining blistered eyes and a smeared mouth, it gazes mournfully at him.

Brokk cannot understand how such a vague entity can exist let alone mutate into any form he commands. Its taloned hands swipe at him and pull across his stout body like clotted rags. It wants to eat, but the dwarf is made of god-stuff by the gods themselves, and the lamia cannot draw sustenance from him.

The dwarf drags the limp thing after him through the forest following the dim melody of a goat bell. Through a stand of pine and barberry, he lumbers and stops when he sees a salt peddler walking a forest path with his goat, the animal laded with sacks of Droitwich salt and dried seaweed from Rameslie.

Brokk throws the lamia at the salt peddler, and it attacks with a hot scream. The peddler jerks about, and for an instant his eyes open wider than seem possible. Then his floppy cap and jerkin shred away, flying off in rags like gusty leaves, and his rib cage flays open, spilling the glisteny viscera the shapeshifter hungers for. The dwarf crosses his arms and watches it feed, watches it ripping the flesh, bursting the joints, cracking the bones to release the effluvial heat, the lifesmoke that it absorbs.

When it is done, the dwarf hangs it again from a sunbeam and admires the sleek, silken contours of its body. Its hair streams like the powdery lavender of twilight, and its skull-visage clacks its fang mesh in the cold that chills the corpse. It wants more.

"Later," Brokk promises, and removes his grinning dagger to butcher the goat. Watching the lamia feed has whetted his desire for blood-sticky meat, and though he does not have to eat and usually thrives off the electrical sap of the Storm Tree, he guts the bleating goat and gnaws its living heart.

As a raven, Brokk circles above the forest until he spies a caravan on the Roman highway that leads toward Camelot. He spools downward and lights on a dray cart. From there, he learns that this is Chief Kyner's entourage, and he is delighted. He has found his way to the sword Lightning!

Carefully, he studies the chief, committing to memory every detail of the large man's physique—

the ropelike braid of his graying hair, the small brow blunt as masonry shadowing hard eyes with a calm and a blue stolen from the sky. His dense mustache hides his mouth, yet it must be severe, for the jaw below it thrusts forward belligerent as a pike's. He wears Roman armor even in this summer heat—a red leather cuirass embossed with the Christian chi-rho, wrist straps on forearms swollen with muscle, the hair glinting like coarse copper shavings. His famous sword, the Bulgar saber Short-Life is missing, and instead, he carries a plaited belt, ivory-trimmed scabbard, and a *gladius,* the short Roman sword. Beneath the scarlet fretted hem of his blue tunic, his knees grimace like twin faces knotted with muscle. The crisscross straps of his sandals attach to soles studded with hobnails. To the last inch, he is a fighting man.

His son Cei, a dimmer version of himself without the mustache, the severe mouth revealed with its razor lips, rides up. "The fork at the old willow is coming up, Father. Let me take the lead. You've been riding point all day. Go back to the wagons. Lie down with a wet towel and read the clouds for a while."

"At the willow perhaps," Kyner says. "The road enters the forest then. It will be cooler."

"You might have a good word for the women when you go back," Cei enjoins. "You've not shown them a joke or even a smile since we left White Thorn. That troubles them, and then the children worry and little goes right with the clan."

"I'll find my wit again when we get to Camelot," he answers sullenly.

"It's Arthor, isn't it?" Cei probes testily. "You worry he won't meet us there."

"He's able. No grief will come to him from the brigands, and Aelle has promised him safe passage. I worry only that a feisty milkmaid might waylay him. He has a pagan's lust about him."

Cei shakes his head with regret for the chief's blindness. "It won't be a milkmaid that keeps that scoundrel away. He's done with us. Done with the Celts. His wild Saxon blood has spirited him away. You were purblind to give him Short-Life, Father. You'll never see that blade again."

Kyner reins himself away to keep from cuffing his son. "I'm going back to the wagons," he says, turning to ride along the line of drays and ox-drawn covered vans. "Watch for the willow's fork."

Brokk flies ahead of the trundling caravan, and, around the shank of a hill, he finds the fork in the highway. The landmark willow lies several lengths down the south curve of the road, partly obscured by a stand of shimmering alders. The dwarf places himself close to the fork's northern swerve, which dips into a long, forested valley, and he unfurls the lamia.

Growing a thousand slumped shoulders, he sways to the likeness of the willow and waits, weaving sunlight through his listless branches. The caravan rumbles by. He glimpses Kyner asleep on his back in one of the rocking carts, a flaxen daughter brushing the flies from his brutal face.

Brokk waits until the caravan wholly disappears into the dark tunnels of the forest; then, he yanks the lamia away from himself and stuffs it into his hip pouch. Briskly, he climbs the shank of the hill, and with the strength of two men dislodges several boulders. They crash through the bramble, digging up a torrent of smaller rocks in a fuming earth slide and smothering the fork of the highway. Finally, he mutters a dwarfish curse that will obscure all exits from the valley.

With that obstacle firmly in place, the dwarf pulls out the lamia, wraps it tightly around himself, lathing his body to a spear of sunlight, and hurls himself into the sky toward Camelot. He flies among cloud trails, and the sky turns white. When he explodes into blue space, the construction site of Camelot wheels below, a scattered nest of rocks and girders cradled among pine mountains. The River Amnis descends from these virid earth summits in wide, shiny loops. Then the forest soars closer, and he returns to a green depth of branches, into a river gorge of birch islands and erratic boulders dissolving in mist and haze.

Brokk lands among lime shrubs beside a boulder at the base of a knoll. He unwraps the lamia and shakes it out like a sheet, fitting it over himself to fit his memory of Chief Kyner. Parting the shrubbery, he sends several wrens hurtling toward the calm clouds. Above him, atop the grassy mount, the sword Lightning stands in a silver-black stone big as an anvil.

No one else appears to be on the knoll, and the dwarf strides uphill as Kyner. At the stone, he stands gawking like an astonished lover, arms outstretched, sidling back and forth, regarding the sword from differing angles. He does not touch it at once, fearing the magic that has placed it point down so firmly in the stone. Bending closer, he examines the rock with its freckles of orange rust. *Is it a Dragon's nerve?* he wonders, feeling the magnetic abundance of the boulder and fearing that to touch it would alert the planetary beast and draw it upward from its chthonic trance. With the lamia, Brokk suspects that he could loft swiftly into the sky and avoid the Dragon—but then, maybe not.

"It is beautiful, is it not?" a gruff voice speaks in Brythonic from behind the dwarf.

Brokk leaps about, startled to confront a Celtic warrior with braided, brindled hair, heavy mustache, and an eagle's stare pressed into his elderly face. He is taller than Kyner and wears old-style garb—a chieftain's browband of reeved leather, sword strap across his naked chest, fawnskin leggings, and soft boots.

The old chieftain laughs mightily. "You're getting old, Kyner, when a tired elk like myself can sneak up on you." He slaps Kyner's shoulder and lifts his yellow eyebrows. "But you are a solid old man, nonetheless. You feel steady as an oak."

Brokk gropes to determine who this Celtic chieftain is—Urien or Lot? "Greetings, friend."

"Friend now, is it?" King Lot smirks behind his immense mustache. "What of my soul burning in eternal damnation, then? Last we spoke, I thought you loathed me for spurning your Hebrew messiah."

Brokk shrugs. "Turn the other cheek, love your enemies, that's the Christian's way, is it not?"

"Is it?" Lot tilts his head skeptically. "You seem not at all the stern messenger of your desert prophet that I remember."

"It's the sword," Brokk declares, turning to face the shining blade—as much to hide his bewilderment as to admire his own craftsmanship. "In truth, it has bewitched me. Behold. Is it not the most beautiful weapon you have ever seen?"

Lot puts his hand to the helve of gold and sees the wonder in his warped reflection within the mirror-polished serif of the handguard. The sleek haft feels chilled even though the summer sun touches it. "Will you try your hand at it then, Kyner?"

"Nah," Brokk immediately dismisses the idea. "The magnetic flux density in this stone would defeat an elephant."

Lot's thick brows knit with incomprehension. "Magnus . . . what? Don't soil my ears with Latin, man. What are you talking about?"

Brokk scolds him without taking his eyes from the luminous sword and the star stone that holds it, "It's not Latin, fool. Magnet. It's Greek. We call it 'lodestone.'"

"The anvil is a lodestone?" Lot runs his fingers over the unreckonable slag with its great lobes and pollen-fine flecks.

"A lodestone the likes of which I've never seen," Brokk says, almost undervoiced, to himself. "Its flux density is incredible. Must be the work of the Fire Lords—the *Annwn*."

"Aye, the *Annwn*, no doubt." Lot regards his old comrade in arms with a puzzled look. "I find it strange to hear you talking of the Fire Lords, Kyner, and—what more was that you spoke of? Flux lines? Is that something in your Bible?"

"Never mind." The dwarf dismisses that with an impatient look and turns away from the stuck sword. "Merlin would know. Perhaps you could find out for me. Ask him how he switches the lodestone's polarity."

"I don't know what you're talking about," Lot gripes. "Ask him yourself. Am I your thrall?"

Brokk wrings his hands contritely, and, taking Lot by the elbow and leading him away from the star stone, speaks the truth. "I would ask him, but I tell you, I dread him. He claims to be a Christian, yet he frightens me."

"I know what you mean," Lot agrees, and lets himself be guided downhill, nodding. "I have always been uneasy with his Christianity and how he stole our queen to the faith you share with him. Not even Morgeu can win her back to the old ways now. And when I brought my sons to meet him upon our arrival here, he seemed—odd."

At last determining who this chieftain must be, Brokk replies, "Ah, brother Lot, Merlin is a demon, after all."

"Always before he seemed so," Lot concurs. "But this time he appeared more a bumbling fool than a demon-wizard."

"A fool? Merlin? It must be a pose. He means to deceive his enemies." Brokk releases Lot and backs away through the abundant grass, lifting his tunic as if preparing to urinate, and stepping out of sight behind a chokeberry bush.

"The wizard certainly has enough enemies," Lot continues. "Even his fellow Christians mean him harm. My spies in the Roman camp tell me that Severus Syrax plots to take the title of high king with or without the sword—with or without Merlin. What do you think of your fellow Christians now?" No sound comes from the chokeberry. "Eh, Kyner?" Lot steps behind the bush. "Kyner?" No one is in sight, only a brown rabbit flitting across the lush sward under giant clouds swept along by azure time.

As the rabbit, Brokk hurries to find Merlin, hoping to spy on the wizard and learn what he can about the magnetic stone of the Fire Lords. But as he approaches Camelot, he slows down and sits for a long time listening to the pine breeze. He is afraid of the demon. Surely, Merlin will see through his disguise and feed him to the Dragon. The Furor sent Brokk to this place not to confront Lailoken, a Dark Dweller from the House of Fog, but to retrieve the sword Lightning.

At the sight of Merlin, in his wizard's robes and tall conical hat of power, standing before the gargantuan ramparts of Camelot, the dwarf backs away. The demon mingles among the revelers accompanying Severus Syrax and his retinue as they march under the ragged clouds of summer to their campsite on the pasture, and Brokk breaks away before he is spotted. He runs toward the low mountains, skittering through tall grass and red wildflowers, seeking sanctuary in the sunny woods, where he can think.

He stops abruptly on a needle-strewn slope among warm fragrances of resin and amber sap. A tall, broad-shouldered woman in a green gown descends among the scaly-barked trees, her masses of frazzled red hair glinting with silica-sparks of magic. Her pale, lunar face bears tiny eyes black as puncture wounds, a small nose like a bat's upturned snub, and a hard, defiant chin. He recognizes her as the sorceress Morgeu, called by the tattooed Picts the Fey, the Doomed.

"I see you there," she calls out, pointing a long-nailed hand at Brokk, "hidden as a smutchy hare. Come out, whatever you be."

The dwarf unravels the lamia and stands up.

Morgeu's tiny eyes widen in dark dismay, and a silver knife streaked black with tarnish and poison appears from out of a sheath hidden by her billowy sleeve. "Keep away! I offer you pain and slow death, dwarf!"

"Do not fear me, Morgeu the Fey." Brokk laughs thickly. "You know me not by sight but by name, whereas I know you by both, for you once sought to work magic with my master and creator, the Furor, the All-Seeing Father of the north gods."

Morgeu waves her poisoned knife before her, aghast at the squat troglodyte and the cawing specter with its bone face of fatal contagion. "Years ago I offered myself to the Furor as a bride—as my mother had before me . . ."

"But the Furor would not taint himself with your earthly flesh," the dwarf completes for her. "I know. You sought my master's power to help you in your famous hatred of the demon-wizard Lailoken."

"Who are you?"

With a smile of thick, square teeth, he announces, "I am Brokk—"

"The weapons master of the north gods," Morgeu speaks in an awe-drenched whisper, and lowers her knife arm. "Why do you seek me out? And what is that hideous thing you hold?"

Brokk has not sought her out, but now that he has fortuitously stumbled upon her, he states with bold command, "I need your help to retrieve the sword Lightning for my master."

Morgeu humbly lowers her cold face. "My magic cannot undo the power that holds the sword to the stone. That is the work of the Fire Lords. I am but an enchantress and work my magic by trance."

"You are too modest, Morgeu." Brokk can see the amethyst carats glinting in her aura, showing the interior music of her tranceful magic. "Among the dwarfs, you are renowned as a sorceress."

Morgeu watches through the jagged red veil of her hair the thing in the dwarf's hand writhe. Its eyes of powdered glass glint hungrily in their sockets, and she replies, "My sorcery ended years ago, when the demons who empowered me were driven off by their brother Lailoken. I am but an enchantress now—and I do not like the look of that thing you hold. Tell me, Brokk, what is it?"

"A shapeshifter," he answers, shaking it so that its mildew features smear to a silent howl that shows a mesh of fangs. "Sometimes called a lamia."

"Lamia eat the cryptarch in human blood," Morgeu says with a shimmer of fear to her voice, the stained dagger rising. "Keep it away from me. Or are you here to set it upon me?"

"Set it upon you?" Brokk had not thought of

that, but it seems now a useful idea. "Not if you do as I ask."

"What do you ask of me?"

"Go to Merlin," he answers at once. "Use your skills as an enchantress and learn for me how to reverse the polarity of the magnetic stone that holds the sword Lightning."

Morgeu backs a pace, baffled. "I do not know these words—*polarity*—*magnetic*."

"Merlin will know them."

Morgeu waves her knife nervously before her. "If I go to him, he will use his magic on me. He could well kill me. And I cannot have that. I have a great work to do."

"Oh?" Brokk works the lamia's molten form between his massive hands and packs it into the steel-stitched hide pouch at his hip. "What work is that?"

Morgeu sheaths her dagger. If the dwarf had come to slay her, there would be now no conversation. She brushes back her startled-looking hair, and answers proudly, "I will find the son of Uther Pendragon and my mother and enchant him with lust. I will make a child on him—a son."

The dwarf rubs his weighty chin. "You can do that?"

She nods, her slight mouth bent to a tight, certain smile. "It is the magic of the Old Ones, Brokk— Mother magic, *shakti-Kali-Durga* that we Celts call *Morrígan,* the female orgiastic magic that ruled the world in the ages before the chiefs and warlords—the tantra that warps, stretches, weaves the womb's life-force into magic. That is the power I have. Fifteen years of trance work has won me that magic of enchantment, and I will use it on my half brother to weave a true ruler with his seed in my womb, a son of *Morrígan,* to be named Mordred, who will drive out the Christians and do honor to the Furor and his brethren, the Celtic gods of the Daoine Síd."

"That *is* a great work, enchantress," Brokk agrees, impressed, his eyes aglint like mussel blue shells. "My master would be pleased with that. And I will help you with it—if you will help me retrieve the sword Lightning."

"Lailoken is a powerful wizard, Brokk—" She opens her arms to reveal her strong-shouldered yet lavish female form. "And I am but an enchantress."

A cunning smile bends the dwarf's hard features. "Lailoken is a demon—but Merlin is a man. And men can be enchanted."

Morgeu sucks breath through her teeth. "It will be dangerous, very dangerous, Brokk."

"Without doubt," he admits, stepping closer, attracted to the violence embedded in her eyes, "yet that is why you are called the Doomed, the Fey."

"It is not a name I wish to fulfill." She does not retreat when he steps close to her, and the air wrenches with a brash smell of cave tar and rock fire.

"And yet that is why you have danced with demons, stared into my master's wroth eye, and survived," the dwarf says, and takes her hand. A relentless charge of horrified excitement passes between them—he feels it for a beauty that is foully organic, and she thrills to it for touching a grotesque creature exaltedly divine. Together, she realizes, they will lift the hem of the vastness and share dominion.

Chapter Fifteen

A starved moon peers into the glade where Melania sits among the Thunderers. Aelle and his men lie in the grass picking their teeth, sharing flagons of fruit wine. The wine, the braised pig—now just a heap of bones—and the baskets of bread and vegetables are tribute from Hammer's Throw, the village beyond the forest. Melania has eaten none of the food, hoping to weaken and die.

Cissa squats before her, his hairless, reptile-stenciled body looking bruised in the moonlight. His eyes, rolled up into his skull, gleam like two soap bubbles aswirl with rainbows. He calls upon the Furor. The emerald dark of the night sky wavers as if with boreal lights, and the furious god is among them.

Aelle and the others cannot see him, but they sense him and rise from their pillowstones to dance in his presence. Melania raises her weary face to watch the god standing on the moon's white road, taller than the trees, his falcon's hat blotting the stars, his wild beard a moonstruck cumulus, and his one eye a prism full of nebular colors. She wants him to kill her, but he only smiles down at her, grim and tense as any lunatic.

Since her capture by the Thunderers, the warrior-priest Cissa has used her to work his magic. Usually, captured women are slain unless they grovel subserviently enough to offer promise as slaves, and then the tribe's women must decide. There are no women in this war party trespassing the Celtic forests. These warriors have come to retrieve one of Aelle's sons, Fen, or, failing that, to raze in vengeance as many hamlets and farmsteads as they can before winter drives them back to their nomad settlements in the east.

The Thunderers believe Melania is a witch. She brought them the lamia, which killed one of their own. The sphinx-handled urn that held the monsters hangs from Cissa's loinwrap. Around his throat, he wears the viper-patterned guardian band, and at his hip is the lode-knife that can kill the razorous specters. She is for him yet another of these magical possessions, a thing to be used for the worship of his gods.

Moving like quick shadows through the glade, the Thunderers dance past her, their greasy bearded faces glaring hatred. They want to kill her slowly, cutting off pieces of her as they sing the praises of their dead comrade killed by the lamia. But Cissa squats close to her, keeping her for himself and his magic.

She is the shell, the husk, the hull of his power. Poltergeist strength plucks at her secret parts until they shine with a painful pleasure that burns coldly through her like abhorrent intercourse, like a devil's sexual intrusion. She is damned, and she screams. Her cries crawl out of her, heavy and cold as ether. When she is emptied of everything but an ovarian glow, the goddess comes down from the Night Tree and fills her body.

Then she floats to her feet, filled with otherness. A soulful beauty saturates her. It is a beautiful despair becoming other than herself. It is the glorious grief of the Furor's mistress occupying the lighted shaft of her body. As inflamed with loveliness as Lucifer, she dazzles. She is Keeper of the Dusk Apples. She is the Furor's lover. She inhabits the created world under the totem moon with a supernal grace wholly indifferent to the animal that carries her.

Melania gazes out from herself as if from another life. She is the unhappy reality far back in the mind of the goddess who uses her body. Keeper of the Dusk Apples has come to earth to stand with her lord in the dangerous rootlands of the Storm Tree. Here in the muck of the world, in the magnetic rubble of the Dragon's hide, they can touch each other in new ways, so wholly different from their luminous lives above.

The Furor pours himself into his priest and stands in the garment of Cissa's body, his bright eyes brimming with the rain of joy and wonder to meet her here like this.

"Where the forests fail, the fields begin," the Furor speaks, and Cissa's body is not big enough for his voice, and he quakes in all his physical joints so that his body appears about to burst apart from some enormous internal pressure.

This terrifies Melania far back in the stunned distance of her alertness. When Keeper of the Dusk Apples answers her lover, the horrified woman feels her skeleton jangle with a pain wilder than fire. "All this will be yours in time, One-Eye," the goddess says. "And the fields will again grow trees. And the trees will gather to forests."

What else they say, she does not know, for she swoons from the pain. When she wakes, everyone is asleep in the pearly darkness except for Cissa, who watches her with a desolate clarity. Too confused to cry, she anguishes to remember who she is and why this tattooed pagan regards her with such exquisite sadness. When she does lift memory out of its stupor, the blue-white knuckles of her hand fly to her mouth, and she prays again to die.

"When I was an eagle," Cissa tells her, "you were the salmon I plucked from the river."

Melania lies back in the dew-shining grass and closes her eyes. She smells the morning. Across the channel, in the valley of the Loire, Great-grandmother lives in her stone tower, waiting for her to return, and the same morning light touches the old woman as well. Silent grief rises, and she curls into herself.

Night seeps down into the forest among trees full of summer and birds singing colors back into the world. Not far into the woods, Arthor and Fen arise from their leaf beds. Merlin is gone. During the night, he and Master Sphenks slipped away, to stroll off to

Hammer's Throw. The wizard dares not enter the camp of the Thunderers. Cissa would see through his disguise instantly and call down upon him the wrath of the one-eyed god.

"We are close to my people," Fen announces, after relieving himself in the bushes. Arthor has unbound his wrists after visiting the bushes himself. "You heard them in the night."

"I heard thunder under the moon," Arthor says, saddling his horse. He wears a white tunic emblazoned with a Celtic cross in scarlet. His shield, cuirass, helmet, and sword lean against the tree under which he slept.

"That was the Furor's voice, hiding the singing and laughter of his warriors," Fen tells him, stepping close. "But I heard their jubilation, because I am of them."

"Then we won't have to ride far, will we?" Arthor gently but firmly pushes the Saxon away so that he can bend to tighten the cinch strap without fear of taking a blow.

"Do not fear me, Royal Eagle of Thor. I will not try to kill you now." Fen's white hair glows, and his pale face looks blue in the dawn haze.

Arthor casts him a cold look. "You will not have a second chance."

"You were stupid to throw your sword away and leave a weapon within my grasp. You should be dead now. But the gods spared you my death blow. Such is battle luck. At your age, my father took an arrow between his eyes and was not felled. Perhaps the Norns— the Fates—spared you so you could meet him."

"Saddle your horse."

They ride through forest tunnels hung with dawnsmoke. The lonesome cries of night birds tarry in the cavernous dark, and from the dense boughs mist and dew drip like spider's milk.

"Leave me here, Royal Eagle of Thor," Fen says, drawing up beside him. "Go your own way now."

Arthor says nothing and rides on.

"The Thunderers are not far from here," Fen adds. "The gleeman and his wise dog knew well enough when to depart. They saved you once. Let them save you again."

"I am returning you to Aelle as Kyner commanded."

"Ever the obedient dog," Fen smirks, "even unto death."

Arthor glares at him. "If Aelle breaks his word, many will die—and you will be first."

"A grand boast, Royal Eagle of Thor. But these are not hungry, masterless brigands you will face. These are hardened warriors handpicked by Aelle for this mission. They are men with their own battle luck, men who love death and so are loved by their rabid god. Do not go among them."

"Why do you care? Yesterday, you wanted me dead."

"Don't you know?" Fen gazes hotly at him until he sees that the boy does not know. In an exasperated voice, the Saxon answers, "I am a Thunderer. If I return with your scalp and your weapons, I hold my place in the tribe. But if you return me like a battle-prize, like some warhorse exchanged between chiefs,

I will have no place of honor among my people. They are not like the Celts. I do not have the rights of respect and authority that the oaf Cei possesses simply because he is Kyner's son. No. Each Saxon is judged by his deeds alone. It matters not that I am Aelle's son. He will scorn me."

"Scorn you?" Arthor scoffs at him with a curt shake of his head. "I think not. Why then did he risk himself by coming after you, here in the hill forests of Cymru? Why did he give Kyner information that doomed other Saxons?"

"You do not understand the Saxons. They are not a nation. They are many warbands that speak one tongue. Death's Angels and Sons of Freeze angered my father when they joined the Foederatus, the union of Saxon, Pict, Jute, and Angle that holds the eastern lowlands of this island. But Aelle goes his own way, always has. Exposing Foederatus raiders to Kyner, even though they were Saxons, was no betrayal for him."

"I still do not understand how you can say Aelle scorns you." He watches the sadness that the Saxon's face carries. "He and his handpicked lovers of death will be destroyed if they are found here in Cymru by the Celts."

"That is Aelle's bravery. It adds to his legend song. He has not come out of love for me—as Kyner would for you. He comes out of pride, as if I were a warhorse taken as coup." A hurt mix of anger and fear cuts a crease between his blue eyes. "Do you see now? If you take me back, I will be shamed."

"Then you will be shamed." Arthor looks away. "That is no concern of mine."

"It is your concern," Fen pleads. "It must be. You have Saxon blood in your veins. We are brothers. I am in your power. What does it matter to you if I ride into my father's camp alone? You have fulfilled your task. I am returned."

"My task is to return you directly to Aelle."

"Why? You say that you will never see Kyner again. Why must you do as he says?"

"I must because I will never see Kyner again." Arthor speaks without looking at his hostage. "This task frees me of him and all his commands. I will never serve him again. I will never serve anyone. Ever."

"Then stop serving now. Let me go on from here alone."

"No." Arthor looks at Fen, his yellow, slant eyes caged, offering no compassion.

"Why? Tell me why."

"I don't have to tell you anything."

"But you have a reason? You are not simply Kyner's dog?"

The sides of Arthor's face flex. "Kyner gave me his sword, and I gave my word. That is all I have now. If I betray that, I have nothing."

"If you ride into that camp, you will have nothing. The Thunderers will kill you."

"There is no shame to die in battle."

Fen sits taller, and the arched bones of his face seem to sharpen. "So you know of shame—and yet you will shame me to preserve your precious word— a word you gave a man who has treated you like his loyal dog since he found you as a puppy in the forest."

Arthor remains silent and looks ahead into the eddying fog.

"Eagle of Thor—" Fen speaks tightly. "You are not one who cares about the honor of your word. That is what you say. But the truth is in your blood— your Saxon blood that has no tribe to tame it. In truth, you are cruel."

No further words pass between them until after the portals of the forest open on a sunny clearing where the Thunderers wait. A dozen bare-shouldered men with salt blond hair and beards sit in the pigweed and saw grass sharpening their swords. Their legs are braced with thong sandals fitted with daggers, and they wear odd, frightful garments—dun loinwraps belted with vertebrae, kilts sewn from scalps, short trousers with shriveled faces smeared by the tanning of human leather.

At the sight of the riders emerging from the forest, the Thunderers stand and gather around the one tent that sits at the edge of the glade, narrow and green as a conifer. The flap opens, and Aelle emerges, big as a bear, his ruddy mane, beard, and hairy shoulders glistening like fur. He carries a spear and, at his mail-wrapped hip, a Roman *gladius* taken in battle.

His wolf-pelt boots trample the grass in giant strides as he advances toward the riders, the Thunderers sweeping after. He stops in the middle of the clearing and waits for the riders to reach him. The flat look he gives his son has the heft and hardness of a boulder.

With a gruff shout, he calls Fen down from the horse, then seizes him by his white hair and twists his head as he looks him over. A hand sign brings two warriors forward, and they seize Fen and hurl him to the others, who rip off his cassock and drag him naked through the grass.

Arthor watches impassively, though his heart gallops.

"Where is the big chief?" Aelle asks in deep-throated Latin. "Does he lurk in the woods? Have him show himself."

"I come alone."

"Alone?" A grin of disbelief glints in his wide beard. "Who are you that Kyner sends you alone into the camp of the Thunderers?"

"I am Aquila Regalis Thor."

Aelle steps a pace closer, glacial eyes growing smaller. "I have heard of you. You have slain many Saxons. You are Arthor. Kyner's son."

Arthor shifts uneasily in his saddle. "Your son has been returned," he announces. "The agreement with Lord Kyner is now complete."

Aelle smiles easily. "Yes, the agreement is now complete, and we can kill each other again."

Arthor backs his horse away.

"Wait, Arthor." Aelle tilts his spear toward the camp. "Come with me. I have a token to give you, proof of bond for returning my sorry son to me."

Arthor surveys the line of lean, silent men dressed in the remnants of their victims. Some still have swords in their hands, and they watch him menacingly, with a vile candor, loathing him for his shield with its eerie image of a dolorous goddess and his blood-crossed tunic, the circle of the sun cut by the intersecting lines of Roman punishment—the god of crucifixion who invades their land.

"Do not be afraid, Arthor," Aelle speaks with authority. "I have sworn a blood oath. No harm will come to you in this camp. Come."

The war chief turns and strides back toward the narrow green tent, and his men follow. Arthor watches, unmoving. He wants no token, no proof. He wants only to be away. In particular, he does not want to see what will become of Fen. He has kept his word to Kyner. Now he is free to go. Still, he feels compelled to follow the Saxon chieftain. The transaction is not yet complete.

He nudges his horse forward and rides into the camp of his enemies. Aelle waits for him before his tent and gestures for him to dismount. Arthor complies and ties his horse to the nearest tree, where apples have dropped and melted in their skins, reeking with a sour sweetness.

The chieftain disappears into his tent, and Arthor stands uneasily beside his horse, prickling from the heat of the staring warriors. When Aelle emerges, he holds a necklace of what looks to Arthor like dried figs.

"Bring these to Kyner," the Saxon chief rumbles with laughter. "Martyrs' relics—emblems taken from priests, monks, and nuns who have met our sword during our time in Cymru. You see, their nailed god is no match for the Furor."

With a stab of shock, Arthor recognizes the green-blackened fig shapes as dried ears and noses threaded upon a twine of scalp hair.

"Take them!" Aelle shouts with laughter, and the Thunderers echo his mirth and clack their swords together. "We will find plenty more."

Arthor backs away from the Saxon trophy. "You have your son. I need no proof."

Aelle gusts with laughter, shaking so hard tears spark from his shut eyes. From behind him, the flap opens, and a bald, sinuous tattooed man appears, green and black as a snakeskin. He hisses with outrage, and Aelle casts an angry stare over his shoulder at him. They exchange irate words in their own brute language, and then the mansnake snatches the necklace.

Behind him, inside the tent, Arthor glimpses a woman. She has dark hair massed in Mediterranean curls and a long-nosed, full-lipped face from a Roman statue. Her large, Byzantine eyes seize urgently on him. She makes the sign of the Cross, then lifts her arms, gesturing in dire supplication.

"Who is that woman?" Arthor asks.

Aelle shoves Cissa back into the tent and throws the flap into place. "She belongs to my son Cissa."

"She is a Christian woman," Arthor states.

"She is Cissa's woman." Aelle rests his spear against his thick shoulder and motions helplessly. "He does not want you to have the necklace of relics. I am sorry. Perhaps there is another emblem you will accept. My men can offer you a scalp shirt. It is not the hair of priests but good Christians, I am sure."

Arthor's mind races, and he looks about, purchasing time. "What has become of Fen?"

Aelle's humor withers. "He is there." He jerks his

bearded face toward the slender trees nearby, where several of the warriors are smearing Fen's nakedness with rotted apples. "He will be whipped for surviving when the other warriors with him died. If he lives through that, he will have other chances to prove himself worthy of the Thunderers."

Fen shouts something in his native tongue, which Arthor does not understand, a warning to his father: "Beware the boy! He is the wild flame that jumps from the fire!"

"Take your pain in silence!" Aelle yells back. "You are no judge of men, you who live on their leash like a dog!"

"The Christian woman in the tent," Arthor says. "What will become of her?"

"Put her out of your mind," Aelle warns sternly, turning to him with a harsh light in his cold eyes. "Take the scalps we offer and go. My blood oath will not protect you if you challenge me."

But Arthor finds he cannot go—not without her. He knows in that instant that if he leaves her behind, she will stay with him forever in that charred place of the soul called regret. Her pathetic plea to him makes the air collapse in his lungs. He cannot simply walk away from her, even if to stay means death. Then, surely, she is the lovely face of his death.

"I want the woman," Arthor insists, heart pounding, mouth dry, words like ashes in his throat. "She is Christian."

"So?" Aelle gnashes his teeth with a sound like wood snapping in fire. "She is Cissa's. Go—now. When we meet next, I will kill you."

Arthor backs away, his eyes very thin. A luminous intensity shines from out of the depths of things. Softly, the wind stirs. His chest burns as if wounded by the impact of his wild heart, and a strict sanity puts everything precisely in its place. He sees the stations of all the alert warriors arrayed around him, edging closer, eager to be the first to put their steel in him. Two indigo buntings flit out of the apple tree in a wide arc and come back. In the soaring summer clouds, rays of sunlight are wound infinite and tight. Aelle peers into him. The chief knows Kyner's son will strike and waits with staunch patience for the tension coiling in the boy's muscles to release.

With a bold cry, Arthor draws Short-Life, feints toward Aelle to push him back one step, and spins off sideways toward the tent. A wide pendulum strike severs two of the tent's guy ropes. Another blow and two more taut ropes shrivel. Grabbing the loose canvas, Arthor runs toward the Saxons, sweeps it over their heads, and leaps into the exposed interior.

Melania squints into the gushing sunlight and tries to push to her feet at the sight of the Christian soldier but falls immediately to her knees in a swirl of dizzy fatigue. Cissa, who has been trying to coax her to end her fast and drink the broth he has prepared, drops the bowl and reaches for the lode-knife in his belt. Arthor swipes him across the jaw with the butt of his sword, and the snake-priest collapses.

Swiftly, Melania yanks the guardian band from his throat and grabs the lode-knife. Arthor takes her arm.

"Come with me!" he cries, hoping to get her away from the tent before the others come at them. But she wrenches free, defying her weakness to scramble across the tent and reclaim the sphinx-handled urn.

Aelle and the Thunderers shred and trample the tent, and Arthor spins Short-Life from hand to hand, ready for mortal combat. He gazes into the pale eyes fixed on him, cold and fierce as the malign north that bred them, and he knows that he is going to die in this place.

But in the next instant, Melania opens the urn, and the lamia sizzles into the air. The sun's milk goes sour. Aelle screams, shrill as a woman, and scurries away. Arthor has to squint in the morning glare to see what frightens him. Transparent fumes wrinkle the air to a hideously implausible shape, a taloned wraith with hooked arms and clustered ribs like a spider's husk, a disembodied skeletal shape drained of all its tissue reds, extending a bodiless bone face of fanged jaws ravening for blood.

"Stay close to me!" Melania yells, and claws for him.

He slides toward her, not taking his startled eyes off the monstrous apparition, and they bump violently. She drops the urn and the guardian band. Her shaking hand inadvertently shoves the throat band farther from her as she takes possession of the urn, waving the lode-knife with her other hand.

One of the Saxons dives for the band, and the shrieking lamia strikes him even as he clutches at it. The impact flings the metal band from his spasmed clutch, and his body rises feetfirst into the air and splits like a cocoon divulging its startling red-ribbed interior.

Arthor pulls Melania after him, toward the palfrey that skitters and neighs nervously where it is tethered to the apple tree.

"The guardian band!" she cries. "We need the throat band!"

But the lamia has finished with the Saxon who last touched the torque, and it swivels like a cobra, searching for the amulet. The band has spun to the verge of the slender trees, into the grass before naked Fen. He has seen the whole sequence, from Arthor's rending of the tent to the Thunderer's desperate lunge for this black metal crescent. The screaming woman and his instincts assure him the throat band offers survival before the glare of this ghostly monster that rears above him, filling out with shrill colors from the man it has split open.

Fen throws himself at the guardian band, and the lamia plucks him upright. The metal band wobbles in his grip, but he does not let it go. The lamia's talons reach into him, ripping a choking howl from his lungs, yet he holds on to the talisman.

Arthor leaps upon his horse and pulls Melania after him. The Thunderers have fled across the clearing, and they offer no threat as he pulls his steed hard about and charges for the opposite tree line.

The hoarse roar of Fen paints the morning with agony.

Once, Arthor looks back. He sees the Saxon twisting in the air in the livid flames of the unearthly creature.

Melania, clutching him from behind with all her might, whispers with husky despair, "Don't look back!" And he turns away sharply and gallops toward the dark alleys of the forest.

—BOOK TWO—

KEEPING
THE WHITE BIRD

Chapter One

The lamia squats inside Fen. It wants to burst him apart and swell stronger on his bloodheat. But it cannot. Fen has placed the guardian band about his throat, and that draws all the sky's vast strength into the woven cells of his body. The lamia, dressed now in arteries and bones, fills its host with unspeakable seductive power. Nimbly, he flows to the ground and spills naked across the clearing, bounding toward the terrified Thunderers.

Fen feels powerful as a frost giant, cold with might and hunger. Boldly, he charges at the men who stripped and kicked him, who pelted him with rotted apples, who would have whipped him to a shameful death.

They see him coming, furred in tiny lightnings, a man-beast of wolfish fire, his muscles gorged with an internal force swelling veins to blue snakes and twisting his face like a thundercloud. Fleeing, they fall over each other. The man-beast pounces upon the two that tormented him the most and smashes their heads together so forcefully their skulls explode like glass and splash brains in the grass.

Reluctantly, Aelle waves his spear at the fiery swollen beastliness of Fen but cannot find the strength to throw it. His hulking son billows larger, inhaling the bloodsmoke of the dead men. He turns an evil face toward his father, and Aelle's knees stutter under him.

"Fen!" a rageful voice booms from across the glade.

The blazing man-beast swirls about and sees Cissa stalking across the clearing, beating his chest like a drum. Cloud shadows swarm rapidly over the grassy field, darkening around him, and the lamia knows that he is summoning the furious god, the one-eyed giant powerful enough to strip it free of this human animal.

Fen feels the lamia's urgency to escape, and he flies so swiftly across the wild field that he leaves feathers of flame floating in the air behind him. He is confused, but this much he knows: He does not want to lose this stupendous new power, nor does he want to stay with the Thunderers any longer, because he knows that now Aelle will surely kill him for spilling the lives of his men, dead by violence and unavenged.

Smooth as liquid, he streams into the forest, lissome ball lightning, bouncing through the dark cellars, fleeing the Furor and the Thunderers, stalking Arthor. For it was that Christian boy, with his arrogant pride, who orphaned Fen from his tribe. He refused to let Fen return to his people alone and without shame. Now Fen will find him, and the lamia will yank Arthor's cruel heart from his ribs.

Strong with the bloodheat of the three men it has

slain, the lamia thumps among the trees with anxious impatience. He will kill Arthor and that damnable woman that carried the living terror inside him to this island, that delivered it to the Furor and separated it from its twin. And after it kills them, it will wander the forests and fens hunting for ways to spend its rage.

Agile as the wind, Fen runs—yet seems to go nowhere. Like Roman sundials, the trees throw shadows that swing weightlessly into the future. Clouds rush swift and blind through the treecrowns, sweeping the glitter of morning into golden midday sheens and then the soft pastels of sunset. And though the ground, springy underfoot, offers no resistance, he takes three steps into darkness.

Magic! Fen wails, and the confused lamia does not recognize where it is in the dense forest under the fleece of stars. Expecting the Furor to loom out of the night, Fen crouches in the leaf mulch. Faeries swarm like hornets against the day's last streaks of cinnabar. They blow closer on a fragrant, aimless sigh of the wind and carry the splendor of sleep. The last image Fen sees before succumbing to the fleeting waters of a dream is the bright commotion of the faeries spiraling upward through the trees toward the invisible pivot where the North Star kindles.

Only after Fen is sound asleep does Merlin emerge from among the cloistered trees. Master Sphenks sniffs at the naked Saxon and retreats, whimpering and tail-tucked. "You smell it, too," the wizard whispers to his cur. "The evil."

Master Sphenks snarls.

"No, we dare not kill it," Merlin answers his wise

dog, and backs away into the darkness. "Already I have spent too much magic to stop it. The Furor will recognize me—and we dare not call him down upon us. We have done all we can to help Arthor this night."

The wizard and his dog hurry to where the moon stands among the trees. He knows that Morgeu the Fey will also have felt his magic, and once she perceives that he has left Camelot will certainly surmise that her half brother is in these woods. He must go to Arthor's side and protect him—but not immediately.

Anxiously, he peers over his shoulder for the Furor. Tripping the lamia-possessed Fen into a time-ditch a day deep may alert the god to Merlin's presence, though not necessarily to the significance of Arthor. Hurriedly, the wizard travels away from where the young man and the Christian woman he rescued have fled.

Who is she? he wonders. *A sorceress?* Watching Arthor from afar, the wizard could sense the evil of the lamia but nothing about the woman. He will have to scrutinize her up close to know for sure. Perhaps at this moment, young Arthor is bewitched by a demon's minion. *No hope in worry,* he reminds himself, scanning for the Furor as he and his wise dog slip through the narrow lanes where the forest drinks moonlight.

Earlier in the day, Arthor had ridden past these same gnarled trees with the strange, beautiful woman sitting behind him, her arms locked over his chest, her cheek pressed to his back. She was exhausted, and when Arthor felt that he had traveled deep enough into the woods to elude pursuit he stopped, and she slept deeply.

From a high bough of a tree that summer had woven in ivy, he searched for the Thunderers and the terrible thing that had laid hold of Fen. Far off, where the forest goes white with dogwood, he spied the Saxons moving away. Only after he was convinced that they were not circling back his way and that Fen was nowhere in sight could he descend and sit beside the woman he saved, studying her smudged loveliness.

But the sight of her only imprisoned him deeper in his loneliness. Unlike the milkmaids and farmers' daughters he had grown up knowing, this woman, even in her disarray and smirch, is different—she has an aristocratic presence, a lady forever inaccessible to a misbreed such as himself. He may flee Kyner, he realized soberly, and escape Cei's scalding insults, and he may even extend the wings of his soul as far as his fingertips and travel to the limits of the Christian world, still he would never merit a consort as noble as she.

Pained, he averted his gaze and sought comfort from the image on his shield of Mother Mary. She alone soothed the venom of his self-loathing with the truth that he will someday outlive his life and change to spirit, a ray from the star of God's love, immutable and heedless of the ludicrous inequities of life. Until then, he must endure. Even in this beautiful woman's presence, he must somehow endure.

He examined the empty urn, tracing his square

fingertips over the twin-coiled vipers and the winged and bearded sphinxes. He held it to his nose and recoiled at its stink of feculence. The thought occurred to him that she is not what she seems, this beautiful lady. Kyner used to tell him skin-rippling stories of vampyres and ravenous werebeasts that the Romans and Phoenicians brought to this island and that Kyner himself stalked in their dark dwellings among ruins and caverns. Until this day, the youth had thought those stories but fabulous tales for children.

And how primitive and unlikely a weapon is this lodestone dagger, he observed with curiosity. He hefted it, ran its dull edge across the back of his arm, and returned it to the sleeping woman's waistband. The warm feel of her breathing body stirred him, and he quickly tried to return his attention to the Virgin.

Now, under clouds like haystacks and sunlight blinking through the leaves, Arthor wanders about, gathering berries, setting snares, and talking to himself, hoping to defeat his hopeless attraction: "You're free now," he tells himself. "Free of the Celts, by God. Free of servitude. Don't let desire make an unholy slave of you. Deliver this lady to Hammer's Throw and be on your way."

A tattered shawl of butterflies covers a blackberry bush, like an old woman bent in the kitchen of a cypress grove. There, he collects mint, elecampane, ginger root, veneria tuber, and galingale. In two of his snares, rabbits wait with desultory timidity. He breaks their necks with deft twists, eviscerates and skins them, and braises them with the herbs.

When Melania awakes, she finds the sky truffled with fire. The evening wind carries a spicy whisper of leaves and cooking aromas. Stepping through a curtain of ivy hung among sighing spruce, she finds the fair young man who has saved her life turning a spit of mint-glazed rabbit. He rises and, in curious lilting Latin, asks, "Are you hungry? You slept all day."

"Yes, thank you." She joins him in the fire circle, and he uncovers birch-bark trenchers of root and berry salad. "I am Melania—of Aquitania—and I am indebted to you for risking your life to save me from the Saxons."

Arthor passes her a flagon of water for the dry rasp of her throat and introduces himself. She listens, eating hungrily yet delicately of his food, and after he explains his presence in the camp of the Thunderers, she tells her story.

"There are *two* lamia?" Arthor finally asks, awed. "Yet, who was the dwarf that took the other away?"

"I don't know," she answers frankly. Facing this young Christian with his yellow eyes and sun-streaked hair shining short and sleek as a badger's in the firelight, she feels she can confide everything in him. "I must tell you, Arthor, when the lamia's strength was still within me—I saw the Furor, the chieftain of the north gods. He stood taller than a cedar, and his mantle billowed blue as the sky. I think the evil dwarf is his creature."

Arthor accepts this with a nervous glance into the darkness. "If, as you say, he uses the lamia to shape-shift, he can be anywhere around us."

"I think not," she says, pausing thoughtfully

before helping herself to more berries. "I don't know what Cissa said to him, but he left with purpose in his stride. I do not believe he lingers in these woods."

"And Fen? What will become of him?"

"What became of me." She shakes her head grimly. "He will have supernatural strength—so long as he feeds the lamia."

"You say they eat only human lives."

"That is their craving."

"Then we are in danger," he says tersely. "He will surely come after me for returning him to Aelle."

Melania puts her hand to the weapon in her waistband. "I have the lodestone dagger. That may well keep him away, for it will kill the lamia. There is so much easier prey in the villages."

Arthor's youthful face closes around that thought. "If he attacks the villages, I will have to track him down. I cannot have the blood of innocents on my hands. Mother Mary would never permit that."

"No, she would not," Melania agrees, peering at him with a sweet expression. "I will come with you, Arthor. I have the urn. Perhaps we can recapture the lamia."

He blows his anxiety into the fire. "Far easier, I would think, to kill it outright."

"Then how will we find the second monster?" An expression of soft alarm creeps into her large eyes. "I cannot live with myself knowing I have released these horrors into the world. If we capture one, it may lead us to the other."

Arthor tilts an appraising look at her. "You ask a great deal of yourself."

"Do I?" She reaches out and clasps his big-knuckled hand. "You could well have walked away from the Saxon camp and left me where you found me. It is you, Arthor, who ask much of yourself. I ask only to travel with you, to reclaim the lamia I carried to this island. Will you help me?"

He places his other hand atop hers, and assures her, "The Virgin Mother will help us."

For a moment, an unspoken fidelity binds the two strangers. Then she removes her hand and rises. "This meal was very good, Arthor. It has nourished me—as you have comforted me. Now I will sleep again and gather strength for what lies ahead."

Melania slides through the ivy screen to her leaf bed, and Arthor sags under a sigh of longing. He lies back with his head in his hands and gazes up through the dark branches at the vapor trails of stars. He prays to Mother Mary, wanting to disenthrall himself of this exotic woman whose fate he has married. But already, haunting dreams of incurable desire burn outward through his skin.

Chapter Two

At dawn, Morgeu finds her husband outside their tent coming back from his ablutions in the woods, the sun like a spoonful of honey in the trees behind him. "I will go now and face Merlin," she tells him, and he waves away the young servants who approach to braid his long, wet, and brindled hair.

"Why must you go?" he asks, peering sadly into her small black eyes, the eyes of crows. "Ignore him. Make yourself forget him."

An ugly moue twists her scarlet lips. "You know the terrors born out of the forgotten. I cannot ignore the murderer of my father." She places both hands on his broad, bare chest, and her sharp fingernails bite him gently. "You are a good husband, Lot. Only you, my soul, have given me peace in this life."

"Yet not enough peace to keep you with me." He moans, and puts his weathered hands over hers. "Stay with me, Morgeu. Prolong our happy season together."

Morgeu bites her upper lip to keep her tears from starting. She has not lied to him. This fierce man of regal countenance seamed with age has been the tender joy of her life and the fulness of all promise. Together, they have climbed pleasure's heights, plumbed each other's sorrows. In his arms, she has forgotten her pain and her vengeful mission and been surprised time and again when that devilish hurt remembered her. She puts her mouth on his mouth and feels the remaining warmth of the fire that has gone by. It warms the hope that she will return.

"I will kill him for you," Lot says, when she peels away. "I will bring you his head."

"No. That is not your way, my king." She smiles a tilted, ironic smile. "I am called to this by my fate. When it is done, if I live, I will return to you."

He bows his noble head, and his brindled hair shines like the current in a river. She cossets him, and when he looks up, his pale eyes shine with sorrow. "You must tell the boys. You must not go until you tell our boys."

Gawain and Gareth have left the camp already and gone down to the river to spear for fish. They stand on their reflections in the shallows among ghostly boughs, ragged curtains of moss, and luminous egrets. Fish light the black waters with glints and shimmers like stellar atmospheres, and at first the boys ignore their mother's call.

Morgeu wades toward them until the pulse of the river knocks at her knees and her voice easily penetrates the green gloom. "I am called away."

The youngest, Gareth, splashes closer and plunges his spear into the mud so that he can grasp for his mother. "Who calls you away, Mother?"

"It is a fateful call, child."

"It is magic." Gawain knows. He pushes his spear into the mud and slogs to Morgeu's side. "You are called away to work magic. Isn't that so, Mother?"

She nods and puts her green-robed arms about her boys. "You know I work magic for our people."

"Like Grandmother," Gareth says, "before the priests of the nailed god took her magic away."

"Yes." She smiles at him and brushes the orange bangs from his eyes. "Like Grandmother Ygrane, of whom the people still speak. She worked strong magic to aid the crops and baffle our enemies."

"Are you called to fight the storm raiders?" Gawain asks, confronting what seems the worst.

"No. But what I must do is just as dangerous. And I want you to know, because you are both old enough now to know, that the legend of our land is yet unfinished. We all must work for the salvation of Cymru and her people. We must give everything we have."

Gareth presses his face to Morgeu's shoulder. "Are you going to die, Mother?"

She kisses his brow, feeling as though her heart has been thrown into the depth of this pool, and the waves close around the dream that was her life. "We all die, Gareth. How we live is what truly matters. You know that."

"I believe he means to ask if you are coming back to us," Gawain says, and swallows.

She meets the dread in his eyes with a steady calm. "I don't know," she answers, and keeps all her grief coiled tightly between her ribs. "That is why I have come to say good-bye."

"Mother, let us go with you," Gareth pleads. "We are old enough for battle now. We will protect you."

Morgeu takes his chin in her hand and speaks to the backs of his eyes. "This is my own battle, Gareth. Soon enough, you will have your battles to fight. And then, you must be as brave as I must be now. Help me to do what I must by promising me that you will be brave and strong in your love of Cymru no matter what happens to me."

Then she looks to her eldest, and says, "Remember, Gawain, all I have taught you means nothing if you forget your limits. Freedom is devotion. Keep to your father and your brother. Keep to your people. Do not be swayed as your grandmother is by the lore and promise of a foreign god. Love the land that made you and love its gods." She steps back from them, and her slender pale hands retreat from touching them to cover her breasts. "In my heart I carry the memory of you both. In your hearts, carry me. Look for me there."

In a steep meadow above the river, the dwarf Brokk waits for Morgeu. As he paces through the rye and the bushes of purple mallow and orange daisies overflowing in late, rough-headed blooms, he drags the lamia after him. It will have to eat soon, but before he bothers with that he wants to be done with Merlin. He wants to learn how to free the sword Lightning from the magnetic aerolite; then he will feed the lamia and use its heightened powers of disguise to flee with the sacred weapon.

"Why do you tarry?" he complains, as Morgeu

ascends through marigolds and eyebright from the river gorge. "The morning is already old, and now the wizard will be among the people."

"Then we shall meet him among the people," Morgeu answers curtly, and strides past him. More than the dwarf, she wants to be done with this lethal confrontation. Magic turns like smoke in her, folding into itself and pushing out, growing stronger with her fear that she will never see her children again. The empty hands of sunlight that the trees let down to touch the earth offer to lift her out of her body. That is her most powerful magic. But she hoards that strength. She compacts her trance power so that she feels as though her body were a garment of bright particles ready to blow apart into a radiant weightlessness. In the secret sexual place of her core, she compacts her magic. It will not be enough to face down Merlin, but it is all she has of her vehemence with which to fight the demon-wizard—and for her children's sake alone, it will be enough.

Brokk pulls the lamia over him into the shape of Chief Kyner and follows Morgeu the Fey up the sun-stained slopes to the large fields around the nucleus of Camelot. A crowd has gathered, and Merlin is visible among them, working his magic. To Morgeu, he does not appear as she remembers him. He seems smaller, more contained. What has become of his sinuous posture, his tiger's slouch, his disjointed gestures? He possesses a wholly human demeanor now, and this frightens her all the more.

Hannes does not see Morgeu or Brokk approaching. He exults among the people who have

gathered to celebrate his position as wizard of
Camelot. Successfully he has defended the citadel
from the grasping ambition of Severus Syrax, and he
has withstood the scrutiny of King Lot. Even Chief
Kyner, who rumor asserts entered the vicinity the day
before, has kept his distance, and Hannes remains
convinced that, as improbable a counterfeit as he is,
he inspires awe.

When Lord Urien's party arrives, Hannes leads
the jugglers and musicians across the pastures to greet
him. In the dense summer sunlight, the carpenter
summons starlings to spin circles in the air, creating a
gentle breeze with their wheelings. Urien, his long
white hair and silver mustache streaked back from his
bony face in the bird-whirling dazzle of wind, laughs
and shouts praises to Merlin.

"You tricky shapeshifter!" the Celtic lord calls
from his cart filled with singing and laughing children. "I see you've learned to make yourself look
more like a man, but your magic displays you for
what you are, you old demon." He leaps down, and
though he is aged and etched with the scars of many
battles, he lands with lithe ease and takes Hannes in a
mighty hug. "Show us a good time, wizard!"

Hannes does not disappoint. He brings on whirlwinds of butterflies and laces the air with floral per-
fumes. To the accompaniment of the musicians,
squirrels perform acrobatics among the squealing
children, and gusts of flower petals roll like clouds
across the sky and drizzle over the jubilant throngs.

In the midst of his proud display, Hannes notices
a surly, ferocious dwarf in the crowd wearing a fiery

blue-and-red tunic bound with heavy leather straps.
He has a square head and devil-slit eyes that peer
angrily at the carpenter. A delighted scream from the
audience turns Hannes's head in time to see birds tan-
gling in people's hair and squirrels pouncing on the
tables, scattering offerings of nuts, berries, and
cheese. With a shout, he sets the animals performing
again, and when he looks for the evil dwarf, he sees
instead Chief Kyner—and beside him, the tall, big-
shouldered figure of Morgeu the Fey.

Quickly, Hannes concludes his amusement and
modestly waves away the applause and cheers of the
multitude. He tries to lose himself in the crowd and
avoid Merlin's fabled foe, but it seems that whichever
way he goes, the backslapping people turn him about
so that he is led ever closer to the still and staring sorceress in her green robes and wild, scarlet tresses.

"Merlin," Morgeu says with soft happiness as he
thrusts up close to her, and she sees that he lacks
entirely the elongated eye sockets, those ghastly and
atavistic bonerims of reptile skull that terrify her, as
much as the sinister silver eyes that peer from their
pits. Instead, this Merlin has jug ears and startled blue
eyes in a round face creased and ledged more like a
monkey's than a demon-wizard's. "Merlin. Merlin.
Merlin."

The enchantress's voice seems to sift down from
the islands of cumulus, and Hannes finds himself
floating somewhere like a froth of seeds on the silver
wind, drifting very small away from the people,
across fields of saffron and goldenrod, drifting uphill
toward a slope of skinny trees and blue clouds of gen-

tian corollas. A hard slap at the back of his head pitches him face forward to the ground and sends his hat toppling as if in a stiff wind. With a shrill cry, he rolls to his back, staff raised to block another blow.

"Who are you?" Morgeu demands, her moon-pale face severe with scorn. "Where is Merlin?"

"I—I am Merlin—" he stammers, looking about for the jubilant crowd and seeing that he is deep in the woods, far from everyone. He sits up with a jolt at the sight of the evil dwarf standing behind the sorceress, squat as a boulder with a hyena's muscular, scorched face. Then, realizing he cannot sustain the ruse, adds forlornly, "I mean to say, I am Merlin's apprentice."

"Where is the wizard?" Brokk grumbles.

"I don't know," the carpenter says, and feels within the pocket of his robe for the summoning glass. Is this the moment to summon help from the elves? he asks himself fearfully. "I am Hannes, a master builder that Merlin has appointed to watch over Camelot in his absence. Truthfully, I don't know where he went."

The anguish that has been building in Morgeu, all the dread in anticipation of confronting the demon-wizard, suddenly lashes from the enchantress with bitter fury. Invisible hands wrench the staff from Hannes's grip and send it spinning upward into the branches. His frightened face blears as a scream of ripping fabric tears the robe from his back and flops him naked on the forest floor.

"When did Merlin leave?" Morgeu wants to know.

"Days ago," Hannes answers swiftly. "Before you came."

Morgeu gazes with revulsion at his withered nakedness, her tar-drop eyes cold and past mockery. "I want to know where Merlin has gone." She speaks in a deeper, slower voice that widens to include the sullen, buzzing morning, as if the bees on the gentians and the dew itself in the disheveled grass speak to him, pure as music.

Spellbound, if reluctantly, Hannes recites all that has transpired between himself and Merlin. When he is done, Morgeu stamps the ground angrily with her foot. "This one knows next to nothing," she says in disgust.

"Then let the lamia feast!" Brokk calls out, and snaps open his steel-rimmed hip pouch. A stink of soured flesh poisons the morning, and vapors waft from the pouch soft as the breath of a sleeper. They spool in the grass serpentwise, coiling upward into brightness, and a deathly visage takes shape; its sooty eyes open, cobra jaws unhinge, and talons flex in great scorpion arcs.

Hannes's eyes bulge. He squirms against the speaking silence that the enchantress has placed upon him. "I know nothing—nothing—" he pleads, his voice sodden from where he floats in the underwaters of trance.

The lamia, weak with hunger, slinks closer to its prey and begins to glisten as it draws body heat into itself.

Paralyzed, Hannes watches as the lamia rises before him like lunar steam with the skull of the moon for a head, its cancerous face drawing closer. The carpenter screams soundlessly, all his bones ringing. In the spongy echoes, far, far back in his memory, Merlin speaks again, "You are a wizard now. The power—all the power—is in your hands. Do not look anywhere else. There is nowhere else to look."

Hannes whimpers and pulls from within himself all his magical strength and strikes outwardly with it so forcefully that his shoulders wrench from their sockets and pop back in again. The pain winces him blind. But when sight returns, the lamia is gone.

Morgeu steps back cautiously from the panting old man, whose fish belly white flesh has suddenly gone glossy violet as a liver. Brokk, looking fatally stricken, falls to his knees and picks desperately among the leaves and flowers for the smashed lamia. He comes up with his fingers webbed in viscous ectoplasm.

"Look what he did!" the dwarf groans. He drips the wounded lamia into his hip pouch and jumps angrily to his feet. "You nearly killed it!"

Morgeu puts a cautionary hand on Brokk's thick shoulder. "Leave him be," she warns. "Merlin has opened in his body the gates of power. Leave him be."

"Keep your distance from us, Hannes," Brokk speaks in a dense voice of threat. "I like you not!"

Morgeu turns away and drifts downhill through the spindly trees, pondering what she has learned. The old carpenter has just informed her that Merlin will be returning with the king of Britain at his side. That tells her that he has gone to escort her half brother to Camelot. She must find her way into trance. She must listen deeper for the chance to attack with tenderness all that she hates.

Brokk glares at Hannes and follows angrily behind the enchantress. He will have to unlock the sword by his own ingenuity. And that will take time. And time requires disguise. And disguise needs the lamia. And the lamia needs blood.

Hannes watches the wicked dwarf and Morgeu the Fey dwindle among the overlapping branches and sparkling sunlight, and he swerves to his feet and puts his quavering hands to his aching shoulders. "I did it," he mutters and hugs himself. "I drove them off! I used my magic against evil!"

He hops a small dance, until his thudding heart drives out the last of his chilled fear, then retrieves his robe. It has burst along the seam and will require very little trouble to repair. Nimbly, he climbs the tree holding his staff, drops it to the ground near his hat, and swings down after it. Robe knotted into place, hat worn at a jaunty angle, and stave in hand, he strides proudly through the radiant declivities of sunlight among the trees.

—— ◦◦◦ ——

Chapter Three

Hay dust smokes with morning light as Brokk thrashes in the dry grass at the top of the valley above Cold Kitchen. He must feed the lamia. Beating a path through golden grass taller than himself, the dwarf seeks a vantage from which to seek prey. Atop a humpbacked boulder, he watches a young girl bringing her three sheep and two lambs to the clover patches under some myrtle shrubs that the Roman legionnaires planted generations ago. He gnashes his teeth with disappointment, for her size will not provide as much strength as the weakened lamia needs. But then, she will be easier for the monster to subdue.

Brokk lopes along the chine of the valley until he finds himself directly above the myrtle grove and the young woman in her hempen gown. But she is not alone. Her sheep sense the intruder before she does— a burly, cleft-jawed man in a soldier's tunic with the black-and-crimson shoulder panels of Severus Syrax's infantry. He has come to take his pleasure and makes no effort at seduction. With one hand, he grabs her shepherd's crook and, with the other, rends her gown.

She stumbles backward and collapses, and the soldier leers over her at the exact moment that Brokk lurches from the brake of crackling myrtles. For a baffled interval, the infantryman stands back, gawking at the homuncular dwarf who holds a fist-ful of smoke toward him as if in blessing. Irate at this ugly intrusion, the soldier draws his sword, yet even as the blade rings from its scabbard, Brokk is upon him. The dwarf's grip cracks the ulna and radius bones of the aggressive sword arm, and when the large man goes down on his knees, the dwarf smears the lamia's vaporous remnants onto his grimacing face.

The soldier's harrowing scream bounds across the valley, chasing the frantic shepherd girl and her sheep down the path to the hamlet. When the village men clamber into the myrtle grove alerted by her terrified report, they find the soldier's split-open corpse hung head down, his viscera dangling from him like obscene fruits.

By then, Brokk has returned to Mons Caliburnus in the shadowy gorge of the River Amnis. Disguised as Chief Kyner, he gruffly sends away the handful of curious soldiers and pilgrims who have gathered to view the legendary sword, and he paces around the stone, scowling attentively, seeing no clue to its struc-ture, until in frustration he kicks it and sits down in pain. Crawling through the feathery weeds, he seeks a lever and finds none. With his dagger, he cuts away loaves of minty earth around the stone, seeking some buried apparatus.

Morgeu watches him for a while from where she

sits, secluded among the incense shrubs of lime at the spur of the mount, her back leaning against a glacial boulder. Satisfied that Brokk will remain busy for the time being and that no one will disturb her, she closes her eyes to the grove's teal blue sky and green shadows and listens to the quiet thunder of her pulse in the rushing darkness. Trance fills her bones with fog. Narcotized by magic, she drifts all day within the empty kingdom of herself, listening, waiting.

Leagues away, Merlin digs a magical ditch hours deep and trips Fen into it. And as the lamia-possessed Saxon falls toward night, Morgeu finally feels the demon-wizard's magic bending the span of distance and time, feels it with an acute precision that snaps her alert. Orange caravels of cloud sail toward an immense red sun. The river flows molten among fiery islands of willow and birch. And crystal lakes, arctic green and blue, hover in the sky among the layers of twilight.

Morgeu staggers giddily upright. *I've found him!* A circus of wrens chatters in the bushes and bursts into flight as she shoves her way through. *At last! I've found him!*

She locates Brokk on the sheer side of the mount, nimbly dangling from the draping ivy, feeling among the black lilacs and blue and white periwinkles for a lever to move the magnetic stone. He waves her away when she calls to him. "Away with you, woman. I must unlock the sword now. Kyner and his clan will be here soon enough. I've no time for your wrathful magic."

Unable now to rely on him to watch over her

tranced body, Morgeu seeks other sanctuary. By
amber light, she makes her way to the riverbank,
where night gathers its mantles of mist. Dark spires of
trees burn like tapers at their tips. She situates herself
in a remote root-cove, and the ground under her
wobbles with liquid rhythms, buoyed by the watery
understory of tree roots afloat on the river.

The last glycerin streaks of day relent to night,
and Morgeu gives herself to her trance. She has eaten
nothing all day, and her body is transparent. Easily,
she shines forth from herself and glides into the dark.
The cold onyx light of the Amnis guides her downstream a long way before the forest canopy opens, and
she flies higher under an uproar of stars.

Following the reverberations of Merlin's magic
that she sensed earlier in trance, she journeys over the
dark world. Faeries sparkle ahead. She follows their
presence into the nightheld forest. For a long time,
she swims among fluid moonlight and wooded hills
that seem to have no beginning or end. The moon
blazes, and hurrying clouds race with its brilliance
through the forest.

She passes over Melania and does not even see
her, for her magic has one ambition, to find her
blood-kin. And then, as if rising from the well of a
dream, he appears—a young man asleep beside a fire
whose embers breathe purple with weariness. She
recognizes him at once, even in the nebulous moonlight and nightshadows, for he has their mother's leo-
nine brow and square jaw. And she knows that if he
were to open his sleeping eyes and if there were light
for them to hold, they would be yellow, the bestial

color inherited from his Roman father, Uther Pendragon.

Watching him sleep, so young and yet with bold features already hardening toward manhood, she feels ruth as in a dismal rain. This youth knows war's sudden hot violence but not yet its lingering legacy of grief nor the original brutal necessity that suffered him into being and by which he must live and die. He sleeps quietly, his unmarred face soft, even gentle. She can see the child in him. Inspired by his beauty and their kinship, she wants to whisper to him all that she knows and fears to know about their destiny.

Then the hurt of what he is to her—child of her mother's faithlessness, born by her father's death—and the mad anger that grows from that hurt assert themselves and pull her away from the sleeper. Stunned that at last she has found him, Merlin's creature spawned on her mother by Merlin's proud Christian warrior, she glows with pain. The sight of the boy's shield leaning on the tree alongside him inspires more anger. The icon of the virgin mother of Jesus watches over him with a kindly sorrow that seems reserved for him alone.

He is Christian, she realizes with a pang of anguish from her memories of this foreign religion. It had been the faith of her father, Duke Gorlois. But that did not save him, and so she loathes it. *Of course he worships the nailed god. He is Merlin's creature.*

All the more determined to use Merlin's own creation to wreak vengeance upon him, Morgeu soars into the night. Now that she has seen him and knows where he is, she will come to him in her body and use her body as a weapon of lethal cunning far more precise than steel.

The hurried return to her body startles her awake under the transparent night. Leaves rustle in the dark with the susurrations of the river wind, and the root mat upon which she floats bobbles as she rises.

"I have found him," she whispers to herself with icy glee. "Now, a horse. I must ride to him at once."

While she slowly wends her way back through the night forest beside the sultry river, Brokk mucks amidst the silt at the bottom of Mons Caliburnus. The water laps at him as he yanks at the ivy tendrils on the rock face. He touches the slick rocks and the pelts of moss with his wise fingers, feeling for magnetism.

His flesh, woven of god-stuff, prickles at the nearness of a powerful magnetic field. The flux lines are so strong he should have sensed them much earlier, except that he has been looking in the wrong place, atop the hill, near the star stone. The magnetic counterpole is here at the bottom of the mount, its presence hidden by the hill of earth above.

He gropes among the rock lozenges that Merlin has jammed into the crevice to hide the lever that reverses the polarity of the magnetic star stone. *Clever!* he thinks, admiring the Fire Lords for the ingenuity with which they constructed the machine that holds the sword Lightning in place.

A thrashing commotion and a splash wrench Brokk full about, and a nervous cry creaks from his lungs. For one instant, his heart frosts with the fear that the Dragon rises to claim him. Then he spies a gliding owl, its claws holding a lively rat snatched from the river, and he blows a relieved sigh. The Fire Lords placed the star stone in this gorge because here, the Dragon's claws can easily reach through the earth's crust and strike at any gods who dare trespass. Even dwarfs, small as they are, are not safe from the terrible beast. All entities made from the energy of the World Tree, the electromagnetic field of the planet, are suitable prey for the Dragon.

Inspired by dread, Brokk claws away the obstructing debris from the horizontal crevice and takes hold of the magnetic lever. It is a rough-hewn lobe of rock, the star stone's twin, and when the dwarf heaves it toward himself it grinds over ferric bearings and spits sparks. In that infernal strobe fire, the chthonic man grins with impish delight, for he feels the magnetic polarity shift. From above, a silver peal rings among the stars like a cry broken from the moon.

Brokk clambers excitedly to the top of the mount and meets Morgeu there. She stands before the anvil rock, tall and pale as a candle, pointing to where the sword Lightning lies on its side.

"I heard it fall," she says in a breath of awe, and reaches for the weapon. "It cried like a bell."

"Don't you touch it!" Brokk adjures, scrambling to the star stone. "This is the Furor's blade. I alone am commanded to return it to him."

"Oh, let me not impede you, mighty Brokk," Morgeu speaks scornfully, and stands aside.

The dwarf seizes the sword Lightning and twirls it expertly. "It is yet whole! The Fire Lords have not damaged it." He clucks a satisfied laugh to see the silver blade skirl the sheen of stars and moon to liquid blurs in the air. "The Furor will be pleased. I am off to him!"

"Wait, dwarf!" Morgeu speaks sharply. "I helped you, and you have agreed to help me."

"Helped me?" Brokk's sour features contract. "You did not help me."

"We agreed that if I confronted Merlin with you, you would help me find the son of Uther Pendragon so that I may take his seed for my tantric magic." She boldly steps within range of the sword, her tar-drop eyes cold as boreholes of the night. "You promised me, Brokk."

"We did not confront Merlin." Brokk flaps his lips with a loud, mocking rasp. "You led me to an old carpenter who knew nothing about the magnetic structure of the star stone. I had to figure it out for myself."

Morgeu stiffens. "I went with you in good faith to meet Merlin. That it was not Merlin is more of Lailoken's devious ways, no fault of mine. I kept my word, though it might well have killed me had we indeed encountered the demon-wizard. *I kept my word, Brokk.*"

The dwarf holds the hilt in his fist and the blade in his palm and pugnaciously thrusts forward his big face. "And now what do you want from me, sorceress?"

"What you promised. Come with me to the

forest where I have located my half brother. Help me
to work my tantric magic with him."

Brokk snorts and turns away, executing nimble
sword swipes at the stars. "I cannot be bothered with
such mortal folly. Seduce your brother on your own."

"You are reputed to be wise, Brokk. But it is not
wise to break your word to Morgeu the Fey."

"I am not afraid of your petty enchantments,
witch."

"My enchantments may indeed be petty to likes
of you," Morgeu replies, her sinuous voice lowering
to a tone of threat. "But I am no stranger to the Furor
or his followers. The Picts themselves named me the
Fey, the Doomed. They respect me. And I will tell
them—and make them believe with my petty
enchantments—that Brokk is a liar. He does not live
and work for the Furor as he proudly claims but for
the Furor's wicked brother, the Liar—Loki."

Brokk swings about and waves the sword menacingly. "Watch your tongue! I could kill you in a
blink."

Morgeu steps closer so that the sword tip touches
her breastbone. "Then kill me now," she challenges,
the black fire in her eyes flaring with indignation,
though within she feels sick with fear of the dwarf and
disgust that she should die like this, slain for her stubborn pride when fate calls her to so much more. "Kill
me now, for if you let me live, I will sing to everyone
of your perfidy."

"Be silent, woman," the dwarf grumbles angrily,
and lowers the sword. "I am Brokk, the Furor's
weapons master. My word is good. I merely question

the validity of our agreement. The carpenter was *not* Merlin."

Morgeu's stomach unclenches, and she softens her tone, "You asked me to help you take the sword. You have the sword. Would you have been so bold in attacking the star stone with your agile mind had you not known Merlin is absent? My courage in facing him and uncovering the truth at least afforded you that assurance."

Brokk swings his slung head like an unhappy bull, unable to refute her claim. "Where is this brother of yours?"

"In Crowland, near Hammer's Throw."

The dwarf stalks off down the mount, muttering irately, "Use your enchantments, then, and get us some horses. Be quick about it now. I'm not walking to Crowland."

Morgeu lifts a silent shout of triumph to the moon and skips after him. The moment they fade into the night, the furtive shadow-figure of Hannes rises from his covert under the hackberry shrubs near the star stone. Chanting a spell of invisibility, he has lain for hours among the cedars and then here in these shrubs, watching, listening. He had hoped to stymie the dwarf with his magic, but the sight of Brokk shapeshifting to Chief Kyner terrified him. Then, when the sword fell, he thought to leap up and seize it—but the appearance at that moment of Morgeu the Fey stabbed him again with fear.

Now he dances around the empty star stone, waving his stave frantically, trying to grasp out of thin air what best to do. He throws a desperate look to the moon among her flocks of stars. *What would Merlin do?* he asks, then immediately quails, *But I am no Merlin! What can I do? What can this befuddled carpenter do?*

A lugubrious necessity occurs to him: He must pursue the horrible dwarf and the sorceress. He must retrieve Excalibur, else he has failed Merlin, and the king to be, and all Britain as well.

He swipes his hat off and dashes it to the ground. "Why did I let Merlin talk me into this?" he moans aloud. "I can't leave the stone empty. By dawn the others will see it. Surely, there'll be hell to pay then!"

Magic! he thinks. *I must work a magic greater than any I've accomplished so far.*

He sits on the stone and holds his staff in both hands at arm's length. After wriggling himself into a comfortable position, he wills the stave to transform into the shape of Excalibur. The pith of himself from where the life's potency that is magic originates tightens, quivers, and aches with what is asked of it. Figurations of mist seep from the gnarled stick and vaguely outline a sword shape. In a breeze, it drifts away.

"No!" he shouts his frustration; then conks himself on the head with the staff to punish himself for his outburst. "Patience, Hannes. Supreme patience, now. The night is yet with us. Take your time. Reach deeper."

Hannes closes his lids and opens his eyes inward. There he sees the spinneret of his soul, the magical

organ within his marrows that spins the threads of his
blood, that grows the filaments of his hair, that
weaves the mosaics of his bones, and that knits the
reality of his dreams. It is itself a white thread, a very
fine needle of lightning, a single, tenuous ray of
starlight that is his life.

He sets the spinneret of his soul turning, and
fine, diaphanous silks of energy haze within the
inward darkness of himself. Carefully, with the same
tedious attentiveness he once applied to working
fragile and rare woods, he shapes the magic. From
memory, he binds the energy to the precise image of
Excalibur. The effort is excruciating, especially the
blade itself because of its utter simplicity, empty as a
mirror. The detailed rowels and circlets upon the haft
come more easily to the craftsman, and when they
are in place he must return again to the silver
reflectance of the blade.

When the image is replete and he opens his eyes,
dawn lies like a fleece on the horizon. He stands and
wedges the stave into the cleft of the anvil stone.
Then he steps back and wills the stick to assume the
shape of Excalibur.

This time, his viscera cramp so tightly, he feels
the magic wrenching him inside out, and he crumples to his knees with a withering cry. Dizzied with
pain, he kneels with his brow to the wet grass and
gasps for relief. When the hurt subsides, he wearily
unfolds. Eyes half-lidded, he gazes at the glare of
morning light shining from the boulder and winces,
blinded. His hands shield his averted face until he can
see again, and then, through the narrow slits between

his fingers, he witnesses the triumph of his magic—
golden rays of reflected sun piercing the misty morning, streaming in flame jets of aurous fire from the
naked blade of Excalibur.

Chapter Four

Rain drizzles out of a blind sky as Arthor and Melania ride through the woods of Crowland toward Hammer's Throw. They seek Fen, hoping to tear the lamia loose from him and return it to the urn. Arthor has no idea how they will do that, yet he trusts the brown-eyed woman, with her classic face of a Roman Venus, who claims her stone dagger will be sufficient.

In his mind, her beauty vouches for her wisdom. She appears even more lovely now that she has had the chance to bathe in a stream, rubbing away the grime of her captivity with wild rose petals and river kelp. With her sable hair coiled in rope braids and worn over her right shoulder, gathered with a twine of purple clematis, she looks disarmingly regal despite her tattered, faded, and drenched gown.

Angels of fog stand among the trees. Arthor proceeds warily, his senses alert, gazing through the billows of shadow and smoke for Fen's pale figure, listening past the dismal seeping whispers of rain for footfalls. He interprets the silences as well. The punctuating calls of birds must come at hopeful intervals, or he stops and listens deeper, trying to smell danger beyond the lingering, mulchy scents of sodden loam.

Melania gladly clings to his back. His muscular solidity comforts her, soothing the anguish she experienced in the ethereal, hollowed-out trances that Cissa forced on her. With her arms around his taut torso, feeling the straps of strength in his chest and stomach tighten and relax as he surveys the way ahead, she feels anchored in actuality, far away from her disembodied suffering. He smells of horse and male musk. His bronze-blond hair curls in wet streaks across his pallid brow and white neck, shorn in the Roman style, in defiance of his Celtic foster family. Even this bitterness, which she saw harden the boyish planes of his wide face when he told his story yesterday, pleases her—for now she knows he will not abandon her. He has nowhere else to go.

She watches him smelling the wind to find where to go, and she rests her cheek against his wet back, closes her eyes, and lets the rain trace its cool fingertips over her face.

"Who goes there?" Arthor calls out.

Melania straightens and peers over his shoulder. In the forest tunnel hung with the rain's soft incense, a tall, lanky old man approaches, leading a gray and a blond mare. A small black dog with a white splotch around one eye steps pertly at his side.

"Ho! Arthor!" the old fellow calls in a voice sonorous as a cavern's echo. "'Tis Master Sphenks still suffering the company of his gleeman, that being Hannes, myself."

Arthor feels Melania stiffen behind him, and he speaks to her, "Don't be afraid. I know this old man. His dog saved my life two days ago. He is a harmless old fool no matter his gruesome aspect."

"He is indeed gruesome," Melania whispers. She sees the demon in Merlin, the preternaturally long skull, his rut-warped brow and eyepits huge as an adder's sockets, and his mummied flesh, hollow of cheek as though he drinks the wind. "I don't like him, Arthor. Ride by."

"I see you survived your visit with the Saxons," Merlin says in his big, hollow voice, "and now look—you came away with a southern beauty far more desirable than the fiend you delivered. You fared much the better in that barter, son."

"This is Melania of Aquitania," Arthor says, and the woman thumps his back with her fist.

"Ride on, I say!" she whispers hotly. "The man is evil. Can't you see it?"

Arthor twists about and reprimands her with a frown. "Hannes is a Christian. And he saved my life, I tell you."

"But look at him, Arthor! He has the devil's eyes. And behind that beard, I will dare to say, there are a predator's fangs."

"Hush. You're not an ignorant woman. A man is judged by deeds, not appearance."

"I bartered well myself, Arthor," Merlin goes on. "Behold the two fine mares I took in trade for a pouch of drachmae Master Sphenks earned by the amusement of a Syrian merchant. Silver has no legs, yet it runs swiftly. But not as swift as gold, eh? And it's gold Master Sphenks will have for these magnificent horses in Camelot. And where are you bound, my boy?"

"Hammer's Throw," Arthor replies. "And you'd best come with us, old man. There's a monster about. A lamia."

"A lamia!" Merlin wears a frightened expression. "Master Sphenks and I have seen the likes of such horrors in our travels through Dalmatia. They are shapeshifters, young son, and with a mighty thirst for human blood."

"Will you ride with us, then?" Arthor asks, and hears Melania's groan.

"Not to Hammer's Throw," Merlin answers, wiping the dew-lapped rain from his haggard face. "There's no one in that thorp powerful enough to fend a lamia. We are off to Camelot to sell these steeds to the warriors gathering there. That's where you'll find the might and experience to track and kill lamia. Come with me. The lady may have her own horse for the journey. We'll make good speed and seek help from those that can give it."

Arthor shakes his head. "Not Camelot. My fate calls me elsewhere."

"Fate, is it?" The gleeman looks down at his wise dog, who looks up at the hermetic figure and sapiently shakes its head side to side. "What do you say to that, Master Sphenks?"

The dog leaps straight upward, spins about, and lands with a bark.

"Master Sphenks says we should talk about this thing you call fate," Merlin replies, and points to a grove of maple. "Let's shelter here briefly. I've victuals from the hamlet. We shall eat and talk about fate, eh?"

"No." Arthor nudges his palfrey forward, and Melania hugs him more firmly. "There's a lamia about. We must keep moving."

As the couple step past, Merlin gestures to the bulging saddle pouches on his mares. "I've blue cheese, rye bread, and crisp apples," he says temptingly.

"Enjoy them, old man." Arthor nods to the glee-man and salutes his wise dog. "May you fare well on your journey to Camelot."

Merlin gnashes his teeth and throws his grass hat to the ground as Arthor disappears into the arched vaults of the forest. He dare not use magic again. The Furor is somewhere nearby. This gray weather is his aura. If the north god finds the demon-wizard, death will come swiftly to Merlin in a bolt of lightning. The best he can hope to do now is what he has been doing all along—watching from afar and anticipating the young king's needs.

In the maple grove, he ties off the horses, drops a wad of dried meat for the dog, and crouches under the drizzling rain, listening for evil.

Melania can still feel his eerie presence as they ride among the rain-lit trees. The time she spent possessed, first by the lamia and then by the Saxon's gods, has heightened her psychic perceptions. "He is not a natural man," she warns Arthor. "We are well to be away from him."

"Yet I wish he had come with us," Arthor says. "I owe him a debt and would be unhappy if the lamia kills him."

They ride on in silence through primeval woods that the rain, fine as powder, has drained of natural hues and stained in seven shades of lavender. Among a holt of willows that offer some seclusion, Melania asks to stop to relieve herself. Arthor complies and holds her hand as she dismounts. Her dark, curly tresses, glossy and heavy with rain, lend her the appearance of a Babylonian princess, and the longing that Arthor feels for her grips him like grieving.

She retreats behind the willow curtains, and Arthor ties his palfrey to a thin mulberry tree among tangled lupines and lilies glittering with pearls of rain and strides into the obscurity of the forest. He leans against a twisted larch, pulls aside the loinwrap beneath his tunic, and listens abstractly to the stream of water sizzling among the fallen cones and needles. He wonders if he can win Melania's love. *Perhaps,* he contemplates, *I can win the fortune she needs to reclaim her estate.* Yet he cannot imagine how he can earn that much gold with his sword.

Short-Life is my sword now, he reminds himself, adjusting his loinwrap. *I've earned it fairly by doing as Kyner commanded—and it led me to Melania. Now, if God wills, it will lead me to the fortune I need to make her my own.*

He approaches a slantwise and wild chestnut, places both hands against it, and extends his right leg behind him, pressing the heel to the ground to stretch his taut hamstrings. Nearby, among breeks of kingscord and puffballs, blue chicory blooms. He considers harvesting several stems to chew as they ride—and suddenly the chestnut heaves forward.

Its branches sweep down and snaggle Arthor as he falls backward, and the scalloped fungus that ledges its trunk folds back around a leering face riven in the bark. Leaves snap like sparks. Branches squeak and cry. Mounded roots suck loudly as they pull from the soaked earth. And Fen's countenance unwrinkles from the brown moil of wood and knots. In an eye-blink, the naked Saxon stands before him, the guardian band about his throat glittering like living snakeskin, and his clawed hands gripping Arthor's shoulders.

"You gave me to the Thunderers," he speaks accusingly through a slack and unhappy smile. His silver-blond hair locks writhe like worms in an updraft of blue wind, and his body looks sinister, the muscles unnaturally swollen and chocked with electric veins. "Now I will give you to death."

Arthor draws Short-Life, swiping the blade through the Saxon's midriff. Ether fire sprays like green blood from the abrupt wound, and Arthor jolts with shock, the meat of his body jumping on his skeleton, twanging tendons, searing nerves. He howls as much with fright as pain to see Fen's cleaved belly heal itself like so much quicksilver bleeding together.

"You can't kill me," Fen cries with a rabid laugh. "I have become more than man."

Arthor sags, and the taloned hands lift him off his feet. In a panic, he hacks at the thick arms upholding him, and they slice like water. The splash lights the grove with spectral radiance and jars through his sword arm and into his chest where it strikes his beating heart.

He hits the ground breathless, energy like blue mold tufting from the tips of his cheeks, nose, and chin, and he thinks he sees his naked bones in his hands, hollow shadows in his shining flesh.

With a sucked-in scream, he pulls breath back to his lungs, and his bruised heart thumps so hard against his ribs he nearly passes out. Fen's severed arms spin brilliant wires of blue light and reattach themselves to the cut elbows with a wind-muted thump of thunder.

"I am made of wind and lightning now." The Saxon laughs at him, his skull glowing through his flesh and rubbing the air around him with a trembling halo. He towers above his fallen prey with eyes like fierce stars, laughing with maniacal silence, a god of dementia.

Arthor crawls backward, abandoning his sword, whimpering to see the silver claws of the beast open, webbed with milky bleedings, reaching for him. He does not have the strength to rise, and as he falls flat under the pressure of terror, Melania steps over him. Her lodestone dagger slashes once, and the grasping claws shrivel like torched grass.

Fen bawls, and the stars snuff in his eyes. Their smoke wreathes his once more human face, a face wrung with shock and pain. "You!" he gasps, clutching his cut hands to his mortal chest, looking thin, pallid, and frail. "Who are you?"

Melania replies with a thrusting jab; Fen hops back, falls over a root-ledge, and scrambles away tucked over his pain. Where he once stood, a burned smell slithers in the pattering rain.

Arthor sits up, his heart banging at the door of his head. At first he can hear nothing else, and Melania's lips move soundlessly. Then she presses very close. "He is gone."

She slips the stone knife in her sash and rubs his shoulders. The white fabric there bears seared claw marks. "He taunted you," she says in a voice that reaches him, "or you'd be dead now. We must stay close. We have only this one weapon to protect us."

He stands and retrieves Short-Life. At the spot where the illusory chestnut had stood, a miasmal haze rots the air with a fetulent stink. The forest extends through rings of darkness in every direction, and he peers anxiously into those shadows for the hollow eyes and the chewing jaws.

Melania takes his arm and guides him back to where the palfrey nibbles at the leaves of the mulberry tree. The gleeman and his wise dog are standing there with the two mares. "Master Sphenks smelled trouble," Merlin says, eyeing Arthor for damage, unhappy to see pallor in his cheeks and tremor in his eyes. "'Twas the lamia, yes?"

Master Sphenks bounds atop the palfrey's saddle so that it stares eye level into Arthor's fright. It takes the reins in its teeth and stands upright, bobbing as a rider would.

Melania, who has stood back at the sight of Merlin, laughs outright, a short, helpless gust of mirth that penetrates Arthor's torpor. The shadow falls from his numb face like the skin off an insect, and a vague smile appears.

"Master Sphenks wants you to ride with him to

Camelot," Merlin interprets. "Surely, now you see there is no hope in going on to Hammer's Throw. Come with us to where the lady may find true sanctuary among the chieftains and warlords of Britain."

Arthor looks to Melania, who nods. If the lamia had slain Arthor, she would be alone again in these woods, prey once more to the viper-priest and his cruel tribesmen. Far better to seek safety among the Christian lords of this island, even if she must abide the presence of this haunted man with the bleached beard and wizened wax cadaver's face. Perhaps, too, her tolerance shall be rewarded if she finds a British prince willing to return to Aquitania with her for adventure and profit—or marriage.

"Will you escort me to the gathering of lords in Camelot?" she asks Arthor. "I have the will but not the might to master the lamia I set loose on your island. Let me at least confess this trespass to those who have the means to right my wrong."

Arthor does not protest but looks into her as if reading a coded message. All hope of defending her from the monsters that assail her withered away when he hung in the predacious grip of the lamia. His heart still speeds like a runner leaving no tracks. No longer does he believe he can protect the innocents of the land from Fen's bloodlust, and he even doubts that he can defend himself.

He shivers, sensing the cold designs that death has on him and in him. Now he simply looks to see in this beautiful woman what remains of his amorous ambition. He knew when he first saw her that she would never be his, but he had aspired to overcome that somehow with valor. The lamia stripped him of that. If they part here, she will leave with his pride.

"I shall ride with you to Camelot," he agrees, "but I cannot escort you to the festival itself. I have sworn to go my own way in the world." *Though I never thought it would lead to such abominations as this,* he thinks to himself, knowing full well that Fen will come back for him, and he may never live to reach Camelot.

Master Sphenks barks approval, drops the reins, and licks Arthor's face. Arthor wipes the slobber from his cheek and pushes the mutt off the saddle.

Melania accepts the blond mare, and Merlin climbs onto the gray. They ride back the way they had come, Master Sphenks leading the way, and soon Arthor relaxes into this decision. The dog will not be fooled by the lamia, whatever shapes it may assume. He puts a hand over his thudding heart and slowly convinces it to calm down. Never before has he been so frightened. Doom seems to surround him. Evil shadows loiter in the mist-brewing trees, and the rag ends of fog among the shrubs hide threats and violence.

With accuracy, Melania reads his sullen mood, and says to him quietly, "Arthor, do not fret. You are the bravest man I have ever known." Her large eyes brim with sincerity. "Fen hunts you because you saved me from the barbarians. If you had been less courageous and had left me, you would have no troubles now. I owe you my life." She holds out the lodestone dagger, presenting him the silver-bound haft of quartz. "Take this. It will serve us best in your hand."

Merlin, riding ahead, pretends not to hear or to notice the glow of pride that brightens Arthor as he accepts the weapon. The wizard will have much to teach him about the lure and allure of desire that burns all the keener the closer it comes to the flame. But for now, it is enough that he has drawn him toward Camelot, and the dangers between here and there preclude all the elections of love.

The faithful enemy lurks somewhere in the cool rain. At nightfall, as the drizzle drums to a downpour, Merlin feels the Furor closing in. When he purchased the mares in Hammer's Throw, he smelled the weather and had the foresight to pack canvas waxed with cerate. The travelers cast it over a capacious hawthorn bush on a knoll and create for themselves a shelter against the torrent. The wizard leaves them there eating apples, cheese, and rye loaves and sets Master Sphenks as a guardian while he goes out into the stormy night to spy upon the one-eyed god.

The black-faced wind carries the Furor's scent, and Merlin follows it to a covert of interlocking elms on a higher hill. The rain oozes through in thin vines, and the wizard curls into a dry, hollowed bole and listens deeply to the heartbeat of the storm. He has no trouble locating the furious god of the barbarians, who presides with his slithers of lightning among the Thunderers at the far end of Crowland.

In trance, Merlin listens to their music, their femur-bone flutes, percussive skulls, and drums skinned with human hide. He feels the ritual power of their shaman, the viper-priest Cissa, as he sways to the dance that binds him with the frenzied bodies of his tribe. Cissa pitches forward into his own trance. But he is not seeking Merlin, or Arthor, or the lamia-possessed Fen. The shaman writhes on the mossy earth to bring the Furor into flesh.

Merlin relaxes. For a while, he lingers in the tree hole on the hill's backbone, observing from afar the one-eyed god's indulgent desire to throw himself into a human body. It darkly amuses him to watch this electromagnetic majesty nosing the earth for the honey of a blood-and-guts existence. His amusement shines darkly, because he knows that the Furor comes to flesh covetous not of human life, which seems contemptuously meager to him as to all gods. The Saxon god of war shrinks to the trembling moment of man to taste for himself the honey of his people's awe.

The old prophecies promise him these western islands. In time, they will be his. Neither Merlin nor all his magic can stop that. Soon enough, the Saxons, the Angles, the Jutes, the Picts, and the Gaels will rule these lands, erect their tombs and altars, and sing praises to their war god. The Furor stoops now to sip that rare, effluvial nectar of anticipation, condensed to the utmost sweetness of imminence in the fervid brains of his worshipers.

So absorbed is the wizard in his tranceful observations that he does not sense Fen's approach on the knoll below. Master Sphenks, lulled by the rain, has curled up and fallen asleep against Arthor, who dozes lightly, listening through the sinuous rain for rustlings in the underbrush. Melania shifts restlessly. Something large as the night summons her.

Fen squats nearby, his bloody fingers hooked about the guardian band clasping his throat. He wants to yank it off, throw it into the night, and let the lamia devour him. When the monster glowed with strength after consuming his tormentors among the Thunderers, Fen exulted. But since Melania cut his hands with the lode-knife, the power has drained from him. Now the lamia wants to eat. It licks the salt in the blood of his wounded fingers and jangles the harp of the rain with its needy moans.

If Fen pulls the band from his throat, the lamia will kill him and the shame of his capture by Kyner, his humiliating return to the Thunderers as a boy's gift, the sickening hunger of his possession will end. But there may be a better way. The witch who wounded him perhaps can take this demon off of him.

The storm returns the night to its original blackness, and he uses it to hold his beckoning. Like a prayer, he beseeches the night to bring her to him. If she is a witch, she will hear him, he reasons. But it is the lamia that hears him and calls to her through the urn and her blood, the two containers that once carried it. Her blood remembers the lamia's possession. The urn on the ground beside her amplifies the summons.

A feeling like something of loveliness, like something wild and her own, draws Melania out of the shelter and into the night. She thinks she swelters and needs the cool caress of rain to soothe her. The darkness among the trees glitters like ebony and opals, a bright darkness the envy of angels, and she goes to it.

Fen is there. Slender in his nakedness and shivering,

he has no shade of threat about him, and his silver-whiskered face with its acute cheekbones looks anguished as Christ's. He kneels under a spruce, his hurt fingers grasping the guardian band, but when he sees her, he lets go and sways to his feet.

"You came!" he sobs.

Melania shudders, suddenly alert and surprised to find herself here. She steps away, alarmed.

"No—don't go," Fen calls. "I will not harm you." The lamia lifts away from his slashed fingers and gleams like the merest thread of sunlight in the starless gloom, revealing the glistening bark of the spruce and Fen's long body shining with rain. "Stay, please. The monster that holds me—I will not let it harm you."

Melania glances about for others and sees only the impenitent darkness of the forest. She hugs herself against the rain. "You called me here."

"Yes. I prayed for you to come—to remove this thing from me. Will you help me?"

The lamia suddenly sweeps open, fangs gleaming in its skullface, its shaggy mane a shroud of boreal lights.

"No!" Fen cries, and clasps his will to the monster. It buckles in the air, inches from Melania's startled body. Exerting every muscle of body and spirit, Fen drags the lamia away from its prey. "Run!" he shouts, and the thunderbolt scar upon his chest writhes with his strenuous effort. "I cannot hold it long! Run!" He cries to the gods of darkness, and the black legends of pain open within him. He bears their telling, rending his body's muscles and the fibers of his soul, until the witch has fled. She is his only hope, and she must not die.

Once Melania has gone, the lamia turns on Fen. But its gnawing at his open wounds is the smallest cruelty after what he endured to hold it back. He knows he will never again have such strength, and he turns away and hobbles into the night. From under the rain-singing flap of canvas with Master Sphenks at her side growling into the storm, she watches his distant white shadow disappear like a light without a body.

Arthor rises from out of the dark interior, lode-knife in hand. "Did you hear a cry?" he rasps.

"It's Fen," she answers, and tells him what has transpired.

"Where's the gleeman?" Arthor asks, gazing into the torrent. The horses stand under the trees where they are tied, heads bowed, rain sparking off their wet hides. "The lamia must have killed him—called him out the way it called you."

"I don't know," Melania mutters, her teeth nattering from the chill. "But, I tell you, Fen stopped the lamia from attacking me. He wants help. He thinks I can help him."

Arthor doffs his tunic and hands it to her. "Take off your wet gown and wear this. If the cold seeps to your bones, you'll get ill."

Melania accepts and thanks him. In the dark of the tent, she does not see his avid, crystalline look of ardor as she drops her gown and slides into his dry tunic, still warm with his body heat. Her mind is on Fen. The anguish she saw in his strong face brands her soul and fills her with a vast caring—for she knows painfully well the impossible effort he exerted to save her from the lamia. That was a strength she never found in herself during her possession. Then, when the lamia fed on innocents, she ran away, stoppering her ears with her hands to blot out their screams. But Fen did not run away—not until she was safe.

Sitting in the dark, staring into the relentless rain, she marvels that he called to her and she went to him. And she wonders where he is. But there is no imagining his despair as he staggers through the night forest with the lamia teetering after him like a black fume loosed from a nightmare. He climbs and descends root stairs, bruising his bones in the dark, scratching his eyes, and lashing his body. The rain's cold feathers clothe his nakedness.

Fen runs through the knives of hedges and crashes across streams with the night between his teeth. Time and again, he reaches for the guardian band at his throat, and each time screams his grip free. He wants to die as a warrior in battle, not like some cow split in half to cool in the rain. So he plows the night with his body, running through the forest of knives and arrows—until suddenly a hand big as the wind grabs him.

The rain stops. Clouds open and display the glass-works of constellations. His head swings wide with wonder to take it all in, and he sees the one-eyed god above him, darkness coming through his empty socket like a falcon.

"So, you have returned home to us, little brother," Cissa speaks, stepping out of the trunk of a sycamore tree. And around him, the Thunderers rise up from the earthsmoke like the dead.

---✧---

Chapter Five

Hannes leaves Mons Caliburnus with the wizard's staff standing in the star stone and looking like Excalibur in precise detail, even blazing with the illusion of reflected sunlight. He must catch up with Brokk and Morgeu the Fey and take back the sword they have stolen. But he is afraid. He has spent his magic disguising Merlin's stave as the sword, and even if he possessed all the power that the wizard opened in him, he would be no match for the dwarf and the sorceress.

From the pocket of the robe, he takes out the small summoning glass that Merlin instructed him to burst if his troubles became dire. He looks at the tiny blue rose pressed flat inside the glass wafer, quivering like a blossom underwater. Then he lifts his gaze to the wind blowing through the trees and knows that he will have to travel that fast to catch his foes, who are on horseback and more than an hour's ride ahead of him.

He drops the flake of glass onto a fist of rock and smashes it with his heel. When he lifts his foot, the star-burst dust crawls away like smoke.

The surprising scent of snow blowing off firs announces a presence, and Hannes peers into the morning's slanting rays and sees an apparition forming among the clustered trees. The figure of a tall man emerges from the dusty light, and the switching grass does not bend beneath him. He comes forward and stands before Hannes with red hair wild as the setting sun and long, green, Mongol eyes that light up his whole face. He wears no hat or sign of rank but by his cinched vest of animal velvet, royal blue tunic, leather leggings laced with scarlet braids, and yellow, tasseled boots, he looks noble.

"Why have you summoned me, man?" the elf asks darkly, the harsh angles of his milk blue face lowered in threat. "Speak up. The fumes of the blue rose cannot long hold my image in the daylight."

Hannes grimaces as if gulping dark medicine. "I—I, uh—Merlin said that—"

The elf plucks at the wizard's robe with a quizzical grin. "You are Merlin's man?"

"Yes—yes, I am. He told me—"

"Ah, so you've lost the sword," the elf notices, looking up Mons Caliburnus where the illusory weapon stands in the stone, the air around it polished like a soap bubble. "That fancy bauble won't last long. But longer than I can stand visible before you under the sun. Speak, man, and tell me what has become of the sword Lightning."

"The dwarf Brokk took it," Hannes blurts, "with Morgeu the Fey. They left on horseback before dawn—for Crowland—to work some dark magic on the king."

"The king?" The elf thumbs his beardless chin inquisitively. "Oh, you mean Merlin's hope for a king. That would be Ygrane's son, Arthor."

Hannes blinks with surprise. "Arthor—that is not a British name."

"You would prefer a king named Eril, perhaps, or Lanval, Fand, or Cador? A good British name, eh? Ha! A name is but a scabbard. In time, the sword wears it to its own shape. And your name, old fellow?"

"I? Oh, I am Hannes the master builder, apprentice to Merlin, wizard of Britain."

"And I am Bright Night, prince of the Daoine Síd." Sunlight swirls through him like spirits-smoke. "You have heard of me?"

"My lord prince, alas, no," Hannes answers in a nervous fluster. "You see, I am a Christian man, of Christian parents, and their parents Christian before them. The priests discourage talk of elves."

"Then perhaps you should summon the priests to find your king's sword." He glowers, sullen as a smoking lamp. "Though I think they will have little pleasure finding you in Merlin's robes working magic."

"Please, Lord Bright Night, I cannot face my master with the sword gone, lost on my watch. I beg of you—"

"Do not beg anything of me," the elf says, raising a hand to silence him. "I have already sworn to aid whosoever summons me by this blue rose. That is worthy enough work for me."

"Can you truly take Excalibur back from the hands of the wicked dwarf?" Hannes asks in awe. "He has the might of an ox in his two arms."

"I fear his strength less than his cunning," Bright Night admits. "Brokk is the Furor's weapons master. He crafted the sword Lightning you call Excalibur and wields a blade as well as any swordsman under the Storm Tree. I dare not fight him. And any faeries sent against him would be dispatched to oblivion."

"Then what are we to do?" Hannes asks with chilly alarm. "Can't you shoot him with elf bolts? Kill him from afar?"

"A dwarf is not so easily slain. He is a creature of the Storm Tree. If the Dragon were not asleep, Brokk would make a toothsome morsel." Bright Night gazes into the narrow avenues of the forest, and his green eyes float like a dreamer's. A moment later, the ground moves under a tremendous thump, and the air flares with a hot, sweet, and frantic fragrance of horse. "My steed is here. Mount up behind me."

Hannes sees nothing yet feels the steam rising from a huge beast and the earth juddering under its stamping and its great lungs huffing. Bright Night swings high onto a lithe, moving transparency that shimmers like the shadow of smoke. He holds a hand out. Hannes takes it, and the steed rushes off, snapping him behind sharp as a flag.

The prince pulls Hannes out of the wind and into place on the muscular, churning back of the elf-horse. They ride like clouds going by. Trees drift in loose green threads of speed, and the rush of their passing moans like the misery of the wind in the pines. Even the sun in the high, open heavens floats along the horizon like a fiery barge.

Soon, the hills rolling under them slow, and the

snorting horse prances to a stop on the crest of a hummock overlooking a lake leveled with mist. Along the shore, Brokk and Morgeu ride colts, moving with alacrity toward a curtain of shaggy trees.

Prince Bright Night lets an ominous laugh roll from his chest. "They dare to run on the low path to Crowland. This is better than I had hoped."

"Why?" Hannes asks. He relaxes his grasp around the prince's waist and shivers to notice how the inner flesh of his forearms gleams like abalone. Suddenly, the spirit horse rushes forward, and he lurches to hold on.

"The ledge roads would have been slower for them," Bright Night shouts against the rushing air, "but on the ledges there are no ways into the hollow hills!"

Hannes does not understand until they blur past Brokk and Morgeu, and the lake mist swirls after them. The hammer of the sun vanishes. Night swarms from over the horizon, and orbs of orange and blue stars crowd the sky.

"Where are we?" Hannes yelps.

"We are in the hollow hills," Bright Night answers through a laugh. "And look—we are not alone!"

Brokk and Morgeu struggle to control the wild fright of their sinewy colts. Mist blows around them like reckless wraiths, and their foul cries rush off in disarray under the preternatural night.

Chapter Six

"I warned you to take the hill trails!" Morgeu cries above the screaming of the colts. The cinderous sky glows with orange-and-blue spheres, the electromagnetic nodules of the Storm Tree's roots.

With brutal force, Brokk reins in his pony, and its head pulls to its shoulder, its eyes flinty with pain. "Silence, woman! And silence your mount or be damned! I must take the measure of our situation."

"I'll measure it for you, dwarf," Morgeu cries angrily, chivvying side to side on her nervous mount. "We are an onionskin's thickness away from death. We are in the hollow hills!"

"I know that," the dwarf barks at her, his lumpy ugliness bunched into knots of rage. He holds the sword Lightning high, ready to lop off her head. "But how? You claim the Dragon is asleep. Yet here we are in his lair! You lied!"

Morgeu levels a mocking sneer at Brokk's accusatory scowl. "It's not the Dragon lured us here. Don't you see?" She points toward the wrought flames wavering on the jagged horizon. Against that seam of subterranean fire, she beholds Prince Bright

Night and Hannes astride a magnificent tropical cloud shaped like a steed with eyes of green African heat. "There, look! That is Prince Bright Night of the Síd."

"The Síd?" Brokk gawks about in alarm. He sees only sharp boulders of slag under a night of spectral globes. The air is hot and full of the acrid nuances of burned rock. "Where?" The tight boreholes of his eyes scan the terrain of shimmering flameshadows, and he thinks he sees in the distance sparks, ember motes, fire spray. "*Those* fireflies?"

"Put the sword down, fool." Morgeu has steadied her colt and reins in closer. "He baffles you with a faerïe spell. The sword is his target. Put it down, and the spell will fall with it. Then you'll see who led us here—to our doom!"

Brokk lowers the sword, and where he glimpsed tenuous glitters, he spies a stallion shimmering like dawn and carrying two figures: a grinning elf and a startled old man in a wizard's hat. "I see him! He laughs at us! And beside him—beside him is that carpenter in Merlin's robes! Damn his eyes!"

"They led us directly into the hollow hills, Brokk, and there's no escape." Morgeu watches in despair as the elf-prince and the carpenter vanish in a bounding streak of sunrise that lapses instantly again to the scorched night. She wipes a lather of sweat from her white brow. "We could wander these roots of the Storm Tree for ages and never find the way out."

"You have been here before, witch," Brokk speaks through a snarl. "You must know the way out."

"I have only been here with the demons who hunted Lailoken," she answers in a voice constricting with distress. "They had the might to come and go as they pleased. But they are gone from me many years now—and we are here alone. We are doomed!"

"Silence." Annoyed, Brokk turns his attention from her despair to the thermal dust in the burned black sky. "I must think."

"Think!" Morgeu screeches, near hysteria to find herself so easily duped by the Síd and led to death in the infernal depths. "Think on your foolishness in taking the low trails that led us here. If you had listened to me, if you had taken the hill paths as I told you, we would be on our way to Crowland. But you were impatient to gloat about your success before your god. Now you will never see your god. Never. No one escapes the hollow hills."

"Silence, I say!" Brokk reaches into his hip pouch with his left hand and unrolls the lamia. In an instant, he has shaped it over himself in an image stolen from her past, taken by the lamia's psychic pincers from her memory: The image glares at her as her father, Duke Gorlois, his big jowls quivering ragefully, his small goat's eyes slanted with anger. "I am not the fool you think me," Brokk scolds.

"Pah!" she shouts at the scornful image in Roman leather and brass. "Take off that shape, dwarf. Do not torment me with my father's ghost."

Gorlois's minatory face pushes spitefully closer. "Will you shut your mouth, then? Will you not speak until spoken to?"

"Yes, yes." She averts her gaze, raising a tremulous hand to blot out the image of her heartache. "It matters not. We are lost. The elf-prince has gone to gather the Síd. They will slay us."

"Be silent this moment," Gorlois commands. When she lowers her head and remains mute, Brokk speaks, "Good. Now I shall get us out of this hole."

"Out? We are in—"

Brokk glares and shakes the leathery shroud of the lamia with its woeful eyeholes and downturned mouth, and sparks fly like drops of sweat. Morgeu's lips whiten, and she keeps her silence. Satisfied, Brokk returns the lamia to his pouch, and says, "We are not here alone as you claim, witch. Behold the sword Lightning." He wields the sword against the blotches of fire in the lightless sky. "I shaped this for the Furor's hand, and it served him well. Even now, it remembers him. With it, I will summon him, and he will lead us out of here."

"He will not come." She says this quickly and shuts up.

Brokk lifts the thick boot of his chin defiantly. "He will come. Why should he not? What is there for our god to fear? The Dragon is asleep, as you say."

"But he does not know that."

The dwarf brushes her objection aside with a silvery streak of the blade. "Then he will send others to get his sword. One way or another, we shall be free of this hideous place. Now keep your silence while I concentrate."

Brokk's hard features blur as he presses his apeledged brow to the mirroring blade and slides it back and forth, greased with perspiration. His prayer to the

All-Seeing Father enters the weapon and goes deeper, beyond the crystalline matrix of atoms and molecular congruity, into the black that floats light, that creates space and time, that unifies all form and motion in the singularity whose depth is the universe itself—and instantly he is heard within the nuclear lattice of the Furor's being.

Sprawled under an ash tree spangled with sunlight, listening to the singsong of whetting stones, Cissa's eyes deepen like tiny glaciers, and Aelle knows. The Thunderers know and stop their sharpening, sit up in the rusty grass, and listen for the commandments of their god. Fen, hanging upside down from a high branch, his face purple as an eel's, hears the lamia inside him calling to its twin.

The cry goes down into the earth, full of need. And the cry comes back from underground, lorn and cold.

"I hear Brokk," Cissa announces, his words twisting from his throat like a musical ache. "He is calling to the Furor."

"Does he have the Furor's sword?" Aelle inquires, and leans forward on his sword, one thick-knuckled hand tugging at his hay-nest beard, anxious to please the one-eyed god and quit Cymru.

"Yes."

The word levitates the Thunderers. They stand around the viper-priest, loose in their joints, taut in their eyes. They, too, are eager to complete their mission here among the enemy's hills. They have retrieved their chieftain's unlucky son. Now only the war god needs to be fulfilled.

"Brokk holds the sword Lightning," Cissa breathes. "He has taken it from Camelot."

"Where is he?" Aelle wants to know, pushing to his feet.

"In the hollow hills."

"No." The Thunderers share small, dark looks. "He summons us from the hollow hills."

"The Síd have him," Aelle concludes, and slams his blade into its scabbard. "Then he is lost. The sword is lost."

"The sword Lightning is in his grasp," Cissa informs them in a tone that smolders with distance. "The Síd have not yet taken him. He needs the Furor's help to get out."

"It is a deception." Aelle steps back to stand among his warriors, speaking for them. "If the Furor goes after him, the Dragon will devour them both."

"The Dragon is asleep."

"This I cannot believe," the chieftain says, and the Thunderers murmur agreement. "It is a trick, I say."

"Brokk calls. He needs help to bring the sword Lightning out of the hollow hills."

Aelle twists a braid of his faded beard. "What are we to do?"

"The Furor wants his sword."

Releasing the twist of beard, Aelle looks up into the ash at his hanging son. "We will send Fen," he decides. "If this is a Síd trick, we will know. If not, he will serve as our guide."

Two men climb into the tree and cut Fen down. They lower him, gaunt and discolored, and he lies in the grass, with the flies visiting him. Hairless, viper-stained Cissa bends over him and adjusts the guardian band so that Fen can breathe easier.

The Thunderers slink away, find watching places in the splintery sunlight under the trees, and wait to see if the lamia will rise. It does. Mist pools in the hollows of Fen's prone body, gathers to a second skin, and luffs upward in the summer breeze. Its face of pain with its burning tendons, its body fluttering in waves of heat, glisten. If the wind shifts, it will fly to pieces.

Cissa claps his hands over its oily rainbow smoke, and it seeps back into Fen's inert body. The lamia is weak. The viper-priest nods to two of the Thunderers, and they run off into the woods. The afternoon sun cuts low through the trees when they return with a British charcoal seller. His hands, black from his work, clasp in prayer even though he is grasped under both arms by his captors. The wild look in his smudged, whiskery face attests to the surprise ringing in his brain that he is yet alive.

Fen has recovered enough from his torment to sit against the ash and breathe strength from the pollen-rifted air. At the sight of the terrified Briton, he knows what will happen, and he bucks to his feet with a cry. Cissa punches him between the eyes with the heel of his hand, and Fen sits down hard, eyes distracted like someone hearing his name arrive from far away.

The lamia unspools from his chest with a shriek, and the Thunderers release the charcoal peddler and flee. He, too, turns to flee, but before he goes even a few steps the flanged jaws pierce him behind the neck and the talons crack his sternum and flay his rib cage. And then he is on the wing. He flies up into the ash, feet tumbling over his head, blood shaking through the leaves. He hangs upside down, the rictus of death on his horrified face inverted to a rigid leer.

While the lamia feeds, Cissa pounds his chest, drumming the Furor closer. Clouds clot the sun, and a rope of lightning dangles in the distance. When the thunder rumbles in, the Furor comes with it. He pitches through the blue-black sky in a thrash of hot rain that melts the sheet of blood on the corpse's clenched face.

"All-Seeing Father," Cissa intones, arms outstretched to the god in the divinity's dark mantle of storm, "open the way into the hollow hills. Send Fen down the stairs of night to your dwarf Brokk, who holds your sword Lightning. Send him into the depths of the sleeping Dragon."

A thundercloud blooms directly overhead like an orchid and lets down a stem of voltage that cracks the air to fiery heat and a dizzy smell. At once, Fen lurches upright, compelled by a force wide as the sky, and bounds in giant steps past Cissa and the Thunderers crouching among the trees and Aelle with his heavy arms upraised in awe. Fen hurtles through the forest, whirling, running backward, leaping sideways, dashing forward again, flying faster as if he is about to spin off the earth. The lamia shoots after him in a screaming vapor trail.

The green shadows of the forest explode to darkness, and Fen falls rolling, tumbling, skidding into an eternal night of flaming rock and slag smoke. He sits up dazed, dying as far as he can tell. Maybe dead already, he feels, and in the dark kingdom of the witch Hel.

But then, the lamia unwinds. Strong from its feeding, it clothes his bruised nakedness in its colorful shadows so that he stands lithely in the hot stink of sulfur fumes and soft steel. Fen looks down and sees his loins trussed in cool silk, his feet shod in python-skin sandals.

The stinking heat of the underworld sloughs away, and the lamia's chill presence soothes him. There is a place to go, a thing to find for its masters, a thing that must be found to earn for itself the next meal of spilled blood, and it rides Fen hard into the scalding dark.

Across the shuddering horizon, Hannes and Bright Night approach. The drastic heat and stink rip breathing to short gasps, and the master builder holds on to the prince with one arm and puts a shining hand over his nose and mouth. The frosty fragrance of conifers from the elf's sweat cuts the sick smoke and drags the whole heart of himself toward a dream. He almost nods off and has to drop his perfumed hand and smell again the putrid gas.

The spirit horse charges toward Fen. But the riders do not see him, because the steed abruptly dips behind a smoking scarp and plummets into a sink-hole. The torrid stench peels away before a fresh, floral wind, and the darkness ruptures to a tumultuous green vista. Monkeys chitter a strange summer into place: cloud plateaus surge in green sky lakes above a triple-canopy jungle of silver-trunked trees scalloped with gold wedges of fungus. Rainbow-splashed birds click, fret, toll, and chime, and the monkeys—troops

of them in green, auburn, and black—screech and
scatter through the high galleries above the ghostly
tree boles.

"Where *are* we?" Hannes gasps in the dense,
sweet air.

"Not very far from the Happy Woods," Bright
Night replies. "This is the jungle of the monkey gods.
It is very ancient, and we are not welcome here. We
must move on."

"Where are we going?"

"We cannot face Brokk alone. Not with the
sword Lightning in his hand. I must gather my troops.
They will be in the fields and groves near the Happy
Woods, where the Piper plays and the Celtic dead
dance themselves into their next lives."

They stream through a welter of hanging air
plants and across sepulchral chambers whose brown-
green atmospheres dangle luminous root tendrils and
parasitic loops. Among the ponderous leaves in the
somber naves of the jungle, where the dazzling light
from the sky lakes is muted by the weight of vegeta-
tion, giant apes watch sullenly. From vapors like tattered sails protrude broken glimpses of feathered
clubs and quartz-tipped spears.

"If we do not stop, we are safe," Bright Night
explains, his voice muffled by the excited jabbering of
the jungle. "The monkey gods are the oldest of our
kind who sought refuge in the hollow hills. They
have lived a long time here in the roots of the Storm
Tree. When the Dragon is awake, they sacrifice their
own to appease it. But they are not averse to seizing
strangers for their blood rituals."

The green cataclysm of floppy leaves, tangled vines, and monkey screams dims away as the elf-horse bounds into a chaparral of dwarf willows and golden grass broomed by an alpine wind. Hannes spots swarms of faerïes—yellow-orange darts of being, half-insect and half-human, like peelings from the sun. Above, a semblance of the moon floats in an ice green sky, a swollen moon of peach color, so large that pocks and rings of craters are visible.

"As above, so below," Bright Night intones. "The celestial energies captured by the branches of the Storm Tree are reflected here in the roots. These energies are distorted in the underworld, yet still I think they are beautiful."

"Yes—" Hannes agrees, breathless. He grins, stupid with joy. He must ask himself if he dreams, and he pinches his fingers. And still it persists—the astonishing vista of the netherworld's day sky with its peach moon and clots of stars in stellar vapors twisting like chimneys of smoke.

"Down there are the sacred fields, where the holy souls of saints and righteous heroes contemplate God and decide whether to live again as people or to leave our world entirely."

Hannes looks below at an emerald expanse of savanna and far-off huts touched by silver sunlight. Then the galloping steed veers and bounds along the pink-sand beach of a glassy lake cluttered with rock spires and boulders. Mermaids sun on rock ledges above the indigo shadows of deep water, their iridescent tails and salt-sprinkled hair glittering.

"To live here, they must feed the Dragon, too,"

Bright Night continues. "In these pools, many a sailor has been fed to the Drinker of Lives."

"Where is the Dragon?" Hannes asks, spellbound by the tiniest details of his trespass in the underworld: sun rays hanging in the long grass, a fog of mayflies near the lapping water, a quick blur of salamanders through the weed stalks, and the far-off music of the mermaids, whose soulful songs slash and glide with the algal breeze and the smack of small waves on the ruddy shore.

Bright Night feels Hannes's grip slackening and reaches back to shake him loose from the tranceful singing. "Fall off here, Hannes, and the mermaids of the sky lake will show you where the Dragon slumbers—but you'll not come back from there."

Quickly, Hannes jerks free of the song-induced lethargy and tightens his grasp about the elf's waist. He stares down and notices that they are ascending. The amethyst sky lake gleams on a level above the saints' savanna, which itself encloses the faerïes' chaparral and, far below, the strangled greens of the monkey gods' jungle. Now they mount over crackling tundra toward purple peaks.

"Will we see the Dragon?" Hannes asks timorously.

"Not if our luck holds. The Dragon curls around its sleep deep within the fiery depths." Bright Night motions ahead toward a gateway of lavender snow peaks. On the far side, griffins swim in the dusk, tawny shadows with weighty cries that rend the air like bells. "Over these peaks are the Happy Woods of the Daoine Síd. There we shall find allies willing to fight for the king's sword. But we must be swift. Already I sense the Furor's shadow among the roots of the Great Tree."

The shadow that the elf-prince detects is Fen, who moves flowing with an inhuman grace through the black terrain of burning rocks. The lamia inside him ignores the caustic fumes and the lamps of pain glowing in his lungs. And when he jumps with alarm at the strangled voices in the melting rocks, the lamia calms him. On narrow, enamel ledges above a blind abyss chuckling with spilled stones, his feet crush tiny yellow flowers of sulfur, and the lamia steadies him. He moves swiftly, because the lamia knows time hunts him.

Fen does not want to try to free himself from the monster: not in this dangerous place. He is glad for the alien thoughts that lead him safely on these obscure pathways where boulders unfurl to flames. He wants to accomplish whatever he has been sent to do and offers no resistance. Even when the scarlet shadows thrown by sudden fires lead him toward a dwarf with a brutal face waving a spectacular sword, he does not hesitate.

He strides into the weapon's range, and he cannot stop looking at the blade, even though the dwarf is speaking gruffly, demanding to know who he is. The steel blue of the razor edge is quiet with dreams. He does not understand at first. The sword rises, threatening to strike him, yet he stands unmoving, caught by something he did not know he loved. Then, he realizes, *this* is what he came for.

The entombed voice of the lamia's twin ekes

sadly from nearby, and the monster inside Fen startles
alert.

"I say, who are you?" the dwarf demands irately.
"Speak or die."

Fen cannot find his voice. The lamia churns
within, luminous and angry.

"Is he the one you summoned?" a deeply reso-
nant voice asks, and a tall woman with small black
eyes in a moonly white face emerges from the red
shadows. The heat has wrung her crinkled hair to
long, garish streaks, and diamond sparkles of sweat
bead her face. Though she is thin as a cat, she has big
shoulders. "Look at him, Brokk. He does not sweat.
And his wrap and sandals have an odd shimmer, do
they not? Do you think he is one of the Furor's own?"

"No." Brokk glowers, his nasty eyes barbed with
menace. He feels the lamia in his pouch squirming,
and he peeks in just long enough to see its red grin.
"Something is wrong. The lamia is excited. This is a
Síd trick to get the sword."

"Are you of the Daoine Síd?" she asks, striding
forward. "This heat—this stink—we've had enough
of it. Summon your prince. We would talk with
him."

"What are you saying, Morgeu?" Brokk interrupts, pushing her aside, and pointing the sword at
the thunderbolt scar over Fen's heart. "No terms with
the enemy."

"I am not your enemy," Fen's voice croaks from
him, and the lamia rises high into his chest. "The
Furor sent me to get his sword."

"You lie!" Brokk thrusts, and the lamia in Fen

impels him backward, flashing an enraged fang-face through his ribs. "By the Norns! Another lamia!"

Fen gapes about, confused—then sees the pale green smoke leaking from the dwarf's pouch. "You have a monster, too?"

Morgeu stays Brokk's sword arm. "Who *are* you?" she asks suspiciously.

"I am Fen, son of Aelle, from the Thunderers. This gruesome thing is upon me, because the Furor has used it to send me safely here to get his sword."

"I do not believe you," Brokk states coldly. He notices the lamia drooling from his hip pouch, snatches it in one wringing hand, and stuffs it back.

Morgeu smears the sweat from her face and, ignoring Brokk, wearily expels the stink from her lungs. "Lead us out of here, Fen."

Fen gestures to the pouch, feeling the lamia's dark call touching the inside of his skin. "The lamia want to be together."

"Bring the Furor to me," Brokk says, "and I'll have no more need of this shapeshifter."

Morgeu pushes at Fen, not caring if he is Síd or Saxon, craving air. "Lead us out, Fen. If you are as you say, then the shadow I leave behind us as we go will be all that the Furor will need to find his way down here to his sword."

"And if he is a Síd illusion, Morgeu?" Brokk challenges.

"I care not at all," she confesses, and slouches toward the dark fathoms. "I am sick to death here. I cannot stay."

Fen turns grudgingly. The sword and the twin

lamia are why he has come. But the dwarf stares at him with malefic certainty, the splendid sword unwavering in his grip. Morgeu's slick hand takes Fen's arm and pulls as the lamia echo dark cries in his blood. Slowly, weighed down by longing, he turns to tread the chasms back to the sun.

Chapter Seven

Arthor kneels in the dew before his shield, praying to Mother Mary. The sun has not yet risen, yet curlews cry in the gray light. "Mother Mary, let me be for you the Son you lost. Give me the strength to defend Him now that He has left us alone in the devil's world. Give me the strength to fight for Him until He returns."

Usually, the Virgin's routine reply comes from far across the field of patience, but this time the words sound crisply above his bowed head: Love is first, Arthor. Never abandon. Never abandon.

He looks up sharply. No one stands in the grass flattened by last night's rain. Only torn mist moves among the big trees, light and angular as dancers.

"Mother?"

The forest canopy rustles, and the commotion pushes him to his feet as a shadow rushes out of the darkness. A dove descends and alights upon the top edge of the shield. In the dim air, it glows. Hands clasped, he falls to his knees again. But prayer stalls in him at the dark thought that this could be the shapeshifter. He reaches for the stone dagger tucked in his sword belt.

"It is just a white bird," Melania says, stepping through the beech trees behind him. She tosses a rusk of black bread onto the wet grass, and the dove hops toward it. In her other hand, she carries the serpent-egg urn and places that on the ground with another rind of bread atop it, then takes Arthor's elbow and leads him back into the beeches. "Fen has run off to protect us. He doesn't want to kill."

"He would have slain me last night," Arthor objects, and puts a hand over hers where she holds his arm. "Were it not for you, I'd be a corpse now."

"Look." She points with her chin to where the dove perches on the urn and plucks at the bread. "No lamia would stand there."

Arthor's young face brightens. "Then it is the Holy Spirit."

She looks at him chidefully. "It is a white bird, Arthor."

"No," he insists, earnestly. "The dove came to me while I prayed. It is the Holy Spirit."

"As you say."

The disdain in her voice separates Arthor from her. "I thought you were a woman of faith."

"Faith did not save my father or my brothers," she answers bitterly. "They died defending their land against pagans. *Pagans!* Is their god stronger than ours?" In the winey light, her sculpted beauty seems inflamed, and she speaks with an orphic intensity: "Or is there no god at all? No god—only the scattered rubbish of dead bodies and the blind armies that clash over them?" Her dark, large eyes reach into him defiantly. "What is faith, Arthor, but fear and the bewilderment of pain."

Arthor closes his mouth, swallows his shock, and manages to mutter, "Is that what you believe?"

"Why do you regard me so astonished?" An incredulous smile bends one corner of her full lips. "Young as you are, you have fought battles. You have slain men and seen your comrades slain. I am astonished that you yet cling to faith."

"Jesus is Our Savior."

"What does that mean?" she challenges, her sable locks tossing forward as her head rears back with indignation. "He did not save my family."

"Then you do not understand what it is to be Christian," Arthor reacts sharply. He tries to soften his tone when he sees an irate shadow flex sharply between her eyes: "Were there no priests to teach you? Did you not read the good news in the Bible?"

"As a girl, I read the good news, and I believed the priests," she answers, hands on her hips. "But as a woman, I have seen the power of the sword. It cut away everything good in my life. Jesus could not stop the power of the sword in his life, and he cannot stop it now in his afterlife."

"Jesus is not a warrior. He offers us salvation beyond this life."

"Then why fight the pagans, Arthor?" she scolds. "Let them kill you. Your salvation awaits you."

"This world is a battlefield, Melania, where good and evil clash. We must choose for whom we fight. But we must fight."

"Jesus did not fight. The Romans beat him, scourged him, and nailed him to the cross—and he did not fight."

"He came to die," Arthor replies bluntly. "He was the sacrifice that annuls the past. All our pagan history is paid for in full by his blood. Now we are free to live for love. No longer are we bound to ancestral rites and pagan gods who demand murder, vengeance, and wealth, and who reward the strong and crush the meek. Jesus pardons that sinful past so that we may live a new way, not the old way of the pagans, who worship only might and its gains. We are commanded to build a world of love. And for that love, we must fight."

"*Love?*" She sneers at him, her beauty suddenly ugly with derision. "What love is won by the sword? You speak nonsense, Arthor."

"No." He meets her scoffing glare with a calm assurance. "I speak of the love of justice—a love that protects the weak, the sick, and the poor, that defends the good, and that destroys what is evil."

"You are a child."

He smiles gently at her anger. "'And a child shall lead them.'"

"As you say."

"Not as I say, Melania." He softly places a hand on her shoulder and points through the beeches to where the dove has returned to its perch atop his shield. "Look, the dove of the Holy Spirit has come to me."

She shakes her head and holds a chilled stare on him. "There are dark times ahead for all of us, Arthor. We shall see how long you keep the white bird."

Hurt by how bluntly his childlike faith confounds her losses, as if God had ruined her family out of spite, she barges through the trees, startling the dove to flight, and retrieves the urn. Without looking at Arthor, she shoulders past him. His heart sinks. Sad and long dreaming of love goes away with her, and he lets her go. That such a beautiful woman could have heard the good news and then deny Jesus troubles him.

Walking toward his shield, he plays upon the notion that she is right and he wrong: *What if there is no God at all? No Jesus. No Mother Mary. All this no more real than Kyner's stories of faeries, elves, and monsters.*

But he *has* seen a monster—and now he wonders about what he has not seen that could be lurking in these fog-tinged woods. He lifts his shield nervously and, after peeking into the jade distances of the forest dawn and seeing nothing unusual, lowers a contemplative gaze on the sacred image of the Virgin.

It is inconceivable to him that Creation could exist without its Maker. Since he was a young child, the Mother of God has given him comfort—and he has heard her voice, today more clearly than ever. "Love is first," he repeats, and looks up through the branches at the speeding turbid clouds. "Love is first. So you have taught me, Mother. Yet what of Melania? What love for her has God given?" A moment's thought reveals that, unlike himself, she once had her own family, had known their love, and at least tasted life as a noblewoman, as well. *She questions God for taking away from her what I never had. More pain in having and losing than never having at all.* His hand settles on the hilt of Short-Life, and for the first time, his rage at the inequity he knew in Kyner's household dims.

Beyond Crowland, in the forested heights above the River Amnis, Kyner and the clan wait for him. They will accept him back, if he will take his proper place among them and serve. But Melania has no place—no family but an aged crone, her estate pillaged and occupied by pagans, even her faith despoiled. He wants to save her. Earning the sword Short-Life for himself has led him to her, and by that sword and by his faith, he will find a way to redeem all she has lost. And he will serve—but not as a lowly ward in Kyner's household. He will serve love.

"Ar-thor!" Merlin's hoarse voice calls.

Bolstered by his determination to win Melania and uplifted by his vision of the Holy Spirit, Arthor carries his shield through the beeches back to the camp. The gleeman and Melania have already packed the canvas and mounted their horses. Master Sphenks sits atop the saddle on the palfrey, wagging its sharp tail.

The old man explains that he stepped into the bushes last night and lost himself in the storm. Melania tells him that the lamia must have called him the way it summoned her. Merlin does not dispute that. Secretly, he quivers with alarm that Fen could have approached so close while he sat entranced in the rain watching the Furor. He resolves to stay nearer to the young king until they reach Camelot.

Ingots of dawnlight burn like bush fire in the forest of Crowland as they travel east on a trace hung with spiderwebs of fog. Melania rides close to the gleeman, as far from Arthor as she can get. The young man lingers behind, watching the shifting shadows for clues of danger. Blue distilled from indigo rises toward the flyways of geese and herons, and his searching gaze lingers there until he notices a dove on an overarching branch. His heart leaps, and he cranes to see if Melania has spotted the bird. But she rides on oblivious to it and apparently to all else, for she stares rigidly straight ahead.

The gleeman, too, appears to be unaware of their surroundings, riding with his eyes half-closed. Arthor marvels that any man could have survived so long in this treacherous world with such indifference. He returns his attention to the dark woods and vaguely wonders why the Holy Spirit shows itself to him now. *Love first,* he remembers. *Never abandon.*

Up ahead, Merlin feels the approach of Morgeu and restrains himself from sitting up taller, not wanting to alarm the vigilant Arthor. The wizard has been chanting under his breath a spell of simple magic to drive off brigands. The one small band of cutthroats in the area wake in their weedbeds with slow, dim-witted dread. Not knowing why, they drift away from the trace they usually stalk and are a hill of alder thickets away when the riders pass through the early-morning mist.

The lamia guiding Fen, who leads Morgeu, is distracted by Merlin's simple magic. It mistakes Merlin's chanting for the ghost-scent of the Furor, and it directs Fen up out of the black grottoes of poisonous air toward the wizard's call. They emerge into the aromatic summer day through a sandy cleft in a salty, alkaline hillside overgrown with tamarisk and white velvet moonflowers.

The dank, genital odor of the wet forest nearly overcomes Morgeu with joy. She kneels in the sand, bends to embrace the nacre earth, and stops abruptly. Through the entwined, serpentine branches of the tamarisk, she sees Merlin dressed in ragged clothes and a hat woven of ivy leaves, beside him a young maiden of surly beauty—and behind them, riding bareheaded yet alert, bristle-cut hair shorn close as a Roman's, her half brother.

"Arthor," Merlin calls to him, sensing Morgeu and wanting the youth to ride closer. "Bring me Master Sphenks so I may consult with him where we shall stop for our rest."

Arthor! Morgeu thrills to discover his name. She rises too quickly, and dizziness swarms through her and plops her to her haunches. Hearing only her own ears drumming, she feels the physical strain of her circuit through the hollow hills. By the time she finds the strength to stand, the riders are gone. So is Fen. The lamia has carried him off through the woods in the opposite direction, toward the Thunderers. He will alert the Furor.

Morgeu sits back in the tussocky sand, her muscles languid, a thin fever running under her skin now that she is breathing pure air again. She has not the strength to confront Merlin just yet. But she will find it, and soon. While the sun eats at the shadows, she lies back, and her eyes roll up as though she has been brained by the soft breeze and blue sky. The sulfur reek of the underworld fades. Her fear that she was dead passes. And briefly the stinking dread of lost hope and the sweet possibilities of life intersect, and she lives in two worlds at once.

Merlin still senses her presence but more distantly. Time touches his face like a breeze, and he smells her farther up ahead—her usual musk scent choked with sulfur. *She has been in the hollow hills,* he realizes, and ponders what this must mean.

He is still wondering hours later when the horses drink at a creek pebbly with toads. He sits under a willow and watches Arthor cross a gravel bar to harvest apples and chicory, Master Sphenks at his heels. Upstream, Melania gathers creekwater in leather flagons. Pine martens slink stealthily through the blowing grass, stalking ptarmigans under the willows. Down in his heart, he feels a giant love for this world, though the parts of the world do not love each other.

He recalls his former existence as a demon when he hated all life. Then he thought that living forms were treasonous to the void, a betrayal of the emptiness that holds all atoms and planets in its grasp of absolute cold. Life seemed a stupid turning away from the reality of the vacuum that stole light from heaven in the explosive origin of the cosmos. Demons believe that there is no way back to heaven. Life denies that truth. It builds more and more complex forms within the formlessness of the void. It mocks the vacuum that holds it, because it ignores the heaven where there is no void, no cold, no limits, only pure light of infinite density, infinite energy, infinite being. The Fire Lords build life, thinking they are building their way back to heaven, and the demons tear it down, convinced there is no way back and accepting no substitutes.

Love changed his demonic cynicism. The love he learned from his mother Optima when he tried to possess her as an incubus altered him forever. Now he sees that though the void ripped the light out of heaven, and the absolute cold chilled that radiance to the darkness of matter, life is the memory of heaven as it writhes in the cold of space. And because love is the force that holds life together, the Fire Lords are right to embrace it. He regrets the aeons he vehemently attacked life trying to break it back down to the void, to the emptiness he mistakenly believed was closest to heaven.

Unspeakable sadness swells in him at the remembrance of the violence that possessed him for so long. A dark string twangs in his heart. Like an empty house, his body echoes with the noise of his grief. He tries to rise, to walk off this sudden melancholy—but like a house he cannot budge.

From a helpless distance, he sees her approaching—Morgeu the Doomed, her hair like a rag of blood, her face a moon disc, her small, black, sharp eyes piercing him. She is an apparition stepping down the sky among the doughy clouds. Caught daydreaming, he did not sense her enchantment locking him down with his own ponderous sadness from a past he cannot disown.

Then she sits up in the tall grass beside him, not an apparition at all but muscularly and muskily real, tainted with sulfur, her green gown torn and streaked, her bright hair twisted with sweat, her ardent face farouche as an animal's. Of his greatness, she never doubted, and so she has succeeded by extreme caution and psychic discipline in drawing close enough to cast a paralyzing spell on him. If he had been in possession of his magical stave, which senses invisible presences, this would have been impossible. She exults with an opulent grin.

Tears well in the wizard's gray metallic eyes. Try as he might, he cannot uproot Morgeu's spell, because she has been cunning enough to plant it deep inside him, in his oldest self, his demon mind. It tangles him with memories of his life in the vacuum, of his immutable sorrow at losing heaven and gaining the cold, lightless void. That is a sorrow he cannot quickly budge.

Glancing over her shoulder to be certain that she has not been seen by Melania or Arthor, Morgeu grips Merlin's frayed collar and drags him backward through the curtain of willows. He is light as ash, which surprises her. For an instant, she wonders if she herself has been duped and he is a simulacrum. But no: When she focuses softly, she can see his bodylight, blue as heaven, the color of a supernal being rather than the bloodglow of a human being.

She drags his inert body through a spite of thistles to a hillock dominated by a massive yew. The dense branches of the tree have grown down into the ground, creating a circular wall of stems, many thick as trunks. Within this enclosure, the spongy mass of the original trunk stands haggard and mucronate with fungus. There, she props the wizard and squats before him. What a simple matter now to take his frilled throat in her hands and crush the life in him.

But she knows better. A demon-wizard is not so easily killed. His death flash could well possess her, drive her mad. Just as dangerously, a dagger to the heart could release a noxious spirit that would rip her life from her flesh and whisk her beyond the sky into eternal night. He is a truly dangerous entity and must be respected. Here he will stay, entranced in his lithic sorrow, while she works a far more poignant vengeance with her half brother. When he finally struggles free, the destiny he has devoted his life to create will be stolen from him and reshaped in her womb.

She peers into his prophetic eyes, with their muted anguish of tears. And though she wishes to speak, to taunt him, she says nothing, for even one word could weaken her spell. Instead, she waves a silky laugh over him and slips away through the tendrils of the yew.

Merlin watches her disappear in the cavalcade of sunlight on the thistle field, and he strains to move, exerting himself to the point of blackout before he relents. She has caught him. Speaking to himself has become a self-devouring. That is her spell. He must return to nascent silence and slowly, slowly expand back into himself before he can move again. She has caught him very well indeed.

To save Arthor, only one hope remains. The Síd. Yet, when he calls to them from within the locked vault of his skull, no one answers. A firefly twinkles in the yew gloom. It jounces closer, and he sees that it is a faerïe. *Lead Arthor to the hollow hills!* he shouts in his mind. Does the little thing hear? Tears stream down his harrowed face with the sincerity of his plea: *To the hollow hills lead Arthor!*

Drifting like milkweed on the summer air, the faerïe exits the loamy enclosure and vanishes in the hot light.

"Hannes!" Arthor calls for the gleeman.

"He has run off again," Melania says. "He has a doddering soul. He could be anywhere."

Master Sphenks runs in circles on the banks of the shimmering creek. No longer a wise dog without the wizard, it weaves aimlessly among the willow roots and withy reeds. Morgeu's magic hides the giant yew from their sight, expanding in their minds the clustered willows to cover that ground.

Melania secures the flagons of water to her saddle and mounts. "Let us be on our way."

"No," Arthor says firmly, returning through the creekside grass from his search upstream. "We must stay and look for him."

"Look where?" she asks with exasperation. "We have searched both sides of the creek and all the nearby willow coves. He has wandered off, I tell you."

"Then, we shall camp here till tomorrow." He gathers the reins of the horses. "He will show up again as he did this morning."

"Or Fen will come back," Melania warns. "And the barbarians. Arthor, come. Ride with me to Camelot."

"These are the gleeman's horses." He leads the

gleeman's gray mare and his own palfrey along the gravel beach toward the willows where they had last seen the old man.

"He knows where we are going," Melania pleads, walking the blond mare after him. "He will find us in Camelot."

"No, Melania." He walks the horses through the green tresses of the river trees, Master Sphenks appearing and disappearing in the feathery grass. "We cannot go without him."

"More of your Christian justice?" she asks, sitting rigid in the saddle. "Does justice require that we risk our lives to wait on a senile old man? Even his wise dog cannot find him."

"We have not looked in the willow coves at the creek bend," he answers, and pulls himself into the saddle of his horse. "That's in the direction we want to go. Let's search there next."

Morgeu watches from under an ivy-draped over-hang of rock at the creek bend as the riders approach. She coils her magic, preparing to strike with a cobra's precision. The blow is designed to startle the blond mare and throw the woman to the ground. The shadow of her death has already been imprinted among the washed rocks of the stream. For Arthor, a Gorgon's stare will hold him while she weaves the intricate spells of her tantric stratagem.

The enchantress floats on a tide of voices: These are the prevocalized spells already in her soul that are ready to shape events. She leans eagerly forward and watches first Arthor leading the gray and then the woman on the blond mare pass through a willow's hanging branches. Waiting for them to exit, she watches the trees catch the wind. But the riders do not exit.

The willow hangs from a spill of boulders on a hillside, and there is no back way out. *What are they doing in there?* she wonders at first, until the sliding sun finally outlasts her patience and budges her from her covert. She stalks angrily over the cobbled creek bank and whips aside the willow branches. With an explosive flap of wings, a dove bursts from the green interior and soars away. The tree stands alone. Among its thin wicker shadows, hoofprints in the sand walk serenely into the stone wall of the hill.

Chapter Eight

"Where are we?" Melania asks in a narrow voice. They ride through a night scrawled with pinwheel stars and spidery wisps of luminous green vapors. A pan of dried, cracked slurry and caked ash stretches away toward a horizon staggered with cindercones. Beyond the black volcanic hills, scarlet flames rush from the earth's depths and shake the darkness. "Is this hell?"

Arthor casts her an angry look. "I thought you had no faith in God?"

A hot wind blows a sulfurous stench from the craters, and the horses toss their heads nervously. Curled up on the saddle before Arthor, Master Sphenks whimpers. Melania looks back the way they have come, but the willow they passed through is gone, replaced by jagged lava fields and crawling smoke. She moans, "Where are we?"

"I don't know," Arthor mumbles. Fear worms in his flesh, eating the strength in his muscles, riddling his spine so that he can barely sit up and face the stinking black heat of this night. Under his breath, he prays, "Mother Mary, save us."

From out of the star-whorled sky, sparks flurry

and spin ahead. Several blow close enough for them to see that they are tiny almost-people with kelpy hair, large eyes darker than shadows, and cinnamon streaks of wings attached to naked milk blue bodies without genitals. A powdery light smudges the air around them and streaks the paths of their spiraling flights. Master Sphenks yelps at the glimmering shapes and will leap from the saddle to snap at them if Arthor does not hold it down.

"Be still, mutt," Arthor coaxes. Though he has never seen their likes before, he knows who they are from the fireside chatter of Kyner and the storytellers. "These are the faerïe."

"Yes, they must be," Melania agrees in a frantic pitch. "Look—they are flying into a cave. They are showing us the way out."

The flock of faerïes whirl into a lightless socket beneath a stark promontory of scorched rock, and Melania rides after them.

"Wait," Arthor calls. "The faerïe lead people into the hollow hills, and they are never seen again. The old people say a dragon eats them."

Melania pauses before the cave entrance, and a cool, vegetal musk luffs from a verdant radiance within. "The air is fresh in there. If there is a dragon, it's out here. I'm going in."

Arthor follows her, and as soon as he reaches the threshold of the cave, Master Sphenks leaps from the palfrey and runs ahead, fleeing the sweltering stink. Inside, the night relents. Rime-bearded cavern walls yaw wide to a daybright ledge overlooking an emerald chaparral of stunted willows and gold grass. In the distance, ice green sky lakes flash beneath a deep violet haze of mountains. The wise dog has already run down the mossy slope to the foreland fields of grass swaying green after green under a sunny gauze of golden pollen.

The horses whinny with relief, and Arthor and Melania ride down into faerïeland, obeying its happy gravity so faithfully that they bound into the grassland at a gallop. Even the ever-vigilant young warrior feels that here in the open brightness there is room for error, and he lets the gray mare go and the palfrey achieve its own exuberant freedom. "Thank you, Mother Mary," he prays aloud, surveying the wide terrain. "Thank you for sparing us the darkness and for watching over us here in the light."

Melania laughs at him. "Mother Mary hasn't helped us, you simpleton. It's the faerïe. Look at them!"

Like a single glittering soul, the cloud of faerïes moves as one, sifting into the grass, vanishing from sight, then rising farther on in silvery particles, sparkling school fish, only to fall back and rise again until they ultimately disappear in the distant green depths.

"If we were in hell, Arthor, we've found our way to heaven."

The barking of Master Sphenks flags him in the tall grass as he runs toward a lone tree. In this netherworld's mauve sky, a peach moon floats huge as a cloud, and starsmoke slants over the horizon. Arthor marvels that everything here seems to move in its stillness. *Is this a dream?*

Huge, big as a cedar, with glossy ebony bark, curled boughs, and no leaves but a clustering haze of silver flowers that twinkle in the breeze, this tree looks as though it has been built in darkness by stars. They dismount in its velvet shade and sip creek-water from the flagons. Master Sphenks drinks from Arthor's hands, then stretches beside a root-ledge and naps.

"What has happened to us?" Melania asks, touching the tree and feeling its dry, glassy surface. Fear and wonder flicker in her. "Is this Cissa's magic?"

"The Thunderer's pagan priest?" Arthor wrinkles his nose and sits wearily in the cool grass. "The faerïe of this island serve the Celts. We are inside the hollow hills. I'm sure of it."

"That is bad, isn't it?" she inquires, leaning against the tree, her legs stretched out before her. "In Aquitania, the nature spirits are called Fauni, and the priests teach us that they are the Devil's minions."

"They may be," Arthor concurs, and shuts his eyes. His closed lids glow pink as petals, and in this bright darkness he again thanks his spiritual patron for saving them. "We rode the border of hell to get here. I don't know how we'll get out."

Melania rests a hand on his. "We'll stay together."

Arthor peeks through the slit of one eye. "I have not lost the white bird," he says softly. "Not even in this place."

"I know," she concedes with a contrite nod. "I heard you praying. I would pray, too, if I thought God would listen to me." A pallor taints her cumin complexion, and her large eyes gel coldly as her beauty converges with the world's pain. "I cannot pray. I am condemned, Arthor. God has cursed me and my whole family—killed everyone but me and the crone who sent me into the world—" A slack laugh leaves her. "Sent me out to find a treasure already looted."

"You condemn yourself." Arthor feels her hand tighten atop his, and he goes on, "God loves you. That is why he sent us Jesus."

She removes her hand. "Let's not talk about Jesus again."

"He died for you."

She offers another soulless laugh. "Then why are we here?"

"God will show us a way out," Arthor insists. He grips her hand and tries to take hold of her sadness, of which he knows nothing except the loneliness he has felt since he was a child. And by that common deficit, by that mutual need, he promises, "We will find our way back to the world we know. And if we pray together, now, you and I, I know God will help you. You will find your treasure. You will win back your land."

The beat of her heart quickens. "Do you truly believe that?"

"I have staked my life on this."

Her bright stare lids with relief, and she clutches the boy's strong, hard hand. "Then I will pray with you." She rolls to her knees, bows her hopeful face beneath the dark coils of her hair, and whispers, "Arthor, help me to pray."

They kneel together under the faerïe tree and with quiet simplicity pray from the centers of their edgeless hearts. Of all their desperate needs, for what they most cry is a return to the ordinary. Melania asks the divine to spare her hell for her mortal doubts. She wants to return to the familiar world to make her own way among the common people. That would be enough for Arthor as well. He wants to contend once more in the realm of men, not at the edge of sanity.

Their prayerful energies, focused and outward-directed, stir the currents of the faerïes' chaparral, so that the bright ones rise once more from the sleep of seeds and bloom into the shapes of the conscious-type that aroused them. As tiny winged humanoids, they blur to the sere verges of the savanna, and there a fraction carry the heartstrong energy past the sky lakes and the dirgeful echoes of the mermaids' songs. A few retain the power to swirl like dust over mountains that float like purple islands rootless in the mist.

Hannes sees them streak like meteors through the spectral sky. But the elf-prince Bright Night ignores them. There is no time for faerïes, with their endless prattle about the small doings of their world. He and the carpenter have vital work to do. They are in the Happy Woods, the domain of the Daoine Síd, and have come to recruit a warband to attack Brokk.

Souls flute like birds in the tufted, vigorous pines and spruce around them, calling to others in distant groves. Religious chants sift from towering oaks and victory cries loft out of dense alders. Each type of tree has its own timbre of spirits swollen with particular desires. There are birch groves of kindness and sorrow, white poplar woodlets of laughter, willow bosks of desire, rowan holts of serenity, spindle thickets of prophecy, beech coppices of wisdom, apple orchards of magic, and reed brakes of solitude. In all of them, the Piper's music lilts a different tune. And in all, twilight leaves its golden dust on everything.

Hannes and the prince are in a conifer spinney of tantrum, where angry souls sing war songs and thrash battle dances. The shadowshapes of the dead thrive to the storm-moan and wind-whistle of the Piper and descend from the boughs, sensing the presence of visitors. Hannes cringes at the eerie sight of their smoky, lunatic shapes. The vehemence of the stamping shadow-warriors with their blurred black wings and bituminous eyes stuns him, and all through his under-being run warnings of instinctive alarm. He crouches and tries to hide beside the knees of a battered cypress, whose frantic, knobbed limbs clasp violet emptiness under the kiss of stars.

"Fear them not, Hannes," the elf-prince comforts. "They are but shades. The ones we seek are elves, who visit here to celebrate their own rage with the dead."

Out of the dreamthreads of sunset, solid figures appear. Tall beings, their long manes shining like blood, they slouch closer, strapped in swarthy leather and rawhide cords, sword belts and soft boots clasped with fangs. Thirty centuries of rage burn cold in their long green eyes, intent on outstaring fate. The prince nods to them and, without a spoken word, turns and leads them unswerving through the stormsmoke of the dead.

Hannes leaps up and hurries to Bright Night's side. None of the elfen gang pay him any more heed than they do the squall of convulsing shades. To walk among them—to stride, really—makes him feel as sleek and certain as pure silver. They will take back Excalibur. No dwarf, no sorceress can stand against them.

Soon, they depart the spinney of gnarled conifers. The spirit stallions that will carry them into battle have already gathered in the fields of dusk. They are big animals nosing around in the high, sweet grass. Through the crepuscular light of the netherworld, they shamble like blue smoke, eyes bright as candy.

Above them, Cissa senses their gathering might. To him, they sound like the song of the hive, droning with the endless, tranceful chant that turns the world to honey. He knows that they will be harder to defeat the longer they wait, for they are collecting their powers. Quickly, he reaches into his heartbeat for news from the pit, and he touches Brokk's irascible cries.

Brokk calls furiously from the underworld. Too clever for his own good, he has declined to follow Fen and has sent back the lamia. He wants the Furor to come to him. *The Dragon sleeps,* Cissa hears in the flutter of his heart. *The Dragon sleeps. Send my god to me, for I have his sword but cannot find my way out of the darkness.*

When Cissa explains this to Aelle, the chief swells with anger to cover his fear: "I am not going into the Dragon's lair. We sent Fen to get the sword. Has he failed us yet again?"

Cissa cants his bald, viper-stenciled head as if listening to the sky. "Brokk will hand the sword only to the Furor."

"I am a warrior." Aelle thumps the tree nearest him. "I fight my battles here in Middle Earth, not in Hel's underworld."

"Would you have preferred to attack Camelot while Brokk stole the sword?" Cissa asks rhetorically. He hunkers in the spiky grass, lifting his face with its designs of pain, the better to feel the wind. He listens through an aureole of sounds—bird chatter and leaf rustle—for Fen and hears him nearby. "Brokk has sent Fen back to us, to lead us through Hel's realm to the sword."

The Thunderers, scattered among the trees, some in the branches, all posted to watch for prey and danger, give no sign of seeing anyone. "Fen is not here," Aelle gruffs. "He has fled."

"No, wise Aelle. Fen is nearby. But he will not show himself. He fears we will take the lamia off him and kill him."

"Fears?" Aelle's wiry eyebrows bend angrily. "A son of Aelle fears his own people? He is unequal to heat our fire! Well he should fear us. He set out to raid and allowed himself to be captured—taken by worshipers of a prince of *peace*, no less! He gave up death in battle and the glorious afterlife in the Hall of Light for slavery to weaklings who worship love and peace! When I find him, I tell you, he will hang from the branch of the bright wind until the ravens eat his sad stamina and carry his sickness away from our tribe."

"Well and good, righteous Aelle—but for now, he

alone can lead us to the Furor's sword." Cissa probes
through the palimpsestuous layers of forest noise and
scent—chittering squirrels, jackdaw squawks, thrush
warbles, rosin scents, and pollen flux—feeling for the
bloodhum of his brother's presence. When he locates
it, pulsing all the louder for the audacious passion of
the lamia, he turns to where his father nervously thuds
the edge of his sandal against a root bulge. "Fen is
ready to lead us."

Aelle signals his approval by waving for the
Thunderers to gather. He smothers his anxiety in the
rigors of command, arranging the men around him
in a fighting wedge. "This day, for the glory of the
Furor, we visit Hel's dark kingdom, where cowards
and traitors are imprisoned. Be brave and obey our
Lord, and you will only visit this terrible place—for
you are Thunderers, destined for the corridors of
light high in the World Tree."

Cissa thuds his chest, drumming the storm god
closer. From the sky, a cloud lowers, sifting through
the forest branches and enclosing the war party in a
luminous fog aswirl with mother-of-pearl colors.
Silence swells. Bird noise and the wind's hymnal
cease. As shadow-figures, the warriors advance, following their snake-priest, who feels Fen among the
witchgrass, backing away, retreating from this world.

Acid sunlight blisters and foams at the shadow
limit of the hollow hills. Fen lingers there until he is
sure the Thunderers follow him. He knows he is
dead in their eyes already. Without the lamia, he
would be a corpse. The lamia is his strength and his
damnation. For now, he must endure it. Its lunar fire

lights the way for him over the black snaky surface of
lava rock. Its death chill cools him in the volcanic
swelter. Its strength keeps him running ahead of the
war party, easy as a breeze.

Ahead, among heat-shattered boulders of amber
glass that look exoskeletal as giant insects, the dwarf's
witch waits. "My brother has escaped me," she
whines, and the darkness stains her with the colors of
silence. "I must go with you into the hollow hills to
find them. Take me with you."

Fen does not even try to stop the lamia from
leaping forth to devour this frightful woman. The
monster's fanged thrust crashes into the spun-glass
rocks, and shards fly like small birds. Weaker for the
effort, the lamia slinks back into Fen, who must keep
moving. The Thunderers are coming. The ghost-lit
darkness and the baked stink of the underworld do
not deter them. They run with the Furor, and soon
they will be upon him.

At his side, the witch appears again, night in her
eyes, bloodshadows in her wild hair. "Do not try to
devour me," she threatens, "or your lamia will grow
too weak to protect you in this place."

"What do you want?" Fen gasps, dragging himself among waist-high monticules of ash.

"Only your guidance into the hollow hills, back
toward Brokk." She keeps a respectful distance, this
witch in torn green satin, with the bones of a man in
her shoulders and jaw, and a woman's coy, helpless
smile. "I cannot find my own way down here. I will
follow you."

Fen ignores her. He wants only to complete his

mission and slip away. If he can find again the dark-haired woman with the urn of sphinxes, perhaps he can free himself from the lamia and win a new life.

The lamia churns in him, indecisive about striking at Morgeu again. Wary about losing more power, it decides to put all its strength into crossing this balesome terrain. Surely, the Thunderers will feed it later. Flames run through the unreckonable darkness far ahead, bright as blood, and the lamia puts its focus there.

Then, at its back, a startling wind arrives. Morgeu knows at once what this is and falls to her knees in the scorched furrows of fused sand. The wavering heat blows away in an arctic mayhem of glacial thunder, blizzardsmoke, and frost rays. "Morgeu the Doomed," a wide voice opens in her head, and the red life in her shivers blue. "Is it true the Dragon slumbers?"

"Yes, All-Seeing Father!" the enchantress cries. Without the protection of her old demon allies, she is but a fragile snowflake in the blustery presence of the Furor. "The Dragon sleeps deeply."

The Furor releases her, satisfied. Always before, he has entered these dark regions surreptitiously to avoid the ravenous attention of the Drinker of Lives. Now at last he can storm through these mephitic caverns fearlessly. Nothing here can challenge his power. Shrouded in his blue mantle of boreal wind, he steps over the animal lives of Morgeu, Fen, and the Thunderers, and strides boldly into the hissing darkness of stinking fumes.

A tunnel of snow trails behind the god, and the Thunderers charge through it. Morgeu and Fen run ahead of them, afraid to fall back and be trampled or hacked by their naked swords. The lamia pours forth its liquid strength and sweeps them onward. Fen does not object to the witch clamping onto him, using the lamia's power to fly with him through the fire-breathing shadows and bright vortices of snow sizzling to hot rain and steam. She is another shield from the Thunderers, who want to break his bones to retrieve their pride.

Abruptly, the Furor halts, and lightning staggers around him, shattering boulders and scattering ash in a hot scurf of sparks and spinning embers. Silver rivers of melted ice run away from him, sibilant as snakes among the hot rocks. He shrinks. All godliness seems to melt away from him, and he stands among the rubble stone in the darkness, a robust old man. Reflections of fugitive flames from distant calderas flimmer in his one blue eye, and he seems to perceive as if for the first time the enormous depth of this somber, black waste.

Cissa is the first to realize that the Furor is not reduced. The god sees with an eye ignited by prophecy. He only appears to shrink as his vision goes ahead of him.

"He sees our enemy," Cissa whispers to the others.

The Thunderers stand gawking among melted shapes of smoldering scrog and fulgurite. They peer through shredded steam with raw amazement at their deity, standing ahead of them in the cratered terrain, leaning on his spear like one of their own. Dark light, like steel dust, shines around him. Only that divine sign distinguishes him from a man—albeit a huge man with a massive brow scored by age and dented with war scars; his riven cheeks rise in creases from an abundant gray beard toward an empty socket and one mad, staring eye blue as a sky a thousand years deep.

When they can muster enough heart to remove their adoring gazes from him, they see what he sees. Far ahead, through a black cleft in a lava lakebed, a war gang of Síd elves ride forth on shaggy blue spirit horses.

It is Prince Bright Night and Hannes, leading their warriors to attack Brokk. At the sight of the Furor standing in the underworld surrounded by an energy field more intense than a star, the horses balk and nearly throw their riders. Bright Night signs for them to retreat, to fly back through the cleft to the emerald chaparral of faerïeland and the mermaids' sky lakes. But too late.

An ominous chill runs through the hot chambers, and blue licks of electric fire trace the tormented outlines of magma channels, sockets of dried pools, and slag spires. Fans of celestial brilliance cast grotesque shadows across the enormous grotto. The captured night of the underworld pulses, ever faster, until it strobes sharp, quick flashes of terror from among the Síd.

Bright Night howls for his warriors to fall back. Hannes clings frantically to the prince's back as the wild horses collide and throw riders into the quick shadows. Then the nimble blue flames vanish, and the night ranges return to their wrathful blackness.

The screaming of the horses and the cries of the elves clash for a blind and terrible moment.

Suddenly, from across the dark, the Furor's spear reaches out like a lance of white sunlight. When it lands among the scrambling elves, several horses and their riders vaporize instantly in startling bursts of shadowshapes smeared by radiance, and a whirlwind shock wave flings the others in every direction, like so much world dust blowing into the void.

---∞---

Chapter Nine

The faerïeland's chaparral grass and dwarf willows sway, listening to the nether night filled with lights. Arthor and Melania gaze up with naked awe at the starry heavens of the underworld, wondering how the blotched moon and these misty starwheels can be visible down here inside the hollow hills. They clamber through the curly boughs of the giant black tree and perch high among its silver, clustered blossoms, hoping to see the secrets of this inner sky.

Craters sleep in the ashes of the moon. The whirlpools of stars fling feathers through the lavender void, and the amplified images of the pure night open new mysteries. Melania lifts the lovely shadow of her face toward the wind, inspiring desire in Arthor hard as cold.

All at once, the wonder drains from her placid features, and fear startles her. "Arthor, look!"

The dark arrow of her face points beyond this wide plain of grass ripples to a charred ridge on a niter cliff not visible from below. It is the desolate ashlands they rode down from. At this height, they can peer into the volcanic terrain of burned brimstone and melted rocks and see the Furor. To them, he appears as an enraged giant, his one mad eye bulged out with pain and ire and the empty socket sunken to the skullrim; bone shines through his dented brow and twisted nose bridge, and his great beard and tangled mane haze into the darkness like battlesmoke.

His fabulous falcon hat and mantle blue as a lost piece of sky identify him as the barbarian's chief god. At his feet, they see a swarming troop of blue horses mounted by frantic men with streaming red hair. The radiant impact of the god's spear twists away the faces of Melania and Arthor. When they look again, the blue horses and their riders are erased in smoke. The Furor pulls his spear out of the steaming ground and stalks off through the fiery vapors, a giant lumbering through the ruins of sunset.

Thunder widens across the fields, and Master Sphenks startles awake with a burst of barking.

"Prayer has not saved us!" Melania despairs, and skids along the glassy bough, eager to reach the ground, far out of sight of the murderous god.

Arthor follows. "If the barbarian god is on the black cliffs, perhaps that is where we will find the exit to the upper world."

Melania looks up at him with a horrified expression. "I'm not going back into that hell," she asserts, and slides to the groin of the tree, her gown blossoming with caught air. "If the north god is there, the Thunderers must be there as well—and Cissa. I think they are hunting us."

"Don't be silly." Arthor slips after her down a curved length of bough, swings from a lower branch, and drops to the ground. "We are nothing to them."

He offers his hand to help her down, but she ignores him and plops into the grass, her impact blowing pollen into the wind. She rises and shakes her coiled hair from her eyes. "Cissa used me to anchor the Furor's lover in the tribe. I was important to them. They will come after me."

"Then we should move," he says, and walks toward where the horses graze.

"But where can we go?"

"I don't know." The shadow of the dog glides ahead through the field. "We will ride. We will search for a way out."

"You saw the north god, too," Melania says, running after him and catching him by the elbow. The sixth sense that Cissa opened in her with his snaky magic brims in her again. Did she alone see the mad god from the treetop? A depthful fear arrives inside her chest—a fear that threatens to return her to the mute trance of the viper-priest's nightmare. She squeezes Arthor's arm forcefully. "You saw him."

He steps back from the fixed and desperate wideness of her stare. He has never seen madness before. He thought he had seen it on the battlefield in the wild stares of men facing down death, but he has not. "Yes."

"I am glad." Her frightened face looks relieved and dolorous in the tattoo of light from the branches. "I feared that the magic Cissa worked on me had

made me the Furor's forever." Her eyes search his for
understanding. "He told me that the gods alone
know how lovely the unspeakable must be. And
when the god's lover spoke in me, when the goddess
spoke—the pain—" The peril of tears breaks her
stare, and she looks away. "The pain was bigger than
I could hold."

Arthor ventures to put a hand to her cheek. "You
are free of that now, Melania. Look around you. The
Furor has gone off. He is not looking for us."

She lifts a look of anguish. "Prayer did not work,
Arthor. You said if we prayed, God would show us a
way out."

"Give it time."

"Time?" She steps back a pace. "Why does the
Christian God need time? You saw the Furor. He is
here! He walks among us. I do not think that our
prayers go to a god who hears us or cares."

A prong of sadness lifts his eyebrows. "Have you
no faith at all?"

"I have faith in what I see." She motions to the
anthracitic cliffs. "Who were those people the Furor
destroyed?"

"Faerïe-folk, I think." Arthor rummages for
fireside memories. "Maybe elves. Kyner spoke of
elves."

"Their god did not hear their prayers, either," she
says unhappily—and sadness heightens her beauty, as
though all that is desirable about her hides a secret, a
truth whose terrible cost denies all hope. "We are
alone down here, Arthor—and there is no God to
help us."

The thought that the heaven of mercy and love is tenantless, that a woman with an angel's loveliness could believe this, frightens him. "Stop this." Arthor waves her away in disgust and whistles for the dog. "You are a Christian woman. Jesus died for you. How can you abandon him?"

"He has abandoned us."

"I say no." He takes the reins of the palfrey and swings himself up into the saddle. "We are alive. You are free of Cissa and his evil gods." He leans down, and his golden eyes slim as if with threat. "The Thunderers are evil. And their gods are evil. They hurt you. We both saw the Furor kill the elves, the people of this secret land. That god is evil, and so he walks this world that God has given to the Devil. I tell you, woman, our prayers have been heard in heaven. And now we will find our way out of here."

Arthor's bold certainty comforts Melania, and she nods softly, like a child, and goes for her horse. Arthor blows a silent sigh, not at all sure that prayer can pay the deficit that evicted them from the natural world. But he has nothing else to offer her. He rides to the gray mare, takes its reins, and walks the horses slowly through the chaparral grass and shrubs, wondering where to go.

Far above him, in the yew tree's skeletal silence, Merlin cannot bear the paralysis that keeps them apart. He allows himself to dissolve toward sleep, and as his body slumbers, he glides with his dreambody into the hollow hills. Like a small flame, he shivers in the dark. Quickly, he finds his way over the cinder tracts, following the Furor's massive footprints in the ash.

Soon, he flutters above the impact site of the Furor's spear. The ruptured rocks reflect his spirit light in a crazy mosaic of seared glass. All that remains of the dead elves and their horses has pooled in the rubble to patches of shriveled sludge, a gummy tar in the seams of the cracked rock plates. Circling through the slaggy grotto, he finds several wounded elves cast off by the blast, bleeding to mist. He can do nothing for them. They are already merely waxen shapes, soft limbs and harrowed faces melted over rocks sharp as shards of pottery.

He flits over the crazed stone floor of broken cobbles and spoilbanks of ash, searching for survivors. But he is only a spark, and the spurts of flame that leap from the grouts of broken pavement threaten him. He spirals back upward to his sleeping body, never noticing the limbs sticking out of a scoria dune, his own floppy-brimmed conical hat perched at its crest.

Hannes pushes free of the suffocating soot, his round face with its jug ears and pug nose smutted with carbon. He exhales a lungful of chalky smoke, and dust falls from his blinking eyes that wink wide and white as a statue's in his black face. Aching in every joint, he rises, streaming fumes and powdery dross. Magic alone spared his life, though now he wishes it had not.

Anger pulses in him. The elf-prince, Bright Night, is gone, fetched away in the searing blast that evaporated the others. Hannes coughs smoke and swats dusty clouds from his robes. A shuddering sickness competes with his rage at the senseless deaths of the others, and he must stand still and chant a calming spell to ease his stomach back from his diaphragm.

Calmed to a quiet fury, Hannes picks up his hat and staggers through the flame-flickering night-world, a smoking mess. He gradually gathers the pieces of his strength out of the remote reaches of shock and fits them back into his stunned body. *All is lost,* he moans to himself. *The elves dead—Excalibur lost. Hannes, you fool. You murderous fool, with your pawky dreams of wizardry—look what you have done! Why are you yet alive?*

Determined to correct that wrong, to pay for his terrible blunders with his worn and foolish life, he follows the red glim of the Furor's footfalls. Head slung forward like an ocelot, he hurries along, reading out of the darkness the fateful light of his own necessary doom.

If the Furor listened, the god would hear the small man's desperation. But the All-Seeing Father does not pay any heed to his back, which is protected by the Thunderers. Instead, he swings his attention ahead of him, searching out more elves, other war parties intent on thwarting him from reclaiming his sword. In the jade chasm that leads down into faerïeland, he spies Arthor and Melania riding among water meadows. He does not know who they are except that they are out of place, humans in the hollow hills where only elves and faerïes belong. They must be destroyed yet are not worth the effort of a spear throw. He may need that strength for greater dangers ahead.

With a thought, he commands Fen to feed his lamia with their lives. Cissa, who has no desire to distract his god with the annoyingly minor detail that the woman below once helped the Furor to meet his lover in human form, signs for Fen to go.

Morgeu the Fey watches helplessly from behind an obelisk of lava rock as Fen lopes down the shattered steps of the cliff trail to the ledges of frothy moss verging the chaparral. When the Furor threw his spear, she sidled deeper into the darkness, hoping to be ignored. If she moves now, they will see her, and she dreads the attention of the furious god. She must let Fen go. He will slay her brother, and what tantric designs she has for taking revenge on Merlin with her womb will die with the youth. Still, she consoles herself, the demon Lailoken will suffer to lose the pawn he wanted for king—and there yet remains hope that her own son Gawain shall wear the crown.

The Furor moves on, and the Thunderers drift after him like phantoms. Morgeu tarries behind, daring to separate herself from the murderous pack at risk of losing herself in the netherworld. She will have to trust in Fen to lead her out of the hollow hills, and she fades into the squalid fumes and edges toward the cleft that opens to the fragrant chaparral. She does not dare actually enter the faerïeland, fearing that the Furor or Cissa will see her. But here, on a barren weal of sulfur rock, she crouches just close enough to sip the cool air and wait. When Fen has killed the pretender, he will come back this way, and she will entice him to lead her out of this hell.

Fen sprints among the grass swords, eager to be away from the Thunderers and their cruel god. The lamia spurs him on, its mind, white as fog, carries one thought—to eat. Shedding distance like a serpent's skin, he streams through the green reeds and bright haloes of water lilies. The riders have not yet seen him, and he sweeps toward them, low to the soft ground, ready to spring.

The starry skies above thread an eerie feeling through him that competes with the lamia's hunger. With his fist, he presses the thunderbolt scar on his chest, feeling his slamming heart. He is still a man. Yet the vapor-strewn heavens that glitter as if starred with ice make him feel as though he has found the afterlife, and the lamia's turbulent strength in him is the power of a ghoul. The future is as hopeless as though he were already dead.

These doubts weaken his glide through the balmy grass, and when he pounces, the small dog senses him and has time to bark frantically. The palfrey skitters, and Arthor throws himself flat against its neck. Melania's scream skins the still air a moment before the lamia strikes. Its claws scythe the saddle where the boy sat as he flops into the loam. He rolls to his back, and the lodestone knife and the Bulgar saber cut the space above him.

The grin of skeletal jaws lifts away like smoke, and Fen hops back, amazed at the boy's agility. Arthor bounces to his feet, saber twirling, lodestone knife steady. His movements are precise as he advances,

offering no chink of vulnerability, no hesitation, and
Fen finds himself wondering in astonishment at how
one so young can display such deft killing instinct.
The youth's amber gaze burns cold and pitiless, offering malign depths in which the Saxon recognizes that
death alone holds promise.

Already, the lamia has shied away from the killer
and flexes toward Melania. Fen jumps backward,
pulling the lamia after him. He does not want her
killed, for she is the witch who knows how to remove
this monster from his flesh. He calls to her, "Woman,
save me!"

Melania pulls her horse to the side, positioning
herself behind Arthor so that the lodestone knife is
between her and the lamia. "Remove the guardian
band!" she cries out to the Saxon. "Then Arthor can
use the knife to put the lamia in the urn." She holds
up the ornate crock, and it hangs against the dizzy
stars like a black heart.

Fen puts a hand to the band about his throat,
retreating before Arthor's steady advance. "If I remove
this," he says sharply, "the lamia will devour me."

"Arthor will save you with the knife," Melania
promises.

Fen looks into those remote golden eyes and
shakes his head. "No. He will kill me."

"Arthor, tell him," Melania insists, and slides off
the gray mare. "You can capture the lamia with the
knife. I have the urn."

With her hand on his shoulder, he stops his lethal
advance and straightens, sword and dagger poised.

"Put your sword away," Melania orders.

"He tried to kill me," Arthor says, and the yapping dog agrees, sliding back and forth through the grass, snarling at the evil presence.

"It's the lamia, Arthor." Melania presses close to him, wanting to physically impose her will. "When he takes off the guardian band, it cannot hide in his body anymore. We can catch it with the knife and the urn."

"Let me kill him and the lamia." Only Melania's firm grip on his shoulder dissuades him from this. He does not want to drive her further from him by disobeying her—yet Fen has twice before tried to murder him.

"He will kill me," Fen says, and continues backing off. "Melania—take the magic knife from him. Come to me. Help me."

"Don't do it, Melania," Arthor warns. "He's a barbarian. He'll use the lamia on me, then take you to Cissa to earn his way back into his tribe."

"No." Fen stands with his arms open at his side, exposing his bruised and cut nakedness clothed only in the shimmer of the lamia's spidery webs. "The Thunderers are ashamed of me. Without the lamia, they would sacrifice me to the Furor. If you help me, I will not betray your trust."

"If you want trust," Arthor quickly responds, "then trust us. Come closer. Take off the throat band. Let us free you from the lamia."

Fen's heart enlarges at the thought of freedom—but as his hands touch the guardian band, he sees again the remote steadiness of the young warrior's stare. Neither sword nor dagger is lowered, and by

that the Saxon knows Arthor will attack. He will kill
both the lamia and him. The barking dog, who once
saved Arthor from the thrown ax, urges him to save
them from the monster. In an instant, Arthor will fly
forward to accomplish his warrior's vow. And at that
moment, there passes between them a fatal understanding.

Melania senses it and tries to hold Arthor back,
but he is too strong. With a shout, he doffs her grasp,
throwing her onto her back in the grass. He flies forward with incredible speed, saber weaving, dagger
held low, cocked to rip upward. If Melania had not
slowed his initial forward burst, not even the lamia
could have saved Fen. As it is, the silver arc of the
saber caresses the Saxon with its wind, and the lamia
barely sweeps him away before the heavy blade spins
around, light as a bird in the man-child's expert grasp,
and slices through his shadow.

Fen floats off through the waving grass, amazed
to have felt the cold aura of Short-Life and still find
himself whole. The boy is a killer. The only help Fen
can expect from him is the succor of death. And so he
flies far across the chaparral, exiled from the Thunderers and their enraged god and driven from the
witch who can save him.

But now he knows her name. *Melania*. In the
sound of it, the lamia's memories of her shapeshift,
and he bounds through the field in her guise but
naked, her lengthy curls brushing the voluptuous
swerves of her body. As Melania's great-grandmother,
a shriveled crone with one weak eye and one empty
eye, he sits on the leopard-spotted mudbank of the

lake listening to the mermaids singing their faultless songs to the moon.

Melania swims through the tall grass calling for him. Arthor sheathes Short-Life and the stone dagger and gathers the horses. Master Sphenks, sensing some animal, barks from out of sight, charging toward the black cliffs.

"He's gone," Arthor says, leading the horses to where Melania stands staring up through levels of tasseled fields and dusky swales toward the green sky lakes.

She turns on him angrily. "Why did you try to kill him? He has no weapon."

"He carries the lamia. And he's a Saxon."

His callousness brings an irate flush to her frown. "We could have helped him."

"Why?" Arthor asks, restraining his own annoyance at her simpleminded trust of the enemy. "He would not have helped us."

She turns away with a vile expression that chills him. "You are no Christian."

"I am a living Christian," he replies hotly, angry at her for hating him, "alive because I do not trust barbarians. He attacked us. Three times he has tried to slay me. Why do you care if he lives or not?"

She does not look at him but keeps her attention fixed on the ethereal horizons under the mauve sky with its fumes of stars.

"You like him, don't you?" Arthor feels his insides cringe at the sound of his own voice. "Why? Is it his handsome face? It's a barbarian's face."

"Like yours?" she asks coolly, and does not turn to see the sting of her words.

Arthor does not reply. His focus has shifted away from her to a tall, shadowy figure advancing through the dwarf shrubs of the chaparral. Master Sphenks comes running from there, tail tucked.

"He could have killed me and he did not," Melania goes on, not noticing the stranger. "If I can help him, I will."

"Someone is coming," Arthor warns, hand resting on the hilt of his saber. "It looks like the gleeman."

The shadowy shape of Merlin approaches among the scrubby trees. He wears crisp robes, colorful as an angel's, and his beard and long hair float about him like a visual music.

"That is not the gleeman," Melania observes.

"No," Arthor agrees. "Is it Fen shapeshifting?"

"I don't think so." A baleful pallor creeps over her as she watches the stranger looming closer, seeming to float across the cluttered terrain, a rainbow icon swathed in his own wind. "Arthor, I'm afraid. Let us ride from him."

"Yes." He hands her the reins of the blond mare and climbs onto his palfrey. Master Sphenks has already rushed away and disappears in the bush. They gallop in pursuit of its fretful barking.

But the weird figure draws closer under the wide moon. The horses spook and buck, and Arthor seizes the blond mare's reins so Melania can dismount. Then he jumps down himself and watches the horses charge off in a fright through the shrubs and miniature trees.

Arthor pushes Melania behind him and draws the

lodestone dagger. At the sight of it, the flying lamia snaps away in terror, and Brokk hurtles forward and nearly collapses in the shrubs. The sword Lightning flashes out of nothing and stabs into the ground, jolting him to a full stop. The dwarf's large, gold-whiskered face grins upward with unconcealed delight.

The skinny lives before him are his reward for enduring the darkness and the stink long enough to be certain that the Dragon sleeps. Once convinced of that, the dwarf allowed himself to roam freely through the netherworld, swatting at faeries with the Furor's sword, venting his rage at the spool of days undone by Bright Night's trickery in leading him here. "And now look!" he speaks aloud with delight. "I have found again the Roman witch of the lamia!" He leers at Melania, then lifts a menacing sneer toward Arthor. "And you, boy—who are you?"

"It's the Furor's dwarf!" Melania gasps from behind Arthor. "He has the twin lamia."

Arthor draws Short-Life, and Brokk laughs. With a slippery twist of his wrist, the sword Lightning sweeps the saber from Arthor's grasp and drops it into the heavy grass. The dwarf's sword tip cuts fanciful designs of light and bright air and comes to deadly stillness at the crook of Arthor's collar-bones.

"Who are you, child?" the dwarf snarls.

"I am Arthor."

"Arthor?" The snarl deforms to a querying frown. "What kind of name is that?"

"My own name."

A flickering smile crosses the dwarf's bellicose face. "You are a brave young one. But this—" He slashes the Celtic cross of Arthor's tunic, the sword barely moving in his heavy hand. "This is an evil emblem." His hard eyes glitter. "Are you an evil one?"

Arthor cannot hear his own voice for the thunder of his heart. "I am a Christian man."

The dwarf's twisted eyebrows rise. "A *Christian* man in the hollow hills with the Roman witch of the lamia! What a marvel, what a discovery of wonder this is for me. How came you here, Christian Arthor?"

"I don't know." Arthor does not budge his stare from the dwarf's eyes of cracked blue ice, but his eyebrows shrug and he strives to speak calmly. "We rode here—looking for a gleeman."

Brokk's wide mouth turns downward with disbelief. "You *rode* here—on those slow, ponderous horses?" He flicks a motion to where the heavy-chested horses nervously wait in the field of stunted trees.

"Yes."

"Looking for a gleeman?"

"Yes."

"But you haven't found him." Brokk taps Arthor's shoulder with the sword and lowers the weapon. "That is why there are three horses and only two of you, eh? Well, call your horses, boy. We will ride together. If you can ride in, perhaps you can ride out." The sword Lightning touches Arthor's left hand, which still holds the lodestone dagger. "And I will have this stone knife that the lamia fear." He takes the dagger and points it at Melania. "And you and I—" He shows large teeth at the alarm that quakes through her. "You and I will discover together why the Norns have brought us again to each other."

Chapter Ten

The play of shadows through the yew branches shows Merlin how the fugitive hours escape him while he strives in vain to break Morgeu's enchantment. His own inner monkeys yawp and grin. They are the animal powers of his body that have fled their cages in his muscles and will not go back in. They want to run free, the way his spirit ran free as a demon. Morgeu has used his memories of his former life to bewitch him.

Slowly, Merlin must unravel those memories. He must forget that he ever was a demon. But memory is its own unbearable mirror. For a long time, he lies in his stillness, immobilized by sad recollections of the wreckage he has made of numerous beings on many tiny hopeful worlds that he visited in his raging flights across the void. The mind is bottomless. Below memory is darkness—the emptiness that interpenetrates and encloses the neural jungle of his brain—the void that yaws between atoms and galaxies. Without it, nothing could exist. Yet with it, heaven is forfeit. And that is the source of his demonic sorrow.

Embittered memories of losing heaven swarm through Merlin's oldest and deepest memories. Yet, further back than that despair is his remembrance of heaven itself. And that is where he must go to break Morgeu's spell. Far back into himself he journeys, past the old ghosts of his fury, past the initial shock of falling into the void, back to heaven remembered and his faithfulness to the light.

Merlin's memory of heaven welds him to a timeless rapture. At first, he resists it, because he fears that he will sink deeper into coma and maybe not wake for days, maybe never. Then he rails all the more wildly at Morgeu for the evil cunning of her enchantment. And the inner monkeys grin and yawp louder.

At last, the wizard accepts his fate. He returns in memory to the time before time, before the long, long loneliness. He conjures again the light that casts death's shadow, the first light, the pure energy of origin. The light absorbs him. In its radiant refuge, he forgets all shadows—distance, form, and memory— and he exists again without body or mind. He exists like a jewel, like minerals that have dwelt a long time in darkness and are astonished to find themselves clear and full of light.

But this is only a memory. The blood circling in his veins calls him back from his serene recall—and he finds that the inner monkeys are gone. He sits up. The shadows have carried only a few minutes away.

All the more limber from his deep rest, Merlin bounds out of the yew enclosure. The sunlight hurts his eyes as he hurries through the thistle field to the

willow banks of the creek, searching for Arthor. Of
course, he is gone. *But where?*

Faerïes flutter in the willow shadows like moist
starlight, and the wizard hurries there. Behind a green
curtain of willow withes, the faerïes glitter against the
rock wall of a hillside. Underfoot, hoofprints walk
into the boulders, and in the air, the wizard hears the
creaking of saddles.

Morgeu's spell helps him now, because the deep
trance that he had to enter to break her enchantment
has suffused him with more power than usual. He
chants for the faerïes to guide him into the hollow
hills. Like bees, the golden bodies of the faerïes tuck
themselves behind the creepers dangling over the
rock wall. Merlin parts the veil and finds a narrow
crevice through which he must squeeze sideways.

Inside, black acres of cinders and ash crawl
through poisonous air toward a serrated horizon of
windy flames. Dead stars float in the arched darkness
looking like the purple embers of a scattered fire.
Their fumes wrinkle the lightless void with luminescent plasmas, and by their vague light, the wizard
finds his way toward the precincts of flame.

As he advances through the addling heat, discard-
ing his hat of woven ivy and breathing the putrid air
through his mouth, he seeks out the Furor's tracks
that he saw earlier in his trance. They shine with astral
light in the sullage of soot where the god has walked.
So intent is he on finding his way to the Furor, hoping that Arthor has not encountered the war god, that
he does not see Morgeu hiding under an outcropping
of lava.

She watches him pass and keeps her mind clear so he will not hear her thoughts. With her attention focused beyond her sweltering niche, on the plangent breeze from faerïeland lapping at the scalloped edges of the scorched lava cliffs, she eludes detection. The wizard passes, and she squirms out of her blistered crevice and climbs down the niter-crusted rocks to the mossy slopes and purling breezes.

No longer does she care if the Furor notices her. The acid stink of the burned ranges is unbearable. She staggers into the chaparral and falls to her knees before a rivulet of glacial water. She will wait here for Fen to return from his homicidal mission. With her smutched face leaning into the icy water, she rolls up her small, weary eyes toward the bloated moon and the stars in their webs of time, and she prays it will not be long.

While she slakes her thirst, Arthor, Melania, and Brokk ride out of the fields of dwarf trees toward the softer grasslands. The dwarf wants to get close to the sky lakes that gleam like valuable stones in the distance. He wants to hear the mermaids singing while he takes his pleasure with the Roman witch.

Sexuality is not a hasty desire among dwarfs as it is with organic creatures. For Brokk, his whim to penetrate the witch is a mechanical delusion—an unrealistic ambition to imitate the gods and experience something beautiful and unexplained. After he experiments with her, he will ride into the ice mountains and seek there a way out.

The Christian boy will prove useful if any elves appear. They are always willing to trade information for humans, whom they must use for slaves now that the Dragon sleeps and no longer needs to be fed. For an able and young man like this Arthor, the elves will surely show the dwarf the path to the upper world. If not, there is always the sword.

The savor of the dwarf's well-thought-out plan vanishes, empty as a mirage, when he sees at the speckled lip of the lake the Furor, his beard and mane huge as fog. Around him stand the Thunderers, hairy and lean as wolves.

Brokk lifts the sword Lightning in salute and sends forward Melania and Arthor on their horses as tribute. "Hail, All-Seeing Fath—"

"Silence!" the Furor shouts, and the wild grasses jump, and the mermaids' indecipherable songs disappear. "Why have you made me come down here into the stinking roots of the Tree to get my sword?"

"My Lord—" Brokk falls from the gray mare and thuds to his knees. "I sent for you to be certain that the elves did not trick me. I did not want to lose the sword."

"When must a god come to a dwarf?" the Furor asks, veins thick at his temples. "My life is in jeopardy here."

"No, my lord," the dwarf blurts, holding the sword Lightning forward in both hands. "The Dragon sleeps."

"So you say." The god groans, and steps forward to receive his weapon. "The Síd are devious. It were better that you had risked losing this sword to them than bring me here, in the rootlands where the Dragon's claw easily reaches."

The Furor snatches the sword and whirls it over his head so swiftly it flashes like mirror dust. "And why are these two alive? I ordered them slain."

Melania whimpers and moves to pull her horse around and run, but Arthor seizes the reins and steadies her with a hard stare. Flight is certain death. That he knows, having seen the one-eyed god spin the sword like fire. *Better to die facing death than fleeing,* his steady gaze tells her, and she relents and sits in her saddle, lame as a skeleton.

Arthor feels like he is floating. There is no bottom to his fear. He stares into the god as into an abyss, and his heartbeat wavers in him like a dream.

Cissa comes forward, bald and leering. "I will do the ritual killing, here in the rootlands of our enemy, and we will leave this cursed place stained with Christian blood."

The Furor holds the hilt of the sword toward the viper-priest. "Do it."

Cissa takes the sword Lightning and feels the Furor's aura upon the weapon—a salt-sea fragrance that skirls up his arm like wind and makes him feel strong as a tree. A serpent grin widens along his tattooed jaw. He motions with the weapon for the riders to dismount.

Melania's legs cannot hold her, and she sinks to her knees, head bowed, hands fisted in the grass with terrified futility. Arthor slides off his palfrey and takes his shield in his hands. Courage failing, balance fading, he grips the buckler hard and stares intently at the serene and sorrowful face of the Virgin. What she has suffered eats a hole in his heart. Almost immediately, his fright diminishes enough for him to turn and face his killers.

The sight of the Furor, with his dark soul in the empty socket of a face like a cliff, penetrates him with the sun's force and bleaches his strength. Before this tremendous entity, he is no more than a dead white thing. All thoughts of appeal, all words of beggary and mercy turn colorless and silent in his mind with a terror of being. A hot flush runs down his leg from his frightened bladder, and he leans on the air and must grip the shield in his numb hands with all his might to keep from falling.

"Mother Mary," he begins to pray aloud, his voice stony, oracular, "see your Son's enemies before me, heartless in their vanity. See them, Mother, and show me now, in this dire and fatal moment—oh, please! Show me now that your Son's love for us is not perished—even in this hateful place. For though God shall bring every work into judgment by the witness of your Son—yet all mercy shall come from you, Mother. Do not forsake us to evil, Mother! Show us your mercy—for the love of your Son!"

Cissa laughs like a cough of winter gust, and the sword Lightning keens softly as it spins over the viper-priest's head. He says something in his barbarian tongue that makes Brokk and the Thunderers laugh— "Let's see if he sings as pretty with a foretaste of oblivion!"—and he swings the sword tip with a razor's accuracy so that it slashes across Arthor's chest, fluttering the rags of his tunic and inflicting a burning flesh weal.

Arthor drops his shield and cries out but does not

fall. A brush of silver air slices through the space where he would have fallen.

"Courage wins him another song," Cissa jeers, passing the turning sword from hand to hand, "before the wind sings in his bones."

But Arthor cannot find the prayer in him anymore. The searing pain across his chest and the deepening cold of certain death have taken its place. Sweat glitters its sequins on his young, shivering face.

"Kill him, Cissa," Brokk says, eager to be done with the boy and on to the woman.

"Where is Mother?" Cissa taunts, and the sword Lightning rises high for the blurred arc that will swipe the Christian's proud head from his sobbing shoulders.

"Stop!" A voice loud, dark and hot as thunder rolls over the savanna.

Cissa's arm locks up like iron, and he grimaces as if stabbed.

Arthor and Melania turn to look at where the Furor and the Thunderers are glaring. Out of the sere grass, a tall, lanky man with a long, long beard rises.

"It's the gleeman!" Melania sings to Arthor.

The narrow old man throws both his hands up and shouts in his supernaturally big voice a barbarous cry. The sword in Cissa's hand wrenches free and flies on the loud wings of the cry directly at the Furor. The scowling god blocks the thrown blade with his spear. Weirdly, it spins about the shaft of the spear and drives hard into the Furor's shoulder.

A monstrous cry flays hearing to deafness and throws everyone into the grass but the howling god and the skinny old man. From where the sword is ripped free, silky darkness spills upward like squid ink, blotting the onrush of stars.

Arthor clasps Melania's hands, and their shrill faces gawk at each other through the grass stems. "You were right all along," Arthor cries as their deafness subsides. "I don't think he is a gleeman."

"Lailoken!" the Furor shouts, and hurls the sword Lightning at him, which he instantly regrets.

The wizard diverts the flashing blade with another crazed cry that sends it toppling across the grassland. All his strength is nearly spent now, but he is satisfied. He has fulfilled the mission given him by the angels and given all he has to serve his king.

Master Sphenks, who cowers behind him, charges away across the savanna, released from the magic spell that Merlin used to summon it so that he could find Arthor. Had he the energy, the wizard, out of gratitude, would cast over it more of the invisibility that had hidden them as they approached this fateful encounter. But he barely has the strength left to remain standing before the Furor's wrathful immensity.

With the blue veins in his face darkening, the wounded god strides forward and jabs with his spear. Merlin catches the sharp tip under his arms and feels the icy metal against his chest as it cuts through his tunic. Hoisted off his feet, the wizard clings to the spear and hangs for a moment above Arthor and Melania. "Run!" he calls to them, his aged face a rage of fright. "Run!"

Arthor leaps as if spurred and pulls Melania after

him. The Thunderers rise to stop them. But the wizard screams a shrill barbarous command with the last wisps of his strength, and the grass tangles their ankles and yanks them back to the ground.

Shaking with pain and anger, the Furor whips his spear, throwing Merlin free. Then he shambles over him and places the spear tip at his heart. The earth's rotation and the moon's gravitational ambit pivot here in the demon's heart. Rage wants the god to impale him instantly and explode him to chaos. But wisdom won from pain insists he hold him fast under his spear and draw from the fulcrum of his cosmic being the very life-force that binds the atomic seams of his body.

Merlin writhes as the light in his bones bleeds out of him and his life blurs. Silences join out of the spaces between nerves, widening emptiness.

While the enraged god extracts the vitality from the demon that the Furor needs to heal his wounded shoulder, Morgeu watches, thrilled. From her vantage on the agate slopes above the chaparral, she sees the north god in his swarming mane and beard and blustery mantle shining like a glacier's icefalls and seracs. And below his bent, hulking form, the demon's plush heart pools in the field like frost mist.

Merlin dies! she exults, and must restrain the urge to leap and dance.

Across the wide solitude of the savanna, Arthor and Melania charge. Hope bounds joyfully in the enchantress. All the blight of the past and its shame and bitterness dim now before a glittering future that consorts with her proud ambitions. With Merlin dead, Arthor is nothing. No need for tantric magic now. Vengeance is at last and wholly accomplished. Her half brother will fade into obscurity, while her sons Gawain and Gareth ascend the tiers of power to attain supremacy in Britain and even Europe.

Morgeu's serene euphoria cramps at the sight of the jug-eared carpenter who had stood in Merlin's place at Camelot. The old fool crouches in the chaparral at the edge of the savanna. Morgeu can barely see him—but she sees clearly the clouds of faerïes flocking about him. They are busy. Mist rises from their swirling frenzy. *How?*

She is too distant to discern the tiny bodies gathering dew and swatting the clear baubles between their wings, scattering the moisture to humid wisps that gather in their thousands and thousands of thousands to haze, then mist, then depths of sluggish fog. As the smoky coils roll onto the savanna, Hannes reaches into himself for the magical might to grasp a spur of boulders. He shoves at the rocks gathered beneath the ridge rim of dwarf evergreen where Morgeu crouches.

The earth slides, and Morgeu scrambles for higher ground. Thunder unrolls over the chaparral and bounds into the savanna. On its steeply pitched roar, the faerïes swirl upward, carrying their fog with them and outlining the hulking mass of the Dragon.

The Furor straightens rigidly at the first glimpse of the threatening shadow. Not for an instant does he hesitate to challenge the apparition, knowing with horrible certitude the fate of gods seized by the Drinker of Lives. He bounds away, convinced that the

Síd have tricked him into the hollow hills for this gruesome sacrifice. As sop to the Dragon, he leaves the demon behind, too weak to escape, and masters the ache of his shoulder to climb hurriedly into the purple mountains.

Brokk rushes after him, neighing like a frightened horse. The lamia clings to him, startled to see the night above explode to sun-cut brightness. Radiant rays of daylight pierce the rootweave of the domed sky where the Furor gouges a way out of the hollow hills with his spear. Sunshine slants from the mountaintop and rides on the sky lakes like myriad lotus cups.

The lamia screams at the sight of the moon washed away and the stars dulled to quartz nodules in the peaty banks of the earthy sky. Brokk stabs with the lodestone knife, and the clinging, panicky lamia flares up like ignited gas. The dwarf heaves away the knife and its sticky, blazing effluvium and hurriedly climbs the stairs of sunlight into the upper world.

The Thunderers, too, with Cissa and Aelle in the lead, rush after the fleeing dwarf and their god. Up from the depths they clamber, moving in huge flying leaps and enormous bounding steps in the gold sunshine, swept along by the Furor's updraft into the blue hole of day.

Morgeu screams after them, "It is a trick! A trick!" But her cries dim through the distances, and she plops down on the interfingerings of moss and gravel, and shrieks.

Only Master Sphenks hears her, and it stops its barking and mad circling and perks its ears. Then, it smells the day world, the familiar scents of sun-baked dirt, territories of trees, and the damp wind of clouds curling with rain. It bolts after those well-known aromas, running into the moted sunlight on the mountain's flank. Tongue streaming back with its effort, it is determined to return to the world of birds, mice, rabbits, and a dog's life.

Merlin sees it dash by and makes no effort to stop it. He pushes to his elbows and gawks about at the wingspread of sunlight shining across the underworld. Hannes, in wizard's cap and robe, approaches, dragging Excalibur. Faeries swirl about him like bright dust.

"Master, are you sound?" the carpenter asks, kneeling beside Merlin.

"I don't know," the wizard answers candidly. The naked flesh of his chest, where the Furor's spear touched it, shines like a miracle, and his bones feel hollow. "The Dragon—"

"There is no Dragon," Hannes announces proudly. "'Twas only me and the faeries making smoke and thunder. That was their idea."

"Their idea?" Merlin asks groggily. "You can hear them?"

"Oh, yes, Master. Listen."

The faeries swim around them, blearing in and out of human shape. When in their nebulous forms, as indigos of brilliance, they chime faintly, and the wizard hears their happiness. "Well-done, Hannes. Well-done, indeed." A weak smile graces his pallid face, and he lies back to listen more deeply to the murmuring faeries—and to dream himself awake.

Chapter Eleven

Fen watches from the mountainside above the mermaids' lakes, where the sunlight streaming through the Furor's exit shrivels the faërie grass to whorls of powdery gray mold. As the north god rushes toward him, he stands perfectly still at the edge of terror, the lamia squatting over him in the gnarled shape of a fungus-ridden tree. The massive god, with his broken face and winged falcon's cap, shambles past without noticing him.

Then Brokk bounces by, and the feculent stink of the lamia he killed swirls after him. The despair of the shapeshifter for its dead twin nearly collapses its disguise. But Fen exerts all the force of his dread to hold the grief-mad lamia in place. Even Cissa does not see him. The Thunderers dash past him, mad to escape the Dragon.

Fen quakes seeing the Dragon's charred shadow in the roiling fog rising from below, but he dares not move until he is certain that the Furor and the others have gone well away. Better to be devoured by the Drinker of Lives than fall again into the cruel hands of the Thunderers. He watches the searing daylight from the upper world bruise and sour the delicate flora of the Storm Tree's roots, reducing the shrubs around him to coral shapes of ash. Slowly but perceptibly, the exit hole clogs with soot and shrinks. He will have to move soon if he is to escape at all.

The Dragon has retreated. The fog thins and light soaks through. Fen spots the gleeman's dog charging up the mountainside. It senses him and alters its course to climb a slope well out of his reach. The withered grass under it puffs to dust with its passing, and it disappears into the narrowing blue avenue of daylight.

Morgeu the Fey laboriously climbs toward him, emerging from a fuming sinkhole that vents the cinderlands. Her green gown hangs in filthy tatters from her large-boned frame, her pendulous breasts swinging heavily as she mounts the rocky shelves. If she knows he watches, she gives no indication but lumbers past, huffing for breath, her face hidden behind grimed veils of orange hair.

The lamia's hunger supplants its mourning for its twin, and it shivers to attack the enchantress yet does not strike. It fears this woman. She has been a shadow before, and the lamia is loath to waste its vitality attacking a shade. It lets her pass into the smoky daylight and scans for other prey.

Among the last coils of dragonfog that flow up the slopes, two horses gallop. Arthor and Melania ride hard to exit the hollow hills. Fen wraps the lamia about him in the form of Kyner and stands squarely on the path of their ascent.

Arthor reins hard at the sight of the old chieftain, and Melania flies past and must pull around to face him. She sees the startled hopefulness in his face, more boylike than she has ever seen him before. Then she glances at the stranger on the ashen slope above, an old, hulking Celtic warrior in Roman cuirass and sandals, his long, silver hair and thick mustache adorning a weathered and careworn face.

"He is my father," Arthor breathes, blinking with astonishment.

"You have no father," Melania reminds him, and reins in closer.

"My foster father—Kyner." Arthor walks his palfrey closer.

"Arthor, no." Melania pulls around to block him. "That can't be him. Not here, not now. That must be an apparition. Fen! It's Fen and the lamia!"

Its ruse disclosed, the lamia surges forward, and Fen cannot stop it. The fang-flanged jaws of a vaporous skull strike. Melania smacks the rump of Arthor's horse as it rears back in fright and sends it bolting forward under the slashing jaws. A storm wind of horror blows through her as the lamia's viperous face swings toward her.

But Fen will not let it have her. She is his only hope of salvation, and he tugs at the shrieking seraph. Its spider pincers writhe inches from her heaving chest, its jagged visage chittering with pain. She pulls hard away and sends her terrified steed flying up the slope after Arthor. Briefly, she glances behind and sees Fen on his knees, the cords of his body pulled to their taut limit. Then his stretched muscles twang loose from their impossible effort, and he comes hurtling uphill inside the fiery-frilled scorpion-cloud of the lamia, its wide, lurid mouth shining with razorous tusks.

The exit blazes above the cornice ledges of the mountain—a root-hanging hole ripped into the very sky over the rock spire. Around its edges, sunfire illuminates broken sod fallen inward from above: black-eyed Susans and daylilies gleam in the root mats and clods of black earth. A mauve glow of sidereal energies still shines on the dome of the nether sky in the distance, but near the hole, the heavens appear as an earthly fabric of loam and roots.

The ragged gap has narrowed to streaks of daylight barely wide enough for Arthor and Melania to jump through together. Their horses leap from the mountain ledge into the blue day with its green woods and cloud-ruffled sky, and the howling lamia comes rushing after like a burst of fire. They must charge through the woods at full gallop to keep away from its grasping talons. Trunks shuttle past, branches sing overhead, and the horses heave for breath, their wild-beating hearts close to bursting.

As they flee among the trees, their rapid hoof falls muffled in the leaf mold, Hannes emerges from the sunken hole in the earth. He sniffs the air, smelling for thunder, feeling for the presence of the Furor. The surrounding woods glimmer benevolently with birdsong and green sunlight. He eyes the trampled grass and shrubs where the Thunderers crashed through the forest, hurrying for higher ground where the Dragon's claw cannot reach.

After turning a slow circle and satisfying himself that the empty woods hold no hidden threats, he

ducks back into the fuming chute and returns, carrying Merlin over his shoulders. He places the dazed
wizard on a leafbed in a surge of shadows under
wind-stirred beeches and goes back for Excalibur.
When he returns with the sword, Merlin is sitting up.

"I must find the young king," the wizard says
thinly.

Hannes shakes his head and lifts Excalibur. "No,
Master. We must return the sword to the stone. If it is
found missing, there will be war."

Merlin hangs his head in weary agreement. He
does not have the strength to protect Arthor now. It
will be enough if he can return to Camelot and keep
that hope alive for him. "You are right, Hannes. Help
me up. We must not tarry."

After hoisting the wizard to his feet, Hannes
peers a last time into the hollow hills. Through the
rent in the dark green earth he sees tottering distances of mountain slopes, shawls of mist, and
sparkles of faerïe in the margins of darkness, cringing
from the sun rays. He shouts a singsong of thanks,
then props Excalibur on his shoulder and escorts
Merlin through the broken lights of the forest.

The wizard does not have the strength to search
ahead for danger. Darkness fits like muscles on his
bones, and he barely has the self-presence to remain
conscious. The Furor has drained him almost to
absence, leaving him anonymous and separate from
all his powers. He must rely on Hannes.

The carpenter, himself weary, hollowed out by
fear and awe, extends his magical strength beyond
himself to feel for dim movements of threat. Out of

the wind comes the rancid odor of wild men—brigands, no doubt. He does not care to know who they are but uses his magic to project a sense of threat into the woods ahead. He imagines spitting serpents and rampant lions.

The Furor feels the threat even as he climbs the Storm Tree. The sun shakes like a fist in the infinite blue. His eyes have not yet adjusted to the light. His heart, too, still carries darkness from the underworld, and fright wedges itself in his chest.

Not out of fear for himself does he dread a mindless death under the talons of the Dragon. He is old. The coming collapse can only bring him release from his long life of wounds. But the others—the Rovers of the Wild Hunt, and even the dwellers of Middle Earth, the small people like Cissa and his heroic father—what will become of them without him?

From a low branch, he gazes back at earth—the dark rind of approaching night, the pastel fumes of sunset, and the honey plasma that is afternoon. This beauty maligns his fear, as if nothing evil or sorrowing could exist down there among such glorious brilliance. And yet, unlike most of the other gods, he has walked the hide of the Dragon and seen the luckless strivings of the tribes for himself.

The mute moon's face knows. It sees into the darkness, where once the north people had only the night predators to fear and fire to stave them. Then the Romans came with their machines of destruction and their dreams of conquest instilled by the Fire Lords. Now the night holds new terrors. The familiar earth has grown strange with the blight of cities,

roads, fences. In the night, alien dreams swarm over
the people, inspiring them with strange ambitions to
tame the wilderness and cage the free and unreckonable spirits of the earth. And by day, the forests
shrink, the rivers clog with debris, the earth bears the
burdens of the Fire Lords' victory.

What will the gods and the people do without
him to defy the tamers of the wild? For them, he
must live, he must go on. And so, he turns away from
the marbled clouds, the blue swervings of rivers, and
the forests wide as summer. He will climb to the
Raven's Branch, to the crest of the World Tree, and
there hang by his feet until wisdom pours into him.
He will hang until that wisdom shows him a future
beyond his loss of the sword Lightning. Then he will
know how to save the earth from his nightmare
vision of the forest-killing cities with their mills of
smoke that poison the wind and the seas. Then he
will at last understand how to stop the Fire Lords
from their frantic haste to build the Apocalypse.

Far below the Furor, among the stammering
shadows of a birch grove, the Thunderers feel his
retreat and the menace of Hannes's magic as an eager-
ness to get away from Cymru. "We have done all that
was asked of us," Aelle says, standing atop a boulder
and addressing the blue rondure of the sky, thinking
it the wide cape of the Furor.

"He has gone," Brokk gripes, kicking his boot
against a tree trunk and shaking his square head.
"And he is angry at me. He thinks I have failed him.
But how could I have known the Dragon is not
asleep? It has never lain so silent before."

"The beauty of denial," Cissa chides from where he sits at the base of the boulder, "is the sweetness of the wish."

Brokk turns on him with an expression as furiously ugly as a bat's. "You are the Furor's priest. You should have seen the truth of the Dragon before you let our lord walk the roots of the Storm Tree."

Cissa dismisses him with a backhanded wave and stands. "Noble Aelle, the All-Seeing Father has indeed departed. He walks now in the lofty boughs of the Great Ash, grateful to be yet alive. We linger not in his thoughts, which move on now to other strategies. And so we are freed of all charge to remain in Cymru. As are you, loyal Brokk." The viper-priest casts him a sidelong glance. "The Furor cannot spare you to the Dragon. You are commanded to return to your workshop. The sword Lightning belongs now to the Daoine Síd."

With both hands, Brokk rubs his gold-tufted scalp, his frustration as irritating as lice. "I took the sword back from Lailoken—that thief! It was mine again! My own beautiful creation in my hands again."

"Take with you the satisfaction that the demon-wizard Lailoken paid for his thievery with his life," Aelle consoles, stepping down the creased side of the boulder. "The Dragon has devoured him along with the Roman witch, her champion the Eagle of Thor, and our craven Fen. All orts in the Dragon's maw now."

Brokk smiles, but darkly. "You don't truly believe you've seen the last of Lailoken? Just because he calls himself Merlin now, do not mistake him for a common and vulnerable man. He is a demon, older than the gods, and he knows all of wisdom and cunning that pain can teach. Mark what I say, Thunderers. Merlin will walk Middle Earth again."

The dwarf touches each of the Thunderers with an aspect of cold portent. Then, feeling uneasy himself from the near-lethal encounter with the Dragon, he barges into the underbrush and vanishes in a trembling of branches.

"Merlin may yet live," Aelle concedes, "but the Thunderer we came here to take back from our enemy is gone to the Dragon—a just fate for one of our own who chose captivity over death in battle. Let us leave his unhappy memory here in these dismal hills and return now to our clan in the lowlands."

Their flesh still stinking with the fetid taint of the underworld and their souls darkened by the shadow of the Dragon, the Thunderers readily agree. Aelle leads them west into the highbush overgrowth. Out of sight, they will slink like wolves through their enemy's woods to the headland where their boats lie hidden under dunes.

Fen does not see them depart. Wracked by the lamia's hunger, he lurches through briars, exploding thorns and branches with his monster's strength to leap ahead of the horses he pursues and snatch Arthor. But the young rider handles his horse with prescient agility. He vaults a hollow log practically standing in the saddle, then at the jump's peak collapses on its withers and directs the palfrey to turn in midair and dash off askew so that the lamia pounces on empty humus.

The boy rides as though fused to the animal's heart, as though they share a soul. Melania cannot match him. Time and again, Fen finds himself close enough to strike her while Arthor vanishes through a sudden arch of boughs. Each time that Fen holds back the lamia's claws, dire pain tears him. Then, when Arthor spins around to dash back for her, the palfrey leaps and squirms like a hare, and the lamia cannot fix on him long enough to strike.

Melania realizes that she only endangers Arthor by holding him back, and she peels away. Immediately, the lamia squats to a shagbark stump, hoping to trap Arthor when he turns back to follow her. Fen kneels within the illusion, panting for breath, glad for the respite, while Arthor reins his palfrey to a tight circle, looking for the lamia.

Bounding as fast as she can through the torn rickrack of briars where the lamia cut through, Melania returns to the narrowing hole that pierces the hollow hills. It has shrunk to a vaporous gap just large enough for her to leap through without dismounting. Through rags of mist, she gallops down the wide mountain slopes, intent on returning to the sky lakes where they stood before the Furor. She has come back to find the lodestone dagger.

The small hole broken in the sod of the nether sky burns red as a rose behind her, its petals tightening. Open space spreads wide before her, mossy slopes, grassy plains, and the green lakes of the mermaids. Their singing ripples and rills in the wind, full of sadness. The gleeman's gray mare that Brokk rode grazes in tall hay on the savanna.

"Faerïes!" she calls out as she tramples the ferns on the speckled shore of an ice green lake. "The stone dagger! Where is it?"

She cranes about and spots mica flashes higher up the slope, where she had run past. Rushing there, she dismounts with her horse still moving and leaps three big steps before it stops. Faerïes bob their luminous bodies in the strong green grass. When Melania kneels there, she finds among the tall stalks the lodestone knife, its quartz haft and speckled blade intact.

She croons thanks to the faerïes, tucks the knife in her waistband, and clambers onto her mare. Riding hard uphill goes slower, and she kicks and shouts for speed and watches the ruddy shaft of daylight dwindle. Fields of hay heads and feather grass brush past like racing clouds, and with a sweep of shade the hole dims like sunfall.

Melania stops atop the mountain summit, at the crest of the massive stalagmite that touches the turf sky of the hollow hills. Already, the ethereal underlights among the rootweave breathe again, quickening to a misting of stars. Where the hole had been, a cool wind yet sweeps from above. She draws the lode-knife and strikes at the scuts of overlaid moss, opening a fissure in the tightening braids of roots.

Standing atop the saddle, she succeeds in cutting a seam wide enough to filter sunlight. Her hands reach up and grasp clumps of sunburned grass. Exerting all her strength, she pulls herself into the bright cleft and feels the snaky squirmings of the earth. The healing magic that seals the hollow hills penetrates her, cutting off her breathing.

For a struggling moment, she gasps blue, then gains enough purchase with her elbows out of the hole to extrude the rest of herself. As her sandals slip through, the ground stitches together beneath her—and from inside the earth, as if from far away, she hears the frightened cry of the gray mare.

With the lodestone knife in her fist, she runs back through the ripped briars, calling for Arthor. He hears her from the distance where he has roamed, looking for her, hoping she has circled around but fearing she has gotten lost. He thinks her call is a cry hurled from within the lamia's grasp, and he rushes toward her.

At the shagbark stump where the lamia waits, the palfrey shies. Arthor sits up taller, looking for the monster, and Fen unfurls before him with a pain-stained howl and a slavering grin. Half-breathless with blood-need, hot eyes watching through Fen's swollen, pulsing, muscle-gorged body, the lamia strikes over the head of the palfrey.

Arthor slides from the horse's back and hangs from its side—but the lamia's clawed arm uncoils like a tentacle across the terrified animal's back and seizes his tunic. Screaming, the horse twists, bucks, and throws Arthor free before crashing through the shrubs.

Fen stands before the fallen boy horribly transfigured, inhuman with the desperate need of the lamia: Flesh burned with hunger's fire black as toadskin hangs from his elongated skeleton like charred moth webs; eyes of squid swivel in a skullmask above spider-clasped ribs, where the huge, ravenous heart of the monster hangs like the dark, flickering lantern of a hellgate. A cage of fangs opens in its bone face.

Arthor unsheathes Short-Life in a blur that slashes through the abomination. Ichor flies—wobbles in the air in tremulous lobes, then spins back and sheets together like gobs of black mercury reassembling. The lamia's claws slice at Arthor, and he chops again, splattering them to bursts of mucilage. They implode to spinning scythes and reattach to the skeletal lamia. Deft as vipers, the talons strike, and Arthor whacks them again and does not stop hacking. He shatters the atrocity to a writhing mess of worms and newts.

Before the defilement can gather itself, Arthor flees. Yet even as he runs among the crowded trees, he hears the wet, slitherous noises of the thing rebounding. Bulgar saber swinging, he spins around and cuts the lamia in two—but it falls together whole. He hews once more, driving downward, splitting the staring skull to the breastbone and twisting the saber to split it open. And again it fuses whole with an acid sound.

Arthor backs off, waving Short-Life, his shoulders burning from his exertion. The shape of fire passes over the horror, and it assumes the appearance of Melania, arms outstretched beseechingly. "Arthor, help me!"

He gashes her low, across the knees, and she tumbles forward and sprawls into a squamous writhing of tentacles that coil up his boots. Thwacking furiously, he bangs away the grasping tendrils and dances free.

"Arthor, I'm here!"

Heaving for breath and chattering with wild fear,

Arthor jumps about and sees Melania rushing toward him. Short-Life sweeps upward, and she falls back with outraged fright.

"Arthor!" She holds up the lodestone dagger.

A glance over his shoulder reveals to him the true lamia, flailing toward him with hooked arms and a widening gullet of fangs, incisors, and razor teeth. He drops to his knees and grabs the lodestone knife in his left hand.

With the scream of a pierced hawk, the lamia falls back. Its shape wavers watery pale over the quaking filament of Fen's body.

"Take off the throat band," Arthor cries, lunging to his feet. "Take it off, Fen—or you will die with the lamia!"

Fen turns and runs.

"Take off the band!" Arthor calls again, and throws Short-Life in a whirling toss.

The blade strikes the lamia behind the knees and topples it to the ground in a snaky thrash. Arthor closes in, lodestone knife poised.

Rolling to its back, the lamia lashes at Arthor with barbed arms. But a gouge of the magnetic knife shrivels it to an aqueous sheen around Fen's naked and shivering body.

Arthor seizes the guardian band and yanks it free from Fen's throat. The lamia comes with it. Its harrowing face of boneplates and fiery sockets whirls about to attack Fen, and Arthor pierces its skull with the lodestone dagger.

A vibrant shriek and a blast of hot effluvium heave Arthor to his back. Above him, the lamia blazes invisibly, wrinkling the shadows with its heat, its woeful, hideous face shriveling to a black clot and then gone into nowhere. All that remains is a sticky, smoldering gel that drools from the lodestone knife.

Arthor throws it into the grass and sits up.

Fen stands over him, holding the Bulgar saber. Panting for breath, his meat shuddering on his bones, he looks crazed. He raises the sword, his blue eyes wide, startled. "Now your life is in my hands, Royal Eagle of Thor."

"Fen!" Melania shouts. "He saved you."

The Saxon churns with rage, pride, exhaustion, and disgust. The lamia has violated him. And the Celts and this half-breed boy have violated him. His own clan has done the same and whipped and hanged him in shame. He has been reduced to a mere husk of a man. And now he *must* strike before he loses all strength and honor. He must strike to avenge the past and redeem the future. This boy below him, with the remote golden eyes of a killer, understands. He is, after all, the seed of Saxons. There has been a lethal pact between them from the beginning. He knows there is no alternative to death.

Melania screams, and with a war whoop that empties his lungs, Fen swings Short-Life and impales it in Arthor's shadow.

The Saxon totters, drops to his knees, and shrinks over his bones. "Now you are dead," he gasps at the startled boy. "You are dead—and must learn to live all over again."

Chapter Twelve

Morgeu the Fey sits up from the bed of mushrooms where she lay down to rest. Her hip aches against the knob of a root, and her brain feels as fragile as the delicate heads of toadstools around her. The scent of the hollow hills lingers on her—a balsam of sunset and woodsmoke that muzzies her with sleep. She has to shake her head to stay awake.

In a creek running through deep rows of elm, she bathes, scrubbing herself with ground pine and mint. She sudses her hair using a froth of soapwort that she makes from bruised leaves of bouncing bet and fern; then, she sits naked in the yellowed light on a hill's brow while her torn, wet gown hangs drying from a branch. Working a magical spell that restores her clarity, dressing her chilled body in familiar chants and the scents and sounds of the ordinary woods, she grows stronger.

By her blood-bond, she feels Arthor. He has escaped the hollow hills and wanders this forest, and she senses his fright amidst wickedness. Somewhere nearby, he trembles. *Fen,* she thinks. But when she reaches out with the brails of her heart to touch the lamia, she cannot find it. Cold reaches back, and by that she knows that the monster is dead.

She looks up through the treecrowns at the hill-top, at the sunlight wavering in the branches like the shaky light of candles, and she uses that mesmeric radiance to deepen her trance. Soon, her eyes close, she lies back, and a small sun rises in her brain. A body of light, she surfaces through the lake of her face and turns in midair to see her nakedness floating below her, a pale wisp of fog hugging the hillside.

Sunlight burns in the numerous windows of the forest. Butterflies plummet through her as she skims over the dark grass, feeling her way toward Arthor by the hum of his blood. She finds him in awe, sitting naked with Melania and Fen in a rain pond under a thicket of elders and climbing vines so thick the light drizzles into the clearing. They are laughing, the beautiful Roman woman, the thin Saxon, and Arthor.

"The Furor jumped out of the hollow hills like a rabbit." Melania smiles at the forest canopy, lying back in the water, her sable tresses spreading like ink.

Arthor lofts a laugh, then adds, "If he hadn't, we'd all have been eaten by the Dragon."

"And Brokk!" Melania giggles, her breasts float-ing like two slick footprints of the moon. "He flew so fast even the lamia couldn't keep up with him."

"You are brave to have gone back into the hol-low hills for the stone dagger," Fen speaks with the amber water lapping at his silver-whiskered chin. "The Furor himself had not the courage to stay—yet you returned."

"How else to have saved us from the lamia?" Melania says with her eyes closed.

"You could have outrun me," Fen replies. "I couldn't keep up with your horses."

"But you did." She sits up, spilling water over her brow and cheeks. "More than once, you drew close enough to strike me—and you didn't. You held the lamia back."

"I knew only you could save me." Fen stares calmly at her with his quiet, tired eyes. The lamia's possession has shrunken him closer to his bones, and the white cords of his body float limply. "I couldn't let it kill you."

"So *I* became your prey." Arthor groans.

"I am truly sorry for that, Eagle of Thor." The salt white of Fen's long hair spreads around him web-like. "You are a warrior. You have made a death pact with your sword and have taken many lives. Of the two, I chose you for the lamia. But you could have escaped me. Your horsemanship is uncanny."

Arthor accepts this praise with a barely perceptible nod. "I would not abandon Melania."

"We saved each other," Melania adds. "Fen spared me, I went back for the blade that saved Arthor, and Arthor risked himself to free Fen from the lamia."

"We are beholden to each other," Fen agrees, and props himself taller, feet gripped by fingers of sand. "We should go from here together."

"You will not return to your clan?" Melania asks, keen with interest.

"I cannot. And I would not." He regards them frankly and without self-pity. "I am not worthy of

them, because I did not die in battle with the others
in my war party."

"Why did you let Kyner take you captive?"
Arthor asks.

"I was not ready to die." Fen pauses, ashamed.
Wasps prowl across the water with their bright colors
and seem to hold his interest. At last, he admits, "I
did not even want to lead that raid into Cymru. My
father commanded me—to test my courage. I failed
him."

"In failing him, you won yourself," Melania
heartens him.

"For what that may be worth," the Saxon mutters.

"It is worth what you make it, isn't it?" Arthor
says. "That is why you did not kill me when you had
Short-Life in your hands. That is why you said I am
dead and now must learn to live all over again. You
were speaking of yourself as well, weren't you?"

"I suppose."

Melania drifts closer to where the two men lean
against the mossy bank. "We have all died on this
journey," she says. "When I saw that the treasure I
had come to this island to claim was already gone, I
died, too. All three of us must be born again."

"But to what?" Fen wonders.

"Come to Camelot with Arthor and me." She
speaks excitedly. "I am going to recruit among the
warlords and chiefs. I want their help in reclaiming
my estate in Aquitania. Come with us."

"*You* are going to Camelot?" Fen asks Arthor. "I
remember you saying that you would never go back

to Kyner and his clan, that you were striking out on your own."

"So I thought," Arthor admits, contritely, "before I died. Now that I must learn to live all over again, I cannot do so alone. I need a family."

"But Kyner will want subservience from you," Fen reminds him.

"I am ready now to serve."

"Ha!" The Saxon stands up, astonished, displaying a lean body mottled with lacerations and bruises. "The Royal Eagle of Thor serve? You are the best warrior and horseman in your clan—in any clan, I can truthfully say. How can you tell us that you will serve those less than you?"

Arthor glances silently at both of them and weighs his words before he says, "I have been in the hollow hills and seen the verges of hell. I have stood before the Furor and met his wrathful judgment. And I have been prey to a lamia—and been killed."

"And that has humbled you." Melania nods sympathetically.

"Yes—and more." Arthor, encouraged by the open faces of his listeners, dares speak earnestly, "Not only am I humbled to experience the smallness of my life—I have seen the greatness of God's will. When I prayed for mercy to the Holy Mother, she appealed to God for me, and I was saved—we were all saved. For what? That I should go into the world and find more trouble for myself? I am not so arrogant as to believe that God exists to serve me. I have been saved this one time that I should find myself."

Fen sits again in the pool and tilts his head curiously. "And what have you found, Royal Eagle of Thor?"

"I know now that I belong where God has placed me," Arthor answers, head bowed, addressing from his soul the dark water. "God in His greatness has made me just what I am—a warrior in the household of Chief Kyner and his rightful son Cei. They are my clan's leaders. I am but a foundling. If I truly love God, if I am a true Christian, I will take my place, humbly and with wholehearted devotion."

Fen shakes his head. "Your god of love is a demanding one. What god would squander a man of your talents on servitude to an oaf like Cei?"

Arthor responds without hesitation: "A God of justice."

"Justice?" Fen turns a silent laugh to Melania, then back at Arthor. "Is it just, then, that Melania lose her estate to pagan warriors? That you, a man with Saxon blood, who has the battle skills that would make you a chief in a Saxon clan, must serve Celts? What justice is this?"

"It is divine justice, Fen. It is God's will."

"I do not understand it. Do you, Melania?"

"No." She shakes her head sadly. "I have no faith anymore—not since my Christian family was destroyed by the barbarian sword. Our tour of hell and our encounter with the Furor has convinced me that this world is ruled not by God or justice or love but by might alone. Arthor, the Furor fled not from your desperate prayer to the Virgin—but from the terrible might of the Dragon."

"No god cares about our small lives," Fen says.

"We survive by our skills alone—or we do not survive at all."

Arthor faces them with adamant sincerity. "You are both wrong. The God I worship is not a created being like the Furor or the Dragon. Such beings are the powers of this world, yes. But there is a Creator—a God who lives in each part of Creation and yet stands apart, watching and guiding. 'Not one sparrow is forgotten in God's sight. Even the hairs of your head are all counted. So do not be afraid, for you are of more value than many sparrows.'"

"Is that what your religion teaches?" Fen asks, incredulous.

"Those are the words of Jesus," Melania replies, looking at Arthor with an unhappy expression. "Then was God watching when the pagans slew my brothers and my father?"

Arthor lifts helpless hands, water streaming through his fingers. "Are we to question God for those chosen to die? Each of us has our time. And those who live by the sword shall die by it."

"If you are so ready with the words of your Jesus," Fen speaks, "why did you not take succor with him in Kyner's clan? Why did you burn with the desire to flee? Where was Jesus for you then?"

"Not in my heart," Arthor answers sincerely. "I am ashamed to say, I loved His mother more than Himself."

"His mother?" Fen frowns, not comprehending.

"She is the Lady of Sorrows—she understands my suffering. She has always given me comfort, since I was a child. But I did not listen to her. I did not understand when she told me that love is first. Never abandon. Never abandon."

"And now you understand?" Fen asks, trying to grasp.

"I understand that I am, finally, glad to be but a foundling. I would not want to be Cei, to have to fill Kyner's shadow. I thought I wanted that. I used to pretend I was a king. It made me feel important. But now, I see the price of that importance. As a king in this land, one must stand against the likes of the Furor. I certainly do not want that. I never want to face that ferocious god again. I am happy to leave that to the true kings of this land. Let them carry such a frightful burden. I am glad *that* is not my fate. It will be easy now to serve those who must lead."

Fen smiles wryly. "So you have found your place as a little man."

"And happy for it, Fen," Arthor answers easily. "I am going back to Camelot to take my rightful place—as a little man. I will never complain again."

Melania brushes her fingers against Arthor's cheek. "How sad that you must return without your shield—without the image of the Virgin."

Arthor squeezes her hand affectionately. "It is only that, an image. She is with me, yet." He faces Fen with a bright countenance. "Will you come with us then—to Camelot?"

"To a gathering of Celt and Christian warlords?" Fen tucks his chin and shakes his head. "I think not."

Melania glimpses a pale motion blur in the canopy and glances up to see a dove perch on an overarching bough. "Arthor—look!"

Fen smiles at their childlike surprise. "It is just a bird."

"Yes," Arthor agrees, and stands up in naked wonder. "Just a bird—a small comfort for the peace I have made with myself."

Morgeu the Fey has seen enough, and she withdraws through the vaulted spaces of the forest. A fleshy moon hangs among the branches of the day sky, orienting her in the loamy stillness. She finds her way back to the damp sweetness of the creek under the hillside where her body lies naked in the cool amber liquid of the sun.

She fits herself into her flesh, and her eyes open languidly. Wind through the trees chills her. The first taint of evening's camphor rises from the creek where, later, fog will crawl. She rises and reclaims her gown from the branch upon which it has dried to a limp, satiny attenuation of her body.

There is magic in this cloth. That is why she wore it to go with the dwarf Brokk to confront Merlin. When the green fabric falls over her head and slinks down her figure, the ache in her hip vanishes along with the damp chill. A surfeit of power replaces the tenderness of her bones with incandescent ceremony: She stands at the creek's marly edge not as an earthly and prayerful woman but as enchantress.

While the cloud-swift afternoon collapses slowly to the melancholy beauty of summer twilight, she dances. Her bare feet stamp the earth in ritual rhythms far, far older than the island's pagan temples now in ruins, older even than the stone cirques on the plains or the highland cromlechs or even the chalk carvings on the coastal cliffs. She beats the prehistoric cadence of the aboriginal goddess, whose breasts are the sun and the moon, whose sex fills the vast, voluptuous hills with her ache of living fire, green with the world's stubborn desire, spread wide under the semen of the stars.

Her own soft flesh fills with inconsolable yearning as she cants and veers through the tinctures of the setting sun. Goddess-force infuses her with longing and enticement. Pleasure shimmers in green, auric waves from her hips, breasts, and belly, and the etheric glow burns coolly in the dusk. With limber arms, she shapes the viscous light, spins, and weaves its supernatural shine about herself. By the time the midsummer sun dwindles away and darkness crowds the forest under the moon's rays, she blazes with green fire.

The night breathes with fireflies. Attracted by Morgeu's spectral illumination, they glitter after her in a prismatic wake as she walks through the woods. By the time she reaches the masses of hawthorn hedges near the knoll where Arthor and his companions sleep, radiance whirls about her.

She sits. Slowly, with an effort that closes her face, that curls her body around her navel, she compresses the eerie brilliance. The green flames licking her body whorl tighter and gradually pull away from her scattered hair and her hunched shoulders and spool under her breasts into her palms turned upward in her lap.

The quarter moon settles like a pale blue petal through the treetops falling away from midnight. As it blushes toward the horizon, Morgeu completes the preparation for her tantric spell. The ghost fire has contracted to a pulsing emerald she holds in her right hand.

She covers the bright bauble and quietly, shrouded in the moonless dark, sidles through the hedges and up the knoll. Fen, Melania, and Arthor sleep on three separate sides of the hill, the better to thwart attackers and warn the others. Silent as mist, she floats among spindle trees to where her half brother lies on his back in the trampled grass. Crickets sing under the wind's heavy breath, and she calls his name several times before he sits up groggily.

"Arthor—I am here," she whispers from a dark dizzy with stars. "Come to me."

"Who's there?" he calls, hand on sword.

"Sh-h-h—come silently." She rises from the tall grass, a silhouette against the loud stars.

"Melania?"

When he stands, she crushes the gem of green light between her palms and grinds it to a ticklish powder. Then she takes three quick strides toward him, opens her palms to a flash of cold brightness, and blows the lustrous smoke in his astonished face.

"I *am* Melania," she instructs him. "I want you."

The dream dust glinting on his suddenly drowsy features dissolves to a conifer coolness, and his eyes close. A moment later, he rouses himself and blinks as if just woken from sleep. At the touch of Morgeu's fingertip to his creased brow, a curtain of heat snaps open in Arthor's chest, and a mirage of mesmeric beauty unfurls before him. He sees Melania sliding

out of her gown, holding out her hand. When he
takes it, a realmful of desire urges him forward. She
leads him down the hill into deeper darkness.

"What you said while we bathed in the pond
today moves me, Arthor," she says in a hush. "You are
so brave to return to your humble place in Kyner's
clan. You are so brave, I want to take my place with
you."

"Melania—" He gropes for words. Her nakedness blurs with pastel softness under the constellations.

"Don't speak. Not now."

She settles to the ground and pulls him after her.
By feel and scent, he senses mint, borage, buttercup,
and columbine crush beneath them. His awareness
widens to unnatural limits, and he observes the
starlight weaving Melania's features with bright passion. Her nipples point at him like small, dark
thumbs. When she tugs him free of his loinwrap and
takes the wick of his desire in her hand, his whole
body ignites with dazzling pleasure.

Together, they rock in each other's embrace,
brinking on wider dimensions. Time falls away.
Their bodies slap sparks of sweat from each other that
fill the night with stars. Melania's wild face drinks
from his mouth. Her legs clasp him tighter to her,
and the stars begin moving.

Turning over and over, they roll onto, into, and
through each other. And each time that lust breaks
inside him and into her and he collapses in ecstatic
disaster, she clasps her mouth to his and breathes hard
into his lungs—and his carnal fire flares again with

inexorable force. He bucks against her, and they grapple in a whiplash of caresses, their joys stitched into each other, sewn tight and slow to explode.

The spires of the trees rise toward the dawn's greasy light before Arthor finally reaches a deep, abiding truce with Melania. He lies limp in her arms, wrung of all heat. Until sunrise turns buttery, he does not move but hugs her against his lean shiver, glad for their love's leisure.

Then, languorously, he rolls over and opens his sleepy eyes. The soft length of her body is a bunched mat of weed-strands and crushed grass. He sits up, puzzled, and wipes tangled straw from his face. His shoulders bear the hot bruises of love bites or he might almost believe he has dreamed it all, as vividly unbelievable as this lewd memory is.

Rubbing the stupor from his brow, he gathers his loincloth, tunic, and sword and looks about for signs of her. But she is gone. Among the narrow trees and the dark hedges, slants of morning mist totter drunkenly.

Chapter Thirteen

Hannes and Merlin bathe in a black tarn where white herons glow like paper lanterns. Among blunt rocks, they wash their garments and exchange them, each glad to be restored to his proper garb. The wizard, spent by the Furor's attempt on his life, curls up in his robes, hides his face in his wide-brimmed hat, and sleeps.

Hannes watches over him in the cinnamon light of the forest mere. Plying his magical sight, he looks into the wizard and sees a darkness black as the uttermost reaches of the abyss. Quickly, he looks away— yet already, hours have fled. The hollows of the night forest echo with lorn owl calls. Hugging Excalibur to himself with fright, the carpenter lies down at his master's feet and waits impatiently for sleep. Rest does not come. His desperate heart beats in the swamp grass with fearful vertigo for the namelessness of the depths he has glimpsed.

At the first touch of sun, he rouses the torpid wizard, and they slouch away among hanging vines and brown, dusty rays of sun. By noon, Hannes leads Merlin out of the dark and perilous woods of

Crowland into the rolling pastures and cow-dotted meadows of the old Roman estates. Among the lonely ruins of once splendid villas, thatch-roofed farmhouses and rude hamlets cluster. Gold coins lost in past centuries hide in the worm-fill of these regions, under lichenous blocks fallen from sunken temples. With the fine threads of his magic, Hannes feels them out and pulls a few glittering to the surface while his master dozes in the shade.

At a farm cottage, they buy hot, fortifying mugs of chicory brew and two horses from stables under a sour vineyard. When the narrow-eyed vintner appraises with loud awe the remarkable sword that these two old men possess, Hannes speaks forgetfulness to him while Merlin wraps Excalibur in a horse blanket.

They ride along the ancient highway that leads to Cold Kitchen, passing drays mounded with a summer's bounty of grains, vegetables, and fruit destined for the open markets of Uxacona and Viroconium. Hunger thrives in them, their bodies' celebration of their near escapes from death, and they stop at hilltop crofts for meals of salt fish boiled in milk and purees of beans with chestnut cakes—hearty food to restore their stamina.

Merlin eats with gusto but says nothing the entire journey, though Hannes burbles with questions. The carpenter wants to know more about elves, faeries, the hollow hills, the Dragon, the Furor and his dwarf. He asks, too, about magic and how it works. Merlin says nothing. Hat pulled low over his brow, the aged wizard rides like a sleeper. He reaches with his heart's

brails for the young king, wanting to know that he is
safe—but his grasp wavers and shreds in the wind.
The wizard's body feels like a nest of bones, his magic
an egg not yet hatched.

Camelot rises to view in rivermist and moonlight. Hannes leads the horses into a hazel grove, ties
them off, and begins looking about for kindling,
assuming they will ride the last steep miles into Cold
Kitchen with the morning. Merlin unwraps the
sword Lightning. Reflections slip over its blade like
light in a cat's eye. He points with the sword to the
mountain shadows under the hard white stars.
Hellswirls of moonlit mist rise from the river ravines
of those heights.

On foot, the wizard guides the carpenter upward
through the oak forest tunnels where lunar fumes
congregate as in a hall of spirits. They walk past midnight before they look down through shagged walls
of cedar into the fog-drifting gorge of the River
Amnis. Hannes gives thanks for his magic as they
descend rocky spillways and ferny couloirs toward the
loud current. Sometimes, by invisible hands alone,
they grasp vertical slabs of jasper and walk straight
down into the roaring darkness.

At the bottom, they traverse a bankside path over
slippery shale and through bracken selvage to where
the river broadens. There, the indolent current slides
quietly around birch islands and their ghostly reflections in the black water. Mons Caliburnus stands tall
against the moon, and bats spin in the silvery darkness
around it.

After shoving the magnetic counterstone into

place at the base of the mount, Merlin climbs to the
top, and Hannes follows. They pause in the hackberry
shrubs near the star stone. The illusory Excalibur still
stands where Hannes set it. All the night's luminaries
show themselves in its mirroring blade.

"A fine work of magic that is," Merlin praises his
student, and the unexpected sound of his voice makes
Hannes jump. "Hush! There are people on the hill."

Using his magical strong eye, Hannes discerns a
half dozen people on the sward below. Most sleep,
while a couple kneel in prayer.

A banshee's feverish wail ululates from Merlin,
and the startled sleepers and worshipers leap up.
Another ghostly cry from the wizard sends them
dashing for the path away from the river.

Merlin emerges from the hackberry bush. At his
touch, the illusion of Excalibur wrinkles away like
heat, and he holds the gnarled stave in his hand. He
removes it, and as he restores Excalibur to its place,
the blade kisses stone with a clear chime.

With the stave across his lap, the wizard sits in the
grass before the standing sword and gazes up at the
lucid weapon. Instantly, he sinks into trance, allowing
his energy and the sword's to merge within him.
Inside the sword's shafts of diamond light, inside its
destiny, he strives to find Arthor.

Time blurs. Out of its smoke emerges the sword,
pointed upright, suspended in the air. Arthor appears
through the time-mist, naked, dewed with sweat.
Behind him is Morgeu, also naked, her thighs and the
red tuft of her genitals slick with sexual chrism.

Merlin's heart bangs like a thunderclap, and he

reels almost unconscious before the madness of this evidence and its ugly truth. *No! It must not be!*

Afflicted with the hope that what he witnesses has not yet transpired, he reaches out with all the magical power he can muster, and he tries to pull the mists of time over this horrid image of incest. But the haze of minutes and hours slips away from him and leaves the naked couple standing in clear light, their pearly bodies reflected in the blade of the sword that floats behind them—and by this he knows that what he sees is actual.

Morgeu places her hands on her white belly, feeling inward to her womb and the baby of a future Merlin has not anticipated. He groans—and time blurs.

At dawn, King Lot arrives on Mons Caliburnus with his sons Gawain and Gareth, because the boys want to try their hands at drawing the sword. They find Merlin sitting in the grass stone-still and Hannes with his back against the stone, asleep. The king nudges the carpenter awake with his boottip. "You— wake up!"

Hannes judders alert. When he sees the fierce warrior-king glowering at him, he throws a look at Merlin. But the wizard sits entranced.

"Who are you?" the king asks, sternly.

"I—I am the master builder Hannes," he stammers, "apprentice to Merlin, wizard of Britain."

"You told me you were Merlin," Lot practically growls at Hannes, then drops a wrathful stare at the motionless wizard. After examining him, he announces, "This is Merlin. Yes, I recognize his bony face now. But what has become of him? Why does he not move?"

"He wanders the spirit realm," Hannes assumes. "He must not be disturbed."

Gawain and Gareth crouch beside the still wizard and ogle his weird countenance and half-lidded mineral eyes.

"Leave him be, boys," Lot enjoins; then, turning to Hannes again, "Why did you lie to me?"

"At Merlin's command alone, my lord," Hannes answers abjectly. "He feared that if his absence were known, fighting would ensue."

Lot nods curtly. "His fear was sound. Now tell me, where did he go when he left you in his place?"

Hannes speaks to the warrior's boots. "That is for him to say, my lord."

"Mother!" Gareth cries out, and leaps off the stone, where he has been futilely tugging at the sword. "Mother has returned!"

Morgeu rides up the hill path on a white mule, accompanied by several of Lot's brawny guards. During the night, she left Arthor entranced and used the tantric power she had built with him to summon a spirit pony from the hollow hills. She had never ridden one before, but the ancient magic emboldened her. Upon the rippling chinebones of a violet creature with white-hot eyes, she rode to Camelot faster than the wind and dismounted in the pine hills above Lot's camp. Reefs of stars still shone in the heavens when she returned unannounced to her tent.

Refreshed, she now appears with white ribbons in hair and wearing a gown of reds, purples, and blacks. Her maids worked hard, deftly applying cosmetics of powdered seashells and minium to obscure the bruises and abrasions from her rough adventure, and when she dismounts to embrace her sons, she looks fresh and pale as morning mist.

The boys do not ask where she has been. All their lives, she has come and gone, worshiping by moonlight in desolate places, assuring the well-being of their kingdom. When she returns, the magic in her hugs lifts them like song into the wind—and this time her touch is even brighter than usual, filling them with a superlative dazzle of well-being.

For Lot, there is a charmed word in the ear, and his hot blood feels strung like a harp, jangling with amorous music. He smothers his face in her fuzzy hair, and its meadow fragrance crowds his heart with love. "Come to my tent with me now," he whispers to her, and tries to guide her away from the wizard she hates.

But Morgeu has come to exult over Merlin. She gentles her husband with a soft kiss and pushes him airily aside. Then she approaches the wizard.

Hannes steps back from his master, feebly protesting, "He is entranced and should not be disturbed."

Morgeu laughs tautly and stands over the sitting wizard. She knocks off his hat, and with a hand chill as a midnight breeze, she grasps his brow and pushes him backward.

The surge of power in her touch breaks his trance, and he sprawls awake on the grass and squints into the rising sun. Morgeu eclipses this radiance and bends close with a mocking leer. "I have taken my revenge," she proclaims in a voice pitched for his ears alone. "My father's blood has earned a way to the throne not through grief but love. Go ahead, Merlin, and create your high king of Britain. I will not thwart you—for I carry his successor!"

Morgeu steps away brusquely, and daylight bewilders Merlin. He shades his eyes with his hand and sees Excalibur stuck in the stone, a ring of refracted light surrounding it. The myth of the one true ruler of Britain that he strove so hard to create, he sees now, is a bubble. It is destined to float away on the wind and burst.

But look how the clouds and trees shine! he tells himself, watching the morning wind preening the green branches. Here in the real world of weather and forests, the bubble remains intact. Arthor is alive. *And I am alive!* Merlin marvels, remembering with a giddy shiver the miracle Hannes worked to save him from the Furor's wrath.

He looks about and watches Morgeu retreating downhill with her family and their warriors. Gareth rides the slow white mule, one hand spinning over-head as if taming a wild stallion. Gawain has an arm about Morgeu's waist, and Lot holds her hand. They are the very image of a loving and happy family, wholly unaware of the hurting dark she bears within her.

With weary effort, the wizard struggles to rise, and Hannes helps him to his feet. "Why are you smiling, Master?"

"Am I?" Merlin asks, groggily. He leans on his

staff, puts quavery fingers to his beard, and feels the shine of joy within him. "I suppose I am smiling. And why not, Hannes? Excalibur has been returned, none the worse and no one the wiser. Arthor lives. And so do we. Why not smile?"

"Morgeu the Fey broke your trance," Hannes says apprehensively, searching the old wizard for signs of dementia. "She seemed to whisper a terrible curse in your face."

"Yes—there is that." Merlin frowns, and Hannes hands him his hat. "But, as experience has taught me, where is there truth without falsehood? Where a mountain without a valley? Morgeu could have burst the bubble."

"I don't understand, Master."

"She could have killed Arthor, man!" he says sharply but not to Hannes, rather to himself, in reproach. "He was in her grasp and I too weak even to know it, let alone stop her." He puts on his hat, the shadow of its large brim covers his face, and from within its darkness he mutters aloud his thoughts, "But she didn't kill him, did she? And she won't. She won't use her magic against him. Not anymore. She wants him to live now. She will protect our bubble. She will guard it with her life—oh yes, with her very life. At least, for now."

"Master, I still don't understand."

Merlin looks up abruptly and seems surprised to see Hannes before him. "Oh—Hannes—yes, of course. I'm mumbling, aren't I? Never mind. This does not concern you. You have done enough for me, good fellow." He takes the carpenter's shoulder in his grip and squeezes it affectionately. "I now release you from your charge. You are free to go."

"You don't seem sound, yet," Hannes observes with concern. "You're still weak. I will stay until you recover."

"I'm well enough. The Furor took the wind out of me, but I'm whole. I'll be fine." He sits on the edge of the star stone and draws a deep breath to clear his head. The trees billow with the giant pulse of the wind, and he experiences again a rush of relief at surviving in the hollow hills under the Furor's spear. "I owe you my life, Hannes. I would like to reward you."

"That is not necessary, Master." Hannes shakes his head, yet his avid blue eyes do not budge from watching the wizard. "The wonders I have experienced these past days are reward enough for this old man."

"Even so—" Merlin gestures expansively. "The world of magic is wide. Horizons forever! I have opened the first four gates of power in your body. Now, let me open the fifth. That will empower you with the heart's brails for feeling deeper into the world."

"Master, please—" Hannes looks pleadful. "I don't want to feel any deeper. Actually, I have been thinking to ask you—when you are well enough, that is—to take away the magic you have given me."

Merlin leans back. "Take it away? But you've become so adept."

"You warned me that the magic does with us as it pleases." Hannes sits down beside the wizard, leans his elbows on his knees, and nods. "I see now the truth of what you say. I had dreamed that magic would make of my old days a youthful adventure. And it surely did that. But I am not a youth. My heart is a horde of ghosts. They wonder why I am cavorting with elves and faeries when I've grandchildren who have yet to learn my trade." He flexes his hands and proudly holds them up. "These, I realize now, are all the magic I wanted. My own life back in my hands. I am a master builder, Merlin, not a wizard. When I lost my hands, I lost my work—and then I lost my mind and started dreaming of a new life. But, after all I've seen and done these past days, I would be glad indeed for my old life. Just leave me the use of my hands."

Merlin smiles, wisely. He recognizes here the human spirit that belongs to its work, that finds itself in what it creates, only thinking it wants more clarity, power, life, while knowing blindly it exists not to want or even to have but to be. "You don't want to be a wizard?"

"No, Merlin," Hannes admits and stands up. "I want to be what I am."

Merlin rises and looks the carpenter squarely in the eyes. "Well said, Hannes. Well said. You shall have your hands. You shall be again the master builder you always were." The wizard speaks forgetfulness to the man.

Hannes's eyes flutter, and Merlin steadies the carpenter until he snaps alert. "It is done," the wizard tells him. "I have fulfilled your wish."

Holding his strong, flexible hands before his face,

Hannes grins. "My hands—you have restored my hands."

"As you wished," Merlin says. "Now, I believe, our agreement is satisfied. You have built me the round table—and I have granted you one wish."

With tears in his eyes, the master builder hugs the wizard. He rants for a while about what joy this is for him, what creations wait to be released from his nimble fingers. Then he bids fond farewell and merrily strides away, eager to return to Hartland, where his family and his work await.

Merlin watches him dwindle and finally disappear in the far warp of the land among cedar giants the Romans planted here centuries earlier. Then he turns, walks to the sheer hem of rock atop the mount, and balances, gazing down at the snakewise river with its mottled skin of morning fire and forest shadows. And he waits patiently for the fragrant wind to send him messages of the young king and to stop whispering about the river's adventures in the lost valleys and its slow journey to the blue embrace of the sea.

—⟨⟩—

Chapter Fourteen

Clouds heave over the forest hills and budge against the dawn, promising rain. Fen and Melania sit upright, embraced, joined below the waist, legs about each other's hips, soles together, foreheads touching, in deepest communion. The fast beat of their hearts outpaces their rocking bodies. And when the mounting pleasure becomes unbearable for her, she lifts her face, shy and desirous, and her eyes open and see him watching her from far away, deep in the dream life of animal ecstasy.

She puts a hand on the muscled pad above his nipple and covers the thunderbolt scar that marks him as a Saxon clansman and chieftain's son. Then his hands release her and brace the earth behind him as he levers his hips, reaching with his bright tine for the core of her need. She's startled by the sound she makes, bites her lip, and lashes his corded neck and straining shoulders with her long hair.

They ride their shared climax equally amazed and collapse together into shapeless exhaustion. For a long time afterward, they lean into each other, not wanting to interrupt the union that has delivered them to the first true joy of their lives.

Neither of them can account for this passion that has fused not just their bodies but seemingly their fates. Beyond the sheer truth of desire, they find they both reach for something more, an initial hope that each echoes for the other. In Fen, Melania has found her champion, who can help her reclaim her estate. And for him, she is the home he can win for himself by displaying the best traits of his heritage—by daring, martial skill, and strong spirit.

Throughout the night, while Fen plaited for himself a grass kilt under a sky choking with stars, this is all they spoke of. Their faith in each other requires no god, no clan, no magic but their own sole desire to take back what the world has taken from them. They recognize themselves as counterparts of one destiny. And now that they have physically sealed that union and tethered themselves by bonds of love, they unclasp and face each other with equal measures of expectancy, dread, and amazement.

Relieved and released from passion, they look at each other for something more naked than their bodies. Fen speaks first. "I want to go with you, to Aquitania—just exactly as we discussed when we lay together in the dark, when we could not see each other, only our dreams."

"It is day now," Melania says, and glances at the blush of dawn. "Dreams must prove themselves in this clear light—or fade away."

Fen takes her hands in his. "I will not fade away."

"You are a very different treasure than what Great-grandmother sent me to find."

"I will prove as valuable," he promises, relaxing all force in his voice and lifting his silver-bearded face to reveal his sincerity.

"Oh, I think more so." She smiles and kisses him.

Arthor shoulders through the hedges, still straightening his tunic from his passionate encounter in the night, and he stops short. "Melania!"

Melania snatches her gown and covers her nakedness.

"Arthor—" Fen speaks with surprise, then shrugs with good humor, and entreats, "Please—we need to be alone."

"Alone?" Arthor shoots bewildered ire at the couple. "Melania—what of our passion?"

"Our passion?" Melania asks over her shoulder as she crawls into her gown. "What are you talking about?"

"Our passion together—last night."

She pulls the gown into place and turns a befuddled look upon him. "I was not with you last night."

"Of course you were," the flustered boy insists. "You came for me. We lay down together in the field."

She passes her frown to Fen, then back to Arthor. "I don't know what you're talking about."

"Melania and I have been with each other all night, Arthor," Fen says as he secures about his waist the hemp cord of his grass kilt.

Arthor rocks his jaw, eyes narrowing, trying to see through to the motive of their lies. "I don't understand." He steps a pace closer to Melania, accusatory finger pointing. "I saw you—I touched you, held you. We were together until just now."

Melania shakes her head solemnly and stands up, dropping her gown fully into place. "That was not me."

Arthor, hands on his hips, turns his head and regards them out of the tail of his eye. "You are tricking me—the two of you."

"Arthor—look at me." Fen steps up to him, his face grave beyond all jest. "Melania and I are in love. We have given ourselves to each other."

"This is true," Melania eagerly confirms, standing behind Fen and taking his arm. "We have spent all night preparing for our lives together."

Arthor's arms drop limply to his side, and his chin tucks in. "Then—who was I with?"

Melania lifts her eyebrows inquisitively. "An elf-woman from the hollow hills?"

"Or the witch," Fen murmurs darkly.

Arthor makes a face. "What witch?"

"The witch with the dwarf," the Saxon replies, nearly shivering to remember the lamia's possession, full of prism, hunger, and power. "She called herself Morgeu the Fey."

"I've heard of her," Arthor mumbles, recognizing the name from overheard conversations at hearthside in White Thorn. He knows she is King Lot's wife, a sorceress much loathed by Kyner and his Christian court. "But the woman I was with looked exactly like Melania."

"I was not with you, Arthor," Melania says sadly, pitying him for the strangeness that has found him in the night. "You were under the spell of an enchantress."

Arthor nods, stunned. He backs away, too numb for words, then turns and retreats into the hedges. A heavy rainlike mist settles through the trees. *Morgeu the Fey?* he says to himself. *Why would she come to me?*

He returns to the field where he lay with the enchantress. The rising sun smears through the misty clouds—green, ocher, purple—hues runny as a disease. From the matted grass where he and his lover thrashed, he tries to spot her footprints. In the wild grass, they are obvious, and he traces her steps among bent shafts of wild ginger, Solomon's seal, deer's-tongue, and trout lily. Soon he finds himself among husky spruce, where the trail of footprints ends.

What did she do—fly? he wonders, searching vainly for further signs of her.

Eventually, he relents and sits on a root-ledge, chin in his hands. Mist flares to a drizzle and soaks him in its chill aura. Hard as he ponders, he cannot think why a sorceress would seduce him. All he can surmise is that the strange gleeman who led them into the hollow hills and saved them from the Furor and his warriors is not yet done with them. They are all under a terrible spell. *Why else would a Christian woman and a Saxon fall in love?* he reasons. *We are charmed by eldritch powers—elves and witches.*

He berates himself for not having heeded Melania when she first warned him about the gleeman. Because the odd man had professed Christian faith, Arthor had ignored his grotesque appearance. But now, recalling those weird metallic eyes and long bones, he knows that this warlock cast his magic upon them. *But to what end?* he asks himself, aware that twice the magician saved his life—first with his wise dog snatching Fen's thrown ax out of midair and then sparing them the viper-priest's deathblow. *Did the warlock save me for the sorceress? Why?*

"It will all come clear in time, lad." A dark, gleaming voice speaks from the leaning evergreens.

Short-Life flies to Arthor's hand. "Who speaks? Who is there?"

"Over here, boy."

In the tenebrous rain shadows among crisscrossed spruce, a vague figure appears. Arthor wipes the dripping rain from his brow and shifts sideways, raising his sword defensively when he sees that the tall man in blue tunic and yellow boots who steps from the forest alcove looks transparent as water. The apparition shows the misty woods behind him. As he approaches, the wounded details of his battered body reveal themselves: His scalp gleams fire-bald on one side, hackled with singed red hair on the other, and his long, green eyes gaze out from a scorched face lacy with blisters and hot sores.

"Who are you?" Arthor asks in a fright.

"Bright Night," the ghost replies in a shining, shadowy voice. "A prince of the Daoine Síd."

Arthor steps back, waving his saber. "Stand away from me. I am a Christian man. My soul belongs with Jesus—not your Dragon."

A luminous smile winks from his burned lips. "I'm not here for your soul, lad."

"What do you want of me?"

"I've come to return something you left behind in my realm." Bright Night's image wavers in the trembling rain as he turns and gestures toward a bank of empurpled clover. "We don't want the likes of it in the hollow hills. It belongs to you. Take it."

Arthor's shield lies on the ground, beaded with raindrops, the doleful image of the Virgin full of beautiful silence.

"Mother Mary!" Arthor sheathes his sword, steps through the clover, and takes the shield in both hands to be sure it is not an illusion. The solidity of it floats a smile on his face. "You've returned my guardian!" He marks all the familiar dents and scratches and touches his brow to the Virgin. "I did not think I'd see this again." Yet, even with his protective icon in his hands, he feels the edge of fear within him and knows its source. He stares across his shoulder at the wounded entity, notes the ester fumes seeping from his burned flesh, and the velvet stink of pond decay. "You look more like a devil than an elf, Bright Night."

"Aye, that I do," the prince admits, looking at his tattered hands. "I've been wounded—struck by the Furor's spear. I would be gone from this life now had not my warriors used their own brave bodies to shield me. But that's my pity, for I'd as soon be dead."

Arthor hears depths of grief in the elf. "Why?"

"Need you, of all people, ask? You, a Christian?" Tensions of sorrow and anger draw tight lines across Bright Night's scalded forehead. "Your faith is what is killing the elves. The love your gentle Jesus preaches holds much appeal for the Síd—elves and faeries alike. But when we take on your faith, we leave the hollow hills, we leave the underground of the Storm Tree, where we have taken refuge these many years, and we return to the great cycle of being—of birth and rebirth. Our numbers are growing less when we should be multiplying, increasing our multitudes, the better to fight our way back into the Great Tree. But we'll never walk in the upper boughs again now that we are losing ourselves to your god. We are doomed—and I'd rather be dead than see the Daoine Síd fade away."

"Jesus promises eternal salvation—"

A laugh harsh as a shout cuts through the elf. "The wish is the keyhole to the soul, lad. Don't we all wish to be eternally saved? But, I'll tell you a truth, unless you practice emptiness and disadherence and silence, you will not be saved. You will return, form after form, to experience life in all its flamboyant complexity, until you are whole enough to be one with our Creator. Ah, that wholeness is lifetimes away for the likes of us."

Arthor recoils from the elf's bitterness. "That is not what my faith tells me."

"Then listen to your faith, lad," Bright Night says, and steps back into the feathers of rain dropping through the branches. "Who am I to gainsay your Jesus? Perhaps love is enough. Yet I am an elf, and for me love is a fiery call. I love the flame of life. I love the warmth of the sun. I love the brightness of the moon and stars. Until I win my way out of the hollow hills and back into the luminous boughs of the World Tree, I am not ready for the eternal salvation you preach." He fades into the silica shadows of mist.

"Bright Night," Arthor calls after him, holding his shield high. "Thank you for returning my guardian."

"May it help your sword teach the strong to tremble," the prince's dark voice shines out of nowhere. "Our faiths may differ, young warrior, but our enemies do not."

The last words wobble into echoes, as if falling down a well, and by that Arthor knows Bright Night is gone. Only then does it occur to him to ask what the elf meant when he said that the meaning of Arthor's encounters with the warlock and the sorceress would come clear in time.

"Arthor!" Melania's cry trips through the hollows of the forest. Fen's shout follows, "Arthor!"

The young warrior walks toward the sound of their voices. When he emerges from the woods into the field where he lay with Morgeu the Fey, Melania and Fen share a look of surprise to see him bearing his shield. He lifts it proudly, and relates his encounter with Bright Night.

Rainsmoke wanders off while he speaks, and the morning sun drops a hard-edged rainbow into the far fields.

"You are blessed by the faeries," Melania says. Even with her torn gown a soaked rag and her wet hair heavy as eels, her resolute beauty congests Arthor's chest with yearning. "Share your blessing with us. Come to Aquitania."

"Your sword will ensure that we win back Melania's estate," Fen states, then looks down at his grass skirt. "But first, we must get me some clothes."

"We all need new clothes," Arthor agrees, plucking at his shredded tunic. "The village of Telltale is not far from here, and I've enough coin in my saddle pouch to buy us some fine garments and a good meal, as well. Let's go there."

"Then you will come with us?" Melania asks enthusiastically.

"As far as Telltale," he answers, and refrains from putting a hand to her cheek and touching its shades of spice. "I am destined to stay here on this island of my birth. I believe that's why the elves returned my guardian. They want me to fight our enemies."

"There are enemies of Jesus enough in Aquitania," Fen asserts.

Arthor kicks at the grass. "It's not only Jesus I'm to defend. It's Britain."

"Britain?" Melania wears a mask of open disdain as she looks around at the ragged walls of aboriginal forest adrift in a slurry of fog. "Britain is a remote and desolate island, Arthor. The world is far more grand than this primitive place. True civilization awaits you in the south. Rome, Ravenna, Byzantium all touch Aquitania with their trade ships and their missions for Jesus. There you will meet wise men of deep learning and beautiful women of true refinement. You are but a boy. Think of the wonders you will experience in the big cities—Arles, Toulouse, Bordeaux. Come away from this bleak and haunted island, Arthor. Come away from elves and faeries and seek your fortune with us, with people who are building the Christian kingdoms of Europe."

Arthor blows a hollow sigh and rubs his beardless cheeks. "I cannot, Melania. Perhaps someday. But for now, I am done with adventuring. I have been to the hollow hills and stood in the Furor's shadow. Last night, a succubus ravaged me. In the face of these frights, my anger at life, at my father and my brother—at myself, really—it all seems so petty now." He shakes his head, amazed at the profound misunderstanding of his earlier life. "I just want to go back to where I belong. I want to serve my people—the ones who adopted me and made me their own. They loved me then despite my bitterness. And now that I'm purged of that rancor, I owe them my service—my love. I owe them at least that."

"That is right," Fen says, with a taunting grin. "You have found your place as a little man."

Only a flicker of eyelids betrays the sting Arthor feels at the Saxon's tone. "I am a little man, Fen. That is what God made me. And I am not ashamed of that as once I was. Now I just want to go home."

"At least you have a home," Melania complains. "The barbarians have seized mine."

"You have Fen," Arthor assures her, and this time does touch her cheek, enthralled by her loveliness. He steps back. "And he has you. Together you will make a home for yourselves." He faces Fen, and says stoutly, "You are always welcome to stay here—on this bleak and remote island. I will speak to Kyner on your behalf, Fen. He is a good Christian and will make a place for you in our clan."

"I don't want a place in any clan," Fen grumbles. "I want my own place in the world. Melania and I discussed this. We are beholden to no clan, to no god, to no one but ourselves. When you are done serving those less than you, when you can truckle no more to the demands of inferior men, like that clod Cei, then *you* seek *us* out, and we will welcome you to our household in *our* own land." He thumps the thunderbolt cicatrix over his heart, and his stridency breaks off abruptly as he gazes down at his naked chest and grass-kirtled waist. "But for now, let's get some clothes and some food."

Melania laughs with Fen, and their mirth sparks shared joy in Arthor. He feels happy for them, glad that they have found themselves in each other, because this proves to him what, in his loneliness as an orphan and a mongrel, he has always needed to believe: that love is bigger than clans and transcends even the strict precincts of faith. He laughs with them, and together they stroll through the wet grass and mobs of flowers to the hill where the palfrey waits patiently in the soft sunlight, nibbling weeds.

The journey to Telltale is lighthearted, a morning walk with friends. They speculate about the eerie gleeman and decide he must have been the elf-king. How else could he have had the strength to wound the Furor? And they also wonder nervously if the dwarf and the Thunderers, driven from the hollow hills, still haunt these woods.

Both Fen and Arthor are good trackers and, seeing no signs of trespass through the wild broom and swaths of knotweed and wildflowers, proceed fearlessly. By noon, they arrive at Telltale. A small party of pilgrims bound ultimately for Galilee is departing as the wanderers enter the thorp, and the opportunity to join them seems too propitious to ignore.

Arthor gives the couple his coin pouch and receives a hasty kiss from Melania, a clap on the shoulder from Fen. And then, abrupt as a wafting cloud shadow, they depart. The last he sees of them is their laughter and their jubilant waves from the back of a wagon rocking through a noonfield of citrine flowers. Melania tosses her head, her sable hair flowing over her shoulders, and she smiles at the man she loves.

The sudden absence of his companions leaves Arthor feeling lonely and eager to be on his way. After spending his last coin for bread and cheese and a hemp jerkin to replace his rent tunic, he rides off. The memory of Melania's loveliness lingers, and several times he pauses to turn back, to join her on the quest to reclaim her ancestral estate. But the amorous mystery of last night's enchantment stops him each time. He feels uneasy with her now that he has made love to her wraith. Beautiful as she is and haunting as her memory remains, she belongs to Fen, and only her shadow has given itself to Arthor. If he pursues her, he will be chasing a phantom.

At last, when his heartache becomes unbearable, he stops in an alder grove dripping pollen, and among lightsplinters and butterflies scribbling in the wind, he kneels before his shield and prays. *Mother Mary, I have lived angry all my life. I burned with desire for what I could not have. Now that my anger is exhausted, I still burn for what I cannot have. But not for the power I once craved. Not that, because I learned in hell*

that power means being alone with a loneliness many times
yourself. I want no part of it. Let Kyner and Cei have that.
I will serve them gladly now, happy and protected in my
anonymity. Only ease this burning desire for what I cannot
have. Take Melania out of my heart.

He looks up to heaven, and wind turns the
leaves in the branches and reveals a kingdom of
clouds. They are his childhood dreams of a majestic
domain all his own, which he is glad to see blowing
away. The domes and streaming pennants of his
puerile ambitions dissolve and take with them the
responsibilities of power he is now relieved to let
go. Whip strokes of lightning glint in the far distance, where the Furor patrols his own realm.

The clouds part, and the sun makes him lower his
eyes. The Blessed Mother gazes gently and wistfully
from his shield. Her answer to his plight remains the
same, he is sure, and he speaks for her: "Love is first.
Never abandon."

For a while, he sits in the hot light thinking about
love. He suspects that love is only desire until it is
returned. And that is why the succubus came to him
last night, while Fen was welcomed by Melania herself. That decided, he hangs the shield from the saddle peg and mounts. He rides decisively now, sure of
his destination. His head high, he stares above the
horizon into the blue that, like loneliness, goes out as
far as he can see. And the wind travels with him.

Chapter Fifteen

Days have entangled themselves while Kyner and Cei argue and lead their caravan along forest trails and hill traces, vainly seeking an exit from the valley where Brokk trapped them. Grapevines curtain whole walls of the forest, attesting to the lingering remnants of ancient Roman invaders. Now and then rubble from a lost mill or granary, some of it with Latin inscriptions, appears among the profuse dodder.

Several times a day, Kyner calls the lumbering caravan to a halt to pray. Everyone kneels in the drizzle of sunlight that falls through the dense canopy and strikes the leaf litter like flint. Yet, though the prayers are intoned by the elders and the chieftain with strenuous sincerity, no pathway appears out of the tall forest.

Cei wants to abandon the wagons and carts and walk the horses out of the valley. But Kyner refuses to forsake their property. He remains convinced that earnest prayer will reveal a trail. "The Romans were no fools," he keeps saying. "They surveyed more than one way into a valley. If we look, we'll find a way that the avalanche has not blocked."

When it rains, the chambers of the forest glisten and drip as if inside a cave. Motes of pastel daylight glint like minerals. Behind the overcast, time sits still, and the caravan trudges on morosely.

The children stopped singing early on, when Kyner and Cei began yelling about who was at fault for taking the wrong fork into this benighted place. The elders separated the chieftain and his son. Then, for a while, the youngsters taunted Kyner with mocking singsong rhymes, especially when the narrow hill paths he led them along dwindled away or, as happened once, ended in a clutter of old stones and a graven satyr with a laughing face. The children had no fear of the chieftain, because he could never bring himself to punish them; when he got most furious, he would line them up against the wagons and beat their shadows.

After a while, even japing the chieftain lost its appeal. Now the children play in groups while marching alongside the caravan or join the women in the wagons and busy themselves helping with stitchwork. Kyner's voice as he prays contains more frequent registers of frustration, anger, and aggrieved justice, and he turns a blind eye to the small offerings of honeycomb and herb sachets left behind on the trail for the faerïes.

At the watery hour of twilight, when will-o'-the-wisps run along banks of orange saprophytes sprouting in a rocky creek bed, Kyner is willing to follow. The caravan rattles and groans on the riprap, and the fleet, gaseous gusts of light disappear and circle back, clearly leading the slow line of wagons. At last, the fox fires bleed off the wind into an open sky jammed with stars, and the wanderers find themselves on a Roman highway at the throat of the valley.

Leagues away in Camelot, Merlin feels them emerge from obscurity. He has been searching in trance for Kyner but has been too weak to find him until now. Vigor has been returning slowly to the wizard since the Furor tapped deeply into Merlin's potency. Puffed and sleepy, he paces the great hall of the citadel, listening to but not hearing the distant music and cheers of the bonfire festivities. He wants to bring Kyner to Arthor, to protect the young king on the last leg of his journey to Camelot. Without the full verve of his magic, he must rely on the faeries.

Ghostly flits of radiance come and go through the tall, empty windows where night stands in its glittering black robes. The faeries bring news of Arthor asleep in a forest glade while the moon rummages through clouds. They urgently warn of a wildwood gang camping in the dense grasses nearby. Surely by daylight they will encounter each other.

"Guide Kyner to Arthor," Merlin instructs, swirling his staff through the air, whirlpooling the sparks closer so that his words touch each of the tiny visitors. "The chieftain won't obey you, so you must go directly to his horses. Talk to them. Get their help. Do you understand?"

The faeries flare up to the cedar rafters and splash among the timbers, signaling their assent. And then, they rush into the night, pulsing like fireflies, and are gone. With them, they take a little more of his energy, and he slumps exhausted to a workbench and rests his head in his arms on a sawyer's table strewn with curly wood shavings and blond streaks of saw-dust.

Morning's rust-colored light shines on the sills when the stout, red-faced foreman rouses Merlin with his loud voice: "Wizard, forgive me for waking you."

Merlin lifts a woozy face of matted beard and sleep scars. "Leave me rest. Work later."

"I'm not here to work," the foreman announces in his big voice, and marvels yet again at the strange way the wizard's face changes from day to day. "Lord Severus bids me announce his presence."

"Tell him to go away," Merlin mutters, and lowers his head toward the blackness of sleep.

"Wizard, he will not go away," the foreman says, and leans his thick arms on the table to say more softly, "He has gathered together all his Britons—Lord Marcus's camp and Bors Bona's army, too. The Celts—Lord Urien and King Lot—have arrayed their warriors in response."

"Oh, please!" Merlin groans, and pushes heavily to his feet like a swimmer a long time in water risen to land. "What is Syrax's game?"

Merlin takes his hat from the table and, not even bothering to brush off the sawdust, puts it on. He swipes a stool out of his way with his staff and marches under scaffolds and trestles, muttering grouchily to himself. Through the arched portal of the great hall, he exits into the inner ward and a flawless morning. Severus Syrax, in shiny brass cuirass, turbaned pith helmet, red silk tunic, and military sandals, strolls, hands behind his back, examining the workmanship of the lathwork on the main doorframes.

When he sees Merlin, the *magister militum* steps back. The wizard appears more formidable than when last they met—taller and more angular. One can see the skeleton in him. And as he draws closer, Severus is astonished by the skull-like hollowness of his face, the gnarled features above a beard of bleached sea kelp, and those weird devil's eyes staring so brightly from their dark pits they make the warlord feel suddenly woken from the dead.

In a booming voice, Merlin asks, "Why are you here, Syrax?"

Severus bows curtly, his painted face composed but with a deep pallor that tells of his fear. "It is time, wizard."

"Time for what?" Merlin stands so close that the frightened man can smell the wizard's slow-burning blood, the cold mauve resonance of a man not quite human.

To his credit, the *magister militum* holds his voice steady, though his rib cage itself trembles. "It is time for what we agreed."

"We have agreed to nothing."

Fear and its frantic isomers of dread and stress congeal to cold anger at this apparent betrayal. "Are you twitting me, Merlin? You agreed I am the man you seek for the throne. I have come to hold you to your word."

"Ah, I see." Merlin finally realizes that Syrax must have confronted Hannes. "My word."

The warlord holds his voice flat, almost devoid of

emphasis, as the initial shock of confronting the wizard eases to the icy comprehension that this devil has lied to him. "I have been warned that you are the spawn of an incubus, and that your word is as changeable as your face. I see now you wear a frightful face. When last we spoke, you preferred a more comic countenance. But I am prepared for your capriciousness."

Merlin lifts a tufted eyebrow. "Are you now?"

"Do you not hear?" Severus lifts a hand in a confidently fey gesture toward the bulwark that partitions the outer ward. The coughs of horses and the shimmer of men's voices sounds from the near distance. "Then, behold!" The *magister militum* claps, and the inner ward's temporary lumber doors swing wide to reveal scores of horsemen and foot soldiers in chain mail and bronze helmets. Blond as a Saxon, Marcus Domnoni, holding the chi-rho banner of the Christian battle hordes, drifts through the martial throng on a white charger. Bors Bona, a small giant with a boar's visage and stubbly gray hair, sits at their head astride a huge warhorse, Medusa-masked helmet in hand. He grins without glee at the wizard.

Merlin sighs. "You cannot seize the throne, Syrax, not even with this host."

"That is not what we agreed, Merlin." Severus, all fear abated and flush with pride, twines a sharp prong of his black, precisely trimmed beard. "The sword. I have gathered my warriors and the armies of Bors Bona and Marcus Domnoni this morning to witness my drawing of the sword."

"Oh, is that it?" Merlin comprehends, lowering his head and stroking his beard.

Unfazed by the wizard's obvious reluctance, the warlord adds, "The Celts have rallied their numbers as well. Now all shall witness my ascendancy."

"Lord Kyner is yet to arrive," Merlin protests.

"I can wait on him no longer," Severus says in a bold voice, then turns and strides toward the large war party. "He is days late. Let him learn of today's important events in the bard's songs."

Merlin shakes his head wearily. "As you will."

A groom leads a black stallion forward for the *magister militum* and an ashen mule for the wizard. Under a boiling sunrise, they ride out of the citadel and across the grassy range, where the crowds who have gathered for the festivities mill and cheer. The Celts wait on the hillside pastures. When they see the wizard riding with the British, they lower their weapons and join the procession.

Merlin leads the multitude down the long curving road to the vagrant river. They ride among trees squabbling with birds and shining with a meaning more than they are, as if something miraculous is about to happen.

Severus Syrax prances proudly through the complex veils of morning mist peeling off the river and takes the lead as the parade approaches Mons Caliburnus. He dismounts among the dew-sequined lime shrubs and, followed by Merlin, Bors Bona, Marcus Domnoni, King Lot, and Chief Urien, marches to the summit.

Merlin thinks the *magister militum* plans to give a speech, because he pauses before the star stone and gazes out at the crowd on the hillside. But he only wants to be certain that all eyes are watching him. He looks to the wizard briefly, searching for a sign that does not come. Yet that does not dissuade the swarthy Briton. Confidently, he seizes the hilt of Excalibur and tugs.

The sword does not budge. He pulls again, one foot propped against the edge of the stone, body leaning back. But Excalibur remains fused to the stone.

The anguish in Severus's kohl-rimmed eyes tweaks pity from Merlin, though the warlord's humiliation is proper and inevitable. A thin wind picks up like laughter looking for a definite shape and finds it in the throng below, whose silence dissolves into frothy murmuring, then outright glee and mockery from the Celts.

Bors Bona puts a hand to his sword, and Merlin fixes him with his silver eyes and breathes one word, "Don't." There is no magic in his voice. But he needs none, for his chill look of implacable authority is enough even for the bellicose Bors.

Merlin crawls onto the stone and stands, arms and staff raised. "Who laughs that has not tried his hand?" he shouts. "None are denied the chance to be proven high king of Britain. None. And those who laugh scorn all good men's hopes. Severus Syrax should be cheered. I say cheered, because he dares aspire to unite us one and all against our common enemies. That his noble aspiration has not been fulfilled now or in these past fifteen years does not diminish our dire need—nor weaken the dream that one day we *will* be united."

Merlin points his staff at the mob that has been

creeping up the slope to hear him. "All you who have faith in a united kingdom—all you who are loyal to our king, whoever he may be, whenever he may come, cheer now this man, Severus Syrax, who has foisted pride for hope—the hope that must not die if we as a people are to live."

Bors Bona throws his fists into the air and cheers. First the Britons and then, gradually and in mounting force, the Celts join in the cheering. And soon the river gorge rings with their jubilant cries, and Severus Syrax slowly raises his arms in the happy triumph of his defeat.

Merlin sits down and slides off the star stone. He walks into the crowd that streams forward to congratulate Syrax and to try their own hands at drawing the sword. Around him bodies jostle and fingers snatch at his robes, hoping to draw luck from contact with him. His silence is so loud, his quartz eyes so luminous in their big bonepits, that no one actually dares confront him, and, with his progress thus unimpeded, he gradually makes his way through the dense gathering to the mule that will return him to Camelot.

This immense summer morning of rushing birds, tumbling butterflies, and fat, ample clouds offers no consolation to the wizard for the diminishment of his powers. Time alone can restore him to the magical clarity and force he once knew, yet time stands against him and the fragile hope he has created for his people. The longer Arthor is alone in the woods, the greater the opportunity for the forces of chaos to defeat him—and with him, Merlin's vision and purpose. Then Morgeu the Fey, with that abominable child in her womb, will be all that remains of Uther Pendragon's sacrifice, a mockery of the future.

Riding atop the mule, Merlin shivers. The sun's heat feels cool. Seed tufts drift onto the river, and the current pulls them away from land, into its own seeking. Somewhere Arthor travels like that, swept along by fate. What can I do? Deprived of his magic, Merlin feels helpless, and the cosmic climate looks bleak. He is far better off not knowing that at this moment Arthor faces death.

A dozen rabid men in motley garb and crude animal hides have surrounded him, boiling out of the underbrush. They arrive from downwind while he refreshes himself at a brook. So abruptly and fiercely do they burst through the screen of hedges, there is no time to mount the palfrey. He seizes his shield and sends the horse splashing across the shallow water before whirling about, Short-Life in his hand.

The wildwood gang fans out, encircling their young prey, harrying him with shouts and thrown rocks that make him twist and crouch. With animal grease glossed on their faces and limbs to fend biting insects, they shine in the strong sunlight as if lit with inner radiance. Their destructive knowing charges the air with their shrieks, their bestial stink, and the agile speed with which they deploy to enclose him, signaling each other with hoots and whistles, and Arthor realizes that these men are adept at killing.

"I have nothing!" he shouts against their wild cries. "I am a Christian man! I have nothing but my horse!"

His horse they will track down later. Now they want his fine Bulgar saber, that quartz-hafted dagger in his sword belt, and the colorful shield he bears. All these will be theirs, and his sandals, as well.

Arthor realizes he must get to higher ground, away from the uneven footing of the brook. But whichever way he goes, his back will stand exposed for fatal moments. Driving off the palfrey was a mistake; he grasps that now, standing without cover, rocks banging off his shield and smiting the ground around him. Hard as he tries to gauge the array of men around him, the more they seem to shift, sliding past each other, ducking close to pelt him, then hopping backward and darting away. No targets present themselves.

A stone smacks Arthor's shin and drops him to one knee. Immediately, two brigands rush him from atop the embankment, one with a knife, the other bearing a sword, both held low to slash upward. Behind him, he hears others sloshing across the brook. He decides that the water is where he will stand, and he whirls upright and lunges into the narrow stream. Three men meet him there, two with swords, one with an ax, all cold-eyed and wrath-faced, the ropes of their throats taut with screaming.

Arthor begins his death-dance. Short-Life blurs once over his head in a feint that stymies the three in the water, then arcs backward, spinning him after it and catching the two behind him off guard. The saber pierces the man with the knife in the groin and slashes slantwise across the forearm and chest of the swordsman, dropping them both to their backs, bawling with pain. Following the heavy blade's momentum, Arthor pirouettes to his original stance, Short-Life whirring over his head.

The men in the stream back hurriedly away, stunned by his lethal display. But in the next instant, a rock punches Arthor between the shoulder blades and throws him to his knees in the water. With a yelp, the axman descends on him, and the shield covers him just in time to deflect a skull-splitting blow. Short-Life gouges upward, penetrates thigh muscle, and twists to separate it from bone.

His weapon caught briefly in his enemy's fleshy part, the others converge. Another rock bashes his shoulder, wrenching him forward. He cries out and shoves hard to get to his feet. The axman collapses before him, thrashing in agony, and Arthor shimmies backward downstream.

Rocks impact around him, and he ducks and holds his shield high to protect his head. Turning quickly, he keeps the brigands at bay. The three men he has cut lie screaming in their blood. Their comrades, infuriated by their unexpected losses at the sword of this beardless youth, attack with a renewed frenzy, pelting him from all sides with rocks.

Arthor prepares to die. In the furious moment of this acceptance, he regrets only that he has not yet had his chance to serve the people who reared him and who received from him only scorn and the benefit of his battle rage. And somehow now, with the war whoops of his killers closing in, that seems just, for the unfortunate darkness in him merits this death, while what he has found of goodness does not deserve the love of those he abandoned but will find favor in heaven, where Mother Mary will speak for him and where God already knows the depth and significance of his contrition.

Like the soul that has already fled Arthor's body, the palfrey flies down the brook, out of the ditch, and into the wind-shaken trees under the grazing clouds. It runs from the sounds of shouting men, through the forest's glittery darkness, its eyes wide-open to everything.

Not far away, on the Roman highway, a faerïe flies into the ear of Cei's horse while he squats in the bushes. "Stop!" he yells, as the steed pulls free of its tether and heaves through the underbrush. It runs, spirited by the faerïes' command, touched by Merlin's wish to lead Kyner's Celts to Arthor. It knows none of this, only the urgency to crash through bushes and bracken until it sees its bright double under the sewn stars of the forest canopy.

Moments later, Cei and a guardsman arrive on their horses and pull up short when they spot Cei's runaway nuzzling the palfrey. "That's Arthor's horse!"

"Listen—" The guardsman points into the air at the sounds of distant shouting.

"Get the others," Cei orders, and urges his mount forward. He rushes through the forest's tangled byways, following the palfrey's hoofprints in the duff and leaf litter. When he arrives at the brook, he spots Arthor upstream curled under his shield, turning slow helpless circles before an enclosing gang of rock-throwers and swordsmen. He draws his weapon and charges.

At the sight of the galloping horseman, the brigands fan out again. They scramble onto the embankments and stone the rider as he closes in on their prey. But he bounds up one side of the brook and bears down on the men gathered there, swatting them with his sword. They scatter, and he dashes across the stream and attacks the enemy there.

Arthor, with his bloodied knees on the brook cobbles, raises his face to heaven, and even as his prayer of salvation begins, he sees Kyner and his band swooping down from the forest, trumpets blaring, lances and swords glinting. And slowly, weighted with astonishment, he gets to his feet, all he could pray for already come to pass.

---◦◦◦---

Chapter Sixteen

Arthor washes Short-Life in the brook, and when Kyner dismounts and sloshes toward him, the boy drops to one knee and presents the saber to him hilt first. "Your sword, Father."

Kyner stands motionless, the blue of his eyes tucked into the leathery seams of his face, peeking out as if unwilling or unable to trust what they see. He takes the sword and motions for Arthor to rise. "Get up, son. You have no need to kneel before me."

Arthor stands, still heavy with amazement that death, which had nearly driven his soul from his body with thrown stones and fierce cries, has now turned to save him: The clangor of steel and the screams from the shorn lives of the brigands brattles the morning air. Arthor, grateful that this miracle has granted him a chance to fulfill the love he has found for himself and his family, embraces Kyner.

The old warrior returns the hug, strongly yet with a tentative heart, not yet sure of the character and significance of the change that he sees in his young ward. Not until later, after the brigands have been run down and slain and the warriors regathered, does he sense the authenticity of Arthor's profound transformation. Cei, with a gloating smirk, leads the palfrey to Arthor, and says, "So this time we took your toasted biscuits out of the fire, eh, Arthor?"

"Thank you, Cei." He looks up at the horseman with a soft, grateful smile in his pale face, his slanted amber eyes aglint with happy tears. "You might well have left me to die for all the heartache I've put upon you in the past."

Cei's vaunting sneer fades. "Aye—well—let this serve as a lesson in Christian fidelity to you. I take care of my own—no matter how untamed. Perhaps now you'll show more respect for those better-born and stop whining about where God has seen fit to place you. You would be waiting for the Resurrection right this moment if not for me."

"I will never forget that, brother," Arthor readily admits. Without his sword and garbed in his hempen sack-shirt, with his short hair stiff as a hedgehog's and his pale rosy-cheeked face free of its familiar scowl, he looks more like a boy than a warrior. "And you—and father—have my solemn word, I will keep to my place. And gladly."

Cei shares a surprised look with Kyner. "Clearly, Father, you were right to send him off with Fen. The trouble of it seems to have worked some good sense into him." He nods to Arthor. "Here's your horse. Let's get back to the cortege."

Kyner utters a silent prayer, thanking God for fulfilling the chieftain's prior petitions for Arthor's safe return. They ride back to the caravan in happy silence, and the chieftain asks nothing of Fen's fate or the disposition of Aelle and his Thunderers. The wind in the trees no longer carries the curling echoes of stabbed men. Kyner's warriors file back through the stippled shadows, not one of them wounded.

After receiving the subdued greetings of the clan, who have few joyful memories of him, Arthor rides beside Kyner at the back of the procession while Cei takes the lead. How wide the sky looks now to the young man. The road opening into the future seems painted in new colors, and when he tells his adventure to the chief, it feels strange in Arthor's mouth, like a story that happened to someone else.

He holds nothing back. He reveals his heart's reasons for wanting to carry Short-Life into a world that does not know him. He speaks of the immediate passion that seized him when first he saw Melania in Cissa's tent and how he envisioned her as his death, lovely and beckoning, and went to her willingly and would have died then and there under the hacking blades of the Thunderers—but for the lamia. Shaking his head, he talks of the mysterious gleeman and his wise dog.

Kyner recognizes the description of the old, bearded man with the long, bestial skull, deep sockets, and eyes of moonstones. Merlin! But he keeps his silence, wanting the boy to tell all of what poisoned and killed his former self and be purged fully of it.

Arthor recounts his journey into the hollow hills. His voice grows soft as he describes the nether sky of sod with its mauve glow that shadowed forth misty swirls of stars and the fat, peach-bright moon. Softer still, he narrates the terrifying confrontation with the Furor, before whose vast mutilation and ancient, haunted presence it was impossible for him to be brave.

He whispers of his escape from the mad god and the lamia. Finally, like a sleeper mumbling by heart what he carries out of his dream, he retells his seduction by the ghost-double of Melania. When he concludes with the bitter truth of Melania's love for Fen and their shared devotion to the wholeness and joy they found in each other, his words are empty air.

But by then Kyner does not need to hear any more, for that part of the story is so old it became song in the first generation of the first people.

"You did well to return, son," he tells the morose boy. "I'm happy to see you with us again—and not just because I have returned to me my sword and my best warrior—but because you've changed for the better. I will thank the Furor for that myself should I see him."

Arthor peers up sharply from under his lowered brow. "Don't even jest about it, Father."

Camelot appears above the highway with the afternoon's first gold. The silver rays of the noon sun brighten the top girders of the tall, unfinished spires into golden crowns suggesting the work of radiant beings. Music floats in waves from the pastures where round dances and flower frolics engage the crowds between martial displays of archery and horsemanship. At this distance, the people appear as dark and colorful grains on the tilted fields, brightening and fading under the vast sweep of cloud shadows.

Cold Kitchen bustles with busy merchants and farmers loading wagons with goods for the festival: amphorae of fruit wine, kegs of mead, baskets of bread, racks of butchered meat, and mounds of vegetables. The whole town is a market. The sight of so many busy, laughing, shouting people delights Arthor. His sadness at the departure of Melania thins away before the joy of seeing so many happy, productive Britons and Celts striving shoulder to shoulder, and he grins to be among his people—to have a people to be among!

Crosswinds ripple the meadow grass on the steep road to Camelot, and an ocean of sky expands around them—all contributing to a reckoning of vastness. Arthor remembers his last visit to this place five years earlier and how the huge vista had awed him then. He expected the site would appear smaller to him now that he was himself larger. But, contrary to his expectations, the mountain shoulders heave taller, the summer pastures furl wider, and the horizon plunges deeper into an immaculate clarity of river scrawl and forest.

Looking ahead at the clustered turrets and broad ramparts of the citadel, he realizes that the terrain looks larger because Camelot has risen to a noble stature and heightened the human perspective of the surroundings. What had been stubby foundation blocks have grown in five years to proud spires and tiers of parapets and tall vallations. The sight of ant-tiny workers moving atop the high battlements lends the prospect a colossal dimension.

Jugglers and musicians greet the caravan as it

trundles onto the champaign before the bastion's outer wall. The soldiers, women, and children of Kyner's clan spill out of the wagons to follow the pipers and fiddlers and acrobatic tumblers to the playing fields. There, feast tables and colorful gaming tents surround wide, grassy tournament grounds, where children compete in pig runs and tug-of-war, and adults dance and cavort or meet the challenges of target shooting and equestrian races.

Kyner takes Cei and Arthor aside as the others rush toward the festivities. "You're both old enough this festival to come with me to meet and show our respects to the chieftains and warlords," he tells them.

"Father, we've arrived late," Cei complains. "The tournaments have already begun. Look, you can see the sword contests are under way in the upper field. That's my best event!"

"Don't whine, Cei," Kyner rebukes, pulling his son away from his horse and waving for the groom to lead the steed away. "You'll be chieftain yourself soon enough. You must know your peers."

"But my sword," Cei protests, unbuckling the scabbard and holding up the weapon. "The haft has jarred loose. I ruined it in the skirmish with the wildwood gang. I'll need time to find a weapon. And the contest has already started!"

"So it has," Kyner observes with a note of impatience. "But we have not come for the contests alone, Cei. There's the business of the kingdom to attend to."

Cei rolls his head backward in frustration. "But I'm not chieftain."

"You need to see how chieftains and warlords contend in conference," Kyner insists, and strides toward the grand pavilion of yellow tent canvas with purple pennants that occupies the range before the citadel's main gate. "Come along."

"Arthor does not need to attend," Cei points out, striding beside his father. "Let him go to find me a sword to replace the one I damaged saving his hide. I'll then at least have a weapon ready when we're done palavering."

Kyner nods curtly. "Arthor may do so, if he will."

"I will, Cei," Arthor quickly agrees. "I'll find the best sword for your grip."

"Good." Cei claps the lad on the back and shoves him off. "Then, go. And be quick about it."

"Wait." Kyner stops the boy as he skips off. "Arthor shall go, as he has agreed. But first he, too, shall be presented to the nobles. Now, come along, the two of you."

The pavilion has tent walls decorated with both Christian symbols and curvilinear Celtic emblems, and within its airy, luminous interior a small, mock round table has been erected. Three chairs of Celtic design stand to one side, three of Roman fashion stand on the other. A seventh chair of plain, dark-stained wood is positioned at the table between the two groups, and behind it stands a tall man in midnight blue robes and a wide-brimmed hat with bent conical top, both garments subtly stitched with crimson astrological sigils and alchemic devices.

As a ten-year-old, when Arthor attended the last festival, he saw this stark, shadowy figure often in the distance and knows he is the wizard Merlin. But when the herald at the pavilion entry announces, "Chief Kyner, his son Cei, and ward Arthor—" and the wizard looks up, Arthor's breath twists in his lungs. Merlin is the very gleeman who led him and Melania into the hollow hills and who suffered to free them from the Furor.

The wizard nods to Kyner and Cei and, with eyes like shattered glass, holds Arthor's wide stare, waiting for him to speak. But Arthor finds he cannot untwist his breath to speak. He is not constrained by magic but by the wide expansiveness of his own surprise, which swallows all his thoughts. Kyner sees the dizzy look in Arthor's face before the wizard's sapient and silent patience and says nothing, for this is not the place to expect secret disclosures. The moment passes. The wizard gestures to the others, who stand around the table marveling at the work plans for the fortress-city.

Lord Urien, silver braid caught in a gold clasp at his naked shoulder, lowers his chin in acknowledgment of but spare deference to the Christian Celt. Severus Syrax, swarthy Persian features framed by coiffed black curls, comes forward to greet them with an obsequious grin in his elegantly trimmed beard. While he clasps their shoulders in his beringed hands and leads them to the table, square-headed Bors Bona and blond Marcus Domnoni, both beardless and attired in Roman tunics and leather breastplates embossed with lamb and fish symbols, nod. King Lot's eagle-browed stare meet's Kyner's blunt gaze, but the monarch of the North Isles does not deign to offer any greeting to these Celts who have abandoned their heritage.

Arthor does not notice, for he stares at the scarlet-gowned woman beside Lot. Morgeu the Fey openly returns his gaze, and he feels his marrows congeal. This tall woman with her muscular shoulders, flame-wild hair, and small, tight, black eyes in a moony face bears no semblance to Melania, and Arthor can hardly believe that Fen is correct and that this big-boned woman is the enchantress with whom he knew such strenuous passion under the packed stars. Yet the way she regards him with a maniacal glint in the coal-bits of her stare and a small, tight smile hooked sharply at the corner of her mouth tells him this is so.

A flare of fear radiates through him, chilling him to the roots of his teeth.

"Arthor, you're done here," Cei reminds him in a hot whisper, nudging him strenuously with his elbow. "Get going now. Find me a sword. And hurry."

Arthor jolts free of his mesmeric fright. He glances at Merlin, who has returned his attention to the scroll of work plans, then he looks to Kyner. The chief has been led to the table by Severus Syrax and leans stiff-armed over the designs, listening to the wizard.

"Go!" Cei mouths, and angrily motions for him to depart.

Arthor bolts from the pavilion. He would give Cei his own sword, but Kyner has not yet returned it to him, and, owing the old chief his life, he feels awkward asking him for his weapon. It will be returned in time, he knows—when next Kyner needs him in battle. For now, he must find another weapon.

But where? he asks himself, scanning the wide fields that slope and roll on all sides. Everywhere, the Celtic clans and British families mingle in summer activities: feasting, dancing, and competing. Who among them would have a sword for Cei? He must go to Cold Kitchen and find the lane of armorers and weaponmakers. For payment, he will offer his word as Chief Kyner's ward, and if that is not sufficient, he will offer his palfrey.

That decided, he runs to the sprawling grove of elms at a rill under a mossy bluff, where the horses are stabled. The draft horses of the caravan wagons are still being unbridled and led to water, and his palfrey stands at the rill with the other warriors' steeds, its saddle still on. Even his shield has not yet been removed from the saddle peg.

Out of a haze of horseflies, he rides from under the giant elms to the road that leads into Cold Kitchen. Dust from passing wagons glistens in the heat, and though he wants to gallop, he knows his horse is tired and does not hurry it. There is much to ponder. Merlin is the gleeman, and he stands this minute in the same tent with Morgeu the Fey, who ensorcelled Arthor with his love for Melania. Why?

He recalls the wounded elf-prince who returned the shield with the icon of the Virgin telling him that all would come clear in time. Portent rises with the dust. Thinking of the knowing way the wizard and the sorceress looked at him, he feels pale and smoky, as if with a sudden turn of the wind he might blow away.

At Cold Kitchen, he moves slowly among the merchants' stalls, where yet more goods are being packed and loaded for the climb to Camelot. The alley of armorers is empty. A portly woman in a flour-dusted apron steps from the adjacent lane of bakeries to inform him that the armorers and sword-makers have gone to Mons Caliburnus this afternoon to display their wares before the visitors who gather to gawk at Excalibur.

Arthor feels he must hurry now. Surely, the con-ference in the pavilion is concluded, and Cei waits impatiently for his sword. A smile flickers over his face as he rides fast out of the hamlet and descends past staunch maples into the cooler emerald light of the river gorge. In times past, he would have let Cei muddle about for his own sword. No warrior in his right mind would loan Cei theirs, knowing what a brutish swordsman he is. By the time he found one, the day's contests would be over, and he would spend the night lamenting about the victories deprived him. At least now, if Arthor hurries, Cei will win or lose by his own merit, and the evening feast will be more pleasant for all.

Invisible chains of birdsong link the branches of the overarching trees that flank the road to the river. At the approaching thunder of hooves, rabbits startle from bushes in the roadside ditch and jitter across his path. The algal scent of the river's dark measure sweeps over him with a deeper coolness, and the air hums with the current of water-rubbed rocks. He slows to pass a line of cross-bearing pilgrims in wet loincloths, straggly hair, and beards heavy and still dripping from their baptisms in the Amnis.

Around a bend of mulberry trees and lime shrubs, the river swings into view, with its murky burden of tree litter, shadows, and sliding light. Yarrow-wild banks line the road to the gravel fan, where a score of horses stand tethered to a broken-down sycamore or wander grazing through a field of ryegrass and cowslip. He dismounts and ties the palfrey's reins to a lime shrub and runs uphill past more dense shrubs to where saffron banners wag in the river breeze. There, a small but eager crowd has gathered around a long table, upon which are displayed thirty or more swords.

Arthor shoulders among the men viewing the swords, selects a hefty weapon that has the sturdy aspect he knows Cei favors, and declares, "I will have this one."

"A mighty blade," the jowly swordmaker across the table concurs. "If you've enough gold coin, this Saxon-slayer can be yours."

"I've no coin at all," Arthor says. "But I can guarantee payment."

"Of course!" The swordmaker laughs skeptically. "And you'll swear on the Bible itself and every prophet in it, will you not?"

"I've no need to swear," Arthor answers irately, resenting the titters from the crowd. "I am Chief Kyner's ward. He will pay me."

"Fine, lad," the portly artisan agrees. "And when the good chieftain pays me, you may have this sword."

"I need it now," Arthor stresses. "It's for my brother, Cei."

The weaponsmith puts a gruff hand on Arthor's wrist and removes the sword from his grip. "Listen to me, lad. I worked many a day to craft this bone-breaker. You're not walking away with it unless I'm paid first."

"Is there anyone here who will sell me a sword upon the good word of Chief Kyner?" Arthor calls out.

Laughter runs the length of the table, and the swordmakers shake their heads and wave him away. A foot soldier in the black-and-green colors of Bors Bona's army slaps his back and guffaws, "If you want a sword without paying, lad, then try your hand up there." He points uphill to the sword in the stone. "That's the only sword that's there for anyone to take."

"I've a palfrey," Arthor offers. "You can have my horse for a sword. Any sword."

"We're not horse traders," the jowly swordsman gripes. "Be off with you, boy!"

Reluctantly, Arthor turns away. Head hung, kicking at weed tufts, he climbs the mount. He regrets disappointing Cei on his very first attempt to serve his elder brother, and he is not eager to return to Camelot. He looks up wistfully at the star stone. It looks so black it seems to suck light into it. And there is much there at the summit to feed upon, for the sword the stone holds upright shines with an almost inexplicable brightness. Its beauty draws him closer.

Light pulses in the gold hilt, and the simple glyph

of the handguard appears slick as a flame. He wants to touch the sword, even though that makes him feel silly, because he is not some simpleminded pilgrim happy to brag that he has been to Camelot and touched Excalibur. Yet, the blade is truly remarkable—clear and deep as a mirror, as if it has been cored out of the air itself.

He stands in silence before its beauty. A chill snakes through him with the abrupt insight that this sword looks very much like the terrible weapon the dwarf Brokk carried in the hollow hills, and that the viper-priest raised over him—the silver-gold sword that the gleeman—Merlin himself—flung out of the mansnake's hand to wound the god of wrath.

Can it be one and the same? he asks, trembling as though the heart of the earth had throbbed beneath him.

He trudges forward as in a dream. Before him, Excalibur, wiped with radiance, shimmers like running starlight. It *is* the supernatural sword that nearly took his life in the hollow hills! His whole body twitches to face this talismanic weapon *here,* at the crux of his convergence with the gleeman Merlin and the undisguised enchantress who mocked his hope of love with lust. Now he can no longer deny a fateful complicity between these magical personages and his own destiny—but to what intent he cannot guess.

He thinks for an instant of fleeing but instead draws closer to the weapon, fascinated to see it held inert in the stone. Even still, motion glows from within. He stands transfixed by this thing that once almost killed him. It has the enormous presence of something other than a weapon and embodies lucidities that carry far more than the wounds of war promised by other swords.

It shines in his wide eyes full of marvel, full of fright, proffering truths as much of terror as of beauty. If he puts his hand out, if he takes it, he senses with prescient certitude that he will touch what cannot be touched, what already touches him at the heart of everything he believes to be good and beautiful and true. He does not understand this. Yet, he *knows* that in his inmost heart he already holds this sword—and that is why it did not kill him when he stood before the mad god of war. It did not kill him, because it belongs to him.

Filled with a holy passion, Arthor reaches out and takes Excalibur in his hand.

---◆◇◆---

Chapter Seventeen

Merlin stands on the riverbank under Mons Caliburnus. Having sloshed through floating green beds of milfoil and watercress, his feet and the hem of his robe are soaked, but he has succeeded in arriving unseen at this secluded scarp. His magic is yet too weak to baffle people, and he feels proud that by cunning and physical effort alone he has positioned himself here, ready to manipulate the magnetic counterstone that will release Excalibur and make Arthor king.

Morgeu the Fey knew exactly where Merlin was headed when he left the pavilion claiming he needed rest. Of course, she made no move to hinder him. She wants him to install Arthor as high king. Once her half brother is established as the legitimate ruler of Britain, then the incestuous bastard she carries will have a rightful claim as successor to the throne. Thus, for the next few years, the wizard can rely on his archfoe to serve as his ally. She will pose no further threat, at least not until the kingdom has been united and all opposition quelled. After that, however—

The wizard shakes his head. *Every act has its consequences,* he recites to himself the first tenets of wisdom.

*And consequences become themselves acts and ripple into
further consequences. And in this way, no prophecy is certain, for the future hides within itself.*

Briefly, Merlin recalls his mortal mother, Optima, the saint who adopted his demon spirit out of
the void and made a place for him in her womb and
in her heart. The place of her womb became his
body: an ugly, grotesque body born old and growing
younger year by year. The place of her heart became
his heart, a heart of compassion and love for all of
God's creation, so that now the gruesome memories
of his long existence as a demon cause him profound
remorse. But he has not forgotten his cruel life as a
demon. He has not forgotten evil.

The enormous amount of work that Merlin has
accomplished to bring Arthor to this bodeful
moment is only a beginning. The real struggle with
evil lies ahead. The wizard will need all his magic for
that. And the boy, surely the boy will have to be a
man, and the man surely will have to be a king, a true
king, to fulfill the great hope of this orphaned island.

With that thought, Merlin returns his attention
to the immediate task. Timing now is crucial. If the
wizard releases the magnetic hold of the star stone
too soon, the sword will fall before the boy touches
it. Too late, and Arthor will lose faith that he can
budge it at all.

To assure success, Merlin intends to use what little magic he has left to reach upward with his heart's
brails and touch the young man when he stands
before Excalibur. But first, the wizard must find the
magnetic counterstone. Wading through spike rush

and bur reeds, he gropes with his staff in the ivy tendrils, knocking against the rock wall until he locates the crevice where the sliding stone sits. His bare hand clears away clots of starwort before seizing the lozenge of meteoric rock. One tug and it will release the sword.

Eyes closed, the wizard tries to call up from within the strength to reach out from the feeling center of himself. Wrens chatter, frogs tock, dragonflies whir, yet he hears none of it. He remains attentive to the quiet within and to the greater silence inside that stillness.

Moments lapse to minutes before he manages to extend his awareness upward, out of his body, to where Arthor comes walking through yellow clover, kicking at the hawkweed and dandelions. Merlin feels the youth's disappointment unravel to awe at the sight of Excalibur. Then comes the shocked awareness that this is the sword that threatened him in the hollow hills.

The wizard experiences the debates within Arthor as though they are Merlin's own: Should he flee? No. Inward mastery holds him in place, then draws him closer. He wants to face his destiny, he wants to understand the forces that have led him on his circular journey from anonymity in Kyner's clan to the mystery of this sword. His hand reaches out and grasps the hilt of Excalibur.

Merlin's eyes snap open. A dove perches on a jut of rock at eye level, white as winter. When the wizard heaves his whole body into moving the magnetic stone, the dove bursts away, filled with the full frost of noise from the scraping stone.

As the white bird comes clear of the ivy wall of Mons Caliburnus, a flash of reflected sunlight from the summit startles it higher. The hot reflection dazzles several times more, casting from the hill-crest sharp rays of sunlight like beams of a beacon. The dove climbs away from this startling light, rises far above the snake curves of the river, and glides upward with the wind, over tilled fields, toward umber mountains and absolute blue.

Atop a rocky pinnacle, the dove alights. It blazes luminously in a shaft of lucid white sunlight let down from a zenith of towering cumulus clouds. For a while, it becomes more than it obviously is, because an angel surrounds it with his fiery presence. To mortal eyes, the angel is invisible, his face this lambent sunbeam, his robes bundles of wind stirring the gorse on the higher slopes of the mountain.

Sitting among bluebells on a slope of the angel's mountain is an ancient notch-stone erected by the nameless Neolithic people who lived here before the Celts. For one day each year, the angle of the sun aligns properly with the primeval stone so that the notches cast shadow-patterns that suddenly and briefly spell words none among the living know how to read. That day has come and gone and will come again.

The angel well remembers what the inscription of shadows says, and in honor of the star of reflected sunlight that shines from atop Mons Caliburnus, he speaks the secret words aloud: *"The truth of this dreaming world is the turning of the stars, and as the seasons return after long rest, this marks the land where dream*

*returns to its native ground, truth. Here reigns the true ruler
of these islands in memory and in promise. Great is the burden of this care."*

The words of the angel shimmer to rain in the
chill mountain air and ride the wind down the slopes
of gorse and across the conifer highlands. The lustrous torrent finally blows over the broad tableland
where Camelot rises in lordly stature above the river
forests. The sunny downpour sweeps into the round
dances and the martial contests and turns up the
amazed faces of the people to its fragrant coolness.

Standing inside the pavilion, warlords and chieftains watch the sparkling veils of rain furl in the wind
and steam across the fields. A rainbow, bright and
hard as candy, stands as a bower arch over the citadel.

Kyner recognizes at once that something won-
derful has happened in heaven, and he rushes out to
receive the good news, dragging Cei after him. The
old war chief laughs uproariously and swings his
grouchy son around him in a wide frolicking step.

Morgeu, too, feels the magic of the sun-shot rain,
and she takes Lot by the arm and, with a charmed
whisper in his ear, leads him smiling into the brilliant
shower. Gawain and Gareth, who have been tossing
horseshoes behind the pavilion, run laughing to their
parents and hold hands in a gleeful dance.

Soon, Urien, Marcus, and Bors Bona join them,
and they kick up their heels in the wet, radiant wind
and link arms with Morgeu and her family. Elemental
joy pulls Kyner and Cei into their jubilant circle, and
Celt and Briton, Christian and pagan hold hands and
merge in a dance of heaven's celebration.

Even Severus Syrax throws up his hands in dismay when he finds himself alone in the pavilion and prances into the glittering rainfall. His face paint blears away in greasy streaks, and he laughs giddily as he skips with the others, hooking elbows and spinning like a child.

All across the fields of Camelot, crowds dance. The rain, brisk and cold, splashes off the people in a burnished glow. And the angel himself dances among them, visible to their eyes as the solar fire that fills each single raindrop with a world of light.